Jürgen Mann · Time of Desperation

JÜRGEN MANN, born 1951 in Sondershausen/Thuringia, lives since 1961 in West Germany. He studied electro technologies and was thereafter engaged in the management of several international companies, which included also living in the United States for several years. He is married and lives today in Bavaria.

Jürgen Mann

Time of Desperation

The Story of an Escape
from the German Democratic Republic

© 2014 Jürgen Mann
Set and Layout: Buch&media GmbH, München
Cover Design: Kay Fretwurst, Freienbrink
Editor and Production: BoD – Books on Demand
Printed in Germany
ISBN 978-3-7412-8370-3

I dedicate this book to my parents
and thank them for being brave, tenacious and courageous
enough to provide a better future
for themselves and their children.

Thank you forever.

I.

No doubt, we all were totally excited! We were pretty young boys and girls, my brother Roland, me and all the other school kids from our classes. Roland was ten years old, I was just about seven. He was still in fourth grade, I was still in first. I guess this afternoon would have been appreciated also by a lot of older fellows – not to mention our daddies. You had to love those Red Army soldiers for giving us a never-to-be-forgotten experience.

Our family lived in a small street in the upper town of Sondershausen in Thuringia, Germany. Sondershausen is located about 45 kilometers north of Erfurt, Thuringia's capital and about the same distance from the Harz Mountain with the famous top, the Brocken. Its plateau was filled with spying radars pointing west. The Brocken was a very restricted area and proof of the Russian presence. You could see signs of their political and strategic influence everywhere.

Another famous nearby location was the Emperor Barbarossa Memorial in Kyffhäuser; this is where you see his massive body sitting on his throne. All is sculptured in red sandstone. He lived in the 12th century and led several crusades to the Holy Land.

At the Potsdam Conference, three months after the end of the Second World War, the Allies agreed to divide Germany. This middle part of Germany, spanning from the Baltic Sea in the north to the border with Czechoslovakia, became the Soviet controlled zone. The eastern part of pre-war Germany, starting east of Frankfurt at the Oder River was given to Poland. It reached to the Baltic States in the northeast and Silesia down in the southeast, almost like a half-moon sickle. At this time, former Middle Germany with states including Saxony, Thuringia and Brandenburg and the long-term capital Berlin became the new East Germany. Berlin was divided in East and West Berlin. West Berlin became an island and was from then on under the Western Allies' control; East Berlin under that of the Soviets. Many still called this new East Germany "Middle Germany", referring to the pre-war situation, or "SBZ", a German abbreviation for Soviet controlled zone.

Thuringia was a border state to the "free West" and is called the "Green Heart of Germany": Green certainly – but also hilly and sometimes even a bit mountainous. I would compare it a bit with Oregon but also in parts with the British Midlands. A bit of both and definitely not crowded.

A half a kilometer long street, eight meters wide led to our part of the town. Winding up from the town center, it was named Possenweg after an excursion destination up in the forest: the Possen. The street changed from asphalt to cobble stones and then to an earthen forest road leading further up to the restaurant. It would have taken you about a good hour to walk there. People went there for coffee and cake on weekends, a nice walk through the woods. Before the Possenweg actually entered the forest, climbing up from downtown, it split into two other streets. One to the left, our street, and one to the right.

Upper part of town in both senses: geographically, we were located about 100 meters above the town and if you stood in the middle of the Possenweg looking down toward town, you saw the steeple of the church in the center. At this time, there was no real danger in standing on such a street as there were very few cars or other motor-driven vehicles present.

Up also from the status of the people who lived in our part of the town: most had important positions in the town or in the political party SED and were well established. According to the name, the SED was the Socialist United Party of Germany, but it was actually nothing more than the new communist party.

As already mentioned the Possenweg was interrupted by a round crossing with two streets continuing left and right. Certainly the prettiest part was the one going straight further upwards escorted by old chestnut trees. Turning right would have led you to one of the political centers of the town, the house of the FDGB, an abbreviation for the "Free German Unions". My parents spent many evenings there listening to the messages the SED thought important to their members and local development. Also further on this street was our public swimming pool.

Our house was the second on the right side after you turned left, number 4 Edmund-König-Strasse. On both sides of our street, wonderful old houses and villas were lined up, most of them in pretty good shape considering it was after the war.

Number four was also an old villa; once it was a one-family home. I call it our house even though we only rented the large basement condo. We had about 75 square meters, two bedrooms, kitchen, living room, cellars and laundry room, a little bathroom but no bathtub. But we had a nice little garden extending from our veranda that was adjacent to our living room. The garden was definitely a nice place for us children to play in. Two old trees, a cherry tree and a willow tree gave us shade in summer time.

There was a bath in the condo on the first floor that was rented by a middle-aged couple. We were not very close with this couple above us even though Mutti talked to her maybe once a week in the hall way exchanging gossip. Her husband played cello in the town's orchestra. The only stress we had was when he had to rehearse for one of his next concerts – which wasn't seldom.

Above them on the second floor, under the roof so to speak lived an older couple in their sixties and we liked them very much. We called them Aunt Rosa and Uncle Walter. They had a garden adjacent to ours with a few chickens and sometimes we were gifted with fresh eggs. Those were rare at this time, rare as chocolate, bananas, oranges, vegetables, butter and almost every kind of meat.

Except for horse meat. I remember times when I went shopping with Mutti – that's what we called my mother; she very much likes this nickname and even to this day would never accept being called Mother. Sometimes we teased her about that. We stood for hours in long rows with other patiently waiting customers to get any of those groceries. If you had tough luck, you were next in line but the special food or vegetable were just sold out.

Connections to the West, to relatives sending packages of goodies or medical supplies, were worth gold at this time. Unfortunately, the officials from customs and border control always slit the packages open, took what they needed and we got the rest. Our grandparents and other relatives all lived in West Germany; they left East Germany right after the war under very adventurous and dangerous circumstances. People left during the night, approaching the West German borderline where – hopefully – no border police was present, and escaped.

We stayed for a good reason: building up a new country after the war. East Germany needed a lot of officers and policemen and all kinds of educated and willing-to-work people. The police advertised heavily for getting their troops together. My father – we called him Papa – applied for such a job and was recruited as a police officer. That was in 1947. He later became the chief of the town's police department for criminal investigations. The rank was comparable to a Lieutenant. This is, by the way, why our family had one of the very few telephones in the town.

Our house on the right with the number 4 was followed by five others. The mayor of the town lived next to us in number 6. On the left side of the street, the first house with the number 1 was a villa serving as a home for small children and infants. You would probably call it a daycare today or simply a Kindergarten. Next to it stood another wonderful old villa in which two of our school friends lived. Both villas had great acre-sized grounds with lots of fruit trees. Adjacent was a flower field and a green house belonging to a nursery. It was followed by two more single homes. Of course, all were built in brick and with three stories like ours. In most of the houses lived one or two families.

Our street was not paved; it was covered with a mixture of gravel and sand and certainly had some little holes. Nevertheless, we had sidewalks. The street ended after six hundred meters at a small crossing opening the view into a wide valley of corn, vegetable and potato fields. We enjoyed this wonderful scenery not blocked for kilometers by any building. In the far distance, you could see the vague silhouettes of two villages. One was called Jecha. Especially in summertime, when the sun shone over the fields and some big cumulus clouds moved their shadows over, it was a gorgeous sight.

Turning right from there, you would reach the forest within three hundred meters after passing a big row of hedges and a meadow. This was simply a dirt road. We did a lot of sledding and skiing on this meadow, Papa, Roland and I. The meadow was steep enough and therefore also fast enough for our age. Not seldom did we crash and tumble down with our sled or on our skis. Once my brother and I even broke our sled crashing at the end of a furious fast run hitting a hole in the icy ground and ending up in the fence of the nearby field.

Straight ahead from the little crossing, the gravel road continued winding down alongside one of the big potato fields. With the trees on each side, it appeared like an alley. In autumn, when the fields were harvested it was permitted to collect the left-over potatoes or other vegetables on the fields. We did this every year whenever possible. I am sure it was not to save money; it was just that we had a hard time getting potatoes or vegetables. But it was fun! Sometimes, we did it also before the harvest; this was definitely dangerous. If anybody had noticed , we could pay a high price for doing it. Mutti took some risks here to feed the family with more than just bread and a watery soup.

Turning to the left, our street became a paved road, a little street leading back to town passing over a steel bridge with a single rail road underneath. I will never forget the feeling of walking over this little bridge when a train, pulled by those old steam locomotives passed at the same time: the steam from the locomotive covered us in a big white cloud. Unfortunately, the black exhaust also left its mark, which Mutti did not like too much. When the cloud vanished, you saw the road continuing; houses on the left side and a long four meters high dark-red brick wall appearing on the right. One followed the direction of the railway on the right, one the street almost like a prison wall. They were hiding the large Soviet Army barracks. About 300 soldiers were stationed here. To our knowledge, the wall had only one opening about 200 meters further down the road: the big iron gate with one or two soldiers guarding it. The gate was recessed from the street by about 10 meters opening a little place in front of it as an entrance way into the army grounds.

The soldiers were dressed in their typical dark green uniforms with boots and their unique way of having their belts over their uniform jackets. This made the short jackets sticking out almost like a short skirt just covering the waist. Of course, they carried machine guns, Kalashnikovs, named after the famous Russian soldier who invented them. They had to open the gate manually when some of their trucks or other military vehicles either left or entered the barracks. It was rather seldom that the heavy tanks rolled out into the small streets of Sondershausen: rolling down the streets with their metallic tracks clanking and leaving marks in the concrete. The gate was always brightly lit up after dusk with four heavy beaming lamps.

On the right side of the gate, in the corner of the recessed wall, they had built a concrete pedestal of about 100 square meters, about 2 meters high. On it stood a majestic military-green colored tank. It was a T34, one of the Soviet's Second World War models that were built during the war in the Ural mountain plants. Even weighing some 30 metric tons it was still a very fast and maneuverable tank they say. It had a 76.2 mm or 3 inch cannon mounted on the turret and a 7.62 mm or 0.3 inch machine gun sticking out of one of the two front hatches. For us, the tank was not only an impressive site but also a symbol for the presence of "our friends" and the German's defeat in the Second World War.

I have passed this tank many times on my way to or from school or to town. It was still standing there until a few years ago.

2.

School was very influential and beneficial. That was not only in a political sense but also when it came to learning skills for daily life or in the sense of general education. The pure amount of studies we did for our age was amazing. I would find this out at a later stage in my life. The time we spent with the teachers and other authorities also aimed to educate us in the right political way. Being educated about the upcoming German Democratic Republic, its goals and fundamentals, was meant to lead to an understanding that GDR was the supposedly better part of the two German states. The government and its politics were always present: in school, at work or in your leisure time, even in your very private home.

It was very common and necessary to spend a lot of time with "the system". I remember that we started the day in school with a pledge to the flag of the Pioneers, the political, very influential youth organization in the GDR. We had the picture of the President of the time – Wilhelm Pieck – in our class room. We were called "Pioneers" and wore white shirts with the symbol of the organization as well as blue scarves around our shirt collars, tied in a special knot. The whole movement can be compared a bit with that of the boy and girl scouts. Of course, there was always the influence of the socialistic party SED and the government, or should I say the Soviets? Boys and girls were members of the youth organization. It was very well organized with special events and excursions usually held once a week in the afternoon. We did sports, visited sites, monuments or memorials, industrial companies, production plants etc. We also did long hikes through forests and fields and learned a lot about nature and the local environment. Some of the highlights were certainly visiting and being with the Soviet Army, at least for the boys – probably not so much for the girls.

I remember this special morning in school when we discussed the next Pioneer session. It must have been two months before the big summer vacation of around seven weeks; the school year finished in mid-July and started again on September 1st. Our school was about two kilometers away from home and we walked back and forth every day, winter and summer, storm and rain. We did not have bicycles; those were also rare at that time. And if one was available, the parents used it for getting to work or to do errands. We had to walk down the Possenweg about three hundred meters and then zigzag through some small streets. We then passed a Soviet military graveyard adjacent to the school building. It had a big monolith standing in the middle with a large red Soviet star on it. It was surrounded by a little park in which some tall oak trees made it a rather quiet place. We had to pass through it to get to the massive wooden entrance doors of our school. The school was named Käthe Kollwitz Middle School. In short, she was one of the opponents of the National Socialist movement and also close to the leftist parties in Germany during and after the First World War. She was also famous for being an artist and sculptor.

Our school was a big, L-shaped sandstone building formed and was four stories high with angled tile roofs. Inside the L-shape was the school yard. There were also two doors into this yard that we used during our lesson breaks. Our class teacher was Frau Rosenstiel, the wife of the school's director. She was a very good teacher and we all liked her. We had most of our lessons with her: German reading and writing, math, grammar, sports and music. I still have my certificates signed by her with my grades. I was a year older than most of my classmates as I was a bit sickly when I was five and six years old. My parents decided not to let me start school until later.

This Thursday morning, Frau Rosenstiel had invited the leader of the local Pioneer organization. He was in his thirties; I cannot recall his name. After giving us a short rundown of possible future events and plans, he continued with what was very exciting news: "My dear young pioneers, I have planned a very special event with our friends from the Soviet army. I am very pleased to tell you that we will spend an afternoon with the soldiers out in the field. They will not only show us their maneuver field and heavy equipment but also let us ride with their tanks." First it was quiet, and then a little storm of cheers came from the class, mainly from the boys I should say. This was really exceptional good news and we could not stop talking about it for the next three weeks. It was spring after all, May to be exact, and it would be a good time for such an adventure. It was hard to believe this would be happening to us.

Later in the day, my brother Roland told me that some of the older pupils were also invited. I could not wait. We told Papa and Mutti about it as we always told them everything that happened in school. They did not seem to like it as much as we did but I thought that it was just because parents worry all the time about their children. Sooner or later, I would understand them and their reservations. The days went by but we never stopped thinking about it and imagining what it would be like to ride in one of those metal monsters.

3.

It was sunny with a totally blue sky and the temperature was around 25 degrees. Weather you would expect for the month of June. But as we all know it is not necessarily given to have such weather at this time of the year. We were lucky. A real gorgeous day for our event. We had a bit of a wind going which caused a few little dust clouds here and there.

It was Wednesday and we were still in school; this was the big day! It was early afternoon. Lunch was served in school and then we finally gathered in the school yard in a formation similar to soldiers starting to march. Our youth leader gave us a short explanation of what our schedule was and of what would happen this afternoon. We then walked in formation out of the school yard around the school building following the street to the right using the sidewalks. I have to say that very few girls were coming with us, no surprise. Girls have other interests!

It took us only ten minutes to reach the big iron gate in front of the barracks as the street leading to them was just four hundred meters from the school. There we stood, in front of the gate. Some formalities with the guards were discussed; some of the soldiers were somewhat fluent in German, so there was not really a problem in communicating. And of course, they expected us!

We were permitted to walk through the gate. It wasn't the first time that we were inside the barracks. Every year, there was an open day and all people could visit the barracks and see all the amenities and special displays they had prepared for the visitors. Everyone was served a bowl of soup from one of the mobile kitchens we called "Gulasch-Kanone". Literally translated something like a "beef stew canon".

We marched on over the big square yard surrounded by three story high barracks to one of the huge garages. In front of them, several of the open army trucks were parked side by side. The trucks had a front cabin for three soldiers, the driver and two others. In the back, there was a framework of steel tubes combined with wooden planks for loading any kind of material and/or just two rows with wooden benches to carry troops. Army trucks are really not comfortable in any sense. Sitting on those hard wooden benches is not a pleasant way to ride.

I looked around and saw my brother Roland a few meters away. I could see the excitement in his face and he could not wait to go out to the maneuver fields and get into the tank. The boys were all in shorts with the blue scarves around their necks and mostly short sleeve white shirts. The few girls attending were in summer dresses also with the blue scarves around their necks; I wasn't really sure how appropriate their dresses were for the afternoon. Maybe they were just interested in seeing the tanks and watching how the boys were having fun.

One of the girls was Roland's classmate and her name was Bärbel. She was the daughter of the mayor; as I mentioned she lived next to us in number six. I think that Roland liked her a lot and even years later, he still kept her in his memory and even had some brief contact with her. She was pretty with blond hair, big blue eyes and tall; she was also wearing a dress.

We were to board the trucks; we were not tall and certainly needed help from the soldiers as well as from our leader to climb on the platform in the back. I think that we had all in all three trucks with some 16 seats each. Sometimes the wind blew and the boys were laughing as the girl's dresses revealed a bit more than they would have liked entering the trucks.

After sitting down, we were instructed to firmly hold on to the metal bars that usually held the fabric covers in place. We did not need the covers today but we surely needed to hold on tight! We were going for a ride – and what a ride this was!

The fields and maneuver sites were a few kilometers away. They used old dirty and bumpy fields that were not nice and flat for a reason. Ups and downs, steep ramps and hills, flat sections, big holes and hillsides of all kind of grades and angles. Test grounds built by Mother Nature more or less and worsened by the army exercises. There were also some bunkers and trenches to give the proper environment for the soldiers playing war.

Riding to these areas on the Spartan military trucks was an adventure in itself. We were almost flying from the bumps in the road: lifting us up and at the next moment making us land hard on the benches. I heard some girls screaming – and also some boys. I am sure that everybody counted their bruises that evening and the next morning. I was one of them. I guess that we were excited enough to stand the pain but were also glad when the trucks entered the field where they came to an abrupt stop. Dust clouds were all over us and covering the scenery. Did it really matter? No, it didn't.

I forgot to mention that the Russian soldiers accompanying us were unfortunately not very proficient in German to say the least; our Pioneer leader spoke a bit of Russian, which helped us with the most important communication. Russian was the first foreign language we could learn in school, starting in third grade. To advance and learn English, you needed a very good grade in Russian first. But learning English was also seen as not appropriate: after all, English represented to a certain degree the Western capitalist culture.

We left the truck one by one with a little help from the soldiers. Our clothes showed that it was literally a dirty ride. Mutti would have to wash them. Without having a washing machine like in the West, this was hard work for her. God bless her! Of course, we did not realize it and took it for granted having clean clothes whenever we needed them.

We looked around and realized that there was not a single tank to be seen. No noise to be heard which would indicate such a monster coming around the corner or appearing anywhere from behind on one of the hills. Also none in front of us or on the steep ramp-like track on the right a few hundred meters distant. But we noticed tracks and the profiles of the big chains left in the dirt everywhere. We must be in the right place!

We walked around and checked out our environment a bit; every step we made on this dusty ground left a small sandy cloud and soon our shoes and socks were covered. In spite of the open field we stood on, not all parts of the maneuver field could be seen. Also, on the right, maybe 200 meters away, a few rows of trees and bushes blocked the view. In the distance was Sondershausen on a bit higher ground than we were. In front of us, the moon-like terrain, was probably at least a few square kilometers in size if not bigger.

I walked to my brother Roland and asked him: "When do you think the tanks are coming?" He was my big brother and I always looked up to him. He shrugged his shoulders and responded simply: "I do not know but I hope they come soon" expressing that he was at least as anxious as I was.

First, I thought that a bee was buzzing around my head; then I realized that the noise I heard was too much of a rumble to come from bees.

The ever increasing sound of powerful diesel engines combined with the squeaky rattle of heavy metal tracks. The tanks were on their way! We could not see them yet but our adrenalin level rose by the second. Our hearts beat faster and everybody tried to get the first glimpse. The air was vibrating.

Suddenly, at the end of the little forest, one of the tanks appeared; first just the long canon mounted to the turret, then the front constructed with massive steel plates. Seconds later, the full length of a tank could be seen. We watched the left side with the wheels and its track rattling over them. The tank left quite a dust cloud behind it. Coming closer, I saw more and more details like the driver's open hatch, the machine gun sticking out next to him in the front, the metal boxes for tools and supplies on top behind the tank turret. And of course, there was the commander looking out of the open hatch on top of the turret. They came straight toward us at quite a speed. My guess is that they were doing 50 kilometers an hour.

The tank was bouncing a bit coming over some of the bumps and driving through the holes in the ground. It did not have any problem coming down the ramp. We had to cover our ears now as the noise got very loud. In the same moment, a second tank curved around the edge of the forest and approached us no less intimidating or less impressive than the first one. We jumped aside making space for the arrival of the armored vehicles. One of the Russian soldiers waved his arms indicating to the commander where he should stop. Just a few feet in front of us, the first T34 stopped with a loud squeak; the engine was still roaring. Now the second tank came close and made a little turn by stopping the left track for two seconds. This way, it came alongside the other one and stopped ten meters away from it. All this caused more dust flying around and I heard some coughing. Some commands were shouted and finally the engines stopped.

We were in awe. Standing right in front of us were two of these massive war tanks we heard so much about: 30 tons of steel armor with a cannon so big that I could probably put my arm in it and a machine gun that could fire massive amounts of bullets in the air. The tracks were at least a meter wide and must have weighed tons themselves. The turrets were turned straight ahead now pointing in our direction. We could see the head of the pilot through the open hatch in the front.

The first commander climbed out of his hatch on top and jumped on the wheel cover and then down to the ground. He walked to the soldiers and started discussing what we thought were the next steps of our adventurous afternoon. Meanwhile, the second commander disappeared inside his tank. We looked at our Pioneer leader, obviously with very questioning expressions in our faces, because he answered before we could formulate our question:

"As far as I understand the procedure, we will embark a maximum of four of you in one tank. One will sit down in the front below and beside the driver; one will sit in the commander's chair right below the turret hatch. Another one will stand up in the turret with the commander; eventually we have two of you there. There is not too much space inside the tank. You should tell me now who wants to really ride and who does not. Maybe the ones who do not want to ride step back so we can see how many trips we have to make."

We looked at each other and moved forward, not all of us. I guess that the fearful appearance of these tanks left marks in some minds. Surprisingly, two of the girls wanted the ride. From the boys, more than two thirds wanted to do it. That meant that we had four trips to make with the two tanks. We had time enough and of course none of us cared how late it would get this afternoon. Our leader came to the same conclusion; he scheduled about 20 to 30 minutes for each ride. We got into groups of four and could not wait to climb on and into the tanks.

Roland and I were in the same group with two other boys. It would be extra special to ride with my brother, I knew that. We did a lot of things together with our friends from school or from the neighborhood. Most of the kids in our street went to the same school. We knew each other for years and spent hours together playing. Vacation time was very exciting and our rural environment with forests, meadows and fields encouraged us to play all kinds of common games and activities.

The first two groups climbed into the tanks. The smaller kids needed help to get up and in and were instructed where to sit or stand. I saw only one boy standing up in each of the turrets, so there must have been an additional seat of some kind inside. What did I know? It did not matter anyway to me. I would soon see for myself. I felt the excitement rising. Another half hour and we would climb on the tank. Where would I sit? Inside? Standing up? Or maybe beside the driver down below in the front?

My thoughts were suddenly interrupted when the engines started roaring through my brain. Thick clouds of black exhaust fumes were spewed from the two pipes in the back. We automatically jumped aside leaving enough room for the tanks to roll out of our place. The first turned right by stopping the right track from rotating and just moving the left track with the typical squeaking noise from metal grinding on metal. Amazing how easy it seemed to steer this T34 around. It made a half turn, slowly and almost carefully until it headed away from us.

We could now see the back of it. The engine was located in the back under a metal grid obviously providing some cooling. On top of the chassis on the right was a cylindrical metal container, on the left a rectangular toolbox. Also, strapped with leather bands to the back of the turret there was a camouflage net. On the angled back metal plate, two other cylindrical cans were mounted, one left, one right. In the middle of the plate, the two exhaust pipes exited the chassis. All over the sides and on the turret were finger-thick metal bars to hold on or helping to mount the tank. Those especially helped us kids to climb on and inside the tank.

The driver stepped on the gas pedal; in fact, there wasn't any as I found out later. He had some levers to steer and also to accelerate the tank. We had to stick our fingers in our ears. The roaring was overwhelmingly loud. The tank drove away hitting the first bumpy holes and leaving a cloud of dust behind. Now the second one turned by not only stopping one track but also slightly reversing it. Then it also pulled away following the other. We watched them going around in circles, putting on some impressive speed, going up a hill and diving down into some sunken valleys always leaving clouds of dust behind them. At one time, the second tank almost jumped a bit by driving over a big bump of dirt leaving the front half in the air for a second or two. I still regret the fact that nobody took any pictures that afternoon. Nothing left besides good memories.

The tanks came back in the same impressive way they had arrived. It was our turn now to experience such a ride! The tanks were located side by side and after the others had disembarked, we were to mount it and take our places. Roland went first, of course. He had the luck and sat right next to the driver. During the war, this was the place for the soldier operating the front machine gun. There were two other seats inside: one a bit behind the driver and one just underneath the turret. This was the one I sat on. It was a half-bowl shaped metal seat and I remember that I could not reach the ground with my feet. It felt okay at first. I saw Roland down below trying to communicate with the driver. I looked around and saw some more equipment that had purposes I did not understand. There must have been also cases of ammunition and tools. And there was also radar communication equipment. Its antenna was on top of the turret.

During the Second World War, the T34 had a crew of four soldiers which included the commander, the driver, the machine gun operator and the radar communicator.

The top hatch stayed open during our ride. We started, and as I was not standing up. I could only see through the front hatch. Only when the tank was on an upward move, I had a view. The bouncing over the terrain was so bad on my behind and my legs that it really hurt. No padding on the seat and hardly what you would call a suspension. Oh well, it was fun. We did some turns, some runs up and downhill and some little diving exercise like the others did. At one point, we stopped. I tried to figure out what was going on in the darker front below me. Roland and the driving soldier where pointing back and forth and were somehow communicating. Roland knew a few words of Russian, not sure if that helped him here. Nevertheless, I saw him holding the one lever and pulling it. The tank pulled forward for maybe a hundred feet and stopped again. Later, he told me that he drove the tank. Not very far but at least he did.

Our ride ended and we jumped out of the tank with help from the soldiers. My knees and legs were a bit weak and my butt hurt, but who cared. We went to the others and exchanged our experiences. Roland proudly told us about him driving the tank. The other kids had visited some of the trenches and maneuver sites, the underground and earth-built bunkers; certainly interesting to see how soldiers lived during maneuvers but no comparison to our adventurous ride in the tanks. Decades after that afternoon, Roland and I still talk about the event. In fact, it's now possible to even own one of those tanks – you can simply buy them.

4.

At this time, Mutti was in her early thirties, Papa in his late thirties. Papa was the chief crime investigator in the town. The position was important for the obvious reasons but also in a political sense. In such a position you had to be a member of the SED – and Mutti too. You also had to be politically "clean" in the sense of supporting the regime in all aspects of your public and private life. This included no or almost no contacts to the West. No Western radio, news or newspapers, no contact with Western individuals, even relatives. The authorities did not like it but had to realize that family contact with relatives in West Germany could not be totally avoided. If they got even the slightest information about such contacts, you had to report it. You were then investigated and pressured to stop. Being reprimanded once would lead to ongoing observation and investigation about your entire family and its activities and behavior. Those investigations were handled exclusively by the Stasi, the State Security Service or "Staatssicherheitsdienst". It was comparable to an organization like the CIA, of course with different directives and principles.

It was a Tuesday afternoon. Roland and I came home from school almost at the same time. Mutti had gotten a package from my grandma in Nuremberg. She was Papa's mother and lived with Papa's brother and sister-in-law. It was always a highlight when we got a package from West Germany. What was even better this time, it was not opened by the border controls or penetrated with holes from the sticks they put through; it was their way of testing the content. It was entirely untouched. It was quite large, maybe 30 by 40 by 60 centimeters. Mutti opened it and Roland and I watched her impatiently. Why? We could expect that there was chocolate in it, and other goodies we could seldom enjoy simply because they were not available or if we could get them, they tasted horrible. The same applied to fruits like bananas and oranges; you just could not buy them.

We had a large kitchen for a small apartment of 75 square meters; a big double ceramic sink, a kitchen cupboard, a wood-fired oven and a little pantry. For making warm water, we had a gas boiler you had to light to get hot water. I remember that my grandma from Nuremberg visited us once. She had to light the gas boiler but forgot the matches. Well, when she got back to light the flame, a lot of gas had filled the room and we just heard a big explosion. Grandma was fine but she never lit the flame again – and we would not let her anyway.

Mutti got the scissors out, laid the package on our kitchen table and opened it. This compared with Christmas or Easter or birthdays: you just cannot wait to open your presents! The package was really untouched and we could not wait to see what was inside. After removing the first layer of paper, we saw two chocolate bars, a few pieces of chewing gum, three oranges and some kind of medicine. Not sure what it was or what the purpose of it was. We were not sick recently. It was not seldom that we asked for medicine supply from the West as there was very little available here. Especially when it came to special diseases, we had to rely on getting it from our relatives. Mutti did not seem to be surprised, she must have asked for it.

I remember that I had scarlet fever when I was five years old; Mutti went to our house doctor who practiced in a big old white villa at the end of a long street with the name Karl-Marx-Alley. His name was Dr. Dönitz. We liked him, he was very helpful and a good doctor. Whenever we were sick with more than just a cold, Mutti went to him. In fact, I was very sick several times in my younger days with scarlet fever and measles and other stuff. It was just a nightmare to get the medicine to cure us. Quite often the only answer you heard was: "I cannot help you as we do not have the dedicated medicine, Mrs. Mann. You better have some relatives in the West. Tell them what you need, I will write it down for you." Mutti then wrote a letter which took a week or longer and then our relatives would send the medicine to us which again took one or two weeks to arrive. And hopefully it went through the customs.

After we removed the goodies, we discovered some fabric. Looking closer at it, these were pants! Three pairs, one was larger for Papa and two were of smaller size for Roland and me. They were dark green and of Corduroy style. We called them Manchester style pants with regard to the British well-known textile city; Manchester was the European textile center.

We pulled them out and looked at them. They had a belt and two pockets in the front and also cuffs. They looked very classy and would be certainly eye-catchers when worn in public. We liked them and put them on right away. Looking like studs we walked around in the apartment and showed Mutti. She was happy for us; actually, she was and is always happy when good things happen to her children. She is just what you expect and imagine from a fabulous Mom. We were anxious to wear them on our next Sunday walk to town. We were absolutely sure that Papa would feel the same way.

At the bottom of the package was a letter from grandma giving us greetings, wishing us well and hoping that the pants would fit and that we'd like them. No problem there, we really did. Mutti gave us a piece of chocolate and saved the rest; we probably would have eaten it all at once otherwise. She also put the oranges away and kept the medicine.

We changed out of our new pants and into our playing outfits and went outside. It was a beautiful Tuesday afternoon and our neighbor kids were already outside having fun. Mutti's rule was that every afternoon when the church bell struck six times, we had to come home. Mutti insisted on that. We did not like it very much, especially in summer when it was still light and the sun had not gone down yet. Also, the other kids' moms seemed to be a bit more tolerant in this regard.

As usual, today we did what we were supposed to do. Just as we turned into our little street, we heard a car coming up from the town. The two-cycle engine made a hell of a rattling noise leaving a cloud of white steam behind. It was a green car, a police car. They were of the military style, a bit like a jeep but not as strong in design and appearance. They called it a "Kübel". The car turned into our street and we knew instantly that Papa came home from work. He was seldom that early but this had to do with his job. Many surprising things were happening in our town and in the county. He was called sometimes in the middle of the night and they picked him up to go to a crime scene. Other times, he did not come home for the whole night and we did not see him for two or three days. Papa did not drive the car himself; he always had a chauffeur who brought him and picked him up from home or from work.

The car stopped in front of our house and Papa stepped out. We ran to him and greeted him. Mutti also must have heard the car and stood on top of the stone stairway leading up to the door of the house. We went up the stairs and Mutti sent us first to clean ourselves up while she gave Papa a kiss. There was a special glow around Mutti. Maybe it was because of the nice package we got from Papa's mom today. After he put down his briefcase and put on his house shoes, Mutti showed him the gifts we got and also his new pants. He liked them, too. Still, he wasn't as excited as we were about them.

I wondered why.

5.

The reason why Papa came home early that day was simple. Usually, he worked long hours or had to go to crime scenes in the evening or simply had meetings. But today, Mutti and Papa had to go to the party meeting of the SED in the evening. They were never really comfortable with attending the meeting nor did they agree with the government of East Germany and its communist-style regime. The government called it a socialist republic while in reality it was more a dictatorship ruled by the SED with the help and support of the Soviets. The political pressure on everybody was enormous and especially on two adults being well-known in the community like our parents.

My parents stayed in Thuringia after they had to leave their homeland in the latter days of the Second World War; they were from the Sudetenland, a small region of northern Czechoslovakia. Today this country is divided in two autonomous, independent countries.

The Sudetenland was well developed by the Germans who had settled there. Reichenberg was probably the richest town with a lot of textile industry. My great grandparents had a few factories there. Ever heard of somebody with the name Ferdinand Porsche? The guy who built the first beetle bug for Hitler? Which became a Volkswagen! That's him; he was born in the area. He later founded the Porsche factory and built the famous sports car.

To cut history a bit short here: After the war was lost, they were pushed out with nothing but the clothes they wore. This is certainly one of the very tragic parts of German history. All our relatives left with Mutti and Papa and ended up in Thuringia, one of the states that belonged to what was Middle Germany during the war and became East Germany after the Soviets took control.

My parents decided not to go to West Germany at this time and tried to settle and find a new home and work. Papa went to the police and was helped finding a little apartment for them. Nevertheless, my parents were always opponents of the regime and its politics. They always felt that the practiced socialism was really communism in a different outfit. Freedom in speech and free will were suppressed. We were never permitted to listen to any Western radio stations, nor read any Western "propaganda material", at least that's what the authorities called all Western literature. You could not criticize the government or say anything critical about the living conditions or the lack of food or failures of the authorities. The slightest remark could lead to at least a serious hearing, if not to temporary imprisonment.

Mutti and Papa had to be very careful saying or discussing anything critical in front of us children or even in front of friends. Friends were very hard to find and everyone was very careful in talking about the government, politics or actual living conditions in a critical way. Any small piece of information could easily be revealed to people who would use it to your disadvantage, maybe just to get ahead in the system. Or they just did not like you. You always had to be extra cautious in public.

Due to shortages in groceries and food supplies, it happened quite often that Mutti and I had to stand in line to get butter, eggs, vegetables, meat or almost anything, even the famous Sauerkraut. Supply was low for many things, especially when you lived in a small town like Sondershausen. Important cities like East Berlin or Leipzig were better off as the government wanted to show the Western world how well their new state provided for its inhabitants. In fact, the rules and instructions were made by the Soviets; they decided where the goods would end up.

Once we were waiting at a grocery store downtown as we had heard that eggs and butter were available. Butter was a restricted product and you had special food stamps for it. We got dressed quickly and hurried down the long street toward town. Some people knew about special supplies and told their neighbors and friends about it so they could go too and take advantage of the situation. Quite often you ended up not getting anything as it was sold out already before you could even get close to the shop. It was very disappointing when this happened and people got angry. Waiting an hour in line and not getting what you came for was sometimes indescribably hard. You got very frustrated and some people just could not keep their mouths shut.

As we finally arrived at the grocery store, people said that eggs just arrived and supposedly bananas too. There was already a long row of mothers with kids and housewives looking for the extra special offer and probably making out a special dish in their mind for the evening. You stood there quietly and hoped that you would be one of the lucky ones. Mutti always reminded us to be quiet and to not say anything, just to wait patiently. I could not see too much of what was going on in the front of the line; I only noticed that we moved slowly forward. Mutti always checked the people around her; she was very cautious and observant. Maybe being married to a policeman created the extra awareness in her. Especially when men were waiting in line – that caught her immediate attention. I followed her view as well as I could and noticed the man three places in front of us. He was about six feet tall and dressed in a white shirt, brown jacket and black pants. He wasn't really someone that would catch anyone's attention. Just a man who wanted the same things we were waiting for, bananas or eggs or, even better, both.

The line got shorter, pretty soon we would have the pleasure of getting at least some eggs for dinner. Bananas were usually the first to go. Some people had chickens and therefore had fresh eggs of their own. Mutti always made soft eggs for us, boiled a few minutes in water. We always loved to hit the eggshells and open the egg with a spoon. Eating it with a grain of salt and a slice of bread with butter was a real treat. My mouth was watering.

I heard some women talking; a few words went back and forth. Suddenly, it got loud. Something must have happened. I wanted to leave the row but Mutti held my hand strongly in hers and kept me beside her. There was some movement in the front and the only thing I could see was that a few people pushed hard against the shop door. "I have been waiting here now for over an hour", a woman screamed. "I want my eggs!"

"Are there any bananas left?" another woman shouted at the shop personnel. "We have the right to get some. Why don't you have enough? It is probably all in Berlin! " Others were still and did not say anything, distraught and disappointed that their effort went wasted. It seemed that the last eggs and bananas were sold. While some women had already left, the man in the brown jacket stepped forward and addressed the woman who made the comment about the bananas being in Berlin in a very serious tone: "Please come with me to the office!" The woman was stunned and fear covered her face immediately. She did not respond but quietly followed the man.

The man was from the secret service, the Stasi. They did not like the criticism.

6.

Mutti and Papa got dressed; Mutti wore skirts or costumes with blouses most of the time and Papa some slacks, white shirts and usually a jacket. They needed only about three minutes for the 200 meter walk over to the FDGB building just opposite from our street.

The SED meetings started always at eight. All participants were expected to show up on time, or even better, early. Participation was also a must. You really did not want to be on their black list. The authorities and the secret service registered everything about you. They knew your upbringing, your history, your job, your family, hobbies, special behaviors, everything. Especially all information about family in the West, including addresses. If you were not a member of the SED, in their view, you were of lower class and not a contributing member of the society. You were obliged at any time and without any doubt or question to support the regime. Showing the slightest doubt about the power of the government was absolutely not acceptable; it could bring you to court, which in many cases meant prison time. Failures in supporting the government and its authorities were always made public; the secret service would not hesitate to give out the information so it could be presented for example on the party meetings Mutti and Papa went to.

The participants counted about 50 persons of the who's-who in Sondershausen. Again, you had to be a member of the party – if you were a teacher or officer or held other important positions. The evenings, I was told later, were full of presentations and discussion about politics in general and specifically related to the brains of communism and socialism: Marx, Engels and Lenin. The SED had to make sure that their "flagship" members "sailed" in the right direction so to speak. They had to train you in the doctrines of these men and how they could be of any help in our daily lives.

Mutti and Papa were never happy at those evenings. They had experienced Russians' cruelty during their escape from Sudetenland and found themselves somehow again right in the middle of their presence and influence, but they had to play the game.

They came home early that evening; I was still awake. We slept in a big room right beside the living room. The pocket door was closed but had a milky glass insert which let some light in from the front room. The room had a wooden parquet floor and was rather spacious, so we could play there when the weather did not allow us to go outside. Our beds stood diagonally opposite from each other in the corners. The room had also two windows that looked onto the garden. It also had a bigger pocket door that led to our parents' bedroom.

The windows of our bedroom also bring up memories. Santa Claus usually came through them on December 6 and poured his goodies onto the floor. That was after he asked us the question if we were good boys: we always answered – of course – but with a rather quiet and fearful "yes". The other special memory of the window I have is when Mutti and Papa asked us if we would like to have a little sister. There was for some reason no hesitation in Roland and me agreeing with this thought. This time the answer was loud and clear: "Yes". We were told that a cube of sugar on the windowsill would help to tell the Stork about our desire and to bring the little sister at a later point in time. That was last year in October: a few days, after the sugar was placed on the windowsill, it had disappeared.

I heard Mutti and Papa coming in the front room whispering but could not really understand what was said. Then I heard them switch on the radio. After a minute or so the tubes needed to heat up, it made some noise. The radio stood on a little sideboard in a corner of our living room. We had a round dining table in the middle of the front room with four chairs and a sitting area in a smaller square sized extension of the room. A couch, two armchairs and a little table almost overcrowded this niche. In the evening, the windows were closed and the roller shades were down. Mutti and Papa had to be careful; anyone would have been able to look inside, basically unnoticed.

We did not have a TV set; very few people had one. TVs were very hard to buy and very expensive. The price equaled a half a year's salary for most and you had to be on a waiting list. Papa and Mutti had friends who had one. He worked with Papa in the police department and his wife worked in the HO. This was the general shop for groceries, the statewide chain of stores. The friend's last name was Bohne.

Mutti was not too keen about him as he had two major problems: drinking too much too often and staying out late in the Ratskeller, the major restaurant right beside the big marketplace downtown. This was one of the best restaurants. As I heard later, the waitress must have been very nice, good looking and more than very friendly to him; they had an affair for years that many people knew about, including his wife and Mutti too.

I must have been six years old by this time. To visit the Bohnes we had to walk all the way through town: down from our side of the town and up on the opposite side of the town's center. This was quite an effort and about one and a half miles in distance. Every time we visited them, we could not wait to watch a bit of TV.

I recall the first time I watched the little, slightly flickering black-and-white picture coming out of a fourty centimeter tube, rounded at the edges. The TV housing was built from wood and polished like a fine piece of furniture. The TV programs at this time included some entertainment but were mostly censored reports and news. Why did they have a TV set and not us? With these thoughts, I fell asleep and this certainly helped me the next morning.

7.

Mutti woke us up. It was 7 o'clock and time to get up. I noticed that Mutti walked slowly and also seemed not to feel right. She must not have slept well either. After getting ready, we had a little breakfast at the kitchen table with some milk and a piece of bread. I noticed the medicine on the table, the one that came with the package from Grandma the day before.

"Are you sick, Mutti?" I asked her. She looked at me and Roland and answered:

"No, not really. My stomach hurts but I got the vitamins from Grandma yesterday and they help."

"How long do you have to take them, Mutti?" I wanted to know being a little bit worried now.

"Just a few drops every day and for about four to five weeks. Don't worry. I'm also going to the doctor today."

We finished breakfast. Mutti looked at the kitchen clock: "You both have to hurry now to get to school in time. I'll see you this afternoon. Take care and learn something!"

She always gave us a hug and we went out the door. She had to sit down; she was just tired and a bit weak these days. Later she would lay on the couch in the front room and rest.

It was 10 minutes after 9 a.m. when somebody knocked at the door; it was Aunt Rosa from the third floor. She brought Mutti four eggs; very thoughtful of her and always very welcome on Mutti's side.

There was another reason: Mutti needed help going to the doctor and Aunt Rosa had come to accompany and help her. The appointment was at 10 a.m. Dr. Helldorf's practice was just down the street on Possenweg; but in Mutti's condition, it could take a while to get there. She had been there several times now, twice in June already.

It was a female doctor.

8.

June 17. It was my birthday. Like every kid, I loved it. Whenever I told somebody about the date, they realized that it was special in the calendar because of some historical events. But I could not use the official name the West Germans would use: Day of German Unity. It was forbidden to mention this in GDR and would have certainly caused problems for my parents.

Actually, it happened on my second birthday, June 17th, 1953. East German workers, farmers and other political opponents of the regime started a little revolution. In all the major cities, especially East Berlin, people demonstrated against the regime, the system in general, the supply situation, the Soviet occupation (that's basically what it was) and other issues. Later in history, there were other examples like the riots and revolts of 1956 in Hungary or 1968 in Prague. Papa was called right away to work and I think we did not see him for three days.

Mutti always made birthdays special – not only for me, but also for Roland and Papa. My special birthday treat was a dish of "Buchteln". A traditional Bohemian and later an Austrian dish, it was pieces of flour dough baked in a pan and served steaming hot on a plate covered with a chocolate sauce. Yummy! I got it every birthday! Gifts were rare, maybe a little toy car or something. Similar to the food situation, not much was available in those days. Of course, I had to go to school that day; it was a Tuesday that year. I was born on a Sunday, Roland too.

We sat together that evening, all four of us and had a nice dinner on our big round table. We had a noodle soup first, and Mutti had made soft eggs from the four she got from Aunt Rosa that morning. With some bread and butter, this was delicious. We usually had tea with dinner, coltsfoot tea, made from a flower; in German it is called Huflattich. We picked the flowers from the surrounding meadows and Mutti steeped them in water to make the tea.

In a way, we were a happy family even though the circumstances were not as pleasant as they could have been. As a little boy, I did not understand what my parents actually went through and I would describe my childhood as fabulous at any time.

Papa had just finished dinner and seemed to be a little nervous; he looked at us, then at Mutti. After a few long seconds, he said: "Well boys, on this special day I would like to tell you some other exciting news. Remember that last year you put some sugar cubes on the window sill that the Stork picked up a day later?"

Silence, we started to think about this, maybe we had forgotten it and needed to remind ourselves.

Papa continued, "I can tell you boys that pretty soon, you will have a little sister!" We were stunned and had to swallow this news before we felt the same excitement we heard in Papa's voice. A little sister, great. This is what we wanted and what we had wished for – we just did not know exactly how it could be achieved. Mutti looked at Papa and smiled. It was a very happy smile.

For a long while, I could not fall asleep that night and neither could Roland. We talked about the news and exchanged all kinds of ideas of what we could do with her and that we will protect her as her big brothers. And we thought about possible names for her – just in case Mutti and Papa would ask us.

9.

Summer really had begun. By my birthday, the weather was already great, with temperatures in the seventies and sometimes eighties, and blue skies with some cumulus clouds. During June and July, it did not rain much where we lived. If it did, it was a wonderful soft summer rain you could enjoy walking in, not caring about getting wet. Most of the afternoons we played outside with the neighbor kids or we went to the woods with a few boys exploring secret passages, little canyons, the old observation tower named Bismarck Tower, or the platform we called Rondell where a memorial column stood for soldiers killed during the wars. From there, high above the town, we could see for miles, and also our street and house. Sometimes our whole family walked up to the Possen on a Sunday to have lunch or coffee and cake. This was always fun and Papa used to take a lot of pictures with his little Rollei camera he had exchanged right after the war for a half loaf of bread. The pictures were all black and white and he used to develop them himself, either at home or at the police lab. We still have many of these pictures.

Papa had built a glider; a flying model with wings of about one and half meters long. He was a member of the Society for Sport and Technology; this was what they called the enthusiastic group of people who built models of all kinds: boats, ships and planes, some with electronic motors. They met in the evenings in one of the side wings of the castle of Sondershausen. In fact, the Princess Rudolphine of Schwarzenburg-Sondershausen still lived in one part of the castle; Papa met her once.

The glider was built from wood; every part was cut and sanded to perfection and one piece after the other was glued together. The framework was covered with a special paper and then painted with some kind of clear liquid. When the liquid was dry it made the paper smooth and brought tension to its surface. The bad part was that any little crash, sometimes even just a bumpy landing would rip the paper open. This would cause quite a bit of repair work.

It took a lot of effort to trim the glider; the nose was made of a very light wood called Balsa and was filled with little lead balls. You had to try over and over again until you found the right balance. We usually did this in open air on one of the fields not too far from home. Papa carried the glider; we carried the wings and some paper and glue. We also took binoculars in case the glider really flew a few hundred meters. Papa had some from the police.

We arrived at the Eastern corner of the field; we used this place as a base for our little flight experiments with the glider. The ground made a little dip down, maybe six meters or so. We stood on a little hill on top of the rim. We would hold the glider up in the air and then give it a little push similar to throwing a javelin. In the perfect situation with a good trim and the right wind, it flew first a bit downwards and then caught air and put its nose up, gliding straight toward the next field. This is where it hopefully landed without any damage. We followed it with our eyes and tried to see if the trim was correct. One of us had to get it and carefully carry it back just to adjust the trim and try again. I think that the furthest flight I remember was about 300 meters. Unfortunately, this one caused major damage that needed special treatment during evenings in the club.

Later that year, Papa arranged for Roland and me to join the Society for Sport and Technology. Roland started to build a destroyer ship based on original plans; myself, I put a little cannon boat together that had two cannons on top similar to the ones on the T34 tanks. We really got into this and we very much liked the atmosphere in the club.

10.

I also remember the very big white villa not too far from our street behind the train station. The villa was used for cultural events and other special meetings. If you went down the Possenweg for 200 meters, you would cross a single railway. This was the same line that led under the bridge near the Soviet barracks to the east of our house. It was part of the line from our main station in Sondershausen that led first to some smaller towns and villages like Jecha and Göllingen, then onto bigger towns and cities like Leipzig and Halle. If you rode the train in the other direction, you would reach the main station and then towns like Nordhausen or could take another train to Erfurt.

Not all trains stopped at this little southern station. The station had a waiting hall and a ticket counter as well as a nice platform, not just a dirt road. Whenever a train arrived, the gates on both sides of the railway would close for the traffic on the Possenweg. We often stood there watching trains driving by with the locomotive engines pulling five or six cars or sometimes more than 20 box cars with coal or other goods. Sometimes we put Pfennigs on the rails to have them flattened to the thickness of stamps by the steel wheels.

The first Sunday of each month was exciting for me: Papa played chess in tournaments at the villa. Chess was his favorite game. He also played with opponents in other countries by mail. He sent little postcards with his next move to his opponent and those sent back theirs after a few days. Whenever the postcard arrived, Papa was very curious to find out what "he" did. On a little table in the front room, he had the chessboard showing the actual game situation. Papa was so curious that he sometimes even left his coat on and went straight to the board, mumbling "I knew it, I knew it" or "Great, he made a mistake!" It was called "tele-chess" and Papa played five opponents simultaneously. It could take a half a year until the tournament was decided. Papa was a very good player. There was once a World-Championship in Leipzig, I think it was the year 1958. He went there and saw all the big players like Tal and Botvinik. He liked this. He brought home letters showing stamps from the event.

Those first Sundays I went with him to these chess tournaments. After we crossed the railroad on Possenweg we went 100 meters further down the street and turned left, following another street for a half a kilometer. We reached a street crossing. On the opposite right corner of the crossing stood the villa; it had one big meeting hall with enough space to place about sixteen chessboards. Papa knew quite a few people, partly because he had played them and also due to his position at the police department.

I had learned a few moves and some basics, enough that I could at least follow a game. I was a beginner so my comprehension of the game or tactics was still not great. Everything I knew was from Papa teaching me how to open a game, make a strategy and think ahead as much as possible.

You could walk from board to board and watch the different games. Of course, there was absolute silence. I would have loved to ask Papa questions. He knew so much more about chess than I did. Whenever he wanted to explain a move to me, we went into the hallway and he would quietly tell me why and what I should watch next. It was alway very interesting to me. I still like the game very much today. At noon, the games were decided and so was the tournament. Papa and I went home to be on time for Sunday lunch. Mutti liked us to be on time; she cooked and hated it when she had to wait on us.

11.

Being the chief of the police department for criminal issues was a hard job. The only thing that indicated this to me was that Papa was gone a lot and sometimes did not come home during the night. He worked very hard. Crime was at a low level and murder was very rare. The offenses were more commonly theft or property issues and drunken brawls. The investigations were mostly closed in a few hours and seldom lasted longer than a few days. Papa had the title of Lieutenant, a senior police officer. The job required continuous training and schooling, physical exercise and also political discussions. The authorities planned the training. They were located in Erfurt, Thuringia's capital. Sometimes, Papa went there for meetings and discussions.

It must have been in early July; school was not yet over. Mutti showed serious signs of her pregnancy. It was hard for her under the circumstances to keep the household afloat: we helped her as much as we could. We learned to go to the shop and to buy what was on the shopping list or at least we tried to get the items Mutti wrote down. Right behind the railroad on the Possenweg was a little grocery shop. For the little daily items we went there, especially now as Mutti had problems leaving home.

Once she sent Roland to get milk and some other things. For the milk, we had an aluminum can. It had originally a cover; we must have lost it on earlier "basic research" tests. Roland and I were good at this! Oh well, the can was still usable even without the cover. Roland took it and a shopping net, that was a substitute for a real shopping bag. The advantage was that the net could hold a lot of items; the disadvantage was that some items were just too small and could fall out.

I did not go with him. After his return, I heard Mutti talking to him in a bit of a louder voice, unusual for her. I found out later from him what had happened: he had tried out the laws of gravity. He got the milk can filled pretty much to the rim; he also got the other few items he was supposed to buy. He must have heard or learned somewhere that if you rotate an open container fast enough, contents – even liquids – will not spill. Well, he certainly tested this out extensively with our milk can. Obviously, some of his experimental steps toward perfection failed with the result that half the milk was spilled, partly over his shirt and pants. Mutti was a bit angry, I guess. Milk was precious in those days.

That was not a good evening for Roland; Papa came home and read him the riot act. This time it was Roland, next time it would be probably me doing something stupid.

Papa came home with special news: his department had to spend three weeks training in a town called Aschersleben. Several of his colleagues had to join him. Training was a bit like a military school: lessons during the day and a bit of leisure time in the evening. One of them had to take the night watch. The whole spectrum of police work was covered: some sports, some weapons training, as well as investigation techniques. I should not forget to mention the political training that was more like a brain washing. Aschersleben was only an hour and a half by train, not too bad. Even though three weeks is not such a long time, Mutti did not like the timing at all.

That would mean that Papa was gone when we got our year-end school grade cards. And, he would also be gone for Mutti's birthday. "Oh no" we exclaimed almost at the same time. But there was no way around it and we all knew it. Papa had to go. School would be over on July 11th, a Saturday. By this date, Papa would have been gone already a week.

Beginning July, there were not too many things to worry about at school; all of our tests were done and lessons were filled with special education; we sometimes could choose what we would like to do. Mrs. Rosenstiel accepted this. One thing we liked was mathematical tricks; she knew a few and showed us combinations of numbers that had amazing results. Or she would ask us to memorize certain numbers, we had to add and multiply, subtract and divide – and she suddenly knew what numbers we thought of. We were stunned every time.

Once she took us through the park right next to the school, the one with the memorial for the Soviet soldiers; she told us quite a bit about the war and some history. It was clear that the GDR disengaged itself from the historic responsibility for starting the Second World War. Still, it was interesting for us to hear about it. Of course, the political background was a bit difficult to understand.

We enjoyed those days; the only disadvantage was if you expected some bad grades. I do not remember how Roland did, pretty good I think. Me too. Just "Singing & Music", which I had no talent for. Grades were given from 1 to 5. Well, 1 was very good and 5 insufficient. My singing was a 3; all the rest like writing and reading, math and grammar were a 1 or a 2. I inherited the weak singing talent from Mutti; Mutti's father cancelled her music lessons at school when she was small. She was not made for singing – and neither was I.

12.

Rolf Bohne, Papa's long time friend and colleague was fired from the police service. Too much alcohol and too many women – the police could not tolerate it anymore or cover it up. He had to go. Fortunately, he found work, hard work in the slaughterhouse. I remember that I had to go into one later in my life as a technician to repair a phone. Horrible. But there was something good that came from Rolf's new job.

Mutti got worse. Her pregnancy did not go very well; she was in her fifth month. I had no idea what was going on, just that she felt badly. Roland might have known a bit more about what pregnancy meant, but not too much more. When Mutti came from Dr. Helldorf, everything was okay. Well, not everything: her blood was getting worse. I do not know what exactly was wrong; I only remember that her Doctor recommended getting veal liver; she should eat about 100 grams every day. The only chance to get this was through Rolf's job. And it worked out: every second day, he came and brought Mutti a half a pound of fresh liver – he "organized" it. It helped Mutti's blood all the way through the pregnancy!

The doctor also told her that she heard one tone, one heart. Great! Hopefully it belonged to our little sister. It probably was the weight because Mutti had a hard time to get up or lay down and walking was quite a problem. She still took the medicine from grandma and ate the veal liver every day. The drops were pre-natal vitamins.

I did not understand much of this but I did know that Mutti was looking forward to the day when school was out and her two sons could help her all day long.

13.

Only six days of school left, this was the good news. The bad news was that Papa had to leave us for the training at the police academy in Aschersleben. We sadly said goodbye to him Sunday evening as he had to take the train early Monday morning. It was hard for Mutti to see him go for three long weeks. Bad timing! Communication would be difficult but not impossible. We had a phone, number 576, an extension from the police network and Papa would be able to call after the daily training hours; maybe not every day but at least once or twice a week.

The days went by quickly. Saturday was the big day for us: we got our report cards. We were okay with them; would Mutti and Papa also like our grades? I guess this is an ongoing question.

Mutti lay on the couch when we came home. Aunt Rosa from the second floor sat with her. I am sure that she wanted to know how she felt and if she could help. She was very helpful and so was her husband, Uncle Walter. As the chickens were not being very productive we got only two eggs, but Mutti was thankful for anything these days. She would cook them for us the same evening.

After Aunt Rosa left, we showed Mutti our report cards. She was pleased with both of them and even excused my three in singing, "Don't worry too much about this; your mother wasn't great in it either. You inherited this from me." Papa actually had a musical ear; as a young boy he started to play the violin. According to his teacher, he was very good, had the right feeling for it. Unfortunately, his father could not afford the lessons for very long. As Mutti was okay with our performance we knew it would help us since Papa could be a bit more serious about grades. He wanted us to really do our best and get a 1 in all subjects. Well, this was wishful thinking.

Roland and I went out in the garden and played all afternoon. My grandparents sometimes brought some toys from the West. I had a plastic yellow stagecoach with four horses. Roland had a little car. It was pretty warm and the afternoon passed quickly. Mutti slept on the couch. It was almost evening when the phone rang. We were just about to have dinner, so it must have been around 18:00. Roland picked up the phone because Mutti needed some time to get there. The phone stood right beside the pocket door to our bedroom in the front room. We had a marble plate over the heater and the phone stood on it. Roland picked the phone set and lifted it up:

"Hallo, Mann, who is there?"

"It's your Papa! How are you and how are your report cards looking?"

"Very good Papa, Mutti said so" Roland replied. I guess that Roland and I had the same feeling in this moment. Mutti found them very good or very much acceptable, but what Papa thought about them, we would find out later.

Mutti came and took the phone:

"Hallo Darling, good to hear from you! How are you?"

Papa responded probably that he is doing well. He also must have said something about a trip or so because Mutti answered:

"That would be wonderful! I hope I can make it, but the boys will help me. When would this be?"

After a few seconds, Mutti just said "Okay, we will do this! Love you and take care! Call me whenever you can."

She put the set down and looked at us. We were pretty curious about their discussion. Were they planning something? Mutti went back to the couch and sat down slowly. We sat down in the armchairs right beside her not letting her out of our sight and wondering what she had to tell us.

"Well, boys, we will make a little trip!" She paused to see our reaction.

"Where are we going?" I liked trips and seeing new things.

"We will go to Aschersleben by train, the town where Papa has his training. It won't be easy for me so I need your full attention and help. We will go on my birthday."

Mutti's birthday, the 25th of July was a Saturday, a week from today. We had a few busy days preparing for the trip.

14.

The pocket door from my parent's bedroom rattled slightly. I woke up, so did Roland.

"How late is it?" were my first words.

The answer was not very comforting: "It is already seven; we have lots to do before we can go!"

Mutti made it clear that we had no choice other than to get up. It was her birthday and we congratulated her with a few flowers we picked from a field and a birthday card we had signed. She always enjoyed everything her children gave her, no matter how small or how valuable. It did not matter to her as long as it came from the heart. It certainly did – we adored her and still do!

After the typical morning routine, we had a little breakfast. The next thing I remember is that we were packing a bag with things we would need for a one night stay in a hotel. Mutti had told us that we would go by train around 10:00. from our little south station to Aschersleben. We would have a hotel room for the night. Papa would spend time with us. How wonderful – and on Mutti's birthday, even better!

We packed a bigger bag that had two handles; Roland and I would carry it between us, each holding one handle. Mutti would not carry anything other than her purse. It took us a while to pack but with Mutti's help it went well. We had to leave; it was already 9:30. As we had to walk slowly and carefully, it would take us 15 or 20 minutes.

The man behind the glass sold us our tickets; they included return tickets for Sunday. I'm not sure how expensive they were, probably not more than five East German Marks for all of us. This currency was about 1 to 10 in relation to the West German Mark. It was minted from aluminum; we had Pfennigs 1, 5, 10, 20 and 50 and 1, 2 and 5 Mark pieces. The rest were bills.

We waited impatiently while Mutti sat down in the little cool waiting hall. The benches were from wood; slats were laid side by side and screwed to a metal frame. Not very comfortable: you always felt the spaces between. The seats and benches in the train cars had the same kind of seats.

The station had a platform and we placed our bag on it. Only one rail passed the station. Again, this was the railway where we put sometimes a Pfennig on the tracks just to pick up a flat, oval shaped aluminum piece after the train ran over it. We would ride to the east this time. The train would arrive in about two minutes. We would certainly hear the steam engine first with its rhythmic breath.

Then we did hear it! And not only the locomotive, also the squeaking when steel rubs on steel. We stepped to the very end of the platform and looked to the right. The noise became more intense and seconds later, we saw the train coming around the little bend that had prevented us from seeing it earlier.

Mutti called: "Step back from the edge, children!" We took two steps backwards and almost fell over the bag. We saw the train rolling in and slowing down until it came to a full stop. Mutti got up and stepped out of the hall walking slowly toward us. Three doors opened and some people climbed out of the train. We waited and then helped Mutti climb the iron steps into the first car. There were only three wagons behind the locomotive and the coal tender. The last wagon was the one for goods, bigger luggage and the mail.

We opened a sliding door and entered an open seating area with the wooden benches left and right. They were mounted back to back to form a seating area where four persons sat facing each other. Roland and I chose one in the middle of the car and sat down side by side. Mutti took the seat opposite from us. An older man helped us to lift the bag in the overhead bin.

"Please sit down and do not open the window because of the draft" Mutti advised. What a pity; it was fun to hold your face out in the wind as soon as the train would accelerate to its 70 or 80 kilometers per hour speed. Roland and I sat down. Just in time as the locomotive whistled and started to pull the train out of the station with the typical jolt. In this moment, all of the cars got straightened out behind the locomotive. It would have thrown us on the seat.

"How long is the ride?" I wanted to know and "Do we have to change trains, Mutti?"

"It will take us about an hour and 45 minutes" Mutti informed us and that we did not have to change trains in another town.

The first thing we saw was our little bridge on which we stood sometimes just to get fogged in from the steam of the locomotive engines. We passed the long wall on the left that surrounded the Russian barracks. Then we saw the fields where we got our potatoes and finally passed the maneuver site in the distance on the right. More fields, some railway crossings and a few houses along the way whooshed by. Almost like on a film strip. Roland and I could not sit still; we went from our window to the opposite one and back.

Time flew by, almost literally. We stopped only once, in Sangerhausen, which was about half way to Aschersleben, for about five minutes. Before long our train approached Aschersleben main station. Papa would be waiting on the platform to greet us. The train slowed further and further down and finally stopped with a little squeak from the brakes and the famous last jolt. We had arrived. We had to help Mutti off the bench, and Roland ran to the car door to open it with its lever. The door swung open – and Papa stood right in front of Roland on the platform. He must have seen us when the train moved slowly into the station.

Papa grabbed Roland and pulled him out just to hug him and let him down on the concrete. Then he took the bag that Roland had dragged more than carried to the door. I was next to be lifted and got a big hug, too. Mutti appeared in the doorway and smiled. Papa gave her his arm to hold on to standing on the first level of the stairs. They hugged each other several times and I could see how happy they were to see each other. Well, us too to see Papa.

We had to walk a bit but not too far. Mutti would not have been able to go for two or three kilometers, no way. Papa led us to the hotel where he had booked a room for all of us. It was still pretty hot.

We had a very nice dinner that evening and celebrated Mutti's birthday. We had lots to tell each other, so the evening was filled with stories and gossip. Papa had the weekend off, and so we could look forward to a wonderful family Sunday.

15.

Sunday morning. Sunshine and blue sky. How appropriate for this family weekend. We got up, got ready and went to breakfast down in the hotel restaurant. They had some flowers on the table but did not have much variety of food and meat or eggs. But this was secondary. All that mattered was being together as a family. And a week later, Papa would be home again anyway.

He had planned a little tour of Aschersleben before we went to lunch at the Golden Lion, the best restaurant in town. Other than a few memorials and the wonderful townhouses and marketplace, there wasn't really much to see. Honestly, I do not remember much about it. Nevertheless, it was in the oldest town in Saxony-Anhalt, the state east from Thuringia, and had some 35,000 inhabitants. It had celebrated its 1200 year anniversary in 1953. We had seen nicer towns like this one, for example Wernigerode, a beautiful place with a castle right above the town center, medieval streets and buildings and small walkways with little souvenir shops. Tourists were everywhere in Wernigerode, walking the ancient steps. From the Brocken, the top of the Harz Mountains, you could see Wernigerode embedded in a valley below.

The day went by quickly and Papa had to bring us back to the train station. We had to wait a few minutes for the train, and then Papa helped us aboard. Our farewell was not too sad; we knew that we would see Papa very soon.

Actually, we had no idea that it would be sooner than we thought.

16.

Training at the academy was tiring. The police force had schooling all day and sometimes also in the evening, plus sports. Rising at 5:00. was normal, and of course the evenings were long. What we did not know was that Papa had negotiated a free Saturday and Sunday. He exchanged with one of his fellow policeman the night guard duty. When he arrived at the building, he would have to change into his uniform, put on his pistol and report to the guard. It would be a long night for Papa: two hours on guard and two hours sleep. Then again two hours guard duty and again two hours sleep. During the guard duty hours, he had to go around the area and check the other gates and the fences and so on.

It was on his second two hours of guard duty. It was already after two in the morning. Long day! But a wonderful day! He walked around and everything was quiet and there was nothing unusual to see or hear. It seemed that there was no other soul awake. Just him. Suddenly, doing this guarding job did not seem to be that important. Nothing would disturb the silence surrounding him; nobody would see him. He decided to sit down a bit to rest. The fence would be a nice place to lean on and take a little snooze. Just a few minutes, this always helps. Then he would go back and sleep until dawn on the hard bed that stood in the guard house; not too comfortable but better than a fence in the back and no cushion under your backside.

It must have been a bad dream: "Genosse Mann?" This was the official salutation for all SED party members but also used for public officers or other political ranks. It means "comrade" and is socialist terminology. Papa woke up after the second shout and looked up – at the face of his superior lieutenant! Papa jumped up and saluted. Not only was it embarrassing but also dangerous. Having night guard duty but not being on guard? What a disaster!

"You will report to me tomorrow morning at 8 o'clock!" cut the silence. The officer turned away and left. Papa could not believe it. How could this happen? To him? Papa had a lot of military experience as he was in the Second World War as a pilot. He flew the famous JU52 with three propellers, which was given the nick name "Aunty JU". He flew all over Europe and Africa and was even shot down once over the Mediterranean

Sea, paddling in the water for 24 hours. Papa had a small scar on his chin from that. He had a lower officer's rank and knew that misbehavior or failure was just not acceptable and could cause some serious problems. Especially in his position at the police – and it wasn't the first time!

As you know, he liked to play chess. Once during the war he was in Finland, way up north where the sun does not go down in summer. He played chess with a comrade and did not realize that it was midnight already. Bedtime was at 22:00. They put him in prison for three days, which was totally unfair. In fact, his superior officer gave him a week off to fly home and see Mutti as he felt a bit guilty about it.

But this was different; a policeman sleeping during guard duty? In the academy? Papa was nervous. This could be serious, if not dangerous. He went back to the guard house and rested. He tried to calm himself down; maybe it was not that dead serious, maybe I will get a little reprimand and that's it.

It was a turning point for the whole family.

17.

Eight o'clock. Papa knocked on the office door. "Come in, Genosse!" Papa entered. In front of him sat three officers behind a wooden table. They were all of higher rank than he was. One was the officer from last night.

"Please sit down!" Papa took a place on the single chair in front of the table. "Tell us what happened last night!" was the next command.

Papa told them openly what happened; that he just wanted to sit down for a few minutes and that he must have fallen asleep for a few seconds. There was no way he could deny the facts. He said that he regretted it very much and that he would accept any consequence. What else should or could he have said? He thought it was the best defense.

"Are you aware that you betrayed our country and that you did not take the responsibility to defend it? In a serious situation with our enemies, you would have failed badly. An officer with your rank has to be a role model for many others. Your behavior is absolutely unacceptable."

Silence. Papa tried to defend himself by saying: "I always acted in the best way and never allowed myself any failure. This was the first time that

I failed in my duty and it will not happen again. My reviews have always been excellent as you can see in my file!"

All three officers showed no impression and after another few seconds, the one on the left ordered Papa: "We want you to leave the training at once, go home and report to your office tomorrow morning. Further consequences will be discussed. You should be ready for another hearing at any time. There will be a report on the incident written and sent to your superiors." Papa got up, saluted and left the room. It did not look good. He went to his room and started packing. He thought about possible consequences. The authorities did not like failure and always tried to make it worse than it really was – as an example for others.

This will be a black spot on my white vest Papa thought. He signed out and left the training camp, heading for the station. All the way to Sondershausen, he was trying to brainstorm if there was any good way out of the situation; he could not find one. Maybe Helga would know, she sometimes had very good ideas, and something men do not have, at least not to the extent women have it: intuition.

18.

The doorbell rang. It was around 11:30 Tuesday morning. We were not expecting anyone that morning. Who could this be? Maybe the mailman. I ran to the door after Mutti gave me the okay. When I opened the door, I must have screamed "Papa" as Mutti and Roland appeared next to me after only five seconds. It was Papa! He stood there with his suitcase with a somewhat disturbed look on his face.

"What happened?" Mutti asked nervously. She always had this six or even seventh sense and figured that something went terribly wrong. Otherwise, Papa would not be here, not today. This was not Saturday.

Well, Papa told us the whole story. Mutti felt that there could be serious consequences. But she would never show this, neither to her husband nor to her children. She always encouraged us to cope with the problems we ran into. She bolstered her family members and backed them as long as they were willing to deal with it. She still is and always will be a very strong character with an outstanding personality.

After Papa finished, she said: "Tomorrow you'll go to the office and just tell them what happened. They will probably inform the department in Erfurt and maybe invite you a few days later for another hearing. Don't worry too much, there's nothing you can do right now. Let's see what happens tomorrow." Papa felt better and Mutti went into the kitchen to make a cup of coffee.

Wednesday morning Papa went to the office and reported to his superior. He knew Papa for a long time and felt somewhat sorry for Papa. There was nothing he could do; at least there wasn't another one of these tirades of blame. He told Papa to be available at any time. Papa went home. Even though he felt that these harsh words from the officers in Aschersleben were a bit unfair and exaggerated the facts, he blamed himself for letting himself down and even putting his growing family into a very unpleasant situation.

He walked home trying to mentally prepare himself for the expected hearing in Erfurt. It might be good to have a better line of defense, better arguments on why it happened. But what could he tell them? He fell asleep, maybe only a few seconds, but this was a fact and he could not deny it.

Even Mutti did not have a better idea than just admitting it and apologizing for it.

19.

The phone rang. Papa picked it up. It was Thursday afternoon. It could only be the office in Erfurt. During the short conversation they must have ordered him to come in Friday morning for the hearing as Papa just answered: "Yes, Genosse! 10:00 o'clock tomorrow." He put down the phone. Mutti looked at him, Papa looked scared. She gave him a big long encouraging hug. "Just be yourself, there is not too much you can do about it now. See what they say and decide. We have to get up early tomorrow; you need to take the first train to make the 10:00 o'clock appointment. Let's get to bed on time today. We need a good night sleep."

I played chess with Papa for the rest of the afternoon, some distraction. In my early learning stages, playing with Papa was not too much fun as

I always lost. Game after game, sometimes 20 in a row. The games were short as I still made so many mistakes. Yet I learned about tactics, special moves, combinations and some of Papa's tricks. I liked those the most. Amazing what you could do and how hidden some of the traps could be. Thinking ahead as many moves as possible is the ticket. Be smarter than your opponent, put out some traps – and avoid the ones your opponent lays out!

I got better and better over the years. There were times later when Papa had a hard time beating me.

20.

It was late afternoo. Mutti was worried; I saw it in her face. Papa wasn't home yet. He was probably too careful to call from an office phone or any other phone. You never knew if they would wiretap our line, especially as it was an extension.

Trains were pretty regular but it would take at least two hours if not more to come home from Erfurt, which was about 45 kilometers away from Sondershausen. The first recorded mention of the town was in 742 by Pope Zacharias. I visited it once with my school class. I remember the Dome and the Severin cathedral, the big open place in front of them and the wonderful medieval streets including the Fishmarket. The city had many brick and beam houses and little shops, and the Krämer bridge, still one of the famous sites today.

Mutti was pacing in the front room when the doorbell rang. This must be Papa! It had started to rain a bit. Mutti walked to the door and opened it. Papa looked shaken and entered quietly our little hallway. He hung up his jacket and went in the front room. I guess we were staring at him and Mutti could not wait to hear the news.

"How was it?" she asked. Mutti sat down right beside him. Papa touched her hand and said: "Not so good. They were horrible. The bottom line is that they will put me down a rank, and I am not sure what my next job will look like. I might have to do a normal police job on the road or with the public police. Everything depends on the top guy in Erfurt."

"They cannot do this to you after all these years of hard police work!"

Mutti shouted. "You always gave your best for them and the community, day and night. This is outrageous!" Mutti got up and started pacing again.

"Yes, they can, Helga. They can do whatever they feel like. They are mistreating me and put me down and will continue to do so." Papa responded. "You know them."

"When do they make their decision?" Mutti asked nervously.

"Not sure, but within a few days. They will call. Until then, I am suspended from all duties!" This did not sound good. Mutti sat down again. You could almost see how her brain was working. She looked at Papa who made a pretty helpless expression.

"Let's wait on their decision, but I can tell you right now: if they demote you, we will not accept it!"

21.

First week of August and Mutti had another doctor's appointment. This time it was with another doctor for an examination. Papa was home and so he went with her. We stayed home playing with some of our toys in our little garden. It was another nice day with sunshine and around 30 degrees.

Years later, Mutti told me that the doctor was the one just down the Possenweg, 200 meters from home. He had cared for Mutti during her pregnancy. The regular examinations never showed any special result other than that Mutti would have a baby! Girl or boy was not clear. I guess that the examination instruments in those days were not as good as today and predictions were a bit harder. After the new test, Mutti and Papa sat down with the doctor. Of course, they were curious to hear if everything was okay. In two months, Papa would turn 40 and Mutti was just 35. I had turned eight in June, Roland was 11. So, there were quite a few years already between the newborn and us two brothers.

"Everything is fine! Don't worry! I do not see any complications. But, one thing is different from what I saw last time." He paused and Mutti and Papa suddenly got pale.

"Believe it or not – I hear two hearts!" I guess that Mutti's and Papa's chin must have dropped as far as their jaws would allow. Mutti recalls that they must have stared at the Doctor in total surprise. Two hearts? That meant twins!

"Are you sure? What is the possibility that your result is wrong?" Mutti was shocked.

"I am pretty sure, as sure as I can be at this time."

"But Dr. Hellberg never said anything to me about it three weeks ago!" Mutti was still in total disbelief.

"I would put it at a 90 percent probability", the doctor said, "I know that this is unexpected but please do not worry, Mr. and Mrs. Mann. Please come back in about two weeks and then we should do another examination and then we'll be absolutely certain."

Papa and Mutti went home thinking about all the consequences this might have – especially in light of the job situation Papa was in. 'What if?' was the big question. They did not tell us anything that day.

Two weeks later, there was absolute certainty: Mutti was having twins! Two hearts were beating in her tummy. Whether the two hearts belonged to boys or girls or a boy and a girl – that was not yet defined.

We were in for a nice surprise!

22.

The officials in the Erfurt police department had made their decision: Papa would lose a rank and would do lower level police work. They had called him and made it clear that there was no other way for them to decide the case. They would not change their minds. They wanted to set an example. Poor Papa. He also noticed that they started what we would call mistreating today. He was on the black list, so to speak.

At the end of August, he went back to work. His colleagues felt badly for him but of course could not do anything about it. Papa's long time driver and his closest colleague tried to encourage him to accept what was decided. It was still not clear what exactly his next job would be. But Papa had to think about his family now. Mutti was now in her seventh month.

We would be a family of six, which was an unexpected big responsibility and load on his shoulders. He would be able, somehow, to cope with what Erfurt decided. He had to! He saw no way out other than to accept his new job – whatever it would entail.

Mutti and Papa had long talks about it. In the evenings, when we were already in bed, we heard them talking and discussing possible next steps. You have to imagine that there was no TV, and radio reception was bad and somewhat restricted: it was especially difficult to tune in to West German stations.

Our evenings were full of conversations, playing games or reading books. My parents tried to listen to the Western stations anyway. Even fractions of sentences were better than no information. As mentioned before, my parents did not agree with the socialist dictatorship the East German government represented. The food supply had not improved in recent years, maybe it even got worse. TVs were rare and expensive, some 5,000 East German marks. You had to wait for your Trabant – the two-cycle engine GDR car – for about 18 years and had to put the money down up front! A good monthly salary was about 400 Deutschmarks at this time. Therefore, very few people had the money, and most did not have the patience to wait that long.

As far as I remember, the Trabant, or "Trabbi" for short, cost about 10,000 East German marks. Its name was related to an event in October 1957. The Soviet Union had sent the first satellite into an Earth orbit, beating the Americans to the punch. Trabant is the Germanized, foreign word for satellite. The GDR built luxury car was the Wartburg and cost about double. It was built in Eisenach, the famous town where Martin Luther translated the Bible while being in exile in a castle named Wartburg.

The government had continually increased the political pressure on the people and many felt like they were in a prison. All industrial activities were government owned and directed. They had a five year economic plan that had to be achieved. Industrial output, efficiency and quality were reported and the results were used as propaganda. Companies were referred to as VEB instead of Limited. This was an abbreviation for "People's enterprise" and meant that the East German people owned the company – of course they did not. Free speech had been out of the question for years, and criticism of the regime would certainly put you behind bars for a while. Now Mutti and Papa felt those pressures more than ever. Roland

and I knew about some of these restrictions but of course did not fully realize what they meant. When we went by the Stasi office we had to be quiet and should not look into the windows, just straight ahead. Also in school, we were supposed to be very careful about what we mentioned about our family life and what was said or what kind of mail we got from the West.

Regardless, we had a great childhood and this was certainly because we had loving and caring parents!

23.

September came quickly and we started school again. I was now in the second class, Roland in the fifth. Whenever possible, we helped Mutti in the household, went shopping and did errands when requested. Papa was still struggling with his destiny at work. His new position was yet to be determined. The nice thing was that he wasn't gone as much as in the past, came home at more or less regular hours and had more time for us and especially for Mutti.

Mutti was still furious about the decision of the Erfurt police officers; she never felt that this was a fair procedure; it seemed to her more like an execution. Papa was ready to give in – Mutti was not. She made that clear.

"I think you should resign from the police", Mutti opened another round of discussion. She waited for Papa's response and as he did not say anything, she went on with her reasoning: "They will never stop reminding you on the failure, they will always bring it up when convenient for them. You will never get rid of this in your records. They will pressure you and your career is pretty much over at the police department." Papa frowned. What was the right thing to do? Mutti made very good points and he knew that she was right, but what about his responsibility for the soon to be family of six? He had to take care of them! And a regular income was essential, obviously.

"Are you sure?" was his response following her arguments and conclusion.

"I need work and an income!" He tried to make his point.

"Yes, definitely! But that does not mean that you and I have to suffer for the rest of our lives!" Mutti had made up her mind. And if she did, there was no way to change it. "Let's write a letter of resignation and tomorrow morning you will bring it to the office so they can forward it to Erfurt." Papa was stunned about Mutti's move but nodded slightly; he wasn't really convinced yet but knew that something needed to be done.

It needed several drafts, hand-written and copied with blue-paper. Three hours later, the final version was signed and put in an envelope. It was late and Mutti was exhausted:

"I have to lie down, I am tired! You too. Let's go to bed. Tomorrow morning, you go to work and give them the envelope. I wonder what their reaction will be, don't you?"

"Yes, hopefully they do not throw me out right away." Papa was still not 100 percent behind the letter. He did not have a good night, too much thinking, too many consequences to consider. No job, no income, what then?

The next morning, Thursday September 17, Papa went to the office and handed the letter of resignation over to his superior. Mutti had to give a few extra words of encouragement to papa in this morning.

"Are you sure, Ferdi? You really want to do this? Now? You've your family and your wife pregnant? Did you really think this over with Helga?" They all knew Mutti from some of the cultural events in the police community and they knew about the twins coming soon. At least his colleagues still wanted the best for Papa. Everyone knew about the case and felt somewhat sorry for him. But in the end, they had their own agenda and could not change anything for the better. His superior hesitated and tried one last time to convince Papa not to file it. Maybe they felt that Papa was not 100 percent convinced about the resignation. But Mutti and he had finally decided to do this. That was it.

Papa left the superior's office in a hurry. "Strange," he thought to himself, "but I feel a little relieved." It's a natural feeling after an important decision is made that gives you a path forward even though it is very uncertain. His thoughts on the way home must have been all around finding new work to support his family. Poor Papa. But Mutti would stand behind him like a rock; she would not let him have any doubt that this decision they made was the right one. Where did she get this confidence?

Papa came home. A long big hug from Mutti helped to ease some, but not all, of his fears and worries. It was a rather quiet afternoon.

24.

Yet, Mutti's pregnancy was an even higher priority now. It was registered by the hospital and through the doctors that she was about to give birth to twins. The state tried to take care of its people; this was a good thing. There were enough kindergartens and pre-schools, the organizations helped families wherever they could. Nothing went unnoticed.

It was Friday, September 18. The phone rang and a nurse from the hospital informed Mutti that they would send a transport on Monday to bring her to the hospital and prepare the delivery of the twins. Mutti was not very happy about this schedule; actually she wanted to give birth at home. But the hospital would not agree with her and would force Mutti to do as they had planned. Free will? No.

I am still unsure about those days as I really cannot remember how close Mutti was to the delivery. I know from years later that Roland knew about it. Whether Mutti and Papa had explained "the issue" to him I do not know – maybe they did.

Mutti rested most of the day on Saturday. She was not feeling well, we could tell. Papa tried to cook something following Mutti's instructions. Well, we ate it – potatoes from "our" field and a bit of butter and curd cheese. I don't think that Mutti slept that night; Papa stayed in the front room where Mutti lay on the couch. A midwife came on Sunday morning; I thought it was just a nurse. Roland and I had planned to go to the cinema after lunch with some of our neighbor friends including Bärbel.

The clock had just struck noon; we had a bite to eat in the kitchen. Papa was pacing back and forth and seconds later he was called into the front room. He came back and simply said: "Boys, you have a little sister!" We were so happy! Papa smiled and said that everything is okay.

"Can we see her? What's her name? Is it as we decided?" I wanted to know eagerly.

"Yes, it is little Brigitte," Papa responded.

Wonderful, a little sister as we had wished for. It must have worked with that little sugar cube on the window sill I thought! I should remember this for later.

"If you want, you can go to the cinema now. Unfortunately, you cannot see her yet" Papa advised us.

"That's okay," we told him, happy about the good news.

We went out the front door. Bärbel waited on the sidewalk and three of the neighbor boys, too. Bärbel was in a cute yellow summer dress, very pretty! I am sure that Roland noticed it too! We went down the Possenweg to town. The cinema was close to the big marketplace underneath the castle.

Roland wanted us not to say anything yet to the other kids. I don't know really why. Such good news the world needs to know! I could not wait to tell them: "We have a little sister named Brigitte!"

25.

The film they showed was about hunters and robbers and was set in Siberia. Wonderful countryside but very lonely – and cold! At that age, I sometimes did not understand who the good guys and who the bad ones were. So I always asked Roland during the movie. That helped.

The movie ended and Roland and I raced out of the cinema. The other children did not really understand why we would hurry home, how could they! It was a 30-minute walk and we could not wait to see our little sister Brigitte.

Her name was clear from the beginning; Mutti and Papa decided on Brigitte. We liked the name, too. Not sure how they came up with it. Sometimes you have certain memories leading to a name.

We entered our little hallway and saw Papa. We could see by the expression on his face that something was not right. *Something is wrong with Brigitte* was my first thought. *She is sick or otherwise not healthy. This would be terrible!*

"What is with Brigitte? Where is she, Papa?" We stared at him expecting bad news. Papa's face relaxed, "Nothing is wrong with her, she's just a bit small. We have to bring her in a hospital in Nordhausen for a few weeks until she has gained enough weight."

"Why is she so small?" I wanted to know.

"Well, she was born a bit early, my son. So she needs to gain some weight."

Okay, I understood. "I hope they have good food for her!" I was a little concerned.

This was not really bad news, just that we would not see her for a while. That's a pity I thought. I looked at Roland: he did not seem to be very happy either.

Papa looked at us and smiled: "Don't worry, she will be fine – and the other little sister too!"

I swallowed. "What other little sister?" And Papa continued: "After you went to the cinema, Mutti had another little girl. We were not sure but now we have twins. Two little girls, one sister for each of you!" Papa was very happy.

"Another one?" I could not believe this. How is this possible? How can Mutti have two babies?

"What is her name, Papa?" I wanted to know at least her name. Papa hesitated: "We do not know yet, we did not really plan on this. We have to think about it, you too!"

Roland and I were stunned and at the same time excited. Papa bent down to give us a big hug. We would not be able to see Mutti yet, the midwife was still there. Two little girls. Sunday-born children, like Roland and me. How wonderful! We will have somebody to play with and of course we would protect them from bad stuff like real brothers do! We were old enough to do this!

Both our two little sisters were taken away and brought to the hospital in Nordhausen, which was just about 20 kilometers away. An ambulance brought them there. We would not see them for a while, I knew this. They were born prematurely in the seventh month and needed special care.

Monday morning Papa had to go to town to get the birth certificates for them. Mutti felt better. At the breakfast table, Papa suggested that the second girl would be named Karin. There was this precious little girl in the neighborhood Papa admired and he mentioned it to Mutti. She liked it too and they decided on Karin. He went to the registration office in Sondershausen and announced our little sisters as born on September 20, 1959, 12:05 and 13:00.

Roland and I also had to make a decision: Who is his little sister and who would be mine? Well, we did not fight over it and came to a quick agreement: Roland's little sister was Karin and mine was Brigitte. And I told everybody in school, our neighbors and friends.

Sondershausen knew about the happy event in a heartbeat. Mutti and Papa got many cards, congratulation visits, gifts and some phone calls. Of course, our grandparents in West Germany and all other relatives there needed to know. After they got their letters, they sent congratulations and greetings. It was overwhelming. Our family was known in town not only because of Papa's police work but now also because of the twins.

Monday afternoon, Papa's best two colleagues from the department came with a big flower bouquet and a big basket of goodies. They sat down in the front room with our parents. Obviously, it took only a few minutes until the discussion went to the other subject: Papa's resignation from the police force. They both tried to encourage Papa not to make a short-sighted decision.

"You have to stay, Ferdi. It's essential for you and your family! Think about it. There is still time as we did not forward your resignation yet. You still have the job and also a secure future with us. Over time, all is forgotten and life goes on. Don't you think so too, Helga?"

"No, I don't!" She made this a strong statement to not leave any doubt that she wanted to keep it as is. Mutti laid on the couch resting but followed the conversation.

"This is not only Ferdi's decision, I also have something to say here!" Mutti was almost furious about the policemen's suggestion.

"I am not so sure that this would be good on the long run. You are familiar with the system! It is ridiculous how they treated Ferdi and I am not letting them treat him and my family like this!" Very clear words and serious, very much Mutti. End of discussion. Her zodiac sign showed: Leo.

After the guys were gone, Mutti tried to force the issue with Papa. "You keep your resignation, this is best for all of us! Believe me, I feel this. We got a lot of money from the government for the girls and with your last salary included, we can survive 3 to 4 months. There is enough work out there and you had enough stress all these years. Nobody will thank you for your work after all and the mobbing will go on whenever they feel like it." Mutti was clear in her mind. If she had any doubts, they were gone for sure now.

Papa kept his resignation filed and it was sent to Erfurt. A few days later, it was accepted and confirmed and he was released from his duties.

26.

In the end, I think that Papa also felt okay with their decision to resign and his final day in the department was September 30. He knew the system too well to ignore the risks involved by staying and being closely watched by the authorities. Leaving their close radar of observation and keeping some distance to the officials would help. Actually, it was pretty dramatic what had happened over the last eight weeks or so. A new big family of six and Papa no longer had his good job. He was home all day and family life was different. At least, he was with us; as a family we could enjoy him and help distract him.

For every child, the government was grateful and gave the family 700 East German marks. Considering that the average worker made around 250 to 300 Marks a month, this was quite a bit of money. I think that Papa had made about 450 a month, maybe a few marks more. Well, as Mutti had calculated this would bring us through at least Christmas. But a new job was of the essence – that was for sure. But where would he find it?

Papa did not have a real education due to the war. He was recruited right after school at the age of 18, so he had no chance to reach his dream of being an engineer. He loved technical stuff and would have been a great problem solver.

I guess the war spoiled many dreams.

27.

It was just two days after Papa's 40th birthday. We celebrated it as much as we could. After school we took a walk down along the fields starting at the end of the Edmund-König-Strasse where we lived. The weather was cloudy but warm with this typical late summer mellow wind. Mutti felt much better and my parents walked arm in arm enjoying each other's presence and supporting feelings.

We had a typical coffee and cake afternoon at home. Yet, the mood was not really good, too many worries and thoughts in our heads. We went to bed at eight. I must have gone right to sleep. I do not remember anything from this evening. Bedtime was at eight usually, Saturdays around nine. This was not a Saturday.

Mutti said that it was after 22:00 and they laid side by side in bed whispering to each other. There was not too much entertainment those days as I mentioned before: listening to the radio or playing some cards. No mobility basically without having a car. Sometimes, Mutti and Papa went to a cinema. We had two in town. Mutti always needed a handkerchief. I guess the movies were very emotional at this time, movies you can still see today: simple stories with love as the all consuming theme.

The door bell rang. Just once. Mutti and Papa were still awake caught in their own thoughts. Mutti pushed Papa slightly and whispered: "Who can this be? It is ten after ten. Police, Stasi?" She was scared. The bedroom window was open as it was a nice Indian summer night. Papa got up quietly and tried to see out the window over to the right where the stony stairway led from the street up to the entrance door. He could see no one. Somebody nevertheless pounded on the door ever so slightly.

Mutti got up, too. She grabbed her nightgown and went into the hallway on her tiptoes. She opened very slowly the door to the WC. The toilette was on the right between the hallway and the kitchen and probably built originally as a guest toilette. The toilette had a little window leading to the covered porch alongside the front of the house besides the entrance door over to the kitchen window. This covered porch was basically the first floor and came in handy when it rained. Also, sometimes, having forgotten the key, we climbed into the little window into the toilette and opened the door from inside. Roland lifted me as I could easily go through the tiny window and jump inside.

There was the pounding again. Mutti looked through the slightly angled window and observed the street. No car, this was a good sign, but a little Moped parked. Mutti got her courage back and whispered into the night:
"Hallo?"
"Yes, Helga?" Somebody who knew her.
"It's me, Karl Dörre." Relief, Mutti knew him.
"What are you doing here at night?"
"Please let me in so nobody sees me and do not switch on any light!" Mutti passed Papa in the hallway and opened the door. Papa was also

astonished about this unexpected guest. They let him in and guided him into the front room.

Karl and they sat down in the living room. Mr. Dörre was the head of the registration and visa office within the police department. Whenever a visitor came to town and stayed at least one night, they had to register at the police almost like you do at the hotels these days. The police took all your personal data and also asked why you were in town and where you were staying. You also had to pay a fee of 10 West German marks per day when you came from Western Germany or a Western country. The government needed the strong currencies to pay their bills.

Because of this procedure, we got to know a couple from the Netherlands one day. He was from the Sudetenland like my parents and his mom fell out of a westbound transport train coming from there during the final days of the war. She broke her hip and had been in an old people's home since then. When Uncle Oswald and Aunt Winnie – this is what we called the couple – came to town to visit his Mom, they registered in the police. When Mr. Dörre saw that Uncle Oswald was from the Sudetenland, he sent him up to Papa's office and introduced them. That is how we became friends with them for a long time. They lived in Amsterdam. He had a Renault Dauphine, one of the late fifties models. Roland and I used to wash and clean it when they visited, and we were proud when Uncle Oswald used to say that it looked like brand new.

"I had to come at night. I do not want anyone to know that I am here. Please keep this a secret." Karl paused.

"Of course!" Mutti and Papa's nerves were frayed.

"I know about your situation and that you are looking for work. I have friends and they told me that there might be an opening for you. This is top secret and hardly anybody knows about it. You were always kind to me and I would like to help you." Silence. He was certainly not someone Mutti and Papa thought about when it came to their search for a job or help in general for Papa.

The government always claimed that there were no jobless people in the Republic. Well, that was kind of true. But when you were looking for work, you still had to know people who would help you to find a good job, and communication was difficult. Think about it: there was no internet, just a few phone connections available, just one newspaper, everything else had to go via mail and word of mouth. You also could only trust a few of your friends – if at all. In Papa's situation, he was also kind of blacklisted with his disengagement from the police, and there would be some resistance to employ him. No doubt.

"Thank you so much, Karl. Please tell us more about this job. What is it and where?" Mutti eagerly questioned him.

"One of my friends knows somebody who works at Elektro-Kombinat in Göllingen," Karl continued. This company produced electrical motors and accessories and was a "VEB". The GDR tried to suggest that all companies were owned by the people – which of course was not really true. The town was just 20 minutes away by train. One of the smaller railway stations we passed going to Aschersleben.

"The purchasing manager, Mr. Schirmer needs an assistant. You have to hurry before they fill the position. Don't tell them how you know about this but call immediately. This is all I can do for you".

He got up. Mutti and Papa thanked him twice for his effort to help and let him out. Like a ghost, he disappeared just rolling on the moped down the Possenweg not starting the engine. Hopefully, nobody observed him leaving our home!

Mutti and Papa went back in the front room.

"What do you think, Helga?"

"I cannot believe that it is a trap!" Mutti said. "What would be his motivation to do this to us?"

Papa had to think. "I do not see any reason for him coming here than really wanting to help."

They sat a few more minutes on the couch lost in their own thoughts. Then Papa got up.

"I will go there in person. I have nothing to lose." He was determined to take this unexpected chance for a new job.

"First call this Mr. Schirmer tomorrow, Ferdi. This might be our chance!"

My parents could not go to sleep for a while. They tried to consider all options and possibilities. It really looked like the golden opportunity rather than a trap constructed by some nasty people. It could be a new beginning! There was actually little risk; they agreed on this. What chances did they have after all? Time was of the essence and soon we would run out of money. Karl Dörre was from the police but seemed to be trustworthy enough.

The next morning, Papa called the manager; Mr. Schirmer invited him for an interview. There were hardly 20 days gone with Papa being at home and it seemed that our destiny had another round of surprises for us. This hopefully would turn out to be a good one.

It was now the end of October. Papa took the train to Göllingen. He met with the manager. The interview went well; it was a short one. Papa got the job! Mr. Schirmer knew about Papa and his past and also about our family's situation. That turned out to be advantageous for Papa. But that Papa knew Mr. Dörre, his friend, was of course the deciding factor. This was Friday and they wanted him to start immediately on Monday, October 30. He would assist the manager not only on the purchasing tasks but also in some of the communication with their West German and other business partners outside Germany. The money was okay; it would keep us afloat and social benefits were a given anyway. Even Christmas gifts for him and the family were provided as we found out later.

This all was almost too good to be true! Did destiny finally turn our way?

28.

Papa started work. From seven to four with a little lunch break. They had a canteen in the company. Papa had to get up at 5:00 and take the train from our little station. He made it home by 17:00. and we could enjoy him more than we ever did before. Life unfolded to be a bit more normal – if there is such a thing.

Mutti and Papa were always in contact with the hospital in Nordhausen. Of course, we were all missing our little girls. They were doing well according to the nurses and we planned to visit them in the middle of November. Nordhausen was a bigger town than Sondershausen and still is today. The next Sunday, we took the train and walked from the station in Nordhausen to the hospital. It was already November and quite cool. Leaves were turning colors or already falling off the trees. We had to wear coats. As the hospital was in the upper town we had a three kilometer walk in front of us. We all were very excited! We would see Karin and Brigitte. We could not wait. They were now seven weeks old.

We arrived at the hospital. Mutti and Papa talked to the nurse and it turned out that we would not be able to see them other than through a glass window. They were still too tiny and under constant observation. Nevertheless, the nurse had them in her arms, Brigitte left and Karin right. Two cuties and just wonderful Babies! Brigitte seemed to be a little heavier than Karin. The observation was right. She had gained a bit more weight. This was to be an ongoing fact during the next weeks and months. Karin always looked a bit thinner. We waved and smiled at them. It was hard for Mutti not to be able to have them in her arms. But it was best for them and we had to accept this. We did not take any pictures I remember. I am not sure why. As I told you, Papa had a little camera that he had bargained for with bread after the war. He took most of our pictures with it. I still have the camera today.

We left waving at them and the nurse; the nurse actually stood at the window when we looked back as we were walking down the street from the hospital. I will never forget this sight. The good news was that they were healthy and growing. In about four weeks, we would pick them up and bring them home. Ready for the Christmas Fest! Just four more weeks!

We came home late, in the dark. With the picture of Karin and Brigitte in my mind, I fell asleep.

29.

Christmas time was always great. At this time of the past century, you had four seasons in this part of Germany. From late November on we had snow, slowly but surely increasing snowfalls. It was not seldom that by the beginning of December there were already some 50 centimeters of snow.

It was the first Sunday of Advent. There are four Advent Sundays, the last four Sundays before Christmas Eve. The tradition is that you have a wreath on the table that holds four candles. Every Sunday you light one more candle until all four are lit. First Advent Sunday can be in November if the calendar turns out that way. We celebrate those Sundays every year with the family by wishing each other a good and merry Advent time. This year, Advent time would be extra special.

Firstly, Papa's company had a Christmas party – and we were all invited. Even though Papa had not worked very long for the company, they included us in the celebration and we even got gifts. They also thought about the two babies: Karin and Brigitte each got a little gray stuffed elephant on wooden wheels they could pull behind them. As soon as they could walk! Karin still has hers. Roland and I, we each got a Russian fairy tale book with some of the nicest stories I have ever read; it was entitled "The Miracle Flower". Papa also got a Christmas bonus which helped. The two little sisters needed a lot of clothes and expenses for them were on the rise.

Secondly and best of all, we would go to Nordhausen and pick up the babies. That in itself was a challenge. Having no car, it would be a big problem to get them home. The hospital could not bring them. By train was not possible because of the cold weather. Mutti also could not carry them all the way including blankets and food. Papa tried not to take a day off from work in the early stages. There was only one chance Mutti thought.

Mutti went to the police. Papa had a few loyal colleagues who could help. One was Vera; she was kind of an assistant or secretary to him during his days there. She and her husband were also part of a closer circle of friends. Nowadays, there was a bit of a distance between them and my parents. Nevertheless, she could help. I remember her and as usual, we called her Aunt Vera. She was around Mutti's age but had no children. She probably had decided to dedicate her life to the police force.

Anyway, Mutti went to the police building on a Monday morning. The next Sunday, the third Advent, we were supposed to pick the babies up in Nordhausen. Time to find a solution for transporting them home!

Mutti entered the building and went straight to Aunt Vera's office, knocked and entered.

"Hallo Helga! How are you? Good to see you!"

"Good to see you too, Vera! I hope everything is well?"

"Yes, the usual things you know but we are okay. Thanks. But why are you here? I heard Ferdi found a new job."

"Yes. He did. We are glad."

"Tell me, how are the babies? Are they healthy? Would love to see them!"

"Me too, Vera! We had to bring them to Nordhausen, they were born in the seventh month and just too small. Now we need to pick them up. Next Sunday!"

"Isn't that great? I am glad for you. It will be a nice Christmas at the Manns I guess!"

"Yes, Vera, but we do not know how we can get them home. It is cold already. The Train ride is too long and too complicated." Mutti paused.

"Vera, do you think that you could arrange a car for us? I know it is a lot to ask but I do not see any other way than to ask you."

Vera understood. She knew that transportation was always a problem, especially for civilians. Taxis were also hard to get.

"Helga, not sure what I can do. No promises. Let me see. Wait outside, I have to call someone."

Mutti left the office and walked up and down the corridor. She knew Vera would help her if she could. This is not an easy task as cars were rare even at the police force and to arrange one for what was basically a private trip would be difficult.

After 20 minutes, Vera came out and said:

"Helga, no problem, I managed it. It will cost me maybe a few extra hours of work but I don't mind. I arranged the car with Mr. Volkmann, Ferdi's former chauffeur; he will take you to Nordhausen and also bring you home with your two little ones. Keep it a secret, don't tell anyone."

Mutti sighed. What a friend Vera was! "Thank you Vera, you are so kind. This is great! I hope that you can come and visit us to see the girls. Will you call me before Volkmann picks me up?"

"Yes, I will. You are very welcome, Helga. Good luck!" Mutti gave her a big hug and left. What a friend they had in her!

Mutti went home relieved that it went well. They knew Vera and her husband for as long as Papa had been a police officer, and had spent some time together. Mutti would not have to worry and it would be a rather short trip with Karin and Brigitte by car. The wind picked up and was blowing cold. Mutti was glad when she opened her front door and could sit for a while near the big green tile oven warming up. Now she had to prepare Karin and Brigitte's arrival. She still had lots to do.

30.

That Christmas was extra special. We enjoyed our days together. Papa had a few days off during the holidays. Our Christmas tree came from the nearby forest. No problem in those days. Papa and Roland and I went to cut it and carried it home. The tradition was that it was decorated by Mutti and Papa alone and we were not supposed to see it before Christmas Eve. We always tried to get a little sneak peek through the keyhole. The tree had real candles and nice handmade ornaments. Glass balls were not a problem because there were many manufacturers in Thuringia. After Christmas dinner we went for a walk. Normally, Mutti stayed home to watch for what we called the Christ Child, in our tradition and imagination, an angel-like being symbolizing the coming new born Jesus that brings gifts. This is our Santa Claus. It brought all the gifts on Christmas Eve.

We always had a white Christmas; I cannot remember one without a lot of snow surrounding us. It was also not such a hectic season as it is today. Very quiet and joyful. I guess we all know such holidays. After dinner, we went for a walk – without Mutti. Coming home Mutti always told us that we just missed the Christ Child bringing the presents. Surprise, surprise. We never saw it!

We got new skis this time! Great! When Papa had vacation, we went skiing with him. Our favorite place was the meadow where we also went downhill with our sleds. Remember, we did not have to go too far; just down to the end of Edmund-König-Street, then right following the dirt road between the fields and through the opening of a tall and tight hedge. Further up, the meadow ended where the forest started. It was steep enough for us in our early skiing days.

Once I stood between Papa's legs and we skied straight down, not being able to turn before the hedge. We landed in it and had a hard time getting out. I had some scratches on my face. Roland skied pretty well already, and went down some of the slopes leading out of the forest onto the meadow. Once he broke a ski. It cracked right in the middle. We had to get him a new pair. In fact, it was a manufacturing defect. We went to the little factory and got him a new pair.

We had a good time. We usually came home like Eskimos, frozen to the bones and totally worn out. Mutti had to undress us and put our clothes near the green tile oven in the front room. We heated this with coal or wood. The shoes we had to keep on even though it hurt a lot when our feet warmed up. But it is the right thing to do as you know.

31.

It was January 1960, a new decade and lots of expectations. The good news was that the babies were healthy and were growing up. Mutti had her work cut out every day as we did not have a washing machine or disposable diapers. Were they invented yet? At least, we did not have such a convenience. I did not know what a refrigerator was at this time either and that you could have one in your kitchen. I think that the first one I ever saw was when I was ten. Unbelievable if you think about it. Mutti had to fire a stove in the cellar to heat water and had to pour it into a big round tub to wash the fabric diapers and all our other clothes. Very hard work! Did we ever appreciate what she did for us? I hope so.

The bad news was that it was harder and harder to get decent food and nutrition for the babies and for all of us. Starting with some basic things like milk, eggs and butter and including baby food and vegetables. Eggs came sometimes from Aunty Rosa from the second floor; milk was available in limited amounts. Butter was a real problem. How do you feed a family with four kids?

The general supply of goods and food was getting worse from month to month. The government could not satisfy the demand although they said they would or could. In addition, the political pressure got bigger and made life – at least for the adults – harder. As always, you could not say anything bad or you would risk the little remaining freedom you had.

Papa's job went well but he – of course – was not able to solve Mutti's problems raising the babies. For some of the food like butter we had food stamps. Mutti had a few more because she had four children. She always went and gave her stamps to the lady in our little shop down at the railway crossing on the Possenweg to reserve her share of butter and milk. It was clever. As soon as the delivery came, the lady would set the two pieces aside and reserve them for Mutti. It worked – usually.

Not on this Wednesday in January. Mutti came home from town and wanted to pick up the butter at the store. The lady told her that the butter was gone.

"How can this be?" Mutti was upset. What would she do without the butter?

"Mr. Roth came and insisted that this time he deserves the butter and took both pieces. You know, I could not do anything if he insists on it." Mutti went pale. How horrible. She left the store and went to the house on the crossing of our street and the Possenweg.

Mr. Roth was one of the higher ranking SED party members; he had two sons. The older one was in Roland's class, the younger one in mine. Their mother was a bit cheap, and you can imagine that Mutti did not like them. Neither did Papa. But for him it was more the political side of Mr. Roth. Papa hated these blind followers and messengers of the system. No brains but big talkers. Blindly repeating any party propaganda – no matter if it made sense or not. Papa called them communists but in reality they were more socialists in a totalitarian system. The very top secretaries of the SED were probably as capitalist as their Western counterparts. Just that the SED guys pretended not to be.

Mutti opened the garden door to walk up to the house; she was on the warpath. Nothing would ever stop her when it came to the protection of her kin and foremost, her children. She rang the bell. Somebody opened the window and looked out.

"Is Mr. Roth at home?" Mutti shouted. She knew he was.

"No" was the short answer.

"Tell him that I want my butter back or I will get it myself. I will be back when he is home!"

Mutti knew that he might have heard this; she went home outraged about the situation. The Roth's did not have small children; they did not need the butter as much as we did. And they knew about the twins. Mutti would not stop until she got the butter back.

Papa came home and Mutti told him. It was certainly dangerous to go against one of them. It would be an issue at one of the next party evenings. Issues like this were perfect tools to pillory somebody. Papa wasn't happy about what had happened but felt that Mutti did the right thing.

The door bell rang; Mutti opened and faced Mr. Roth. She was just about to start her tirade when he handed her the butter. He just said that he was not aware that Mutti needed it so badly and left. What a lie! Of course he knew! Mutti won the battle but what about the war? It did not matter much now but there could be consequences down the road. It would be a mistake to underestimate the party.

They found out the hard way. The next meeting came and they had to face the nasty comments about their behavior. Right or wrong, my parents had to accept it as there was no way to go against their imputations.

The party made the rules and the people had to follow them. Anyone standing up for himself was a problem for the system and those problems were solved one way or another, no exception.

Mutti made a decision, not very diplomatic maybe, but she was fed up. She would quit the membership of the party and would give back her membership book! As Papa was no longer such a public figure, it did not matter too much. Of course, this would put another nail in the coffin.

She followed her instinct and quit during the next meeting. They made her sign a paper when she returned the book. Mutti kept the paper, she was not supposed to. They chased her for it several times but she denied taking it. She wanted it for evidence. I am not sure what was going on in her head during those days. One thing is for sure: Papa and Mutti always pretty much knew what they wanted with Mutti being more decisive than Papa. They were always thinking about how to improve their own and their children's lives. They had burned two bridges now. This would not be too helpful for any improvement they were striving for.

32.

Oma and Opa, my grandparent's nicknames, were coming from West Germany! They lived in Mönchengladbach, this is 30 kilometers from Düsseldorf and about 45 kilometers north of Cologne. They got a visa for a few days. We were all excited and Mutti could not wait to pick them up at the train station. Papa's mother-in-law was not his favorite person but he would be able to stand her for a few days. We had waited to arrange their visit until spring for two main reasons: better weather, and by then the babies would be seven months old. They always brought us toys from the West. Things we had never seen before. They once brought me the little yellow stagecoach with four horses and some little cowboy figures I have already mentioned. Unfortunately, we could not show them to our friends; our friends would tell their parents at home and it would be seen as another faux pas against the system. You could not give your children toys from a capitalist country! Too bad. We still enjoyed them.

Oma and Opa would sleep in Mutti's and Papa's bed and they would sleep on the couch in the front room. My grandparents were 10 years apart in age: she was 60, he was 70. They were very sprightly and good hearted. My grandpa was still working but would retire soon. They had a little apartment in Mönchengladbach. It would take them the whole day to make the 600 kilometer trip. Sometimes, we looked at maps with Papa and he showed us where he had flown during the war: Italy, North Africa, Norway, Sweden, Finland, Germany to name the most frequent countries and areas. I had no idea where my grandparents lived, only that it must be far away.

They arrived and we welcomed them in our home. Mutti wanted to cook something special for them as a kind of welcome meal. There was not too much choice. She had bought some nice sausages and wanted to make some Sauerkraut and mashed potatoes for them. By the way, prepared Sauerkraut is never sour; it should be served even with a slight sweet taste!

Mutti sent Opa and me to town to get some of this famous Sauerkraut. Opa and me, what a team. We arrived at this store. It had a window front and you had to go up a few steps to enter it. On the left was the counter, way too high for me to look over. So I peeked through the glass. Opa was a tall man, probably 1,90 meters which is around 6 feet 3 inches. Actually, Oma was small compared to him, maybe about 1,60 meter or 5 feet 3 inches. They both were always dressed up and had very good manners. Old school if you want. Better than what you see quite often today.

The store sold vegetables and related products. They did not have too much on offer that day; the display counter was mostly empty.

"Do you have Sauerkraut?" Opa asked the salesclerk. We shopped there often so I knew her and thought that she was a very friendly person. Probably younger than Mutti, blond hair and brown eyes. She wore a white apron over a skirt and a blouse. She saw me and smiled.

"Yes, we do. How much do you want?" They had what we wanted. Great! Opa's answer was misleading to say the least:

"I need two pounds or 100 decagrams." Her face went dark. She looked at me. Maybe for help? Then she responded:

"I'll give you two pounds if that is okay with you." Opa had a grin on his face, maybe it was more like a smirk.

Decagram is an old weight unit; Deca is Greek and simply means 10. So 100 decagrams in the metric system would be 1 000 grams or two pounds as a pound is 500 grams. Obviously, 100 decagrams would be equal to two pounds. My Opa loved to play games with the younger people. He

69

thought it was funny; they mostly did not share his sense of humor. People still use those units today in Austria.

Now it was her turn to be funny, "Did you bring a container?" That question left Opa frowning.

"No. Don't you have one?"

"Only newspaper." No surprise to me!

Packaging material for anything you bought was rare or not existent. The choice was newspaper or you brought your own pot or any kind of container. Can you imagine putting meat or sausages or your Sauerkraut into a piece of old newspaper?

Opa was not used to this and we had not brought a container.

He was thinking, then lifted his hat, turned it upside down and reached it to her over the counter by saying:

"Why don't you put it in here?" Not very funny grandpa! She just left and came back with – a piece of newspaper. Well, we got our Sauerkraut, left the store and went home. I enjoyed being with Opa. He could tell stories and he was a smart man, I learned a lot being with him. By the way, for Roland this was the same; he liked Opa too.

It was a great meal, and did not taste of ink. Mutti always was and still is a great cook. She made gourmet meals out of nothing. She simply mastered those challenges. Papa seemed to be hard to satisfy in this regard although he very seldom had a reason to complain.

My grandparents left us with good memories, always. They saw us too seldom; our wish that we could visit them some day never died. The issue came up every time they came to visit us, but with two little babies now it was almost impossible to make such a trip. Also, the visa regulations were very restrictive, not to mention the recent developments with my parents. There was no way to get a visa for the family, not even for a few days.

33.

Papa had bought a twin baby carriage; not the greatest quality but workable. It had a big hood, good for covering sun or rain. Karin and Brigitte could lie side by side, and the carriage made it easier for Mutti to take them with her to town or elsewhere. We had to help her push when going uphill. The wheels were trouble. They had air-filled tubes which went flat regularly. Getting new ones was impossible, repairing them was a challenge. We managed; we had to. The bottom and the sides were from carton, the hood from soft plastic. The handle was okay, and strong enough to lift the front wheels over the curbs of sidewalks. We made a lot of trips and walks with the babies. Once we had to lift the carriage over a railway and once we tried to push it up the Possenweg to go up to the forest. We could not do it, too steep and too heavy. Nevertheless, we were somewhat mobile and later, this carriage would serve us in a special way.

Papa had started a new round of tele-chess. I watched him and tried to learn from his game. He sat for hours and tried to find the best new move. You have to think ahead several moves and pick your best one. Papa was good at this. I watched him and after he picked his move, he changed the board to a different set up. As said before, he played five different games at the same time.

Another hobby Papa had was stamp collecting. He had already built quite a collection. His favorite countries were Germany and Austria. The German collection was very valuable; the Austrian stamps were very pretty and colorful. I was encouraged and started my own collection with the doubles Papa could spare. We had little albums where the stamps were placed in order of the year and by theme or set. Papa also had a few catalogs that showed particular stamps and their trading value. The only bad thing with the catalog prices is that you get only about 25 percent of it in trading. There are exceptions where you would get 50 percent or more but this is rare. The goal was to get a country completed; Papa had almost completed Germany. He missed out on a few special ones. Like with every collection: you had to wait and see how you could get those at an affordable price.

Papa was somewhat happy with his job. It worked out well with his boss and he must have done a good job as he also received a nice raise after six months with the company. We had enough money to make some trips like to Wernigerode or the Kyffhäuser Memorial where the Emperor Barbarossa sat on his throne.

As far as Roland and I – and the babies – were concerned life seemed to be okay. Summer was approaching and we were looking forward to our vacation. Only Mutti did not seem to be too calm. She was always positive and caring and well balanced. She seldom showed us if she had any concerns. Everybody probably more or less says that they have the best mother in the world – I really mean it when I say this. She still is outstanding in everything she does.

Not sure if something was bothering her, but sometimes I had the feeling that she was in a different world so to speak. Papa on the other side was very quiet; I think that came from all his experience with the police; he was used to not saying anything to anyone and to keep secrets very well – if there were any.

As a family, we developed a certain routine in our daily life like many people would. The babies were the center of all activities and needed lots of attention, and Mutti had a lot of work with them. We enjoyed playing with them, carrying them around and talking with them even though they did not – yet.

Receiving packages and letters from our Western German relatives – especially from the Grandparents – was always a highlight. We heard about the differences in their lives and the typical gossip of what was going on. I think that my parents also felt the difference that was caused by the political and economical circumstances in both parts of Germany. Most of the information gained came through listening to Western radio stations, which was basically forbidden.

I guess that you had to feel somewhat imprisoned. As always in life, the question is how you handle the situation you're in: Are the circumstances encouraging you to make a change in your environment or are you accepting them and making the best out of it?

Mutti would be the encouraged one; Papa would be the accepting one.

34.

It was summer now and we were approaching another round of report cards, always a bit of a scary time. Roland and I were pretty good in school but you never knew if there would be a surprise. Well, there wasn't one this year.

Mutti cleaned house; she wrote several letters to her Mom and she wanted to get rid of some stuff we never used. Maybe Oma and Opa had use for them. In any case, Mutti, Roland and I went to the post office to send a package. Mutti needed us, as I explained before, to push the baby carriage up the Possenweg when coming back from town. The carriage could carry some additional packages and we sometimes put one on top of it or would hang a bag on the handle. The package we took wasn't very big, so that worked out well.

The post office was a big, older, villa-type building almost in the center of the town. It was painted yellow and had a big entrance stairway with about 20 steps. You had to open a big wooden door. I needed all my weight to push it open. There was then a second door that led into a big hall with several counters. The counter on the left side was for letters and all kinds of special mail, on the right was the one for packages and bulky stuff.

The carriage had to stay outside on the sidewalk. One of us – this time it was Roland – had to guard it. Mutti hated it when people looked in and touched the babies. So, our task was to prohibit this from happening. And we did. Some of the ladies would have loved to touch Karin's or Brigitte's tiny hands or touch their cheeks. No way, we had a mission and we fulfilled it. When Mutti came back, we reported how we "defended" our sisters. Mutti was proud of us.

The postman took the package, checked the address, weighed it and glued some stamps on it. The package was for my grandparents. No idea what Mutti had packed in it. What could she send? There was not much from here that they could not buy over there – I guess. Only the handcrafted figurines and wooden smoke men from the Erzgebirge, the mountains southeast of Thuringia, were special. Or the glass ornaments from the same area. At Christmas time, we sent those. But now?

Mutti paid and we went to the other side in the hall to buy stamps for letters. For West Germany, there was a higher fee, no surprise. They literally made you pay for the relationships you had with the West. We always checked for new editions of stamps, too. Papa tried to stay current with his collection. If there were new ones, we bought the whole set, which included always one special one with a higher value. This would be the expensive one in a few years. We also bought stamped versions and if there was a first edition letter, we got this too. Papa would be delighted.

We left and came down the stairs of the post office just in time to prevent another "attack" on the babies. We still had to buy some groceries – at least had to check what was available. We went to the HO. The shop was down the little main street downtown. The sidewalks were so narrow that Mutti had to steer the carriage on the road. Not really a problem as there was hardly a car passing these days. This HO shop was part of a chain in the GDR and the letters were an abbreviation that stood for trade organization. Same procedure: this time I guarded the sisters and Roland and Mutti went shopping.

I watched the people and watched the babies; they were sleeping covered up with a woolen pink colored blanket, enough to keep them warm. They were really sleeping: Karin was laid a bit on her side with her head on Brigitte's shoulder. Brigitte laid on her back sucking on her left thumb. A peaceful and precious picture. Hopefully no crazy woman wanted to touch them. Well, they wouldn't stand a chance with me!

Roland and Mutti came out of the shop. They could not have bought much. I saw just some vegetables and sugar and I guessed the other bag was flour. Oh, maybe Mutti would bake something for the weekend. Now came the hard part: pushing the carriage all the way home. Quite an effort. About two kilometers almost all the way uphill! Babies have it nice!

35.

Vacation time! Hurray! Six long weeks of doing nothing – maybe. At least we could relax and did not have to get up early and worry if we had all our homework done for the next day!

As we could not go too far with the babies, we went for a lot of walks always considering that the two little ones and their carriage was quite some weight to push. Roland and I went to the public swimming pool with friends. It was at the end of the opposite street over the crossing. In other words, we just turned left from the house toward the crossing of Possenweg and the other streets and walked further up the hill passing the unions' big building where Mutti and Papa had their party evenings. Further on, about 300 meters on the right was the pool. You had to pay entrance fees but I believe it was only 10 Pfennings. It was located on a hillside and at the bottom of the hill was this long deep rectangular pool. It was surrounded by large grass-covered grounds where you could put your blanket down, lie on it and enjoy the sun. At one end, the pool a straight slide, maybe five meters high; and on the other end it had 2 diving boards; a one meter board and a three meter. The last one was too frightening for me. Roland did jump a few times.

You had a nice view overlooking the town from here. As all children would have enjoyed such a pool – swimming or jumping or sliding in, so did we. Especially diving in the water was fun – and plunging with big splashes making everybody wet. Most of the children didn't like this but we did it anyway. We had some diving goggles and used them to watch other people under water, or to pick up items from the bottom of the pool. Sometimes we pushed the girls under water and of course they started to scream. I noticed that girls were different in many ways, not only because they had different swimsuits. We spent many afternoons there having fun.

36.

The best thing that happened to me that summer was that Papa had somehow managed to get me a bicycle. Well, it was a black colored old lady bike with 26-inch wheels. It did not look too great and all my cleaning effort did not help too much. Nevertheless, I had a bicycle and it was easy for me to get on and off as it did not have a high frame in the middle like the men's bikes. I could race up and down our street and a bit further. Mutti did not like us to go too far away; she wanted us more or less around the house. She worried about us for a good reason. It wasn't seldom that we came home with some kind of injury or other mishaps. She probably had to think about my biggest accident ever which happened about three years before, in winter time.

The town had worked on the Possenweg, the portion up from the crossing toward the forest. This part was not paved at the time. They widened it a bit and paved it with cube-shaped basalt stones that were 15 centimeters long. They also put in curbs. It turned out very well and I think that we all enjoyed it especially when coming or going with our hand carriages to get wood from the forest. It certainly was better for the few cars driving up the Possenweg.

One of the advantages for us children was that in wintertime we could drive down on our sleds. It was steep enough that we were going quite fast until we got to the flat part of the street where we usually stopped. The new pavement improved the speed. Depending on where you started to push down the street, it was a 300 to 400 meter ride. I sat in front and

Roland in the back steering the sled. We wanted to be the fastest, nothing new. Roland pushed while I was already sitting, then he jumped on and we leant back to increase our speed. We passed several other sleds and tried to overtake another one on the left side of the street. We were too close to the curbstones! We hit one of the misaligned edges of a curbstone with the left gliders. Our sled turned 90 degrees around sideways and hit the curbstone head on. It threw me headfirst into one of the piles left over from the basalt stones. Unfortunately, they had not removed them. You can imagine that being thrown into a pile of stones with head and face first could turn out disastrously! In fact, one of the edges of a stone hit my face under my right eye beside my nose. Blood everywhere. I must have looked half dead.

One of the older guys from the neighborhood grabbed me and carried me home bleeding like hell. As you can imagine, Mutti went pale when she opened the door and saw me bleeding. I had my skin and flesh ripped out leaving quite an open wound. My coat was covered in blood and I did not speak. Papa was still in his office at the police station when Mutti called. I had to go to the hospital as quickly as possible. And no car available! At least Papa managed to get a truck from the police to drive me to our downtown clinic.

It must have been freezing cold on the truck. But what choice did Mutti and Papa have? The doctor took me and laid me on my stomach on a gurney. They pushed me into the operating room and gave me local anesthesia and put a metal clamp over the wound to close it up. I remember all this, it is amazing! They did not want to sew it. What a procedure. We were there for over two hours; at least the truck waited the whole time.

I could hardly speak or eat for a few weeks. I was nevertheless hungry and asked Mutti for a little slice of sausage.

"You cannot chew, how could you eat a sausage?" Mutti was really sorry for me. I have to mention here that I love sausages and still can go several days eating nothing other than sausages or hot dogs. As much as it was understandable, my simple answer was:

"Well, then I will swallow it down." They were laughing! Still one of the memorable scenes in my life.

The accident left a nice scar on my face that is mentioned in every passport as a special sign. It could have turned out much worse! It never hindered me in any way even though I thought everybody would stare at me. There's not much to see today but it's still noticeable.

37.

It was a typical summer and it ended typically: school started and we advanced to the next grade. Roland was now in sixth grade, I was in third. Our classes had about 30 pupils, boys and girls. One interesting subject we all had was needlework where we learned how to sew on a button or how to knit a little potholder. It certainly was beneficial as I found out later. Roland started with Russian, the first and preferable foreign language. As I mentioned, you needed a very good grade to be allowed to learn English afterwards, two years later.

It must have been one of the first days at school; Bärbel, the daughter of the mayor who lived next door and Roland came home from school. Mutti was in her usual good mood. I got this from her and I am very thankful for it. I was home a bit earlier that day and we were waiting for Roland and Bärbel. They always came home together – and that wasn't just because they were in the same class. Bärbel was in one of her nice summer dresses, real cute! She became a little lady and I guess that Roland noticed this. They agreed on doing homework together and waved at each other before entering their own homes. Roland came into the house and sat down with us in the kitchen. Mutti had made a tasty homemade soup with potatoes and some vegetables.

Mutti was always interested in what was going on in school, what they taught us and what the homework was. After his first few spoons of soup, Roland said:

"Mutti, I think I am not permitted to go to high school or university." Mutti put her spoon down and looked at Roland with a serious expression.

"Why not?" Mutti asked also a bit worried what Roland would answer. Was there another political issue or was it because of his parents?

"Well, we talked about education in school" Roland continued. "We live in a country symbolized by workers and farmers our teacher told us." He paused.

"Miss Handke said that only children of workers and farmers should be further educated and not the children of state or government employed parents. We are second class to them."

Mutti tried not to overreact but could not hide her complete disagreement and outrage:

"Is that what they told you? Is this really true?" She looked at Roland and he simply nodded. "Bärbel cannot go either". And Mutti was now determined.

"You make an appointment with your teacher tomorrow and tell her I want to see her!"

Mutti got up and left the kitchen. She went in the front room and sat in a chair. Her mind raced from one thought to the next. Is this really true, is this what this system is doing to my children? Prohibiting them from a better future? Are they crazy? I have to confront them, they have to look me in the eyes and repeat their statement. Tomorrow.

Papa also very much disliked what he heard that evening. They are going to discriminate against my children for a lifetime he thought. What can we do? Going against them? This is hardly possible without risking everything; now that we are already on the blacklist. He tried to calm himself down by thinking that Roland might have wrongly interpreted what the teacher said. Helga will find out tomorrow, my father thought. My parents did not sleep that night. Something was not right.

The next morning, Mutti went to school. She was aware that she might have to wait until the teacher or the director had time to talk to her. Mutti had thought about the situation and all of the possible arguments and questions and answers.

9:45 – end of the second lesson and the long morning break in school. Mutti sat on a bench outside the teacher's room and waited impatiently for the bell to ring. The doors of the classrooms opened and all the pupils went out on the schoolyard to have their milk and their slice of bread and butter. One minute later, Miss Handke came out the door and greeted Mutti. Mutti could hardly wait to tell her off but held herself back.

"I heard that you told my son Roland yesterday that he cannot go to any university or technical college. Is this true?"

Miss Handke took a moment before she answered:

"Well, you know that in our country, we depend on the good work of our farmers in the LPGs and our work force in the many companies and these people need the education the most. The others have to step back." It was true, no misinterpretation, no misunderstanding! LPG was an acronym for the collectivized farms in East Germany.

"How can you decide on this on our behalf and how can you do this to my children? They deserve better and they will go to university after school!"

Miss Handke paused again and simply said, "This is how our country works, these are the goals of our society and of democratic socialism. As you and your husband are very familiar with the rules of our society, you will understand. We all need to comply."

Mutti jumped up and while passing the teacher she only said, "I don't think I will, good day Miss Handke!" And she was out the door trying to catch her breath and calm down. She wanted to scream out loud but thankfully kept her mouth shut and went home.

Her head was spinning with thoughts. Special events passed through her head and many unpleasant moments she had to experience over the years – with Papa, with the SED, with the police, the living conditions and now the school. Mutti started talking to herself, "We cannot go on like this! I have enough of this; my family deserves better and there must be a way out of this!" And Papa agreed with her.

38.

In October, we had what we called potato vacation; it was the time when the potatoes were harvested and we had a week off school. We went down the street to "our" field and collected a lot of the leftover potatoes. All in all, we brought home a few sacks full. While we were digging in the dirt to hopefully find some nice big ones, Aunt Rosa from the attic condo babysat at home. She loved this and every once in a while it gave Mutti a well-deserved break from her twin baby reality. On those evenings, we had boiled potatoes with butter and quark, a soft cheese similar to cream cheese. We liked it very much.

"I will write my Mom tomorrow," Mutti started a conversation. The babies were already sleeping in their little bed that was in our bedroom. Roland and I and my parents were sitting on our big round table for dinner.

"Something special going on?" Papa asked.

"Not really but I need some information. I also want to know how my sister in Austria is doing."

Papa looked at her: "I thought she was in Mönchengladbach recently?"

"That was six months ago, and I have not heard from her since," Mutti sighed.

Her sister Margit was married and lived in Austria. She lived in a beautiful area in Saalfelden. We had seen pictures from there. Wonderful mountains surrounded the town. Her husband was a dentist. Sometimes they drove all the way up north in their VW beetle to visit my grandparents, 1100 kilometers. A long trip. Mutti had not seen her sister since the end of the war when she and their parents escaped to West Germany. Mutti stayed with Papa in East Germany and started a family. It would be great to see her, Mutti thought to herself. "I would like to see her again, I miss her."

I did not feel very comfortable when I saw Mutti angry or worried, I never did; it just wasn't her. Her normal outlook was positive, caring, loving and with a good attitude. She seemed to be distracted lately. She was somewhat nervous. She probably had a lot on her mind and anyway was always thinking about her husband and her children. Yet, she was strong. She could cope with a lot of stress when and if necessary. She could work day and night if requested. And besides that, she had a big heart, a wonderful caring attitude toward family and friends. Honest and reliable, too. A mother anybody would like to have! On the other hand, you would not want to be her enemy; that is for certain. It was not only her Zodiac sign that was a lion, she could fight like one.

It was a long letter to her parents, several pages. I'm not sure besides the greetings and gossip what she communicated. Mutti would not make anything up. Fortunately – or maybe unfortunately – she did not have to with our latest experiences. It took her quite some time to fill the pages. You also had to be careful what you wrote. There was always the possibility that the Stasi would open the letter. They pretty much monitored the mail to and from West Germany.

I had never any doubt that Mutti knew what she was doing. Three weeks later, she got an answer from her mother. Mutti usually read the entire letter to us; this time she cut it short. I did not think too much about it, she probably had her reasons.

39.

Our circle of friends and relatives must have increased; we went at least once a month to the post office to send packages of around a kilo or so to all kinds of people in the West. People I certainly did not know but they were friends of Grandpa and Grandma, so this was okay. It looked like Mutti and Papa were giving things away they did not like anymore or for what they no longer saw any use. As long as they did not take my toys away, it was okay with me. We had a great condo and we certainly were not going to move to another one. So, maybe Mutti was just cleaning closets and some of the stuff could be used elsewhere.

Our family life seemed to be normal – what was normal to us! School, homework, Papa's daily job in the electro company, Mutti's daily job with washing and cleaning and taking care of Karin and Brigitte. They certainly had grown and Karin started to walk when you held her with one or two hands. Brigitte was heavier and it took her a few weeks longer to make the first steps. At least, both were more fun to play with! They were still light enough for us boys to carry them around. The twins were now around 14 months and another Christmas time for them arrived. Not that they would remember the first one, and this one would probably not stick in their minds either. I do not remember Christmases from when I was that age.

Mutti was knitting a lot; hats for everybody and woolen jackets and pullovers. Even socks. She was very good in this regard. Her education as a baby nurse and the lessons she took in what they called a women's college served her well. This certainly helped her raising us kids.

January came colder than expected; we had enough briquettes in the cellar. In October each year at the latest, a big truck came and poured tons of briquettes on the street and sidewalk in front of the house, just a big pile of black coal. We had to bring it into the cellar and stack them on the cellar wall in triple rows up toward the ceiling. We all helped but it took us usually a half a day to do this. And cleaning the sidewalk afterwards was no fun! Always hoping for a rain shower.

Well, during this January we were glad to have enough of the black gold! It was bitter cold, sometimes minus 20 degrees celcius or even colder. Going to school or work was not fun either. Mutti's pullovers and gloves and scarves came in handy and kept us warm. Sometimes the trains were delayed and Papa was late for work. But nobody would blame one another for it. Papa had a good reputation with his boss, Mr. Schirmer. His work was interesting and he enjoyed it – and he liked being away from the stress of the police work.

During the autumn days, Mutti did a lot of fruit canning. Peaches and cherries and plums; we did this for weeks – and enjoyed the fruits during wintertime. I guess that there were more than a hundred glass jars in the cellar, which was cool enough to function as our refrigerator.

The company in Göllingen had a relationship with a West German electrical motor manufacturer in Rheydt, the twin city to Mönchengladbach where my grandparents lived. What a coincidence! Not that this would really bring any advantage or the opportunity to travel there – like it would be these days. Visiting your customers is essential; I learned this in my later life. The company named Schorch Werke Rheydt was a good client to the Göllingen supplier. It wasn't that seldom that a West German company bought goods from their eastern brothers and sisters. East Germany was the best economy in the Eastern Block, no doubt, and the products were pretty good quality.

February was getting better, at least regarding the outside temperatures. It was carnival season. This tradition – similar to Fasching in Bavaria or Austria – was also known in East Germany, and Mutti had to make us costumes every year. Roland once was a doctor with a stethoscope – and I was a nurse! Would you believe this? I felt funny but nevertheless we won a prize in a competition in school! Mutti was always proud of us and there were years in which we even had to go in our costumes through town to visit Aunt and Uncle Bohne. We still have pictures from those days.

Mutti and Papa talked a lot; usually when we were already in bed. Not loud but loud enough that we could hear some words through the sliding door to our bedroom. It seemed to us that Mutti was becoming more and more dissatisfied with our situation. She felt stronger and stronger toward the idea of visiting Western Germany. Her parents and her sister being the major reason she said. She pushed Papa toward letting her go.

Papa was not so sure about it and saw danger written on the wall. Too much had happened and they both knew that they were observed by the police and by the Stasi. There must have been many arguments between my parents figuring out all the pros and cons of such a trip. Like all such discussions with serious background, when the issue is very critical or would be an important step in your life, it takes days and weeks, sometimes months to come to any conclusion. I have to assume that Mutti convinced Papa that she should try to get a visa for a week's trip to Mönchengladbach. Papa's point of view was actually that Mutti would not get a visa at all. He knew the system, how decisions were made and he expected that no one would allow Mutti to go.

You have to understand that the authorities were all over you like a dirty shirt; they knew almost everything about you, your intentions, your relationships, and your personal way of life. Our sisters were still too small to be left home, of course that was not an option and Mutti would not leave them behind. She wanted to take them on the trip to the West. Her thought was also that she needed us, her two big boys to help during the travel. And that was impossible to achieve, Papa argued.

"There is not a single official in the whole Republic who would sign a visa for a mother with four children representing the majority of the family," was Papa's opinion, "Nobody will give you the visa. Except if you go alone."

During those days in early 1961, there were too many inhabitants already fed up with the socialism they experienced, the lack of supplies, the political pressure and the feeling of being incarcerated. Some of them – and of course you did not hear this anywhere other than behind closed doors – had the courage and escaped the country. That was a much too dangerous thing to even think about. The observations of the Stasi were so good that they spied on everybody who gave them the slightest hint of any intention to leave GDR.

Escape was the last resort for many but few tried. Berlin was a divided city; the eastern part of the town was under Soviet occupation, the western under the protection of the Western Allies from the Second World War: USA, Great Britain and France. West Berlin was an Island surrounded by East Germany. Whoever wanted to enter West Berlin had to either go by plane with an airline of one of the allies' countries, or take the painful way over the transition highways with a temporary visa. Those highways were under very strong observation. The Vopos (an abbreviation for the Volkspolizei) would punish you not only with a big fine of Western money but also would take you into custody, if you would leave the highway.

Leaving GDR on the other hand would mean that you had to leave your household and belongings behind and start a new life in West Germany. Who really had the courage to do this? Go through months of fear and sleepless nights? Facing a new life you did not even know? With no money and maybe no job and living at the mercy of other people?

I guess it always depends on the intensity of the pressure you are living under. At a certain level, you do not care anymore, and you have to do something to change your environment. There were people in Sondershausen who escaped during these months; doctors and academics first; then neighbors and other people you maybe knew from a shop or a restaurant in town or a business they had. If you maybe had thought about it but stayed behind, you must have felt deserted and maybe angry with yourself that you did not have the guts to do the same.

Mutti and Papa always listened to Western radio stations; this was the only way to get accurate information about what was going on in East Germany. I do not think that I was very observant but I still overheard comments like "something is going on" or "I don't know, what do you think" or "they will do something". I was a kid and not sure what this was all about. Some politicians were talking. Well, we all know how truthful that can be!

I remember one evening when Roland and I were in bed. Laying in bed and not being tired is horrible for me, still is today. Thinking and thinking and thinking, about everything. Listening to all kinds of noises you hear, yet trying to shut out the world for a few hours at least. So, we talked for a while.

"Do you want to go to Oma and Opa?" Roland asked me.

"I don't really know but I guess it would be interesting," I said.

"They say that they have many toys and big shops and fruits and bananas and oranges you can buy every day".

"Do you believe this?" was my question.

That is what people told us who were once or twice there. Roland was not so sure either, "We will see."

"Are we going? Did Mutti say something or Papa?"

"I am not sure. Yesterday I heard Mutti saying that she wants to try to get the visa," was the information from my brother. And he continued, "Maybe Mutti will go to the police on Thursday. Papa and Mutti know Mr. Dörre who helped Papa get his new job. He handles applications for West German visas."

This was all new to me. Roland must have known more about it than I did. Oh well, at least he told me something! A trip to Oma and Opa for a few days in a brand new world. What an exciting expectation. But you had to believe Papa; he knew that we did not have a chance to get a visa. The next day we went to the post office and sent two more packages to relatives in West Germany.

40.

It seems that my brother was right. It was Thursday morning. The sky was somewhat covered with gray clouds. Mutti put on her best dress, high-heel winter boots and her winter coat with the fur around her neck. And a hat. Mutti looked great in hats. Actually, I think most women look better with hats. It was winter after all: late February and we still had snow on the ground. It was seldom very windy, so that helped.

Mutti was nervous. Today was the day she would go to the police department for a visa application and try her luck. How would it turn out? Did we have at least a slight chance to get the visa? Mutti knew the people but this would not help. It was clear to her without Papa even pointing it out to her.

Papa had warned her, "I am afraid you will not get it for yourself and all of the children. If you want to go and visit your sister and parents, you very probably have to go alone for a few days. Be sure that I will be happy for you and watch the children. You do not have to worry." That deserved a kiss and Papa held her tight for a while. Mutti seemed to be confident that it would go better than expected; maybe this was just optimism. Certainly, this was the right attitude. Nothing to lose and much to gain, she thought to herself.

She walked down the street and looked around. It was a cozy little town and she liked it even though it wasn't her home town. Everything she experienced in the years living here was pretty much okay except for the political things. She had four children and Papa had a good job with the police and now with a civil company. Not all was bad – or nothing is perfect, if you want. Well, she thought, maybe this is not bad after all. But we have no future here! Not us and not my children. Or am I not realistic? Anyway, this thought brought her back to reality. She was on a mission and had to concentrate on it.

She noticed that the clicking of her heels on the sidewalk made some men turn their heads. Mutti was tall and good looking and I think that it was noticeable. Mutti had this winning personality, a very friendly and nice character. She crossed Wilhelm-Pieck Allee, a big street that was used for the May 1st parades. Two more corners and she would be on the street where the big yellow painted police building was. She knew the way, since she had walked it so often to Papa's office.

I remember visiting Papa once: the long hallway in the upper floor toward his office. We waited for him to finish his work and so we could go home with him. It could have been my last day on earth! I was chewing a bonbon and suddenly it all went wrong. I swallowed it and it got stuck in my throat. I must have totally choked on it and could not get any air. Papa and Mutti tried to push my back and it did not help. Believe it or not: they held me upside down by my feet while hitting my back between the shoulders. I had turned blue already. Finally, I spit out the bonbon and started to breathe regularly again. It was close.

Was there any way she could influence the decision? No, she thought, no way. These policemen were highly trained and would not even allow a woman's charm to influence their decision. That only happens in the movies, Mutti thought. She wondered if Karl Dörre was on duty, but whether this would be an advantage was a big question. An inexperienced fellow could provide a better chance. Who knew?

How would they react to her request? What should she say? How should she argue to go with all her children?

She stood in front of the big stairs leading to the entrance. Every step she took seemed to be more difficult than the last. She opened the right side of the building door when she suddenly realized that somebody was close behind her helping pull the door open. She turned around and saw Mr. Volkmann, Papa's former chauffeur.

"Hallo Helga, how are you? How are the twins?" Mutti needed a second to catch her breath.

"Very well, thank you. I am doing fine and so are the twins. Always growing and now walking a little."

"Can I help you with anything?" he asked Mutti.

"No, I am just trying to visit my family and will have to apply for a visa." She stopped. Was this a good thing to tell him? He knew probably her relationships and family ties to the West. Maybe it was, maybe not.

"I think that Mr. Dörre has duty today. Not sure, you will see. Please give Ferdi greetings. How is he?"

"Doing well, thanks. It is a different world for him but he likes the job. I will tell him. Have a good day!"

Mutti left him and looked on the board near the entrance where all offices were shown with their room numbers. It seemed to be forever that she was here. Well, at least it was over a year ago, maybe 18 months or even longer. Second floor, room 217. She went straight to the stairs.

"Hallo Helga!" The voice came from the hallway to the right. She turned and saw Vera. Not now, she thought. I need to concentrate on my mission she thought. Vera quickly approached her and shook her hand.

"You look great!"

"Thank you, Vera. I am feeling fine and to answer your next question: Ferdi is doing well and the twins too." She was hoping that the conversation could come to a fast end by answering the obvious questions.

"I hope we see each other soon. Give greetings to Ferdi." It worked!

Mutti looked at the signs. To the left was Room 217. Through the glass door and a few steps to the right. She checked herself in the glass door. Not too bad she thought. It's now or never. A few more steps. Okay, Helga, take a deep breath and knock.

She did and a familiar voice said "Enter."

She opened the door and looked straight at the face of Karl Dörre.

"Helga, what are you doing here? Very nice to see you. You look great!"

"Thanks!"

"Please take a seat, Helga! I still call you by your first name."

"Of course, we've known each other for a long time," Mutti did not mind. If you give me my visa you can call me anything you like!

"How is Ferdi doing? And the two girls?"

"Oh, they are doing fine, starting to walk a bit. Ferdi enjoys his work, quite a different job from his police work. You probably can imagine! But Ferdi likes to be home every day and every night."

"I am sure. As long as he enjoys the job. You deserve more family life that's for sure. Four children is probably not always easy. Lots of work for you, Helga!" He was certainly right there.

So, now she had to discuss the visa. How should she explain? She thought the best way forward was to inform him about her sister living in Austria and slowly lead him into her desire to visit her parents. Mutti's thoughts were focusing on her family: I need this visa, I want this. I want to go to my parents, with my children. Is it really impossible? Just for a little while, please. They cannot deny this; she tried to talk herself into a positive outcome.

"What can I do for you, Helga?" It ripped her out of her thoughts and back into reality.

"Do you know that I have parents in West Germany? And a sister in Austria?"

She tried to keep to small talk. "Yes, I heard. They visited you twice here, didn't they?"

"Yes, once two years ago and after the twins were born they came to see us, too. You know, grandparents have to see their grandchildren, especially with the twins, they could not wait to see them. But my sister and her husband never made it. I have not seen her for about 16 years. It is horrible for me. I would love to see them all." Let's see if this made any impression Mutti thought.

"Wouldn't it be almost impossible to leave the twins and the boys behind? Even for a week or so?" A straight answer but that is not what I am going to do! I will take them with me!

"You are right, I cannot do this. But I could take them with me. Actually, the boys would need to help me anyway carrying all the stuff and the carriage."

Now I said it! What was the reaction? She tried to judge his facial expressions. He did not seem to be too excited.

"I am not sure if you can do this, Helga. You would leave your husband behind, just him. That is not going to be approved. You know that. I do not have to explain to you how the system works."

Papa was right. They would point this out. No surprise. The country was just afraid of people leaving to the West who would not return. But this wasn't her intention, was it?

"You know that I just want to visit and I have the chance to see my sister as she is coming down from Austria at the same time. It would be just wonderful. I need about a good week to go back and forth, that's all."

"I do not see a real chance for you, Helga. But let me get some forms out here and we will complete the application first."

Mr. Dörre got up and checked a drawer in his cupboard on the left wall – one of these old wooden pieces with drawers in the bottom and two doors at the top. He took three papers out of the second drawer and came back to his desk. "I can fill these in for you but you have to tell me addresses and names. Although I do not think that it will be approved, you have to tell me when you want to travel to the West."

Mutti stared at the papers. No chance, he said. There must be a way! She opened her handbag and handed him a piece of paper. "Here are all the addresses and names. I would expect that our family reunion could take place in Mönchengladbach during May. I am not sure yet about when my sister can drive down from Austria. But they could schedule their trip as necessary." Mr. Dörre looked Mutti straight into the eyes. He did not really judge her she thought, or did he? She tried to appear as normal as possible pretending that her application was not unusual at all. Even though it was. Papa said that he would have the authority to approve the visa. Maybe he did not? If there were somebody else involved in the process, her chances would fade further.

"The only thing you have to do is to sign the application here and I will do the rest." He pointed with his finger at the bottom of the first sheet.

"You know that I do not think that it will be approved but we can try." Mutti signed the paper.

"When would I know if it is approved? What is the procedure now?"

She tried to be as calm as possible but her brain was spinning and her heart was pounding.

"Well, Helga, I have to see. I have to show this to another colleague but that shouldn't take too long. Just need another signature. I will see what I can do. I can only hope for you that the application will be successful. You will hear from us in about five days. We have your phone number and will call you. Is that okay?"

"Absolutely," Mutti replied.

No further indication on the possible outcome, no more word. Mutti noticed a little tension now and decided to get up from her chair. "Thank you so much Karl! I really appreciate that you are trying this for me. I know that you will do your very best!" Was this a good thing to say? She suddenly doubted it. There was nothing more she could do. She did her best and it was just hope and prayer now. Karl opened the door for her and gave her greetings for Papa and for us.

Mutti felt drained. This was pure stress she thought. Whatever you say could be wrong. Doubts and worries entered her head while going down the stairs. They will probably inform the Stasi. They might observe us. We have to be careful. She left the police station and did not realize for a while that it had started to snow slightly. She tightened her belt around her waist and put the collar of her coat up. Then she pulled the hat a bit further over her forehead and thought "I need a warm cup of coffee when I get home!"

41.

The weekend was cold and grey; it had not stopped snowing and the ground was covered with 25 centimeters of fresh snow. We stayed home and played games or read books. Skiing was not really an option and nor was sledding. The snow was too wet.

Mutti was in silent council. She had talked with Papa about the visit at the police station and her talks with Mr. Dörre. Roland and I just knew that it was up in the air if we go and that the decision was pending for a few days. Papa, on his side, felt reassured on his opinion but of course would have liked it differently. They would know at the latest on Tuesday or Wednesday. There was still a chance for the visa but it was a small one. The German saying is "The hope dies last".

Karin and Brigitte were slowly but surely starting to walk by themselves. They grabbed the legs of the chairs positioned around the big round front room table and walked around it. It did not always work out and they fell on their behinds; Brigitte was rather timid; Karin was a bit braver and would get up by herself. And of course, sometimes they started crying when they hurt themselves. The typical learning curve for little children that age. It was fun watching them.

Mutti was busy looking in every drawer for all kinds of valuables, pictures and albums, books and some collectables she saved from home through turbulence of the war. It was not Roland's or my greatest interest to see old pictures from Papa's and Mutti's youth and home town, parents and friends, but they were certainly important memories for them as they are for me today as a grown man. She finally fixed another little package for her grandma.

Papa checked his stamp collection. Everything had to be in fine order, checked and listed in catalogues. I think that there were six albums in total, pretty thick ones. Most of them were German stamps and one book only for other countries like Austria. The stamps certainly represented good value if sold to a dealer. Like any collector, Papa would not like this, but they could serve us in bad times, too.

42.

The weather got better Monday afternoon. Better? Well, it stopped snowing and sometimes the winter sun came out a bit. As we had a veranda, we could enjoy the sun in winter without leaving the warm house. It is amazing how warm the sun is, even in February. As a consequence, the snow melted within four hours. While we were doing our homework and our two sisters were taking their afternoon nap, Mutti cleaned house. She seemed to look for certain things like she was missing something. She usually had everything in nice order – I learned this from her. Not that I am perfectly organized but I have my stuff in pretty good order.

We were almost done when the phone rang. Once, twice, then Mutti picked it up. We stopped working and listened.

"That would be fine" and "I will be there" and "Thanks" was Mutti's part of the conversation. She put the phone down. We starred at her and she did not look too encouraging.

"Who was it, Mutti?" Roland wanted to know.

"The police office," was her short answer, "I have to go there again Wednesday."

"For the visa?" Now it was my turn to ask.

"Yes." She did not show any indication if this was good or bad news. Well, at least they got back to her was my thought.

"Are we going to Oma and Opa?" That question left Mutti with a blank expression on her face. She did not say anything and went back to her work. That's not Mutti, I thought. Something was not right. Or was it just that she did not know at all? Maybe she was left in the dark. They obviously wanted to see her again; maybe some more questions. Who knew?

Papa came home and Mutti told him about the call.

"They did not give you any hint? Not a single indication about their decision?"

"No, they did not. They just want to see me again. They have some questions."

"Well, this is typical behavior as you know" Papa responded. "They do not want to say anything other than in a personal conversation. They are probably still cautious and will try to find out why you really want to go. They just do not believe anybody."

"I will go and find out!" Mutti was determined and seemed to have her ambition back.

"No matter what they say, I will fight it through!" Papa almost looked in disbelief. He should know Mutti, shouldn't he?

43.

Wednesday afternoon. The sun was out on Tuesday and today and it had warmed the air. It must have been some 10 degrees centigrade outside, not bad for February. At least winter seemed to have left for now and streets were dried up from the last snowflakes.

It wasn't the greatest day for me at school. We had our political lessons on Wednesday. Some stuff was interesting, maybe, but my head was somewhere else: Mutti would go to the police department today. She would leave before we got home. How would it turn out? Would we be going to the "West" where all the bad politicians ruled like Adenauer and Heuss? This is what the teachers made us believe. History was divided into the good and the bad Germans; the good ones lived in GDR, the bad ones in West Germany. The GDR had all the economical and political progress on their side after the Second World War ended, and the Soviet Union as the big protective brother. According to them, the West must have suffered tremendously and people were so poor and unhappy. We believed most of this as kids.

There seemed to be more steps today to reach the big door of the police building. Mutti was nervous, very nervous. In a few minutes she might know the decision. What would Karl tell her?

She knocked on his office door. "Come in." It was his voice, Mutti recognized it. She tried to convince herself that everything would work out. I have to be assured of it, it makes a good impression she thought. She opened the door. Mr. Dörre got off his chair and greeted her while he closed the door behind her.

"Helga, how are you? How is the family?"

"Very well, thank you, Karl!"

"Please take a seat and thanks for coming." He paused. Mutti tried to smile a bit. She saw some papers on his desk but was not able to see if it was her visa application. He did not look at her for a moment, almost like he had to concentrate on his next statement. Was this good or bad?

"We had some discussions here about your application. It is unusual and we do not really see why you need to go with all your four children. Ferdi will stay, right?"

"Yes, of course. Somebody has to watch the condo and water my flowers!" Mutti tried to make her answer less serious than the question was.

"He would bring us to the station and also pick us up on our return in Erfurt."

"I understand, I think you mentioned it last time." He paused and looked straight into her eyes. Not that Mutti's eyes weren't beautiful, but it wasn't for that reason. He wanted to know if she was telling the truth.

"When would you go to your parents?" Mr. Dörre asked.

Mutti's tension was gone slightly and she heard herself saying "As soon as I know the travel plans of my sister".

"We cannot give you a visa with your four children just like that". Mr. Dörre paused. Mutti tried not to overreact and wanted to answer when Mr. Dörre continued:

"Unless you confirm to us that you will return to the German Democratic Republic. Also, we have to limit it to 10 days maximum."

He looked at Mutti to thoroughly judge her reaction. Mutti wanted to jump up and scream but held herself back. She just smiled and said:

"I will certainly do that. I would never leave my husband and the children need their father".

She signed the papers. He handed her the formal visa and told her that she has to inform him as soon as she knows when she will travel and what the schedule would be.

"I am glad that you can do this trip and see your relatives. Give greetings to Ferdi and the children from me".

"I will do that, and thank you for your support, Karl!"

They shook hands and she left the office still holding herself back from cheering out loud. After the police building was out of site, she leaned on a house wall and looked in the sky:

"Thank you God!" She shed some tears.

She walked home. Her head was spinning. She thought about her parents, her sister. The trip needed to be organized. But first Oma and Opa needed to hear the good news. What would Papa say? He was so skeptical. But I got it! 10 days, 10 happy days.

It was a joyful evening. Papa was still in disbelief but was happy for Mutti. Roland and I did not find sleep that night.

44.

About two weeks later, we got a letter from Oma and Opa, and they confirmed that we should schedule our trip for May. Mutti had written immediately to them to tell them. In fact, they thought that it would be a good idea to be there around Whitsun, the religious festival six weeks after Easter. Friday, May 19 would be the day when we would take the train to Mönchengladbach. It was exciting. Nevertheless, we were obliged not to say anything to anybody. It was better to keep it to ourselves, Mutti and Papa said. Well, they had to get us out of school for a few days, or not? Whitsun also had the Monday as a holiday but we would need to skip school for the other four days at least.

Mutti got busy organizing. It was now March and there were still two months to go before our trip. But for some reason, she went through all of our closets and cupboards and inspected everything. It looked to me like she wanted to take tons of suitcases on the trip. What did I know! She said that she needed lots of clothes for the babies and for us and herself and that she had to send some things ahead. We went several more times to the post office and sent packages; smaller ones, bigger ones, some addressed to relatives in Nuremberg or to friends of Oma and Opa.

Mutti and Papa stayed up late in the coming weeks; they talked a lot about the trip. For them, West Germany meant freedom, good living conditions, and a future without restrictions. The information they gathered over the years from our relatives and by listening to the Western radio stations was a clear message: the GDR is a prison, a dictatorship that gave little hope for any improvement. The Soviet Union backed this regime and there was little hope for change. Some inhabitants figured that out very early and left the country. Therefore the government was very careful with visa decisions and it was odd that the authorities let Mutti go, even though Papa would stay as a bargain or security deposit if you will.

There was always something to do for the trip. Even the twin's carriage had to be maintained, repaired and prepared. It would be a disaster if it broke on the trip. We even needed to think about a spare tire and wheel. We would not be able to carry the twins outside the carriage plus the suitcases and other bags. So the carriage would serve not only the babies but also as an additional container for all kinds of baby food and bottles and diapers.

Papa and Mutti worked together on the carriage in the front room for several evenings; they even checked the walls and the bottom of it!

Mutti also advised us to take some of our books to read and other things we would like to have. So we prepared ourselves and packed a little suitcase. What would you take? I had no idea. This was the longest trip I could remember ever taking. Well, there was still time to think about those things. We had to concentrate on school anyway. It was the second half of the year and we had lots of tests to do. Mutti would think about everything.

At the beginning of April, Mutti got a letter from the police department for visa applications. It was a reminder to inform them of the schedule for the trip. We had just made the final plan and Mutti would go in the next few days to book the train tickets.

We would take the train from our little southern station in Sondershausen and go to the main station. The next train would take us to Erfurt. Erfurt still is the capital of Thuringia today. Up to there, Papa would be with us. Then, he would just help us change platforms and we would ride to Mönchengladbach via Kassel. That would be the "transit" track – transition from East to West Germany with thorough border control. No problem with a valid visa I thought.

Two days later, we had our train tickets and Mutti let the police know by return of their letter when we would leave and when we would return. The police also had to inform the Stasi; that was for sure.

They surely would watch every step we made.

45.

It was Easter week. We liked Easter. A few days off and the family would take walks and be together. Of course, Easter egg hunting was the most fun part for Roland and me. The eggs were hidden all over the little garden. Mutti would collect at least a few in the last two weeks before Easter, hard boil and paint them. I'm not sure where she got the paint. Sometimes, we got an extra package from Oma and Opa with some goodies. Mutti hid those, too.

The sun was already quite warm and the traditional Easter walks were relaxing. This year, Easter was different. Temperatures were mild and the sun was out and warmed the air. This was not unusual. What was unusual was our spirit. No matter what issue we talked about, we always came back to the trip.

Life really had changed since we got the visa. Everything revolved around our journey to the West. Of course, the babies were still the center of our family. It was pure fun to see them grow and walk and babble their first words or whatever you call those noises. Mutti and Papa were in command and seemed to plan everything with military precision. I was not sure why there was so much to prepare as it was only a 10 day trip; they knew best I thought.

Roland and I, we concentrated on our packing and considered a few little things we would like to have on the trip. We took each a book and a card game Oma had once brought us.

Mutti also had to go to school; we needed permission to miss school for a few days. Our trip would fall around the Whitsun holidays, or Pfingsten as we say. Usually, school was off for a week but we needed three more days. Mutti didn't have any problem getting the permission from our director, Mr. Rosenstiel, the husband of my teacher.

I am not so sure how I felt about this whole thing. I guess I did not really know what to expect in the West. There were so many rumors that people had a lot more things to buy and life was better and more cars and so on. What did I know! The officials always put the West down, and all the news we heard about the West were lies they said. We would see – wouldn't we?

Most evenings, Mutti and Papa prepared special packages for the trip. I was not sure at the time what was needed but thought that they packed things like pictures to show and travel items for the babies, things to wear etc. As I mentioned before, Papa also checked the carriage for the twins: wheels, screws, the handle and the bottom again and again. Most of the material was compressed paper, which was glued or stapled together and not very durable. There was also a hood as wide as the carriage to protect the babies from rain or sun.

The babies probably weighed less than 50 pounds together at this time; Brigitte was a bit heavier than Karin and a little slower walking and moving around. They still fit nicely side by side in the carriage. I also remember that the carriage had no suspension. Between the handle bar was a net that was useful for shopping and for holding Mutti's handbag. All in all, the carriage would be heavy and, Mutti would need both of us strong young men to make the trip!

Days went by with the same routine: getting up, breakfast, school, lunch, packing, dinner, sleeping. Eventually, the big day would come I thought. Roland and I were talking a lot laying in our beds fantasizing about the golden West. Toys were certainly on our mind – and food – and chocolate.

"Can you imagine that we could have eggs and bananas and chocolate as much as we want?"

Roland's simple answer was a clear "No". It was followed by one of his favorite desires, "I heard that they have a lot of cars, fast cars. I would love to see one and maybe ride in one."

Roland was always very into cars (and still is): When he was four years old, he always went to the end of the little street where we lived at that time and went to a company called Otto Stille. They sold paint for all kinds of purposes. Not that they had enough or a lot of different kinds, but it seemed to be a good business for them.

The entranceway to the warehouse and offices was a ramp of about 15 degrees and maybe 50 meters long leading down from the street through a gate to their yard. They had a small truck that stood there to be loaded. Roland loved to watch and got a kick out of seeing the truck driving up the ramp with black clouds coming from its exhaust pipe. I don't remember what type of truck it was. Later I joined him hanging with our hands in the fence watching the men loading the truck, but I was not as interested in it as Roland was.

The company signs are still there today but the business was closed a long time ago.

46.

First of May. This was really a special day in the GDR! In school, we learned a lot about the working class, its fights against the rich and the establishment in history – and the glory the workers and farmers enjoyed in this country.

Preparations for the big May parades were intensive. As pupils and Pioneers, we marched in groups in the parade. Roland and I were members of the Society for Sport and Technology where we built models such as ships and planes. Once a week we went to the Sondershausen Schloss in the middle of town. I think I told you. In one of the side buildings we had rooms with workbenches and materials. Some senior guys watched over us and taught techniques for building wooden models. Roland decided to build a destroyer with canons. I started on a little boat. Papa had built several already that we tried out together.

Anyway, we had to learn to march correctly; we went all over the schoolyard in a two-row formation. It was funny in a way: The tallest girl and the tallest boy side by side at the front and then down to the shortest of our comrades. At this time, I was already the tallest boy, which basically never changed all my life! I remember the girl I had by my side. She was not really my type – hey, I was nine years old. I can still see her face. I would have rather been a few meters back in line. Her name was Doris; I liked her better. Well, mother nature put me up front.

We usually marched in circles and to commands of a whistle like in military service – it had to be perfect. Frau Rosenstiel had to perform and therefore, we had to. We also learned some of the socialist party's songs like "The International". During the parade, we would sing them. The street the parade route took was mainly the Wilhelm-Pieck-Allee, named after the first President – like our school. This street seemed to me so wide and long. When I see it today, it is so little and non-impressive, quite the opposite from my impression in those days.

Uniforms were another issue: The boys in dark blue short pants with a white shirt and the Pioneer scarf bound around the collar. The girls in dark blue skirts with white blouses and the same scarf. Somewhat impressive. We represented the youth and the upcoming working force for the country. A vital sign for the future of the GDR.

The sun warmed us up in those spring days. It was some 18 degrees Celsius that morning, with a light wind. The streets where the parade would go where filled with people. They weren't cheering, but they enjoyed watching. During the whole parade, we held the models we built proudly in front of us so everybody could admire them and with them, our talents. It was a big event and as rather young children, it was certainly a highlight every year.

47.

May 18, Thursday night. I could not sleep, neither could Roland. Too much in our heads, too many thoughts. Between excitement and nervousness, expectations went crazy and ended finally in some weird dreams. We had to sleep at least a little bit for the big trip!

"You have to get up!" Mutti's soft voice sounded in my ear. I opened my eyes and saw her smile.

"You have to get up, Jürgen, and get ready. Today is the big day. Roland is already up!"

After three more seconds, I jumped out of bed. This was the day! I got dressed and ate a slice of bread with butter while the others were busy checking everything one last time. I straightened out my hair and brushed my teeth. I was ready!

Mutti and Papa prepared the carriage for the babies with blankets in case it was cold on the train station platforms. As I said before, the bottom of the carriage was just made from thin pressed carton, and was not good insulation. It was always so windy standing there waiting for the train to arrive!

Food had to be prepared for the babies as well. And diapers, clothes, hats and some toys. So much to think about! In addition to watching what we packed in our suitcases, Mutti and Papa had to look after all the important issues. Mutti was always great in preparing for a trip, she never forgot anything. Still today, things are in perfect order and everything is in its place. Just amazing! Papa seemed to be a nervous wreck. Well, who would not understand this? Such a trip for the family and without him. We boys could not carry too much, and would have to help Mutti with pushing the carriage and getting it up stairways. You could not really count on somebody being around every time to help.

"Do you have all the papers, visa, money, IDs?" I heard Papa asking.

Mutti just said "Yes, yes, I got it all! Don't worry!"

Still Papa did not look as if he was satisfied with that response: "Please check it again, it would be a disaster if you forgot something!" Mutti showed him; it was all there in her purse. Besides the papers, she had a picture from Papa in the side pocket. Papa saw it and gave her a big long hug. There was something sad around this scene; was it just the goodbye or was there something else? I could not figure it out. In spite of being excited, it made me a bit sad too. I would miss Papa during our trip. We certainly loved him and we always had fun with him. Ten long days without him, maybe that's what Mutti was thinking about.

We especially enjoyed Papa's stories about his school years when he was a little boy like we were then. Wow, the things he did! I am not sure what would have happened to us if we had acted like that. A big punishment would have been for certain! But telling us these stories always brought this famous whimsical smile on Papa's face. I will never forget those!

I guess I have to tell you at least this one: They were two boys at home, and in the 1920s they lived in a little village. Always on the hunt for some adventures, the street gang – that's what we would call them today – had an idea, a very bad idea.

Authorities like police or teachers and church ministers had a lot to say and were not always liked. Jokes were played on them quite often. But watch out when you got caught! In those days houses weren't built for all weathers and storms and if it rained hard, half the streets were flooded or washed away. The roofs and the eaves and rain pipes were not as strongly built either. Yet, heavy rains were not seldom in the area where he grew up.

"Let's teach the minister a lesson!" Not sure if it was Papa's idea but I would not be surprised if it was.

"Remember that the minister always has his bedroom window open," he explained to the others. Papa paused to see their reaction.

"The next time it rains, we will divert the loose part of the eaves and bend it so the water will go straight into his bedroom!" The others were okay with the idea. "When should we do this, Ferdinand? We need to get a ladder to climb the roof. And what if somebody sees us?"

"We get there when it is almost dark. I will climb up and bend the eaves. You have to watch that nobody comes around. If someone comes whistle to warn me. It seems that tomorrow is a good time as the minister has an evening mass to celebrate and it looks like a little thunderstorm is coming."

What a plan, nasty and dangerous. Nevertheless, it was agreed although some of them in the end kept themselves out of it. They gathered the next day as rain was expected and managed to get a ladder that was in a barn nearby. Papa climbed on the roof after guards were posted around the house and in the street. It must have been a hell of a job to bend the eaves even though the hooks that usually kept them in place were pretty loose. After a few minutes the job was done. Papa could return the ladder unseen and the gang disappeared.

As expected, it poured that evening. What a rain, buckets full! Some two hundred meters away, the gang watched while the water followed its usual way down the roof and into the minister's bedroom. The boys were thrilled.

The whole thing backfired on them: the minister had seen the boys watching the disaster and figured that there were only a few guys who were undoubtedly involved – Papa was certainly one of them. I will spare the punishment here but it was severe – and not only in school by the teacher, also at home.

For a few days, sitting on his behind was not really an option for Papa!

48.

It was time to go to the train station. We were all packed and ready to go. Papa and Mutti took care of the carriage down the staircase to the street. We took some bags and a suitcase. Papa went back and brought the rest. It was a little chilly but it would warm up later; at least that's what the weather report said.

Mutti went up and carefully carried one baby at a time down and laid them side by side in the carriage, covered them up and put her purse into the net between the handles. Everything was fine. Mutti went into the house one last time with papa while we were watching our stuff and the babies. It was only 6.30 in the morning, so it was still quiet. Of course, there were no cars or motorbikes.

We heard steps in the house. Frau Hendrich – or as we called her Aunt Rosa – came down from their little apartment under the roof. We had said goodbye the evening before to Uncle Walter, as we called her husband – but she insisted on seeing us as we were leaving this morning. Big hugs were exchanged quietly.

After Papa pulled the house door tight, we went down the street without saying a word. Suddenly, leaving the house behind, I felt that some kind of sad feeling came over all of us. At least I felt this way. But the trip would only be 10 days!

49.

As expected, there was a nasty wind blowing on the platform of the little station. We had made the rather short walk of 300 meters or so. We had our tickets and were just waiting for the train to arrive. Papa and Mutti stood close to each other whispering. I entered the little waiting room in the station to look if there were other people waiting. None. Even the ticket counter would not open before seven.

First thing I heard was that familiar ping-ping made by metal bells mounted on the bars and signaling that they go down to close the street. Pedestrians and bicycle riders had to wait at the Possenweg.

There was only one rail as I mentioned earlier. I asked Papa from which direction the train would arrive and he pointed to the left, which was east. This is it, I thought. Now we start this adventure. Going to Oma and Opa for a few days and seeing how they live and bring back a few goodies and toys. I got excited. Where was the train?

Then there was the familiar breathing of the locomotive, the rhythm of the engine blowing steam up in the air. It took another minute before I could see anything. It came toward us, growing from a point to a big gasping monster. We kept a safe distance from the railway. Maybe it was respect as well as caution. The train slowed down and finally came to a stop by using its squeaking brakes. Papa chose a door nearby and opened it. There was a steep metal stair up into the car. Not like today when doors are level with the platform. This would not be easy!

The porter came to help. Lifting the carriage with the babies on board was not easy. Later in the day, we had to find a different way to do this, simply bring the 2 little ones in first and then bring the rest. What a procedure! Well, we did it and finally sat down on the wooden benches. We had two opposite ones, enough space for all of us. This first part was just a 15 minute trip to the main station, so getting settled in did not make sense.

With the typical jolt, the locomotive pulled on the cars and they finally moved slowly but surely away from the station. We passed the familiar streets and houses at a rather slow speed. Everything was well known to us as we lived here for some 12 years – I was just about 10. Three weeks after we would come back from West Germany, I would celebrate my 10th birthday.

How exciting! But first things first.

Mutti had informed Oma and Opa about our arrival time in Mönchengladbach. It would be late at night, around 22:25. They would pick us up and then we would stay with them. They had a little apartment and it would be crowded and not very comfortable. I guess no one really cared about that. There will be a reunion, Mutti's sister was coming from Austria and we would have a good time. Mutti had not seen her since the end of the war.

We had not called them; it was very difficult to get through to the West. But the letter with the information was sent early enough, they should have gotten it on time. Oma was 61 and Opa was 71 at this time; he still worked in a company near their home and so did Oma. She had a job with the British Rhine Army in Mönchengladbach. Not sure what she did exactly but it was some kind of office job.

I am sure that they were as excited as we were.

50.

Our train took a long curve, an indication that we were coming close to the main Sondershausen station. The iron wheels started to squeak hitting the iron rails. The cars were shaking a bit from left to right and vice versa. Roland and I enjoyed looking out the window. We will do this all day today, I thought! Mutti looked at Papa and smiled. They were holding hands the entire time. I know that was hard for them to be apart, even more so for Papa. He was a bit helpless sometimes when it came to household and kitchen duties. And Mutti made it easy for him. He always got what he wanted presented in a very loving and caring manner. Actually, that applies for all of us. What a Mutti we have!

As before, the train slowed down and came to a stop with a jolt. If you were standing up, you had better hold on to one of those bars. Looking out the window, I saw the familiar surroundings. I had been here before several times. The main station had several platforms and around 10 railway lines running through. It looked like we had arrived on number three.

Papa went to the door to open it. We grabbed a few things and followed him. Mutti waited patiently for Papa's return and checked the babies – they were napping! Roland and I climbed down the metal stairs and waited for Papa and Mutti. First Papa went out and took the carriage by the axles and Mutti held onto the handle. This way the carriage stayed kind of horizontal. Slowly, they lowered it down to the platform. Done. Arrived safely! Mutti checked all our belongings before we started walking toward the stairs.

We had to change platforms, yet another challenge. Our train left from here to Erfurt as I mentioned; we had just about a half an hour to get to the right platform. No time to rest. We managed to get to the platform after making sure that the train would really leave from there on the schedule board. We could definitely not afford to miss it. Otherwise our other connection in Erfurt would not work out. A horrible thought!

Papa went to a kiosk while we were waiting on the platform. He bought a newspaper and a pack of cigarettes. They did not have Casinos, only Durf. He hated those, I remember. As you know, from a certain point of nicotine deficit, smokers are okay with anything. Just another five minutes and the train would arrive. We got ready to roll. Another challenge: boarding with everything in a minute or two.

The locomotive came puffing into the station, slowing down the train until it came to a stop. Everything went well and we settled in one of the cars.

Another 45 minutes or so and we should be in Erfurt.

51.

There were very few cars in town, most of them were green and had two-cycle engines. They left this blue oily exhaust behind which did not smell very good, nor was it very healthy.

One of those turned into the Possenweg, accelerated up toward the upper town, crossed the railways and turned left into our street, Edmund-König-Street. It stopped right in front of our house.

Aunt Rosa was cleaning her front room when she heard the car. She ran to the window and took a peak from behind the curtains. Her windows were dormer style openings in the roof. It would have been almost impossible to see her from the front of the house unless you leaned out. Because of the angle of the roof, she could hardly see the car but knew that it was either police or... Why would they come this early? It was before 9.00 o'clock!

Two gentlemen in long trench coats and with hats stepped out of the car and turned toward our gate, opened it and walked up the stony staircase. Aunt Rosa watched them until just before they disappeared under the entrance roof. One second later our doorbell rang.

Aunt Rosa shivered. She was alone; Uncle Walter was at work. Her brain started working through all of the possibilities. Who are they and why were they here? Of course, the authorities were informed about the family leaving today; also that Papa would bring them to the main station in Erfurt and then would return home. Many people knew about the travel plans. The door bell rang again. Should she open it? It was not her duty to do that. What if the Pantels opened it? No chance, she thought, I have to go and ask what they want. Maybe it would be good to know.

She tried to calm herself down. Where is the family right now? She checked her watch: 8.42. So, they must have left Sondershausen already and were sitting on the train to Erfurt, all of them. Okay, let's open the door. She made a brave step to the door and unlocked it.

The door opened half way and she looked in the faces of the two men staring at her. She felt scanned from top to bottom.

"Good Morning! We are policemen and would like to talk to Mr. Mann." Aunt Rosa was stunned. It's like they did not know. Probably a trap to figure her out!

"You probably know that he and the family have left for the station, don't you? This morning. The father is bringing his wife and the children to Erfurt."

The older guy said: "So nobody is here, right?" Pause, "Is he coming back? Did he say so?"

Better play dumb, Aunt Rosa thought: "I think so" she responded, "he did not tell me, sorry".

"Thank you" was all they said and turned around. One followed the other down the stairs, through the gate on the sidewalk. Aunt Rosa quickly closed the door so they would not think that she was watching them. Seconds later the engine of the Kübel started and the car left with its typical sound. Aunt Rosa went up the stairs to her apartment. When she reached the first floor, a door opened. Frau Pantel appeared and walked into the hallway to greet Aunt Rosa.

"Good morning. Who was that?" She could not hide her curiosity.

"I think they were former colleagues of Mr. Mann, I am not sure."Aunt Rosa tried to make it an unimportant event.

"Yeah, but what did they ask?" She was very insistent on knowing.

"I think that they just wanted to wish them a nice journey." Not very convincing Aunt Rosa thought. Well, what do I know?

"Have a good day, Mrs. Pantel." She left her standing in the hallway and went further up the stairs to her apartment. What was this all about? She could not figure it out. When Mr. Mann comes back from Erfurt, I think I have to tell him, definitely! He certainly knows what's going on.

"They should be in Erfurt by now" she thought and put water on the stove for a cup of coffee.

52.

The train slowed down and we slowly approached Erfurt station. We could see the Dome and the Severins church sticking out above the building's roofs. I remembered it. I was there with the school class on one of our excursions, maybe a year ago. It was great. I liked it. I could visualize best the big marketplace in front of both churches. It was a nice setting. Opposite the church were the old brick and beam houses, hundreds of years old our teacher told us. One was from the fifteenth century. Amazing. And still standing!

The brakes started squeaking again bringing the train to its final stop. The big clock on the platform showed 8:54. It must have taken us almost an hour. Well, as we used to say: these slow trains stopped at every mailbox! In other words, in every little town we passed, people came on board or left the train. Maybe for work or just doing some errands.

As in Sondershausen, Roland and I grabbed a few bags and things and left the train. Papa followed with the suitcases and Mutti finally came with the carriage – first the babies, then the vehicle. Here we were, the last stop before the long ride to Mönchengladbach. I only knew that it would take us 10 hours or so. I had no idea what the distance was in kilometers. I never asked Roland or Papa.

"We have 1 hour and a half here," I heard Mutti saying to Papa. In fact, Papa would wait until after we had left to make it easier for all of us to hop onto the final train. It would not be difficult for Papa to get home: trains were frequently going back and forth from Erfurt to Sondershausen.

We decided to go to the café in the station and relax a while. We walked through the big entrance hall with its columns and the stone floor. There were sun beams hitting the floor that made the hall give a better impression than it really held. A little Kiosk, a newspaper shop and the café were about everything entertaining here – other than watching people. Isn't that fun? Always!

Mutti would go for a coffee and a piece of cake, Papa maybe a beer. We usually got lemonade. The babies – amazingly – were still napping. Mutti nevertheless checked on them: soon we needed to wake them up and feed them. Mutti had two warm milk bottles under their covers; they should be still warm!

Roland ran around and checked out the station. Not much to see! And everything was dirty from that black dust. Mutti always reminded us not to touch anything. Oh well, let's make it short and say we needed to wash our hands twice when we came back to the café. Mutti was showing some anger. "Always something with these guys," she must have thought. As long as there was soap we could manage.

Papa was not in a very good mood; I saw how he sat close to Mutti and from time to time held her hand tight. He certainly did not like that we were leaving him. Actually, he never liked it! He needed Mutti more than we needed her, I guess. She pampered him all her life – and us too I have to admit. Papa whispered something into Mutti's ear that somehow did not really cheer her up. In fact, she took her handkerchief and wiped a tear away. What could have been so sad today?

The babies woke up and demanded their food. They were dressed in their knitted little red jackets; they wore pants that Mutti had sewn on her sewing machine. It was a Singer. You had to paddle with your foot and the needle would speed up and make every stitch you wanted going in every direction needed.

Our train would arrive at around 10:15 and would stop for a few minutes. It came from Dresden. We obviously needed the time to get on it.

Papa paid for our beverages; 3.35 East German marks plus 15 Pfennings tip. Those were the days! Pretty cheap considering what we pay now. At this time the exchange rate between East and West German Marks was around 1 to 10. Of course, that does not really apply when it comes to your daily cost of living. We paid much less rent than my grandparents and food was cheaper too.

We got up and grabbed our belongings. We then walked toward platform seven. It will be nice to just sit down and not change trains for a while I thought. But with Papa here, it wasn't bad at all. I watched the small red hand going around the big clock indicating the seconds passing. Every time the small hand reached the 12, the minute hand went one tick further. Once I heard people saying that time stopped for them. It did not seem to be possible to me. I wondered what they meant.

It was now 10:13. The loudspeaker clicked and a voice said that the train from Dresden to Mönchengladbach via Kassel was on its way and that everyone should be careful on the platform and step back. Mutti immediately pulled us back from the edge to a safe distance. You could hear the locomotive already and seconds later we saw it approaching Erfurt station. It seemed that you weren't really sure if it would find the right track to platform seven. But it did.

We had second class tickets and looked for a car that would be close to us. The cars all had cabins with six seats. Just right for the five of us! There were no seating arrangements, except the baby carriage had to be outside the cabin: near the doors, opposite the WC.

The doors opened. Mutti gave Papa a long big hug and kiss. They stood together like they were glued and would not let go. Another hug and another kiss. Finally, they turned to us and then started loading our bags and suitcases. Of course, we helped. Roland went upfront to look for a nice cabin. I followed and we occupied it leaving our stuff there before going back to Mutti and Papa.

Mutti had taken Karin out of the carriage and stepped into the train, guided by us, to our cabin; Papa followed with Brigitte. Brave as we were, Roland grabbed the front of the carriage and as I was the smaller one I went to take the handle to bring it up the metal steps into the train. We managed but only because Papa appeared behind me and helped me to pull it in. It had to stay there in the front of the car by the door as I mentioned. We placed it nicely against the wall so it could not move. Papa did go a last time into our cabin and said good-bye to us. Mutti started crying, too much for her. I have to admit that it was a touching moment for all of us. We just have to look forward to the welcome when we come home I thought. That would help.

A final hug and kiss from Papa and he left the car. He came to our window and watched us. Somehow, I could not wait for the train to leave the station. I did not like this farewell. I heard a whistle. The conductor who stood on the platform checked if all doors were closed and the train was ready to leave. Seconds later another whistle, a jolt and we moved.

We were waving as long as possible to Papa who walked a while with us until we were too fast. He finally disappeared from our view.

There was silence for quite a while between us. Mutti was still crying. She wiped her eyes.

53.

Aunt Rosa was still a little nervous about the morning event. She had her coffee and stayed in her apartment. She could not make anything out of it. What was the reason that these two men came and asked for the family? She thought about us, looked at her kitchen clock. It was just a few minutes to 11 now. They must have left Erfurt already she thought. And Mr. Mann would be on his way home now. Of course, she wasn't sure when he would be back.

Uncle Walter never came home for lunch; it was too long of a way from downtown, about three kilometers. He rode his old black bicycle which served him well. But going home was out of the question during the 30 minute break – and all uphill. He wasn't the youngest either.

He worked in a plant where they built and repaired tractors for the farming industry. In fact, there was no real industry, all VEB and LPG. VEB stood for all companies as owned by the people of the GDR; I think I mentioned this already. On the other hand, LPG stood for the collectivized farms: all farmers were treated as a big family. They had to produce everything for the country and could only keep a small portion for themselves. It was all managed by the government according to their five year economic plan. That was never achieved!

In a while Aunt Rosa would cook for herself some vegetables and potatoes. Sitting on her old chaise longue, as she called it, Aunty Rosa dozed off a bit. She felt tired. All these weeks she tried to help us wherever she could with the preparation of our trip. She babysat, helped with the cooking, helped with the shopping – or if there was anything unusual to buy. You could really count on her.

Pantels from the first floor, were more reserved and lived their own life apart from us. Just the usual hello and good morning greetings. That was it. They had no children.

A noise woke her up. Almost like somebody was banging on a door. First, she did not trust her senses as she suddenly realized that she must have slept for an hour or so. The kitchen clock showed 11:45.

But here it was again. The first thing which came to mind was carefully opening the window in the roof and trying to look down on the street. She was shocked! There it was parked. Another green car like the one from this morning! She was paralyzed. Could this be – them again?

There was the banging again and a shout "Hello, is anyone there?"

Scary, she thought. It took her a moment to make up her mind – then she went down to open the door. She did not want Mrs. Pantel to open the door. She was just too nosy. She also did not want them breaking down the door.

She turned the key in the front door and opened it. Two policemen in uniform stood there with a very serious facial expression. They greeted her with a short "Good Day" and waited for her response. There wasn't any. After what seemed to be a little eternity, the skinny one asked her: "Do you have keys to the condo of the Mann family?" followed by their reasoning, "We just want to see it." Aunt Rosa was shocked. This – is unbelievable!

Her thoughts went wild. What do they have in mind? They just cannot enter somebody's property like this! It would have been very dangerous. What do I do? I cannot let them in, no way. What are they looking for?

"No, I do not have one. I think that there will be somebody home later this afternoon." She surprised herself by being that calm and giving such a good answer. Giving them an expectation would probably keep them from forcing their way in. The two men looked at each other; it seemed like they could read each other's mind. They were trained to do this. They looked around, checking the windows, looked at Aunt Rosa,

"We are coming back." It sounded like a threat. They turned and walked down the stairs. Aunt Rosa shivered again. "This is too much for me," she thought, "I wish Mr. Mann would come back and I could tell him that 'they' were here." She closed the door, locked it and went up to her apartment as quickly as possible. Hopefully, she could avoid Mrs. Pantel. The first floor was quiet. They were gone she noticed. Good! In her kitchen, she sat down and sighed. The clock showed 11:58. He should be home soon.

If they had known that the doors of the condo were not closed! They were open! Just four quick steps and trying the door handle would have let them in the condo!

Just a few days before, Brigitte sat on the couch as she could not yet walk on her own; she was always a bit heavier than Karin and so she did not have the courage or the stability to walk. Karin did already. Anyway, she sat on the couch and had Mutti's full key ring with all the keys from the house to play with. Mutti had to do some cooking in the kitchen. When she came back, Brigitte had lost the keys. Well, not too many options here to find them, right? You would think. They did not find them! Believe it or not, the keys were gone! Even turning the couch and searching the upholstery did not turn them up. So, when we left that morning we could not lock the doors of the condo. Papa only had front door keys. How close to a disaster this was!

Another deep sigh and Aunt Rosa started cooking her lunch.

54.

Papa took another look at the train leaving. He had tears in his eyes too. It just made him realize how much his family meant to him and how much he would miss us. He turned around and walked toward the stairs. He had to go to another platform to catch the train home to Sondershausen.

He looked around. As a former policeman, he would see anything suspicious. He remembered how he was trained to observe every little detail surrounding him.

There was a good chance that "they" watched him or observed him. It was not totally out of the question. The whole situation was serious, not only for the family but also for the authorities. Maybe they regretted giving Helga and the children the visa. Maybe they felt that something was going on. Maybe they were just overly cautious. Everything was possible. The Stasi certainly had a sixth sense.

Once, at police school, the teacher let a cleaning guy in to wash the classroom windows. After he had finished the work and left, the teacher asked them to describe the person in full detail: behavior, type of person and so on. Very tricky but it was a good lesson. "I just have to be careful and watch my environment," Papa thought.

He went down the stairs. At the end, there was a long tunnel leading from the entrance hall of the station to the platforms, twelve of them. He decided to walk toward the hall and maybe have a rost-bratwurst on a roll. These local Thuringia sausages were fabulous! They were grilled on wood-fired grill and tasted great. Good idea, he thought. While approaching the entrance of the station, he noticed somebody following him. In the window of the coffee shop he saw a man with a briefcase. It did not look like he was in a uniform. Papa stopped to light a cigarette. The man walked by without any noticeable interest in Papa. Well, better be safe than sorry. Papa looked for the bratwurst grill. The stand was right in front of the station entrance. He bought himself one of the crispy ones inside a roll. He put some mustard on and had a first bite. "Good food," Papa thought.

55.

The train was going pretty fast; not sure but maybe around a hundred kilometers an hour. The countryside was pretty. Well, it was spring after all.

The trees were blooming, and so were the flowers. The sun wasn't really bright that day but at least it did not rain. Many little villages flew by our window. It was interesting to see how the landscape changed from hilly to flat and to hilly again. The Harz was even mountainous.

Mutti had turned our cabin into a living room! You could expect this! There were beds made for the babies out of two blankets and their two little pillows. They certainly seemed to like it as they were laying quite comfortably. A few toys in reach and food whenever it was desired – how could they not enjoy it! Mutti sat beside them and had the curtains closed so it was easier for them to fall asleep.

We sat opposite from Mutti having the whole bench for ourselves. We had packed two books to read but the view out the window was much more interesting. We also had to guard the baby carriage, which was outside down the hallway at the door of the car. Mutti was very keen on checking on it every half hour; I did not get it. Who would take it? Nobody needed a twin carriage! Oh well, Mutti wanted us to do this for her and we followed her wish. Whenever the train came to a stop on one of the stations we passed, we were extra observant and guarded it until the train left again.

The conductor was a serious man; he checked our tickets soon after we left Erfurt. Mutti also had to show him the visa. It was a thorough check: names, address, destination, and visa validation. It was not that often that almost a whole family went to the West with legal papers so to speak. During recent weeks, we had heard about some people escaping to the West: doctors, other academics, families, as well as single persons. When something like this happened in Sondershausen, it really took only a short time until everybody talked about it. For some reason the number seemed to be increasing lately. I did not pay too much attention to those things; I had my own agenda. And this was not as serious.

Mutti told us about the border; she advised us to be very kind and very polite when we were checked there; the police would come and look into everything: clothes, bags, the carriage, even check the babies. And of course would look at passports and papers. She expected that it would probably take 10 to 15 minutes.

There was still an hour of train ride to Bebra, the border town.

56.

Papa returned to the station and walked toward platform number five. This was where the train to Sondershausen would leave. Another ten minutes and he would be on his way home. He could not stop thinking about us. How are they doing, everything okay? How would the border check go for them? It would be a very serious situation. There was always the chance that something would go wrong – or the authorities simply would find a reason to reverse any of their decisions. Unfortunately, there was no way to communicate; no phones or mobiles like today.

He walked up the stairs to the platform. There were a few more people now. The weekend had started and people were travelling for a relaxing weekend maybe, or simply were going to visit relatives. A whistle was heard and a few seconds later, the train arrived.

As soon as the train stopped, he opened one of the second-class doors; he noticed a man looking at him. Civilian clothes, a cigarette, a gray jacket. You would think nothing unusual. But this is always the mistake you make Papa thought to himself. These are the dangerous persons, the ones who try to appear normal, as they have nothing to hide. Papa was too clever for this and had too much training during his police job. He tried to ignore him and entered the carriage. Papa made a bit of a hesitation like he did not know if he should go left or right. By doing this, he could see if this guy followed him. He did. Okay, Papa said to himself, let's find out who he is.

Papa went down the little hallway in front of the cabins and finally decided to open one of the sliding doors to enter. It must have been the third one. Turning into the cabin gave him a short view down the hallway. The guy was gone! He had not followed him. But where was he? It would have been better if he knew.

A young lady was the only person sharing the cabin. She was reading the "Neues Deutschland", the official SED newspaper and the most widely read in East Germany. Papa went to the window and sat down. Looking around he noticed that it was a non-smoking cabin. Oh well, it is only a half hour to Sondershausen. This was one of the faster trains that didn't stop at every little village.

Two whistles and they were on their way. Papa decided to watch the platforms whenever the train stopped to see if the guy got off. He was tempted to go over to the platform between the cars to see if the guy would be in the next car. But he decided against it; that would be too obvious.

He watched the young lady. She was probably around twenty with blond curly hair. She wore a pink blouse and a black skirt, a light-colored spring jacket and flat black shoes. Blue eyes, a little golden necklace, no lipstick and weighed probably…Stop it, he said to himself, you are not with the police anymore. Those days are over. On the other hand, these skills come in handy.

Back to reality. Where was the guy? The train had stopped twice but Papa did not see him getting off. So, he was still on the train. Maybe I am just too stressed. A few more minutes and he would either see him getting off in Sondershausen or he would stay on toward Leipzig, the train's final destination.

The train wheels started squeaking again and it slowed down. Almost back in Sondershausen. Now what do I do? I still need something to eat before I go home. I have to go downtown. There should be something easy to cook in the HO shop? Maybe they have a Bockwurst or two that I can heat up. A slice of bread with some butter or margarine, and I am done for the day. Listen to the radio or read a book. Take a walk to the fields at the end of our street.

The lady stayed but said "Auf Wiedersehen" when Papa got up to leave. He eyed down the hallway approaching the door. No one else was leaving. The train was slowing further and finally stopped. He opened the door and at the same time checked down the adjacent car. Nobody looked like "him." He stepped down the iron steps and started walking following the "Ausgang" signs. The guy was not to be seen.

The clock on the platform showed 13:08. Helga was now close to the border if the train was on time. Hopefully everything was going well!

Papa left the station and walked down the main road toward the center of town. This would take about 20 minutes. But he wasn't in a rush.

57.

We were hungry. Mutti noticed this and got up to open one of the bags. She was always prepared. Kids and Papa were always getting hungry, that was a fact. It was just a question of when. Mutti pulled out some paper packages, unfolded them and revealed a few doubled slices of bread. Now the only question was: what is on them besides some margarine or butter? Mutti gave one each to Roland and I and took one for herself.

She must have planned on that. There was no way she did not! We had slices of sausage on them. Yummy! We were quiet for a while chewing down our lunch. The train was rattling as we passed a section where the rails must not have been properly aligned. Hopefully, they would not come apart.

We had stopped four times so far and must approach the border soon. At least Mutti told us that it would take about three hours and it was almost 13.30 now. Mutti must have read my mind. "Boys, we will soon be at the border. Please behave yourself when we are checked. Let me talk and you stay quiet. Okay?" We nodded.

"Roland, when you have finished your bread, please go and check the carriage again. Jürgen, you help me with the babies." It could not be clearer and a minute later Roland left the cabin.

I helped by holding Karin while Mutti took Brigitte. She straightened out the blankets with one hand and put her back in a comfortable position. Then she did the same for Karin's blanket, took her and sat her down. She slid open the cabin door to look down the hallway connecting the other cabins. Roland was not to be seen.

Always something with him, she thought. She turned around and said: "I have to see where Roland is. Stay here, watch the babies and do not leave the cabin!" She closed the sliding door and moved toward where the carriage stood, a metal platform rattling and moving but that was a passageway to the next car. The carriage stood on the one side so it would not be in the way of anyone. It looked okay. Mutti took a closer look after she made sure that nobody was watching her. She kneeled down on one knee and let her hand feel the bottom; first from the right, then from the left. Everything okay, she thought. The bigger covers for our little ones were in place and the hood was up. Good! But where was Roland? A lock clicked right behind her, and a second later Roland appeared in the doorway of the WC. "I had to go, Mutti!" he stated seriously before Mutti could say anything. While going back with him to our cabin her heart was pounding as the train started to slow down.

That must be it, she thought. I have to get prepared for the border check! She was pleased when she saw that I had not moved an inch and everything was still in fine order. She grabbed her handbag and searched for her lipstick. As Mutti had light skin, her red lips were glowing.

We have a pretty Mutti, I thought.

58.

As expected, it took Papa about 20 minutes to walk down the street. It was surrounded by smaller trees and the sidewalks were a bit old and bumpy. On the right was the SED party building, and a little further the Ferdinand-Schlufter-Strasse where we lived a few years earlier and where I was born. This was the street where the big sign of the paint company was located. Roland and I watched their truck going up and down the ramp. I told you this before.

On the way he had passed the police building he knew so well. Many thoughts came into his mind. It was a good job but often very stressful: the political pressure, always being on guard, no mistakes permitted, and always committed to the system with everything you do and everything you say. He turned his head and looked up to the window of his former office. That time was long gone!

The post office came into sight, this big yellow building with clinker bricks. He passed it and walked straight to the HO. The Bratwurst he had earlier had not satisfied him. What would you like for dinner he thought entering the shop? Sausages, great choice, what else! Easy to make, no dishes just a plate and a cooking pot. Do we have mustard? No idea, better grab a little jar. I guess we have bread at home, he thought. Well, good question. But the sausages would taste good even without it!

The lady at the cashiers desk gave him a sympathetic look: poor man. Probably no wife, no family. She smiled. "One Deutschmark eighty five" she told Papa, who got out his coin purse and counted the money on the desk. I am still a pretty boy he thought smiling back.

He left the store and went home.

59.

Aunt Rosa had washed her dishes from her little lunch. She could not help being nervous. At the same time, she was anxious to tell Papa what had happened this morning. Maybe he had an explanation. It was not at all unusual that the Stasi or the police would check such situations out, of course not. They would not stop if they had a bad feeling. Again, their sixth sense for events was amazing.

She had just sat down when she heard noises. Different than this morning. Keys were rattling! It must be him. She jumped up, opened the door just a little and listened. Yes! It was Mr. Mann coming home. She had to tell him immediately!

She went down, shortly stopping to see if the Pantels were home. Quiet. Good. She came down to our hall; Papa had kept his keys so he could come into the house anytime. Papa was not in the best mood.

"Everything in order, Mr. Mann?" she asked him.

"Yes, they are on the train. Let's not talk here," Papa sensed that something had happened, Papa saw it in her face. He pointed to the front room.

"Let's go in there," She followed him.

"What is going on?" Now Papa was concerned. She quickly told him about the two civilian gentlemen coming in the morning asking for him.

"I tried to be as calm as possible, but I am not sure if they believed me. At around 11:00 or so, two policemen also came to see if they could enter the condo." She paused.

"They wanted the keys to the condo! If they would have known!" The doors were open.

"If anybody had walked into the condo, Mr. Mann, they would immediately realize that not everything was as it should be."

"Unbelievable, I would not have thought this would happen," Papa was surprised, to say the least.

This was alarming. His brain was suddenly spinning. He looked at his watch. Helga and the children must be at the border. Hopefully it goes well.

"I will leave the house, I am not staying here – at least not during the day. Tomorrow is Saturday and I will leave in the morning and come back late at night. I will go to Bohnes. Just in case they try again to ask or enter the condo." She nodded.

"I do not want you endangered. You have helped us so much! I will knock on your door tomorrow evening when I come back. Please be careful!" She nodded.

"How was it with your family, is everything all right?"

Papa told her that we got safely on the train to West Germany and so far, there seemed to be nothing to worry about. Until 10 minutes ago, Papa had to admit. I have to leave as soon as possible. He let Aunt Rosa out the door and she went up to her apartment.

"Well, at least I should cook the sausages, I need something in my stomach." He ignited the gas flame on the stove. 15 minutes later he left the condo making sure that all doors were closed.

He was aware that the rooms looked a little deserted. They should not see them like this.

60.

"This is the border to West Germany. You are leaving the German Democratic Republic. Everyone who does not have a visa has to leave this train now!" The announcement from the loudspeakers was cold and frightening. We sat in our cabin, quiet, not saying anything. Mutti had advised us to show our best behavior. She had gone into her handbag and pulled out our papers, IDs and the most important thing: the visa.

The train had stopped. It was indeed Bebra, the border town, or at least the closest stop before you would leave the GDR. On the platform we saw many policemen; actually, they were called "Vopos" an abbreviation for Volkspolizisten. These men were trained as border police. They entered the train at every door just to make sure that they had everything and anything under control. It was hard to imagine that something could escape their observation. They had pistols and some had machine guns.

Everything appeared very serious but I still felt a bit of an excitement. I guess Roland did too. He looked at me as if to tell me that his emotions were the same as mine.

I looked at Mutti. She sat there with her legs crossed and upright almost like saying: I am ready! You guys can come and check us out. It wasn't long until the cabin door slid open. The Vopo was tall and had to bend down when he entered our cabin. "Guten Tag, die Papiere bitte!"

Not a very friendly person, I thought. Mutti handed him the papers. He checked them looking alternately at us and the IDs. Then he started a long string of questions:

Where are you going and why; what is the purpose of your trip; are these your children etc. 'Of course, can't you read?' Mutti thought.

"Please open your bags." He checked every one of them.

"Could you lift up the babies?" Mutti did, first Karin, then Brigitte. Would somebody have the nerve to hide something under a baby? Next question: "Do you have a carriage? Where is it?" Mutti got nervous. She pointed to the hallway:

"It is at the front of the wagon. There are only two blankets for the babies in, everything else is here."

"Please show me!" Mutti left us and went with him. He looked into the carriage, lifted the blankets. Moved the hood and looked under it. That's when Mutti got pale. She held tight at the door handle of the WC. Who knows what would have happened if he had seen her face. Fortunately, the policeman was too busy with his search. He put the carriage back into its place and said, "Go back into your cabin. I'll come back later."

Mutti opened the door and fell into her seat. What happened? She looked sick! I suddenly noticed that she did not have the papers anymore. What was the problem? Would they send us home?

"Stay calm and be quiet". We were.

An eternity could not have taken longer! People were moving in and out of the train, shouting, complaining and arguing. Some were guided away with their suitcases.

Every car – I heard later – was checked. Even the locomotive and the tender where the coals were stored! They looked under every car with some kind of two-wheel carriage with a big mirror on top. I heard that people had tried to escape this way.

Well, we had a visa and finally, the policeman came back and handed Mutti the papers.

"Gute Reise." The door closed and when the train started to roll, Mutti had tears in her eyes. We did it, she thought.
"Are we now in the West?"
"Yes we are."

61.

Where should I go? Almost a bit helpless Papa took a long walk through the fields starting at the end of our street. I have to sit down and think. How can I manage the next two days? Maybe I could sit a while in the coffee shop downtown. Not a good idea. Let's not be seen. They might search for me.

He turned around and approached the Possenweg on the upper end where there were no more houses – just benches. It was now around three o'clock. Helga must have passed the border! They must be in the West! If anything went wrong, I would certainly hear about it but then probably not before tomorrow. The thought was horrible.

Following this train of thought he realized that safety was the first priority. You should not be home; just sleeping there would be okay, he thought. Leaving the house in the morning and coming home late when it was dark would be best for you. Not that they wouldn't pay attention or come back and check the condo out if possible – but this was the best way to avoid them.

The police and the Stasi were certainly informed about Mutti's travel plans: times, dates, trains, arrivals and departures of all locations. They knew by now if Helga and the children made it over or not. The border check would create a feed back to Sondershausen.

If Helga made it, the next 48 hours were the most critical in the Stasi's and police's eyes. Most of the family was gone. The possibility during the following days that the rest – Papa in our case – somehow would fall through a hole in the border security was evident. Since the beginning of 1961, the number of people escaping was increasing rapidly. Some went with a visa, some at night over some unobserved parts of the border. Or they made it in to Berlin by going through the East-West checkpoints by foot. Of course, many were caught. A few years in prison was the usual outcome of the trials. The charge was "Attempted Republic Escape". In fact, the government feared that after a certain time they would not have enough people to keep the state up and running.

Papa was talking to himself: "As we had discussed, Helga, I will leave early in the morning on Sunday. But only if I get a telegram from you! I will try not to leave any trail. They might be already all over the place looking for me. They have a sixth sense, no doubt. I need to check the map and consider how to go by train, station by station. Via Leipzig and Magdeburg? Or from small town to small town? Better would be the last choice. Smaller stations would not be that thoroughly observed and I will have a better chance of reaching Berlin. Tomorrow, I might go to Jecha, nobody knows me there. And a good lunch would be fine too."

He got up, looked around and took another walk through the fields not seeing a soul. The sun went down slowly and maybe in a half hour I will go home, he thought.

Hopefully, there was something left to eat.

62.

We did not have to switch trains again until we arrived late Friday evening in Mönchengladbach. Oma and Opa had a busy day: their daughter and the grandchildren were coming. How exciting. Lots to do. They lived in a two-room apartment, probably not more than sixty-five square meters.

Oma was nervous. She had put everything together to make her family welcome and comfortable. Opa had to shop and buy enough food for everyone. Cooking was okay, even though it could be a challenge with this little kitchen. Oh well, it was what it was; this was the best they could do. Nobody had enough money to put on a big party and let everybody stay in hotels. And anyway, this was not the most important thing. Seeing each other after quite some time would be the real joy!

It was getting dark. All day long they thought about us – hopefully everything went fine and we made it through the border control. They knew what kind of a procedure it was, as they had done it twice – pretty scary and always a few nerve-wracking moments. At least we had authorized papers and the special visa. I have to believe that they make it all right,

Opa told himself! Soon we will get ready to go to the station and pick them up. They lived about two to three kilometers from the station. And even as old as Oma and Opa were, they would walk all the way!

They had a little dinner and did not talk too much. Their thoughts were with us. It will be wonderful, Oma thought. I cannot wait to see them!

They left their apartment around 21:20. It would take them almost an hour to get to the main station.

63.

We had gone through Kassel, the first big city in West Germany. You could see a major difference. There was much more life out there. More cars, more people. Lots of nice buildings and it was cleaner, I have to admit. The buildings looked restored and renovated. Of course, Roland and I enjoyed the views, the different buildings – and the cars. Many things were so different. Everywhere they had billboards and advertising, blinking lights indicating or pointing to a shop or a monument of some kind. People looked different: happier? I could not tell. Maybe a bit more relaxed. And they were dressed in different style, modern in a way, especially the women. A few had funny hairdos. I looked at Roland and we smiled.

I was tired. I went back to our cabin. Mutti fed the two little ones. They were hungry! How could they be? We were carrying them around all day long or they slept on the pillows Mutti had given them covered with the blankets. I sat down and Mutti looked at me: "How is it, Jürgen? Pretty exciting out there isn't it?" I nodded.

"Everything is different. Did you see the cars, Mutti?"

"Wait until you are with Opa and Oma. Are you hungry? I have still two sandwiches left, one for you and one for Roland."

She opened her bag and reached for one for me.

"How far is it now, Mutti?" Mutti checked her little watch. She got this once from her Mom for her birthday. Not too fancy with a little leather band and a round face.

"Still four hours to go, Jürgen. Maybe sleep a little bit. Here is one of my pillows."

I must have just swallowed my last bite when I fell asleep on the pillow.

64.

Not much left to eat. But Papa wasn't really hungry. The six sausages were very good; with the bread and mustard it tasted great under the circumstances.

He went upstairs to Aunt Rosa and Uncle Walter. They were sitting on the chaise longue and had the radio on.

"Where were you, Mr. Mann? We were a bit worried."

Papa went pale, "Why? Was the Stasi here again?"

His heart started beating and he sat down on the kitchen chair waiting for the horrible news to come.

"No," was the simple answer. Papa was confused. "They said they would come again, didn't they?"

"I have no idea," Aunt Rosa said, "I was here all day."

Papa looked at them and they just shrugged their shoulders. So, they did not come. They must have something up their sleeve. This was unusual. They say they will come and then they don't. Something is wrong or they might be waiting until tomorrow. "Go to sleep, Mr. Mann, you cannot change it."

Papa got up, thanked them. Aunt Rosa gave him a hug and led him out the door. He went down the stairs quietly, crossed our hallway and went into the kitchen and ate an apple, and then into the front room and put on the radio. Listening to some light music would hopefully stop his brain from worrying and wandering between hope and fear, excitement and depression. Hopefully they made it through, he thought.

I will go to the Bohnes tomorrow. Gerda and Rolf would spend some time with me. She would cook too. So this part was taken care of. I won't be at home and if the Stasi come again, they will not find me. But would this really keep them from going after me? I probably would not stand a chance. Somewhere, they would catch me, open the condo and this would be the end of all his dreams. It was a very risky scheme.

He had also found a bottle of wine that was half full. He had two glasses with Helga the other day. That might put me to sleep. But first I have to think about what route I will take Sunday.

Aunt Rosa had some ideas from her trip to Berlin seven weeks ago. She was very religious and always had a crucifix on her wall in her tiny front room. The Catholics had one of their big events in Berlin, and she had gone there by train to enjoy the event. She had told Papa how he could find the best connections by train and via what towns and cities he should go. He certainly considered her advice but wanted to go over it again in his mind one last time. And at the end, he had to decide which route was best and fastest for him. From Sondershausen, she went to Sangerhausen, probably a good idea as it was a rather short distance and a good start. But then where? Straight to Magdeburg? That is a long ride. Maybe rather through some little towns where you could expect less observation, fewer police.

From Magdeburg to Berlin was easy. This was a city and trains left on a frequent schedule to Berlin. Berlin was the capital – for West and for East Germany. Also, it should not take too long, maybe an hour by train. Papa planned on being in Berlin maybe by early afternoon. Tomorrow evening I have to prepare my papers, he thought: party book, ID and money. He got up and checked the little satchel Mutti had prepared for him. She had put some socks and underwear in and a shaver, toothpaste and toothbrush. Papa had packed his chessboard in another bag with chess figures. It could serve as an explanation.

Well, let's drink the wine, I need some sleep, he thought. He took a sip. His thoughts went back to his family. Have they arrived? He looked at his watch: it was 22:45. Almost he thought. They are probably in Düsseldorf now. In about 30 minutes they will arrive in Mönchengladbach.

He switched off the radio and slid the bedroom door open. It was somewhat cold in the bedroom.

Surprisingly, it took him just a few more minutes to fall asleep. It was a long and exciting day. Helga and the kids must be in Mönchengladbach by now.

65.

Papa had to take a day off from work on Friday, of course. Half a day would be gone by the time he would be back from Erfurt. Going to work on a Friday afternoon to Göllingen did not make sense. He would not have been able to accomplish any reasonable work anyway. He had asked

Mr. Schirmer, his boss; he gladly granted him the day off. No big deal; Mr. Schirmer did not even inform human resources.

Nevertheless, it was noted that Papa was not in the company working this Friday. Colleagues came and asked for him, were surprised but would not ask his boss. But it was unusual. Mr. Mann was not there and no one was informed.

Like in many companies, some people do not like each other. One of Papa's male colleagues was obviously prepared to take Papa's job 18 months ago but was rejected and now jealous. There was always tension, and they did not get along very well. When he saw that Papa was not there, he had a song to sing – at the HR department. Pretty soon the whole company knew.

As I told you before, we were one of the families in the town who had a phone: number 576. It was an outside extension. An extension like you would dial in a company to another office or a colleague. But our extension was still the one to the police department! Even though Papa had left the police, we could keep the phone line. The problem was that we could not say a lot or anything troubling. The police very probably tapped all our phone calls. Still, during Mutti's pregnancy and on other rather rare occasions, it came in handy. We had to tell the operator in the police building who we want to call and she would put us through. So they could keep a record of everyone we tried to call.

The HR department called our home as soon as the absence of Papa from work was evident. The police operator put them through. Nobody home!? More importantly, Papa was not home! So he was not sick and still not home?

Now everybody knew it: the Stasi, the company and the police! They must have driven to our home to investigate. This is why the bell rang a second time this morning: first the Stasi, around 8:30 or so and then the police before noon. Papa did not know about these circumstances or should I say coincidences caused by his absence in the company. Sometimes, things happen totally outside your control.

It was not only the Stasi that were on alert, the police were also curious about Papa not being home. The Stasi saw circumstances where families travelled to the West as their duty to investigate. That was a given. They knew about the visa and everything else, no surprise. You might say that the police knew about the visa too. Yes, but they did not pay much attention as long as there was no indication of something unusual, or unless they were ordered by the Stasi to take over the observation.

Well, the fact that Papa's company was searching for him was unusual. They should know about the one-day absence. This sparked the interest of the police. This was the reason for the second visit later that morning. It was always scary to see how this organization worked so well. They just knew everything, almost everything. And here they got an unexpected hint.

There was something else happening that afternoon that Papa did not know about. In fact, it was just after 13:00 or so when Papa got back from Erfurt. As I told you he walked the long street down to the shopping area to get something to eat. When he passed the police building and looked up to his former office window – he was seen! One of his former colleagues and maybe one of the two men checking our condo that morning had seen him walking by. Unbelievable, but it was the answer to their main question: he is back in town as expected!

"Call the Stasi, they do not have to go again. Tell them that we have seen him, he walked by five minutes ago. We should be okay!" said his former colleague to his partner who called the Stasi office and reported it.

Mr. Schirmer had to apologize to HR and said that he simply forgot to mention that Papa took a day off to bring his family to the train station. All this was unknown to Mutti and Papa until they heard about these things weeks later.

66.

The train slowed down. This is it, I thought. I had slept probably an hour and a half and was fully awake. We would see Oma and Opa in a few minutes. Unbelievable. Roland was excited, too. Mutti seemed not to enjoy the outlook too much. Something bothered her. I did not know what. I was sure that when she saw her parents, it would go away.

We started packing. So much to pack! Our cabin looked like our own front room at home: all these bags, toys, books, magazines and food. Bag after bag was stuffed, and Mutti took care of the two little ones. We always called them the two little ones. Cute.

The lights of the town grew bigger and more frequent. More and more rails appeared to the left and right of the train, a sign that we were nearing the station. Breaks started to squeak in the usual way. We looked out the right window as this was the platform side, which became a wide concrete surface. We tried to look at every face of the people waiting for our arrival. It was obviously pretty dark already, 22:24 the clock showed. No Opa, no Oma? Maybe we overlooked them or they were waiting all the way at the end of the platform. They should be here!

The train stopped with its squeak of the iron breaks; a short jolt and we had landed. Mutti commanded us to wait, "This is the train's final destination boys, no reason to rush. You have to help me anyway. Just take a bag each and go outside, maybe you can see Oma and Opa on the platform."

Roland and I grabbed two bags and ran to the door. A few steps down and we stood – in front of Opa and Oma!

What a joy! Big hugs and smiles everywhere. Wonderful and exciting. They waited all the way at the end of the platform and realized that we were probably more in the middle of the train. So they came toward us. Obviously, they saw us boys before we saw them.

Opa went into the train and so did Roland; he was older and stronger and could help with the suitcases and bags while Opa greeted Mutti inside the train with a big long hug. Mutti cried, she was overwhelmed with her feelings. This could be it, she thought.

"Everything okay?" Opa asked her. She nodded, wiped her tears and pointed to the doorway.

"Let's take the carriage first and bring it down to the platform so we can put the little ones in right away. Roland?" Roland was behind her taking a suitcase.

"Wait here and watch the babies, we'll come back in a minute!"

They maneuvered the carriage down to the platform and Mutti came back to take first Brigitte and then Karin to lay them in their carriage. She covered them up as it was a bit cool. Now the rest.

Minutes later, the family was ready to leave the station.

The plan was that Opa would walk home with Mutti and the carriage and that Oma and us boys would go with the tram. The simple reason was that the doors of the street train were not wide enough to put the carriage in. There were no pick-up cars or other big taxis to carry the carriage of twins. Hard to imagine. Well, Opa and Mutti started to walk home.

Oma led us to the special tram station in front of the main station. We had to go down stairs through a pedestrian tunnel. Wow. Totally new to us. The best thing were the escalators! Unbelievable. One down, a short walk and one up. What a fantastic new experience for us! This was fun!

Roland and I did it several times while Oma was waiting on the little platform for the number seven tram to arrive. I wonder if she enjoyed watching us going up and down several times on the escalators. Finally, we had to quit as the train was approaching.

I looked around: so many lights, blinking commercials and billboards. Cars all around and not so much exhaust coming out of them! I watched Roland; he also inhaled all these new impressions. I read the commercials and brand names – I had never heard of them, did not even know what products they were. Oh well, we would find out.

What was important now was the arrival of the tram. It came in slowly and Oma pulled us back from the edge. "Careful boys, stay back!" The doors automatically opened right after it came to a halt. Oma made us go first, each having a bag. She took the suitcase. The steps up were steep and we had to take big steps to get on the tram. People watched us and we watched them. Everything looked so different. The seats were hard plastic of some kind and we found a place where we all could sit beside each other. We just stared out of the window: it was a different world that was for sure!

Roland and I pointed out to each other all the interesting things we saw. After the train started moving, every second new things appeared. Oma looked in another direction: "If you look over there, boys, you will see your Mutti and Opa walking." We turned our heads and really, there were Mutti and Opa pushing the carriage along the sidewalk. We waved, not sure if they saw us.

It took us about 20 minutes to the stop right in front of our grandparent's apartment. The tram had to make several stops to let people in and out. It was an interesting ride for us and it probably made us even more tired than we already were on this evening. It was a long and exciting day! One we will never forget.

Oma opened the door to their little apartment; we looked into a hallway which led to two rooms: their bedroom and a big living room with a tiny kitchen niche. She must have had prepared mattresses and an additional bed in the front room. Their couch was moved to the side. How would we sleep here? In this room, all together? After all, we would stay for about a week.

Oh well, it will work somehow. We washed our hands, drank some water and waited until Opa and Mutti arrived.

It took Mutti and Opa another hour to reach the apartment. The carriage was placed in the hallway of the house after the two babies were laid down to sleep. Actually, they were sleeping already. Covered with their blankets near what was supposed to be Mutti's bed; they almost slept through the whole night. Of course, before we went to bed, we told Oma and Opa all about our trip, especially about the morning when Papa was with us in Erfurt, the border controls and our new impressions and observations.

"It was very hard to leave Papa behind all by himself." Mutti was sad. Nobody answered; I felt sympathy and thought about Papa and what he might do while we were gone.

"Ferdi will make it" Opa responded. Of course he will, I thought. He was not the greatest cook, but he survived more serious things than this. Oma gave him a serious look and turned to Mutti,

"Don't worry Helga, I have a good feeling!" After some quiet moments, Mutti turned to her father and added,

"We have to go to the post office as soon as possible tomorrow morning and send the telegram."

"Will do. Now let's go to bed, I hope that you and the children have a good night sleep. Tomorrow is another day and we might go for a walk." That would be great, I thought. I was eager to see all these new things. Maybe we could see some of their shops. And more cars. Maybe some toys?

My air mattress was not comfortable. Also, the pictures of the day ran through my head, once or twice like a film.

I must have fallen in a deep sleep right after that.

67.

Papa had some wild dreams; the past day was too stressful and scary on top. Many faces appeared, friends and colleagues – and then Mutti waving at him from the other side of a river. Where are the children? It seemed that she screamed at him with no voice. The distance increased until she disappeared. Then there was this bright light. Like a flashlight. He was suddenly awake!

Still disturbed from his dream, he slowly came to his senses. He looked up – and realized that the sun was up already! Another look at his watch and he jumped out of bed. His first thought was to leave the house as quickly as possible. 8:30, not too late he thought. He slipped into his clothes, washed and shaved and entered the kitchen to find something to eat. Coffee? No, it takes too long. Anything else to eat? Nothing left other than the last apple. Oh well, it was at least something. He put it into his pocket and went into the hall.

He listened carefully: it was quiet. He wanted to tell Aunt Rosa at least that he is leaving for the day. So on his tiptoes he quietly went up to the second floor. The Pantels were either still sleeping or had left even before him. He knocked on Aunt Rosa's door and two seconds later her head peeked through a small opening between the door and the frame.

"Oh, Mr. Mann! Good Morning. Just a second." She closed the door and seconds later opened it again.

"Come in." She was still in her nightgown and Uncle Walter must have still been in bed.

"I just wanted to tell you that I'm going to visit the Bohnes, you know. I will stay there all day and come back at night. Hopefully nobody will come and try to get into the condo." Aunt Rosa was concerned.

"Please be careful, you know how they are. I will try my best to keep them from entering. I hope they will not force their way in!" Papa nodded and realized how critical the situation was. If they have only a little doubt, they would not hesitate the blink of an eye and break the doors open. Actually, they did not even have to do this!

"Okay, thank you for everything. I will go now. Are the Pantels here?"

"No, they are at a concert in Nordhausen and stayed overnight."

Oh, good, Papa thought. He nodded and turned to leave. He looked back and said, "I will let you know this evening if my wife and the children made it. I hope!" He went down the stairs, a last check in the front room and the kitchen; nothing suspicious left anywhere. Hall is okay! Let's go.

He heard a car coming, slowly, two-cycle. He stopped breathing. What now? I have to hide, quickly! He opened the cellar door, closed it quietly behind him and ran down the wooden steps to the washroom. He stopped. Leaning against the wall he listened.

Where was the car? Silence. I have to wait he thought. Better wait two or three minutes. He was leaning on the cellar wall. Still no noise. His heart was pounding. It was nerve-wracking. He listened again. Nothing. I have to be careful when I open the house door! Could be too late! No, I will go into the kitchen and try to see down to the street.

He climbed the stairs and listened. Then very slowly he opened the door. He could see the milky glass of the house door; at least nobody stood in front of it. He slipped through the cellar door, closed it and tiptoed through the hall into the kitchen. He had to be careful here as someone might be able to see him through the window. We had curtains but they would not totally hinder the view.

He knelt down and moved slowly to the window. From one side, he tried to look on to the porch in front. Nobody. He slipped to the other wall and tried to look in the other direction. At the very least, he would be able to look down the street; but there was still a blind angle to observe the front of the house. He did not see any cars down the street. Well, if they were in front of the house, they would have rung the bell already. He looked at his watch, eight minutes since he first heard the car.

He decided to wait another five minutes. Then he walked to the house door again and opened it slowly. Looking in all directions he saw that there was nobody from the Stasi or the police or anyone else; at least there was noone to see! He pulled the door tight behind him and went down the steps to the gate. Another look left and right. There was nobody to be seen. He walked down the street to the crossing with the Possenweg. His brain was working rapidly: I should not take the main streets, just in case they came up from the town. I will take a little detour.

He went over the crossing and straight up the street in the direction of the public pool passing the Union house. Right after he climbed the little hill, he turned right and went down one of the little dirt roads that led to the villa behind our little station. It was more of a pathway than a street and turned at the bottom in an s-curve crossing the railways. Papa stayed somewhat to the west of town using little streets. It was a long way around the center of the town, trying to avoid many of the normal streets we usually walked going to the Bohnes. In general, it was the direction to the main station.

Today, he was not really in a hurry, so time was not a problem. He would sit and talk with Rolf and Gerda all day and would not leave their apartment until it was dark. It took Papa almost two hours for what normally took us less than an hour.

He finally was at their gate and rang the Bohne's bell.

68.

What a night! Even though I was so tired, I woke up twice. There wasn't any time or climate difference between East and West Germany; but as usual, the excitement, the dreams and the new environment did not leave the body at total rest. We finally got up at 7:00 and all of us felt the same way: exhausted; mentally and physically.

Oma and Opa had a little bathroom; well, this was crowded for probably two hours! Just searching for all we needed in the bags and suitcases was an odyssey. Looking halfway decent, we finally sat down at a table that wasn't big enough for all of us. We decided to take turns for breakfast. Mutti and Oma went last. Karin and Brigitte needed their morning procedures too. And how hungry were they!

It was nearly 10 o'clock when Mutti turned to her father and demanded to go to the post office.

"We have to go, Opa! It will probably take all day until they deliver the telegram to Papa. The earlier we send it, the better!" Opa nodded, took his jacket and said to Oma:

"We'll go and send the telegram. When we come back, we could take a walk until lunch."

Oma responded a bit harsh: "I have no time and somebody has to cook. You better pass the grocery shop and buy me some things before coming back!"

Opa took it with humor and just said: "No problem, where is the list?"

She gave him a little paper with the items she needed. Opa looked at Mutti and smiled:

"That's how she is. Can we go?" Mutti was already at the door.

The post office was about 10 minutes walk. It was in one of the next side streets over. They entered through a big heavy door and approached one of the counters. This one had a sign above saying "Telegrams and Phone Calls". The officer looked at Opa and Mutti and asked: "How can I help you?"

"We need to send a telegram urgently to East Germany. Here is the address and the name."

The officer looked at them and nodded. He filled out the necessary papers and asked:

"And what is the text?" His eyes became a bit bigger; obviously, it was always surprising news people would write and he could not wait to hear this one.

"All arrived well."

"That's all?" The officer was really surprised.

"Yes, that's it" Opa responded.

"No signature?"

"No."

The officer looked at both and quietly started to write down the short note.

"2 Deutschmark and 25 Pfennings."

Opa paid and Mutti and he turned and left an astonished postman behind.

Later I learned that the text was decided in advance by Mutti and Papa; they did not want the telegram containing any information that might lead to false interpretation. It was also sent to the Bohnes as mentioned, not to our home address. Papa would hopefully receive it there the same day. Communication between the two countries – the status quo could not be described differently – was difficult and widely, if not totally, controlled.

Mutti was relieved. The telegram was sent; Papa would hear the good news. Hopefully he would get it that day! He needed this information! He needed to make a decision! Tomorrow could be too late. And I cannot call him, this is impossible. She knew this. Frustration was building up again in her. I have to stay strong for my children she told herself over and over again.

The shopping at the grocery took her mind off it a little bit; seeing all the numerous offerings of food and vegetables, sweets and meats, fruits and milk products was overwhelming. Bananas! Oranges! Enough vegetables for everybody. Butter, milk and eggs too. How can it be that they have everything and we have nothing?

We cannot be wrong Mutti told herself. It can only get better!

69.

The door opened and Papa was right away pulled into the apartment. His friend Rolf was careful, too. One never knew.

"We should not give the neighbors any cause for curiosity. You know, some of them could be an undercover Stasi agent!"

Gerda appeared and gave Papa a long hug. "You look stressed out, no sleep?" She judged him by checking his face and his eyes.

"Not great" Papa heard himself whispering. They went into the little kitchen. He took his light coat off. They sat down.

"First of all I will make you a cup coffee."

Gerda Bohne was a nice person, not as attractive as Mutti but lovely. We called her Aunt Gerda. She got up and poured Papa a coffee and gave him some cream and sugar.

"I will make us some breakfast. No eggs, sorry but butter and marmalade. Also, I have a few slices of Thuringia red sausage!"

"Sounds good to me," Papa responded and tried to smile.

"I'll take what I can get."

Rolf Bohne was his long time friend. They shared the police academy and the stressful job from the beginning at the police department. They became friends and so did Mutti and Gerda. It was a friendship like many others in the GDR; the daily problems, political and economical, brought people together.

Hard times make people cooperate and share life, their worries – and support one another. They had spent time together on vacation and trips, celebrating certain events together. I just realized that we called him Uncle Bohne, by his last name but his wife, Aunt Gerda. I never thought about this until today!

"How did it go yesterday?" Gerda asked curiously after she sat down beside Papa.

"So far so good," Papa responded, "But of course, I have not heard anything yet. We were so nervous. Everywhere you see green uniforms or you wonder if the civilian waiting right next to you on the train platform is one of them." Papa paused.

"How were the children?" Rolf asked to get Papa talking.

"Oh, they helped a lot with getting on and off the trains we took. They are good boys!"

"Was the train on time in Erfurt?"

"Yes, alright. They left on time." After another pause Papa was back to the important issue:

"Helga has to send the telegram now and hopefully it will arrive today. I am confident that the telegram will be sent on time but who knows what they do here." There was frustration in his voice, anger and a certain feeling of being helpless.

"She will send it on time, I am sure! Normally, they are also not so bad here with delivering telegrams." Rolf tried to encourage Papa.

"It's the first thing Helga will do today, don't worry."

"I know," Papa answered quietly.

So much depended on this telegram. If it did not come until tomorrow morning, what should he do? The whole plan would be thwarted.

He had thought about this for a long time: What should Mutti's message be to him? They had to avoid any kind of information, any kind of hint, anything that could spark any farfetched ideas about what was planned. It had to be a short, normal message, just a note, a few words or even less. And: no signature. Sent from a West German post office.

After hours of thinking it over, they came up with the following wording: "All arrived well." That's all.

Both knew what it meant. It did not reveal anything other than that we had arrived without problems. A trivial note but efficient for the recipient. They also decided to send it to their friends, the Bohnes. This would not catch anyone's attention, hopefully. That was the plan – and now it was up to the postal service to do their part. And this in itself was scary enough.

Gerda had made a nice breakfast and Papa enjoyed it very much. Some real food for a change he thought. It was a quiet breakfast. All three were caught in their own thoughts. Papa had to think about the past; so many things they had done together, real friends: vacation, excursions, celebrations, birthdays, carnival.

Once they had been a loving couple. Now, with Rolf's adventures here and there, it was a pity to see the downfall. It was never quite clear how much she really knew but at least Gerda must have felt that something was wrong. Rolf wasn't too clever about hiding it.

"Did you like your breakfast?" Gerda asked him, pulling him out of his thoughts.

"Very good, Gerda, thanks. You are a good cook!" She smiled and started to clear the table.

"What do you want to do today, Ferdi?" Rolf asked him.

"We cannot sit here all day and wait. We could take a walk or play some Chess?" Immediately Papa decided on chess.

"Let's play some games. I can show you what a real player is!" Papa grinned at Rolf who shortened his comment down to a "We'll see." Gerda saw that they were getting up to get the figures and the board and knew that she would have some time for herself.

"I will go to the shop and see if they have anything for lunch." Papa and Rolf nodded but it seemed that their minds were already preparing for some battles. Actually, as far as I remember, Rolf had little chance to beat Papa. Still, they both enjoyed playing each other every now and then.

"You can have the white figures." Rolf made his first move as they heard the front door close.

Gerda tried her luck shopping for lunch.

70.

Opa and Mutti came home. What they had bought was inspected by Oma. "Well done, you two! Just the potatoes could have been a bit bigger!" Opa grinned and shrugged his shoulders. Nothing new here, he tried his best.

Mutti checked the babies; they were playing with their toys. Roland and I were outside the house around the corner in the side street. We checked out all the cars. Wow. It took us 15 minutes for each car until we had seen everything inside and out. Volkswagen was written on one, another one was named Opel Record, a third one was a Mercedes. Last one was the most luxurious, an SE 300. Big bumpers, wide tires with white walls and four doors. All chrome and a three-liter engine. The speedometer went up to 240 km/h. Unbelievable. We were about to inspect another car when we heard Mutti, "We are having lunch, boys! Please come back."

"Oh well, we can see more in the afternoon," Roland said impatiently, and we both walked back to the apartment.

Oma was almost ready with the cooking; it smelled funny! I wondered what that was but had to wait until we sat on the table in the front room. Oma and Opa would eat in their tiny kitchen. She had made potatoes with spinach and eggs, sunny side up. Great, just what I liked. Eggs, we had not seen some for a while. And spinach. We had not heard about Popeye yet and the fantastic power he got from eating it. But we liked it. It all tasted great.

Oma was satisfied when we complimented her on her good lunch. After cleaning the table, Opa suggested we go for a walk. We would take the babies in their carriage. They would probably sleep anyway but the fresh air would do us all good. Roland and I liked this idea too – we could see more cars! All shops were closed anyway Saturday afternoon and all Sunday. So, just window shopping and fresh air. Fine with us.

After the dish washing was done, we got ready, and all left the apartment. It was exciting to inhale all these new impressions: houses, cars, people's clothes, street trains going by and shops with TVs and radios – for sale! Many houses were nicely painted and in good shape. Gardens were landscaped with flowers and grass and trees and in good order. Different from what we knew in Sondershausen.

I thought about Papa: How would he react if he could see all this? It would have been nice if he could have joined us on this trip!

71.

Gerda had cooked a good lunch; not sure where she got the meat but it tasted great. Maybe Rolf had brought it from work.

While Gerda was shopping and cooking, Papa had lost only one of the six chess games – and this was probably because his thoughts could not be channeled to the game all the time.

They had finished lunch and sat there for a moment without talking.

"Let's see if there is anything interesting on TV," Rolf interrupted the silence. He went to the little table on which a cubical piece of furniture stood with an almost round glass screen in the front. It was a black-and-white TV with a screen about 15 inches. The enclosure was brown polished wood and had two big round knobs left and right underneath the screen. Rolf turned the right one and it made a little click. Nothing happened until about a minute later. The screen went gray and slowly created a black and white picture. A bit snowy but soon it was visible. It just had turned 15:00 and the news was on, a speaker reading text from a paper. The background showed an antenna sending signals and the badge from the flag with hammer and sickle and laurel wreath.

The news was not really exciting, at least not for the people who knew the propaganda machine in the GDR. Everything was always achieved, great and a common success of the state and its working people. Boring and not all true. It took only five minutes and they started to show one of the early GDR movies which was quite good and usually about stories of the life in the GDR.

Once, Roland and I had seen a travel report of snake hunters in South America trying to catch the biggest one on earth, the anaconda. That was quite interesting and actually the first program I remember that I had seen on TV. Must have been 1958 or 1959. Not sure. Amazing when you are looking back to those days!

Gerda had baked also some cake for the traditional coffee and cake time in the afternoon. The cakes were usually pretty dry just because you were missing good butter and other ingredients you could not get at all or not in the expected quality. Papa enjoyed it. Being with his friends was a blessing today.

He looked at his watch; it was now almost 17:30. And no telegram yet! Gerda read his mind:

"You know that they deliver telegrams at any time."

Papa nodded. "It would be nice if it arrives soon!"

They watched some more TV. It was about sunset and it would slowly get dark. The TV set was still on. Yet, every little unusual noise made them listen carefully: is it the postman?

It was 19:00; still no telegram. Papa was now extremely nervous. There was more news on TV but that was not important now.

Would they work and deliver in the evening? Papa could not sit still any longer and walked up and down the front room, into the kitchen, then the hall, then back to the front room.

"Could we ask the post office or call?" He looked at the couple. "You know that this would be dangerous, Ferdi!"

Papa agreed. "I know, sorry. I cannot stand this anymore!"

"Do you want something to eat for dinner, Ferdi?" Gerda changed the subject.

"No, thank you. I am full. I had enough food, thanks Gerda!" He sat down on the couch and looked at them, first Rolf then Gerda.

"What about a coffee, Ferdi?"

"Okay, Gerda that would be nice. After the coffee, I think I will go home. Nobody knows if the telegram will arrive today. There is still time." Papa calmed himself, "but I would need to know tomorrow morning the latest. Otherwise,…" he stopped. Silence.

They all knew what a tragedy that would be.

Gerda made another cup of coffee.

"Do you have something for breakfast tomorrow, Ferdi?"

"Not really, Gerda. I hope I will get something in the station tomorrow."

"I will pack you a piece of cake to take with you. At least you'll have a bite to eat."

She went in the kitchen and packed Papa a slice of her cake from the afternoon coffee. She put it in front of Papa on the table.

"Do you want to sleep here, Ferdi?" Rolf said. "When the telegram comes, you could leave."

Papa shook his head and after a few more silent moments Papa decided: "I'll go home."

He stood up, looked at them. They read his mind. Rolf confirmed:

"As soon as we have it, we will let you know. Don't worry, it'll come! We will stay up and wait!"

Papa went into the hall, took his coat and prepared to leave. They hugged each other twice. Papa thanked them again and snuck out the door. He turned right, went along the fence for a few meters until the walkway appeared which led down along the little gardens. He did not look back. He stumbled down the unpaved path that led to the street coming from the main station on the right and leading left to the town.

It was a long way home; he knew it by heart. Nevertheless, he kept his eyes open for any unusual sign or person. The church clock struck twice: it was 20:30.

It was pretty dark now; the streets were barely lit up. The government had no money for this and there were not enough lanterns. It was Saturday evening. He met a few people on his way home. They were mostly coming from a movie or a birthday party, maybe. Papa decided to take smaller and darker roads; he just wouldn't like to be seen by anyone, especially not by the Stasi guys. He constantly thought about the telegram and what it would mean not to have it by tomorrow morning, at least by late morning. What do I do if? What was plan B? Do we really have any, do we really have any other choice?

He passed the villa where we played chess, turned into the little street underneath the station. Not a soul to be seen. The wind blew a bit but wasn't cold. He was almost at the end where the street joined the Possenweg. Then he saw it: a police car driving up the Possenweg.

He immediately ducked behind a pillar marking a garage entrance. His heart was beating faster. A police car, now! It drove uphill and could well go to our house! I better wait a while he convinced himself staying behind the pillar. He checked his watch: 21:48. His former colleagues were seldom out that late, he knew this. They must have had a good reason for doing it. It's me!

He tried to calm himself down. Maybe something happened? Like a robbery? Seldom these days but not unusual. I'll wait until they come back, he decided. He listened into the night. No engine, no car. He could not be seen behind the pillar unless somebody walked or drove by; then, there was a chance to make out his silhouette.

Another five minutes went by, or ten? Who knew. He checked his watch again. It was one minute to ten. I have to go, I cannot wait any longer. I'll go. Papa peeked around the pillar; nobody to see up and down the little street. The Possenweg was just half a minute walk from here. I have to go and see where the police car is. He walked to the corner and stopped. He peeked over the fence around the house right on the corner. He could see the railroad crossing. It was always lit up by a lantern. Nobody to see. Not too many houses showed lights. Down the street toward the town: also noone. Good. He turned toward the crossing and walked as much as possible in the shadows and darker parts of the sidewalk. I have to go quicker, he thought. I have to cross the street where there is no light. The street crossing with the Edmund-König-Street was well lit. He walked over the railway and a few meters later, he crossed the Possenweg. The street had a lot of big chestnut trees, good coverage. He reached the turn to our street. Well, almost home.

Before he turned into our street, he looked back. Something in his brain told him to. We all have those moments where we instinctively feel what to do. What was this? He leaned against a brick wall around the big villa opposite from our house. He stared down the street as well as he could while at the same time trying to avoid being seen. He was not really sure, but something moved further down the Possenweg, just about where he came out the little street hiding behind the pillar. He decided to run the 100 meters to the house.

Papa opened the little iron gate carefully and slipped through. Around the house there were enough bushes and little hiding places. He decided to go right around underneath the bedroom window and behind one of the big trees blocking the view to the neighbors. It was pitch dark there. He almost stopped breathing and waited. Being in the house was more dangerous. If these were some dangerous visitors, they would not see him.

Through one of the thinner branches, he could see the corner of the Possenweg and our street. The same place he stood two minutes ago. 'I have to be on guard!' Whoever this might be I have to find a way not to be discovered.

Who were these people? He had seen – at least he thought he had seen – two persons. Long coats. But other than this he was unable to identify anything. They must turn the corner any moment – if they are after me. Another minute passed. Then he saw them. Right, two adults, long coats, hats. Both in pants! What do I do? His mind went crazy. He decided to stay behind the tree. He was pretty sure that these guys could not see him even if they would go up the stairway to the front door. They crossed the street and approached the gate. They opened it and went up the stairs. There was something familiar. Were these former colleagues?

They looked around and whispered something. Papa did not understand what they said. But their behavior was not really like that of the Stasi. Who are they? Papa stayed quiet behind the tree. One of them turned and Papa could see that it was a woman! The other one lifted his hat to wipe his forehead. It was Rolf! And Gerda!

Papa left his place of cover and walked to the stairs.

"Don't ring the bell!" They shrugged, turned their heads and saw Papa coming toward them. What a relief.

"What are you doing here?" Papa was still stunned. Why would they follow him? The telegram arrived!

"We have good news." Papa's face lit up.

"The telegram?"

"Yes." Papa hugged them both. He opened the front door quietly and they walked in through the hall straight to the front room.

"Sit down." They sat on the couch and Papa took the armchair. Rolf opened his coat and pulled out the telegram from the inner pocket.

"The mailman came about 15 minutes after you left. We thought it was better we come right away." Gerda smiled.

Papa opened the telegram; his hands were shaking. Was it what I expected? The paper was pretty brownish but the letters were still clear: "All arrived well."

That was all. But it was all he was hoping for and exactly what he had decided, with Mutti, to be the message. He covered his face and gave it to Rolf and Gerda. There was silence for a while. They all knew what this telegram meant.

"No turning back now." Rolf said it almost without any emotion.

Papa broke the silence. "Now it is my turn!" He said it with determination.

"Is there anything we can do for you?" Gerda asked. She knew that there wasn't really anything they could do other than wishing Papa well for the next day.

"I don't think so. You guys have done so much for me and Helga, you know that we will always appreciate this and will never forget you!" It was a sad moment in their friendship and they all knew for months that this moment would come.

Gerda got up: "We have to go, Ferdi. Rolf, it is a long way home. Ferdi needs some sleep for tomorrow." Rolf got up. He hugged Papa. Gerda had already tears in her eyes, the two men were not too far from crying themselves. She gave Papa a kiss and a long hug. Then they left. Papa closed the front door after waving them good-bye.

Papa went back to the front room and looked again at the telegram. No signature, exactly as we agreed. They made it! He was happy.

I need to pack and go to sleep now. Tomorrow is my big day. He felt encouraged: we will make it!

72.

The little alarm clock rang. 6:00 o'clock. Papa had no dreams last night. He had thought about today and how he would manage to get to Berlin. Then he fell asleep. He had to be very careful. Using all his police sense and experience, he was convinced that he could make it to Berlin. But this was rather the easy part.

He got up. First things first. Shaving, washing, the cake from Gerda to eat, clothes, packing. And checking the house for a last time. As I mentioned, we had no real bathroom. So we washed ourselves in the kitchen. When Papa finished, he prepared a little satchel for his chessboard and a box with the figures. He had all his papers, any kind of identity card or personal ID as well as his red SED party book. All these preparations had been thought through probably a thousand times, but now was the time to put everything into action and try not to forget anything. Also not the money, the East German Deutschmarks.

The money which had only one tenth the value of the West German Mark; but money is so important. He must have had 140 Deutschmarks; enough to buy tickets and something to eat. At a time when a normal worker made just about 250 to 300 Deutschmarks a month, it should be enough.

Papa made his inspection tour. All rooms, the cellar, the veranda. Checking all cupboards. He sat down in the front room checking everything in his mind. What else do I need? Pictures. Do I have pictures? What else? He closed his eyes and concentrated. After a while, he got up. I have everything! Okay. It was 6:35. I need to go upstairs to Hendrichs. The Pantels are not home – that's good.

He climbed the stairs and knocked on the Hendrich's door. It was opened immediately. Aunt Rosa stood in the doorway in her nightgown, Uncle Walter behind her in his nightclothes.

"Good Morning," Papa said. "It is time." Aunt Rosa asked immediately: "Did you get the telegram?"

"Yes! They made it alright."

"I guess that this is it?!" It was not a real question, rather something like a sad and final statement.

"Thank you both for all the good things you have done for us!" Aunt Rosa started crying. Papa hugged her and then Uncle Walter.

"I have to go. My train will not wait. We will write you as soon as we can!"

A last look and he turned and went down the stairs quietly. He took his satchel and left the house. The street was empty and no one seemed to be up yet. Well, it was Sunday after all and Whitsun on top. A holiday, religious, Catholic. In West Germany, they also had the following Monday off, he had heard.

He went down the brick steps and closed the gate; still, he had to look back. That was it. Maybe this is the last time I will see this house, he thought. Almost 10 years we lived here.

He tried to clear his head and turned into the Possenweg down to the south station. He crossed the railways and turned left into the small passageway to the platform and the little station house.

'I will go first to Sangerhausen as I decided earlier. Return ticket, of course.' He was nervous. Was it a good choice? Probably. Too late to change it now.

There wasn't anybody at the station when he entered the building. The counter was nevertheless occupied. 6:51. Papa looked through the window and saw the clerk. It was an older man, probably 55 or so, in uniform. He opened the little round opening in the middle of the window:

"Good Morning! Where do you want to go?"

"To Sangerhausen. Return ticket." Papa had just said this when he froze. In the counter window he could see a green growing shadow right behind him. His heart stopped. That is it. Over and done. They got me!

He could not help himself and turned around after he managed to cover up his fear.

"What are you doing here so early in the morning, Ferdi?" The police officer smiled and greeted Papa. Papa could not believe it; one of his former colleagues! With all his courage, he tried to stay calm and reached out his hand to Wilhelm, a colleague policeman who worked on cases like theft and robbery at his time in the office. They had some cases together but Papa had not seen him for quite some time.

"You know that I love to play chess, Wilhelm" Papa started a conversation. "There is a tournament today in Sangerhausen I want to attend."

"Still this game. You will never give up on it, will you Ferdi?"

"I guess not – if you ask me. Where are you going this early Wilhelm?" Papa tried to keep the conversation friendly and calm. "I am going the other direction, have to visit my cousin in Erfurt. My wife is not feeling well, so I'm going alone."

The conversation was pretty much over at this point. Papa was relieved that Wilhelm did not join him on the train to Sangerhausen. This could have been complicated.

"How is work?" Papa asked to fill the silent gap.

"Hey, okay, you know. Always the same. A little crime here and there, a few hours overtime. Nothing too spectacular." Papa looked at his watch. Another six minutes and the train from the main station should arrive.

"How are the boys and girls? How is Helga?" Wilhelm now continued.

"They are great, thanks. Growing all the time. Helga has her hands full with them." Wilhelm nodded. It was somewhat dangerous not to mention that they are in West Germany; it could be a trap. Wilhelm could have known that Helga made the trip with the children. Still, Papa felt that he should not tell him.

A whistle blew. Great, Papa thought. I will be gone in two minutes. Wilhelm looked at Papa. He had this police look, checking everything out on the other person. Papa could not wait until the train stopped and he could disappear in it. "Get away from here and Wilhelm," he thought.

The train stopped. "Auf Wiedersehen, Wilhelm. Take care!"

"You too" Wilhelm responded. Papa opened a door and climbed the iron steps to enter a car with a smoking sign.

He sat down and looked out the window. Wilhelm had disappeared into the building. Papa's heart still beating double time.

73.

Sunday morning. We woke up. I looked around and saw Roland lying on his thin mattress. His did not look very comfortable; mine wasn't either. But Oma and Opa's apartment was small; we had to cope with the limitations somehow. Just the thought that it would be ten days in all made me nervous. I was sure that all the new experiences would compensate for it.

Mutti was up already and had made breakfast for the twins; two slightly warm milk bottles. Karin and Brigitte looked satisfied when I looked into their carriage. It seemed that they were resting. Oma and Opa were in the kitchen; I hoped they would make our breakfast. I was starving!

Mutti forced us out of bed saying "Off your mattresses. Go in the bathroom and get ready for the day, boys!" It took us another minute to get up and find the little bathroom. It was tiny, I guess it was big enough for the grandparents.

Roland and I got ready, brushed our teeth and got dressed. We were trying to leave the bathroom clean and in order. I still have this attitude; I think it is okay to do so. Let's put it this way: clean and in order according to my standard. There is always this little difference between a wife's and a husband's standard!

We saw Oma and Opa and said "Guten Morgen." They seem to be looking happy to see us rested. We sat down on the table and Oma served us two soft eggs and bread and butter, marmalade and honey – and little oranges as dessert! I could not believe it; we had not seen oranges for weeks or months! Mutti sat beside us and ate a bit. She seemed to be somewhere else. Her mind must have been in the distance. Probably with

Papa I thought. He had to do breakfast and the cooking all by himself! He would not like that.

Opa broke the silence and said: "We will take a walk today, all together; it will be nice. We'll check out the area and maybe we can look at some more cars!" He looked at us and expected a reaction. It was immediate!

"That would be great!" Roland was excited. Well, me too.

"It will be good for you too, Helga" Opa continued. "It will be refreshing, some air and some new experiences for you." Mutti nodded.

When we were finished, Oma and Mutti cleaned the table and we got ready. Opa took the lead in preparing for our walk. 30 minutes later, we were all ready to go.

"What about the telephone?" Mutti asked. "We will be home on time, don't worry. It is too early anyway, I think, don't you?" Mutti looked at the clock on the wall right over the couch.

"Yes, too early." she responded quietly.

We left the apartment. It was about 18 degrees Celsius, not too bad. Just warm enough to walk without coats – just jackets or sweaters. We had lots of those. Mutti always knitted some for us. The twins were cozy in their carriage wearing their knitted pink suits. Mutti and Opa pushed the carriage and we headed to town.

Roland and I took the lead, always checking out the cars. Suddenly, Roland started running. I was wondering why. Seconds later I saw it: a little round red sports car. Must have been something famous, not sure. Roland was! When I came closer and looked at it I noticed a kind of hand-written signature: Porsche. Wow, a Porsche. I had heard the name once from Roland while his eyes were sparking in excitement. So, this was a Porsche. Under the name was another one: Super 90. Wow. Roland could not get his eyes off every detail he could see. We walked around and looked inside. A real sports car! Probably very fast – and very expensive.

"How many kilometers are on the odometer, Roland? Can you see it?" Roland pressed his face on the driver's door window.

"I think it says 240km/h." Unbelievable I thought. That was fast! "Watch out boys!" Mutti had come closer and also looked at the car. "Nice, a Porsche" she confirmed. "You know, the guy who built this was born where I was born and where Opa and Oma are from? He also built the Volkswagen you saw yesterday near the apartment. It looks similar, doesn't it?" Yes, I thought, that is true, somehow similar.

Mutti looked at the houses and stopped at a shop for furniture. She checked the different kinds of displayed items. "Your furniture has a different style," she told Oma. "Well, you know what we have."

Oma looked at her and – as small as she was – hugged Mutti and said: "It will all work out!"

Mutti was suddenly gone with her thoughts. Where was Papa now? Did he get the telegram on time? Was he on his way? He must be so nervous. Hopefully he is on his way. By this afternoon, it could be all over with a happy ending.

She looked at Opa who seemed to read her mind. "He is coming, he will make it!"

He laid his arm around Mutti and we started walking again toward town.

74.

The train had left Sondershausen south station on time at 7:04. Papa sat in one of the left side wooden seat rows in the direction the train was rolling out of the station. His satchel laid right beside him. This was the direction he took every morning to work in Göllingen. It rolled slowly over the Possenweg. The barriers were down. Papa looked quickly up and down the street: there were no cars in sight and no one other than an older couple waiting to pass the railway toward town. He leaned back and breathed a small sigh of relief. He would wait a few minutes and then walk toward each end of his car. There were platforms you could cross if you wanted to enter the next car. They weren't covered like they are on trains today. He just wanted to check if there was anyone "interesting."

The train passed the little gardens of the houses behind our street and went next under the overpass where the barracks of the Red Army could be seen. The same bridge Roland and I would stand on to be engulfed in the white steam of the locomotives – and maybe also some black dust Mutti would comment on. On the right side he looked over the fields where we had walked so often – he and his boys. Letting his little gliders fly or our kites ascend in the summer wind. Memories of Easter walks with the family. Was it all past now? Really? Is this the last time I am seeing this? "Yes," he told himself, "it has to be the last time!"

Suddenly, the nervous feeling he got from being on alert came back. He thought of what would or could happen. He started again to concentrate on his mission. One step at a time. That was the plan. Reaching Berlin sometime in the early afternoon today.

He got up and looked up and down the aisle. The train was running at about 60 or 70km per hour now and it shook him from left to right. He grabbed one of the vertical bars to stabilize himself. He could see both ways through the windows into the adjacent cars. The back of each seat row was low enough that he could see where people were sitting. Just an older lady two rows down on the right. He walked to the one platform. The rattling noise from the iron wheels got louder. Further into the following car, there was also only an older man with a hat. It was early Sunday morning, on one hand this was no real surprise.

On the other hand, one person in a trench coat and a hat could change a lot. But based on the experience he gathered over the years as a policeman and also during the last two days, he would be very careful. He looked at his watch while walking back to his seat. At this speed the train should take another half hour or so to Sangerhausen, unless it stopped at one of the little towns on the way. Why did I not look it up! I need to know these things he reminded himself. Every station or hold was a dangerous place. Police could control the station, not letting anybody on or off the train unnoticed.

I have to get up and watch the stations early enough to see if there are police or any other suspicious persons waiting, he thought. The Stasi was on alert by now and so was the police. Not that they knew any hard facts but they were always suspicious. Who would know? There was no possible way to contact the Hendrichs or Bohnes for information. If he called them, the police in Sondershausen would know at once. He had to manage the situation all by himself now.

Papa thought about Gerda and Rolf Bohne. They followed him yesterday evening and he did not even realize it until shortly before he reached home. How can we ever express our thanks to them, our quiet supporters? Same applies to the Hendrichs, Rosa and Walter. And the risk they took knowing about our plan.

The train did not stop. It approached the outskirts of Sangerhausen. Papa knew the town; he had been there on several occasions. More and more houses were showing left and right and it took just another minute until the train started to slow down. It was 7:47. That was still early for a Sunday, at least for normal people. Papa pressed his face onto the window to look ahead. Unfortunately, the train bent around a curve, slowing down further. He went to the opposite window and saw the station coming up. It was a small one but the two platforms right and left were now visible. He saw a few people waiting. Slowly, the train approached the station aligning the cars into a straight formation. The view to the platforms was blocked now.

Papa walked to the end of the aisle hiding behind the sliding door. This way, he could watch the persons rushing by the window – but they could not see him that easily. Papa checked everybody passing the window. The man there? No, not suspicious. He looked to the second platform, no. Just a younger couple.

"I have to leave the station at once," was his next thought. Get away from this place! There will be a next train and it does not matter if it is a half an hour or even an hour later. Just leave the station! Public places were the first ones we always checked, he reminded himself.

The train stopped. Papa was still checking the platform. He might have overlooked someone! He opened the door and had a good view of the platform. It was the one for tracks one and two. A few people were standing with their suitcases and bags. My bag!? Where is my bag!? He suddenly realized that he had left it on his seat. You idiot! How could I forget it? He turned and walked back. It lay there. Okay, stay calm Ferdi!

He walked back to the door, opened it and climbed down the iron steps. A quick look and he saw the stairs going down into the typical tunnel underneath the rails and platforms. He took two steps at a time. Exit to the left. Good. Get me out of here! Not hasty but with firm long measures he walked toward the exit through the typical tiled halls. Most of the stations he had seen were dirty and blackened from the soot of the locomotive's exhausts . Only in East Berlin did they take more care of the buildings, at least the ones supposedly demonstrating the great achievements of the republic. Sangerhausen was not one of these places.

He stopped at a kiosk to get some Casino cigarettes. The short stop also gave him the opportunity to observe his surroundings. And he needed to find the train schedules to see when his next train would leave. He noticed one of the glass boxes with the schedules. He paid for his cigarettes and walked over to it.

"Let's see," he said to himself, "We figured out two options to leave from here: either straight to Magdeburg or first to Halle and then to Magdeburg." Both were detours as Berlin could be reached in a more direct way. Berlin was about 230km northeast of here, maybe a little more depending on the train's route. But going to Magdeburg first would extend the ride to almost 300km. In other words, at least a good one hour longer to reach Berlin.

Magdeburg was the first choice nevertheless. Aunty Rosa had told him about her experience last year after she went to Berlin for a church reunion. It just would be a bit safer. You could expect that trains directly to Berlin would be the first to be watched. Magdeburg was a big city – still is – but not on a direct route. The only danger there would be the big main station.

Assuming that the police or Stasi had come to the point that they went home and open the condo to see and search for any evidence – they would have found more than enough – all passengers in and around the stations would be checked and observed to find him. That would certainly also apply to smaller towns on the way to Berlin like Aschersleben, Bernburg or Nienburg, Bitterfeld or Potsdam depending on where the trains would stop.

He checked the schedule. Magdeburg would have been easy as there was a train leaving from here in about an hour and ten minutes, at 9:08. That would work out nicely. And Halle? 11:01. That train didn't leave for over three hours.

"No, this is too late. Decision made. Track 3, platform 2, and this time I will write down or at least check where it stops. Let's see: Hettstedt, Aschersleben, and Wanzleben.: Three smaller towns. Hettstedt, he did not know, same with Wanzleben. The last one was just about 25km from Magdeburg, he thought from his memory.

He turned away from the box and left the station. Stations built in this monumental style from heavy stones were always cold. The sun coming up outside gave a little warmth on this early Sunday morning. He walked down the concrete steps of the building and crossed the square located in front of the station. Four streets ended here: right, one slightly to the right, half left, and one very narrow left along a tall brick wall that blocked the view to the tracks.

Almost no traffic and hardly people to be seen, Papa noticed. He felt good about the schedule. The train leaves at 9:08. It would bring him into Magdeburg around 10:30 as it was a faster train even though it made three stops along the way. They were not usually longer than two or three minutes. Aunt Rosa told him about this connection, but he was not sure if it was still exactly the same schedule. They might have changed the plan.

"Oh well, I will take it." Papa was determined.

After crossing the square, he chose to walk down the street with the most shops, which was the half left one. Somewhere should be a coffee shop or a little fast food restaurant. Breakfast would be good he thought to himself. I have not eaten anything since Gerda's supper yesterday! Other than her cake.

He stopped and lit a cigarette. Even though these were the better kind, they still tasted awful. Better than none! He looked around. The street had sidewalks on either side. Rows of chestnut trees provided some shade. A few persons came toward him who he secretly observed. It was now part of his behavior to do this; the police trainings and education made him a very sensitive person in this regard. He noticed a little bistro type café on the other side. It seemed to be open as he saw a ceiling light lit.

He crossed the street and went in. He smelled the coffee immediately but also the cold smoky air that was so typical of such places. The furniture was simple and made from wood: eight round tables each with three or four chairs. The bar was two feet higher and had four bar stools.

A second after he entered, a woman came through a side door behind the bar and greeted him with a friendly "Guten Morgen." She was in her mid thirties and dressed in a beige blouse and a blue skirt, almost looking like she was still with the Pioneers. She looked tired, like she had not had enough sleep the night before. Her clothes were wrinkled and her hair was held together in the back with a rubber band. She was nevertheless attractive. Maybe it was the revealing blouse.

Papa sat down away from the window but still in a position where he could observe the whole room and part of the street. The waitress came to him and Papa ordered a coffee.

"We have fresh rolls with sausage." She pointed to the bar. In a plastic box on the right side, there were a few rolls.

"Are they from today?" Papa asked her. She nodded but not very convincingly. Papa was hungry, "Thanks, one please." Hopefully she had kept them cool. I do not need food poisoning now. Not today!

He looked again at his watch while waiting: 8:18. Not bad he thought.

Good timing. You do not want to be at the station too long before the train leaves anyway he stated to himself. Too dangerous. He checked his satchel. Everything seemed to be in good order. Chessboard and figures, papers, identity card, wallet etc.

The coffee came with the roll and a smile. Papa thought first to pay right away. But this would give the wrong impression. "Yes, the man was in a hurry," she would have reported later. Not good. Papa ate his roll. The coffee was delicious and he asked her for another.

The street in front of the bistro got noisier. Papa suddenly came back to reality. He saw a car stopping on the opposite side and one of two men stepped out and walked further down the street; the other one parked the car around the corner. It was not a "Kübel" like Papa had driven during his time at the police. Also not green! He watched the two men.

The second one had left the parked car and yelled something at the other that Papa could not make out. A few pedestrians stopped and watched them. The men turned around and crossed the street straight toward the coffee shop! Papa's heart started to beat faster. He tried to check the two men but could not see anything disturbing or threatening. Stasi agents would not behave like that; policemen only if they were on a serious hunt for a criminal.

They came straight into the bistro, looked around and went to the bar. The waitress had also watched the scene and she stood nervously awaiting their next move.

"Do you know how we find the Goethe-Strasse? We are in a big hurry!"

She did not respond but pointed in the direction away from the station: "The second on the right when you follow the street." Both turned on their heels and left not even saying thank you. Papa was wondering what their mission was this morning. But he was relieved in a way. And his observation did not fail him. They were not from the police and not from the Stasi! He heard the engine being started and two seconds later saw them driving down the street.

He checked his watch: 8:41. Time to leave. I need tickets too. "May I pay, please?" The bartender came and he paid.

"Some people are crazy," she said and looked at Papa.

"Thank you and have a great day!"

"The same to you," Papa responded automatically, got up, grabbed his satchel and left the bistro. If she only had any idea what a day this was for him!

On the sidewalk, he looked up and down the street; nothing unusual, just a few more people and two Trabbies leaving their oily two-cycle engine fumes behind them. Papa walked toward the station and crossed the street after a hundred meters. Tickets first, he thought. The counter was right next to the entrance; it was open, no problem. Return tickets, of course.

He entered the station and went to the counter. Two people were in front of him. It took three minutes or so.

"One return ticket to Magdeburg, please." The clerk looked at the schedule: "We might be a little bit late today, maybe 10 minutes." Papa did not like this but what could he do?

"Are you sure about the delay?"

"Yes, just got a phone call." Papa checked the clock behind the clerk: 8:58. Should I leave the station? Maybe too little time, if he is right, it's about 18 minutes before the train arrives. The clerk pushed the tickets under the window and said: "They are valid for three days, do you know?"

"Yes, but I will be back tomorrow. How much?"

"Three Marks 80 Pfennings." Papa paid and took the tickets. He could not ask the clerk about a connection from Magdeburg to Berlin, that would also be too dangerous. He would remember him asking.

What now? Using the toilet would be a good idea, he thought. He looked around and saw an arrow pointing to the restrooms. He followed the signs and entered. They need to air this place! The stench was so bad that it made him want to gag. He opened one of the stalls, entered and locked it and sat down on the closed toilet. I have to stay here for another six to eight minutes, he thought. I will survive this stinky place!

At 9:08 he left the stall, washed his hands and checked himself in the mirror: "You have seen better days!" He left the restrooms and walked down the hall toward the sign for platform two, track three. He climbed the stairs carefully and slowed when he was able to just see the entire platform in front of him. Let's check out the people: An older couple with two suitcases on the right, a young girl with a rucksack, two guys with briefcases, harmless. Going slowly, he turned his head to see the other side of the platform. No one else to see. Good! He reached the top and looked at the station clock: 9:12. Another three to five minutes if the clerk was right.

He stared down the tracks toward the direction the train was supposed to enter the station. Was this black smoke in the distance? Papa got nervous again. He walked back and forth and heard a whistle in his back. When he turned around, he clearly saw the black point coming closer and growing into a locomotive. The train came, finally. A few seconds later a conductor made the announcement through the loudspeakers:

"The belated train from Leipzig to Magdeburg is arriving. Please be careful on the platform!" While the cars were passing by, Papa checked the passengers inside as much as possible.

"If there was someone mysterious, I could still leave quickly down the stairs and leave the station." No green uniforms. A good sign!

The train stopped; Papa walked toward one of the cars with a smoking sign. The doors opened and people were going to step out. He helped an older man who could hardly put one foot in front of the other and lifted his little suitcase down on the platform. I hope somebody will pick him up, Papa thought. He let the other people enter first and then got on the train himself. He checked out the situation: maybe better to be with a few more people – who knows. He walked down the aisle of the car and sat down opposite a couple; actually the older couple he saw first when coming up the stairs. They must have been in their fifties. Older couple? Is this old? Funny thought. In about eight years I will turn 50!

Papa put his satchel up into the storage net above the seat and checked the platform and the stairs. Nobody suspicious. Hopefully I did not overlook anyone, he thought. The conductor walked by the window, his whistle in his mouth, ready to blow it. He looked left and right twice. Then a shrill tone and the car jolted to move forward, slowly, but constantly accelerating.

I am on my way! Again. In about an hour I will be in Magdeburg!

75.

It was a quiet Sunday morning in the police station in Sondershausen, mainly because Saturday night had been more or less uneventful. A small break-in in Bendeleben, nothing serious. A fight in a pub in Hachelbich: two young drunk fellows fighting over a girl's attention. The usual Saturday night events. Oh well, nothing other than writing a few action reports. The typewriters were hammering the letters on the paper. The two officers trying to get home after a sleepless night would be able to finish this soon. Their shift actually ended at 12:00 o'clock – after 12 hours of working!

"Would you check my report to see if I forgot anything, Peter?" The first officer took his report out of the typewriter by turning the rubber wheel. He got up and laid it on his colleague's desk.

"I need another 5 minutes, Reiner," he responded.

"Okay, I'll get us another coffee." Reiner checked the clock on the office wall: another half hour. And then a nice afternoon at home! He left the office.

The phone rang. "Sergeant Harder."

"Stasi office, Gebert. I have a few questions!" The voice on the other end sounded serious. Harder listened carefully, "You know about the Mann case?"

"Yes."

"When did you last check on them? The father should be home now. The rest of the family was registered on Friday going over the border at Bebra around 13:00 hours. We want to know where he is!"

Harder was wide awake now and answered: "Last time we were at their house was yesterday morning. He was not home. The old lady told us that he could be with friends."

"What friends? There are a couple of options. Maybe Bohne? You know that they do not have any relatives in town. Just a cousin who lives in Mühlhausen."

"She did not say anything, she said she does not know."

"Okay. I want you to check the condo again. We are not sure about him. Try to investigate and interview the Hendrichs again. And then, drive to the Bohnes'. Just see what they know. I need this report by 14:00 hours!"

"We have a change in shift here at 12:00. I will tell my associates when they take over."

"No, I want you and Koch to do this as you are more familiar with the case. You do the job, understood? I am waiting for your report!"

The phone clicked and the line was dead. Harder leaned back in his chair. There goes my Sunday afternoon!

Reiner came back with the coffees. Not that they smelled very delicious but it would keep them awake for a while. He placed one on Peter's desk. "Here you are, the last one for this shift!"

"You would think! I got a phone call. Guess we need another coffee right away!" Peter Harder told Reiner Koch about the phone call.

"You know Gebert, he is very serious with his demands and we better do what he wants!" Reiner nodded. Damn! And we were planning on a nice Sunday afternoon and an early evening at home.

Peter read his mind: "Me too. A nice afternoon and early to bed. What can we do? Let's finish the reports first and wait for our colleagues. The office should at least be occupied. Then we'll leave to see what we can do for Gebert."

Peter typed the last two sentences, reeled out the paper and gave it to Reiner. They both checked each other's report. Done. A sip of the coffee. Signatures on the report, copies into the files and the original in envelopes for the desk of Solfert, their boss.

The knocking on the door announced their replacements. Two younger officers entered after the "Come in!" There was a short formal transition and briefing. "Okay. Anything special other than what you told us?"

"Yes. We still have to do a special investigation for the Stasi, the Mann case. We'll come back in about an hour or so and have to write another report for Gebert." They both raised their eyebrows: "That serious?"

"Well, he thinks so. And if he does – you better do what he says!" The other two nodded in agreement.

"Have a nice shift, we will see you later." Reiner and Peter took their belongings and saluted. Then they left the office.

"I hope we have gas for the car. Did you check with the driver?"

"Not yet."

"I do not want to walk and we would not make it on time anyway." A "Kübel" stood behind the building with a driver waiting. They approached the car and the driver jumped out.

"Where do we have to go, Genossen?"

"First to Edmund-König-Street." They jumped in and the engine was started.

The Kübel rolled out of the gate and turned left. It would take them not more than five minutes. It was just after twelve now.

76.

The train had reached its top speed. Hard to say but maybe 80km per hour. As scheduled, this would bring them into Magdeburg around half past 10 plus the ten minute delay. Papa checked out the couple: they were not talking too much. Obviously, they were going to visit their children in Magdeburg for a week. So they must be on vacation. He was certainly not retired at this age! People had to work until they reached 65. Retirement was secured by the government but this did not mean that it would be a happy one. The Hendrichs did not have enough to spend and family events like birthdays or weddings or funerals were the highlights in their lives. Uncle Walter would retire in two to three years. He worked hard all his life to make a small living for his wife and himself. They had no children. This couple could at least enjoy their lives. Maybe they had grandchildren.

The train should be close to the first station: Hettstedt. He had never been there. Probably nothing special there other than the nice castle Papa heard about. The town nevertheless was pretty old: first mentioned in the 4th century and officially a town in 1046. Some 12,000 inhabitants. Interesting to us was the river Wipper that we played on – and in! – going through Sondershausen. It had its source not too far away from here. All of these small towns had some history and sometimes you discovered that an unexpected famous person was born there or an historic event like a battle took place there.

The small station came up and the big black and white sign said Hettstedt. The station clock showed 9:37, exactly what Papa's watch indicated. The train came to a stop. Three passengers left the train and another two came on board. Very normal people, nobody who would create any nervousness in Papa's stomach. At least from what he could judge.

After two minutes, the conductor blew the whistle and the train rolled on. Next stop would be Aschersleben, which was located east of Hettstedt. That was where all the trouble in our lives began. Sleeping during night watch! How could I have done that?

Papa was suddenly thinking back to the events of about 18 months ago. It was certainly unfair that they had treated him like this! But everything happens for a reason. He was made aware of how dangerous it was to go against them or to have "failed" them. It also sharpened Helga's and his mind and made them consider their future – and that of their four children. During the last six months there had been signs of stronger restrictions, tougher laws and intentions to limit access to the Western countries. Some inhabitants fled to the West, first just a few; then more and more. It was almost an every day event that news spread about neighbors or doctors escaping the Republic. Papa and Mutti had listened to the Western radio stations a lot; yet, nobody could really figure out if something special was about to happen. The Russians were capable of doing anything to protect and strengthen the Eastern Block. And they would do anything to draw the line at GDR's western borders.

The train started to slow down. After passing a few villages, houses and streets became a bit more frequent. We are approaching Aschersleben, he thought. I will check the little station a bit Papa decided. In fact, a green uniform here would not alert him too much because of the police academy here; there were always some coming and going as he did twice in his career.

He got up and walked to the front end of the car. He looked back and checked his satchel. Nobody would take it, he was sure about this. It would make other people curious if he took it with him every time he got up.

He could see a glimpse of the little station when the train bent left. It looked certainly familiar! He saw only one person on the platform waiting. A woman. That's okay he thought. Not that there were no females in the secret services or the police departments, but it would be very unusual that she would be on a mission all by herself. Papa went back to his seat. I will have a cigarette right after the train leaves Aschersleben he decided. Actually and interesting enough, no conductor had checked their tickets yet. I have to watch this. Maybe he will come right after we leave here?

The train stopped. Hardly anyone got up to get out. He saw the woman stepping into the adjacent car. Also, there were no cars other than a taxi in front of the small long station building. What would I do if I see the police entering the station or waiting on the platform? Good question. I am not really prepared for this Papa thought. Most of the little stations had only one track. So it would be hard to hide. Having police inside the train would mean no escape; that was for sure. You could not jump out – this would certainly end up in a serious injury if not death. I'd better think about it while I have the time! Just in case.

Papa looked at his watch: almost ten. Maybe another minute and we are gone from here, he thought, we will go almost straight north from here.

He looked out, lost in his thoughts. I wonder if the Stasi or the police at home went to the house again. If they did and found out by checking the condo and our household they would certainly have the time to call and inform colleagues in Magdeburg and of course also in East Berlin. This would make it very dangerous and hard to cross the border to the West. My mission could be finished sooner rather than later.

After all it was Whitsun: Sunday and Monday holiday. But did this count? Probably not. If they did check early, they would have gone to the south station in Sondershausen and asked the clerk. He would remember. We had no car, so train was pretty much the only possibility to get away. Sangerhausen was only a few minutes and a phone call away. They could have appeared in the station before 9 o'clock, couldn't they? So maybe they did not check this early. Hope arose in Papa. This gives me at least enough time to go to Magdeburg. If they checked later and found out, Magdeburg could be a dangerous place. Too many policemen, too much Stasi. There was a chance for this option, he could not deny this.

Okay, so what should I do? Papa's thoughts were spinning. There must be a solution to bypass the possible danger. As long as I am not in a bigger town, the chance of finding me diminishes to a much smaller probability. Think, Ferdi, think! I have to consider that they will find out, I have to. Just to be on the safe side. I need to make a plan. There was after all still the danger in East Berlin crossing to West Berlin. But this was the ultimate risk Papa had to take.

He stared out the window. Suddenly the familiar jolt – and the train started to roll away from the platform. Two people were waving. Erfurt came into his mind. The picture he remembered when he walked along the train with his family waving farewell. He saw Mutti smiling behind the window and Roland and Jürgen waving goodbye. They made it. Helga was probably thinking about him every minute since Friday morning. It would be wonderful to see them all soon.

No, it will be wonderful, he corrected himself getting out of his world of thoughts and memories. I have to make a decision: go all the way to Magdeburg or take the option of stepping off the train in Wanzleben. How far was Wanzleben from Magdeburg? Or could I possibly catch a train from there to Berlin? How can I find out? Asking the conductor would be easy – but not a real option. He decided to look for a map. Most trains had a little map at the end of the cars near the platform near the toilet. Toilet? Good idea! He got up and thought about his satchel for a second. Better take it this time. No, let me ask the couple.

"I will be right back" he addressed them both. "Would you please watch my satchel?"

"Of course," the lady responded, "Don't worry!" Papa left and went straight to the toilet. First things first. When he came out of this little box, he looked around at the walls. The map was in the right corner. "I knew it," he thought. Maybe I can just see where and how far away I am from Magdeburg. Wanzleben, here you are. Papa found it. Well, that looks like 20 or 25 km. I could go by taxi – if I can find one. The taxi could drop me downtown and I will carefully make my way to the station. From the little dot on the map Wanzleben appeared about half the size of Achersleben, less than 5,000 people. Small enough to escape the attention of the authorities. From a distance point of view, this would take the train another 20 minutes, maybe 25. Time enough to get prepared. His gut feeling told him to do it: get off this train! He looked down the adjacent car and saw the conductor coming. He turned back to his seat. The lady smiled at him. He grabbed his satchel and opened it to take the ticket out.

They showed their tickets when the conductor came. The older lady looked at him and asked, "How long does it take to Wanzleben, conductor?"

"About another," he checked his watch, "20 minutes" he answered. I was right, Papa thought, great. So, the couple were also getting off there? He decided to ask them.

"No, we are going to Magdeburg. My son and his family live near Wanzleben but he decided to pick us up in Magdeburg with his Trabbi." She paused, "He just got it, brand new! And then we go for lunch, all together!" Pride was in her eyes. Her husband smiled too.

"Well, he waited long enough for it!" She punished him with a serious look and he went quiet. Hopefully nobody heard this.

"Where are you going, may I ask?" she continued the conversation.

"Wanzleben," Papa's answer was short, "Visiting some friends." She nodded.

"How big is the town, do you know? I have never been there." Maybe she could tell me a bit more about it Papa thought.

"It is a cute little town but not much going on there. You have to go to Magdeburg to shop. Much better!" There was this inner smile most women have when talking about shopping.

Papa decided to end the conversation and looked out the window. Fields and bushes were flying by and some farmhouses could be seen. Whenever a street crossed the tracks, the bars were down and the train took a little wiggle. But seldom was there a car waiting. The train travelled at high speed and soon Wanzleben would appear. Papa's head was clear: I'll get off and look for a taxi. If I do not find one, maybe there will be a bus. The whole thing would cost me maybe another half hour. Maybe worth it – who knows. Time will tell.

He looked to the window on the other side. I will make it, I have to!

77.

The Kübel with Reiner Koch and Peter Harder drove up the Possenweg. Crossing the tracks made them bounce a bit in their seats. Not a very comfortable car, Peter thought. But this was really not a new experience for him. These were pretty much the only cars the police had.. They were lucky to have three of them. And hopefully they were not broken when they needed them. Like now. Gas was also not always available. You would think that would not be a problem, we are the police. Well, think twice.

It was a quarter after twelve o'clock, Hendrichs should be home, he thought. Maybe Mr. Mann would be too. It is lunch time. That would make it easier. A short chat, a few questions and we could go. They turned left into our street and parked in front of the gate.

"I will wait in the car," the driver said, "Okay. It might take a few minutes."

They climbed the stairs and rang the bell: Mann. Reiner went along the wall and tried to look into the kitchen window. Nobody was to be seen; the kitchen was empty. Peter rang again, this time a bit longer. Reiner came back and shrugged his shoulders. "Nobody home it seems."

"Should we ring the Hendrichs?" Peter asked.

"Yes, we need to, at least talk to them." Peter pressed the Hendrich's doorbell.

Aunt Rosa was just about to put the food on the table when she heard the bell. Uncle Walter was already seated at the table. He froze. Then he got up carefully lifting his chair so it did not make any noise.

"Who can this be? Police again?" Aunt Rosa made an expression like "I do not want to open the door." Uncle Walter thought for a second; we could be in Jecha visiting relatives, couldn't we?

"Don't open the door, Rosa. Be quiet." He slowly and quietly closed the open kitchen window. All others were shut. They stood in the middle of their little kitchen and did not move an inch. It rang again. Uncle Walter put his fingers on his lips. They had wooden floors, so it was dangerous to move and make any noise. They were not sure if the people at the front door would hear it but better be safe than sorry. They waited another two minutes. No more rings.

"Maybe they really aren't at home," Peter said. Reiner looked disturbed,

"We need some information for Gebert or we'll work until midnight!" Reiner went again to the kitchen window.

"I can't see a lot. Let's go around the house."

They both walked down the stairs and went up the three steps from the garage to walk behind the house. The house had our little garden and you could look into our veranda and up to the Pantel's balcony and even up to the Hendrich's roof window. Peter went to the fence to have a better look at the whole back of the villa. It was dead, the whole house – nothing to see, nothing to hear.

"All windows are shut, do you see?" He looked at Reiner with a questioning expression.

"Seems so," he responded shortly. Peter walked around to the side of the house. Our bedroom shades were closed but this was not unusual; we were gone for 10 days.

"What do you think? Should we get somebody to open the door?"

Reiner shook his head. "No, not yet. If he is not back tomorrow, I would get Manfred and his guys and open the door." Peter was not very happy to wait until the next day. They would be empty handed and Gebert would not like it. But he wanted to get home. Gebert, what would he say?

"Let's go and check on Bohnes." They left the garden and walked through the iron gate and closed it. Peter just wanted to jump in the car. He stopped, turned around and stood in front of the gate thinking. "You know what, Reiner?"

"Yes, I think I do." Reiner was already on the other side of the car. He came back.

"See this tile here? We will leave the corner of the gate exactly at the corner of the tile. What do you think?"

Peter answered almost excited: "Exactly what I thought!" They looked at the position of the gate again and memorized it.

"At least we will know if somebody was here. Our colleagues can check it this evening."

They jumped in the car and told the driver to go toward the station near the "Frauenberg," a hill just behind the main station. In a dead end side street is where the Bohnes lived.

The Kübel turned and drove down the Possenweg with a nice blue exhaust cloud streaming behind.

78.

Papa checked his watch: another ten minutes, plus or minus one. I have to check my satchel again. Do I really have everything? But I have to do this quietly. He went to the toilet with the satchel. He locked himself in and checked all his belongings. Everything there. Good. I will go back to the seat just to say a friendly goodbye. This would appear normal. A minute later he opened the door and went back to his seat. He quickly looked at the couple. Another minute and Papa told them "good bye and have a good visit with your son". They thanked him and Papa got up and went to the doorway.

Wanzleben. He leaned against the wall and looked out the window. Pictures of houses and gardens went by. I must be close. He tried to see the station coming up while the train started to slow down. As he could not see the platform he turned to the other side of the car. Must be on this side this time. The train was now already very slow. Papa saw the little station building and the platform was growing in his view.

He just wanted to turn his head when a flash of green blinked in the corner of his left eye. He abruptly turned his head back: two uniforms, green, policemen! His face must have turned white. Pure fear crawled up his body. The train almost came to a halt. The two policemen were standing in front of the station building and would disappear from his view in a second, hidden by the building. They had machine guns, Papa noticed.

For a moment Papa covered his face with his hands. If they are already here, they might already be waiting for me in Magdeburg. I have to get away from here, now! His thoughts came quickly: cannot stay on the train, cannot leave through the station. It could be a false alarm but I cannot take the risk! There is only one option.

The train stopped. The door to the platform stayed closed but could be opened any moment. Papa had turned around and looked out the other side of the car. No further railway to cross and some bushes alongside maybe hiding some gardens or fields. That is my only chance!

In the next moment he jumped to the opposite door, opened it, and stepped down and jumped the last half meter to the ground. He quickly checked left and right and ran the three meters toward the bushes. Somebody could have seen him, but he had to take the risk. On his knees he tried to look for a little opening in the bushes. There was one about another five meters ahead to the left. 'I can get through there,' Papa thought seeing a bit of a cleared area. He pushed himself into the opening and fell to the other side of the bush. This all took not more than ten seconds.

He laid down on his front to the ground and tried to see if anything was happening at the station. The little gap in the bush gave him enough of a view: nothing – or maybe not yet. He lifted his head back and looked around. As long as the train stood there he was covered. Just 25 meters away, there stood a single little house with fences left and right leading to the bushes. The fences were made of netting wire.

He got up and ran towards this fence. The bushes were obviously the boundary between the property and the station. The garden had some fruit trees and laundry was hanging from three lines waving in the light wind. 'There is my new coverage,' Papa thought.

Right at this moment, he heard the whistle blow and the train started to roll. I need to get behind the laundry! Within three more seconds Papa jumped up and ran the 10 meters to the hanging laundry. He ran through the first row of laundry and got tangled up in the second tearing down some underwear and socks. Fortunately, the first row had some bedding hanging up that was big enough to block the view towards the station. Nobody would be able to see him now.

"What are you doing there?! All my laundry is dirty again. Get off of my property!" It was like somebody shot him. Papa looked up and saw the lady of the house staring at him from the window. I have to run, was the only thing that came to his mind. So he took off, around the house to the adjacent street turning right without even thinking. He ran for about two minutes until he stopped in an entranceway breathing heavily. After a few moments, he peeked around the house corner. The lady did not follow him, neither did her husband – if she had one. The street was empty. The train must have left the station. But where are the policemen? Papa leaned against the house wall and rested for a short while.

During the last five minutes, he had his satchel hard in his left hand. He looked inside. Nothing was lost.

"I need a cigarette – now."

79.

The Kübel with Peter Harder and Reiner Koch entered the street where the Bohnes lived; it was the second to last house on the right. The driver stopped right in front of it. Reiner and Peter jumped out and opened the little wooden garden gate to approach the front door. They looked at each other – and pressed the doorbell. A few seconds later, the door opened. It was Rolf Bohne who opened. "Guten Tag, Genossen!" He seemed to have expected them.

"Guten Tag, Rolf. We have a few questions; can we come in?"

"No problem," Rolf answered.

They entered the condo and Rolf let them take a seat in the front room on the couch. Gerda walked in and also greeted them. They looked at each other and then Peter broke the uncomfortable silence.

"We do not want to beat around the bush," he said, "We are here to ask you about Ferdi Mann."

He paused and watched their reaction. There was no reaction. "Ferdi?" Rolf responded.

"Yes. We would like to talk to him but cannot find him." Another pause and a certain look from both, Reiner and Peter.

Rolf who was still standing up, sat down.

"Well, you probably know that he was here yesterday. Not sure what he is doing today. He left for home yesterday evening."

"When?"

"Gerda, when was this? Maybe 20:00 hours?"

"Could be right," she responded easily. Peter and Reiner looked at each other.

"We tried to see him at home. It is Sunday, we thought he would sleep in and rest up after bringing the family to Erfurt." Rolf was not surprised that they knew every detail but obviously they missed a certain portion of it!

"Well, I am sorry, he did not tell us what he is doing today. There was no reason to tell us. It is Sunday, a day to rest and stay home I guess."

"You have no idea where he could be? No indication from him what he is doing today?" Rolf made an expression like he would think about the possibilities where he could be.

"No, no idea. I am sure he will go to work Tuesday, I don't think he took off while the family is in the West." All sounded very normal – almost too normal for the two policemen.

Gerda broke the silence: "Sorry, but I did not offer you a cup of coffee. Would you like one?"

She asked not overly friendly as this would cause new doubts. "No, thanks. We are working overtime and would like to finish our investigation."

After saying this, Reiner tried to read the Bohne's minds. He looked first to Gerda, then to Rolf. No sign of any reaction in their faces. Another piece of silence.

Rolf tried to give the impression of being helpful: "Did you guys ask the Hendrichs? They live above you know. Maybe they know where he is today."

Sounded helpful but was maybe not very convincing. The answer was short and almost harsh: "Yes. We did. They are not home either!" Their faces went to a serious expression.

That's enough. No more words, Rolf thought to himself. "Okay, Rolf and Gerda. When you hear from him today you have to call us at once! Understood?" That was straight! They are after him!

"Of course, we can do this. I am sure he will be home tonight" Rolf tried to be calm and cooperative. Reiner and Peter raised themselves from the couch and walked by them towards the door.

"See you," was like a warning just before the door closed from the outside. Rolf and Gerda stood in silence for a moment until they heard the Kübel engine being started. "They do not know anything yet from the telegram!" noticed Gerda.

80.

The cigarette was a pleasure. Papa inhaled every puff. He had calmed down and his pulse was slower. There was still the danger of these policemen; the station was just 200 meters away. He had to wait a bit longer. Then he had to find a detour to what could be the center of the town. I need either a bus station or a taxi!

He peeked out of his hideaway but saw no one. The train crossing was another 50 meters down the street. I have to go there, I have to! He started walking. At the railway crossing, he peeked around the end of the bushes blocking the view to the station. He saw the platform and the station building. The platform was empty. So the policemen could be still outside in front of the station. He slowly crossed the rails. Looking to the right, he carefully watched the expanding viewing angle. More and more of the little area in front of the station came into sight. He could not see any of them. Maybe they were waiting in the station or maybe they had left? He walked further always looking towards the station now. The area in front of the station building was empty! "I am just walking normally and will go down the street," Papa told himself. He stepped on the left sidewalk and walked towards what seemed to be the center of Wanzleben.

Sunday mornings were usually quiet; just a few people were out walking or going to church. A couple came towards him on the other side of the street and an older lady looked out of her window checking out what was going on in her street. Papa had passed the station and thought about his next step. I need a taxi, he thought. Busses are okay but a taxi would be more flexible and faster. Suddenly, he had an idea. He crossed the street and went to the window where the older lady was. He walked straight to her and said "Good Morning!"

The older lady was a bit surprised but responded as well with "Good Morning".

"Could you tell me where I can get a taxi?"

"A taxi?"

"Yes, a taxi." She checked Papa from head to toe. Then it seemed that she made an effort to think about it.

"There are no taxis here."

"Any busses? I need to go to Magdeburg." She checked Papa again and responded:

"No, but our neighbors have a car. How much do you pay if they drive you? I could ask them." Papa had to try and cover his excitement: a car! There is a car! Great. They could drive me anywhere! Well, almost anywhere.

"Eventually, I could pay them 20 marks. Could you ask them?" The lady disappeared. Seconds later, he heard the door being opened and there she came.

"Follow me. They live over the street." Papa followed her. They went just to the right and crossed the street. The house she pointed to was a red brick house. On the side was a garden door a little wider than usual. Behind was a wider entrance way – and there it was: a light blue Wartburg. The absolute most luxurious car at this time – beside the Russian Moskvitch.

The old lady rang the bell and a man in his fifties opened. "Good morning, Emma! How are you?" He stared at Papa being interrupted by her answer: "This gentleman needs a ride. You know that we have no taxis. He will pay you." She looked at Papa and he nodded.

"Where do you have to go?"

"Magdeburg. I could pay you 20 marks. I missed the train." The explanation seemed to be reasonable.

"Okay. I need just a few minutes."

That would be great Papa thought. By car. I could ask him to drop me anywhere. I could go to the train station in Magdeburg or get a taxi there and go one or two towns further if it appears too dangerous to hop on the train there. I just would need the schedule from Magdeburg to Berlin. It could even be possible to check outside the station. We will see.

The old lady was still standing beside him. A minute later the man appeared and opened the big gate, locked the gate on the side of the wall and walked to the Wartburg. The engine started and left a blue cloud of smoke. Wartburgs also had two-cycle engines. In a few years from now, they would introduce Otto motors, four cycles. The Wartburg came backwards out of the entrance way. Papa waved him out, walked to the passenger side and opened the door. Turning to the lady he squeezed her hand and said "Thank you" and jumped in.

The man put it in first gear and they left. They followed the road until the first crossing. A street sign said Magdeburg to the right. They turned and seconds later they were on their way to the city.

So far, no word was spoken. The man finally broke the silence: "Where are you from? I have not seen you here before." Dangerous, Papa thought. Such conversations are dangerous. I cannot tell him too much. At the end, he could think about it later and go to the police and tell them about the stranger he gave a ride to. Everything was possible, always. I have to be careful.

"I want to go to Magdeburg to visit some friends."

"Magdeburg is a nice town. Have you been there before?"

"No, never. They invited me." Papa tried to keep the conversation short. Another subject would also help to stop the "interview."

"How far is Magdeburg? How long will it take us to drive there?"

"About 20 minutes depending on where you want to go. Do you have a street name?" Not good. What do I say now? I have no street name!

"I forgot. But they will pick me up near the train station. So, if you do not mind you could drop me there."

"I can do that, no problem."

They drove along a country road and through two other villages. In the distance, Papa could see the city slowly shaping up. More and more houses and side streets, signs and a few shops left and right. Closed of course, it was Sunday after all. The traffic was light. Very few traffic lights hindered their way to the center. The car was certainly more comfortable than a Trabbi or the police Kübel. Still, it was equipped simply and besides an ashtray and a little glove compartment, there was not too much you could get excited about.

The man steered the Wartburg into one of the main streets towards the center.

"We are almost there. See the big building at the end on the right? That is the station." The car rattled a bit over the street train rails and some of the sections had still cobblestones. They approached the station. Papa opened his satchel and looked for his wallet. 20 Deutschmarks. Oh well, money doesn't count now. He picked a 20 mark bill and closed his satchel. The man noticed it and said:

"You know, give me ten, that's okay." Papa thought for a moment and tried to make a very normal impression:

"That's okay. I told you I would pay you 20. No problem. I am very thankful because now I will not miss my friends. We do not have too much time today. I have to go back tomorrow." He took the 20 and put it in front into the little compartment beside the steering wheel. The man had a short look at it. He slowed the car as they were just a hundred meters from the station.

"I'll stop here as I cannot drive in front of the station. It is also easier for me to go back from here – if you don't mind."

"Great Sir, thank you. I really appreciate your help! Have a nice Sunday – and Monday!" Papa opened the door with the little chrome lever and jumped out. A final goodbye, and he pushed the door shut. The Wartburg roared a bit and left. The blue smoke was something like a goodbye wave.

Papa looked around. It was a bit busier here, definitely! Several cars drove up and down the street and there were quite a few people walking. The front of the station seemed to be busy too, people coming and going with or without suitcases. It was true: the front of the station was blocked with guardrails like when there was a demonstration. Well, there was never really a demonstration here. That was futile! There were no police to be seen but they could be inside. I have to carefully investigate where the train schedule is located. Papa started to walk towards the entrance. A few stone steps and he entered the station hall.

It was huge, high ceilings and a few big columns holding them up. The stone walls and ceilings were unfortunately not as clean as you would like but rather covered with the black dust from the locomotives and other pollution. They should sandblast the building Papa thought looking up. He looked around observing his environment and also looking for the glass cabinets with the train schedules. Then he saw it, hung on the way to the railway platforms, on the wall.

Magdeburg had a few more platforms than Erfurt, probably some 10 or 12. You could see this by running down the schedule. Papa checked his watch: already 11:20. He talked to himself, that little adventure cost me almost an hour!

Okay, let's see. His finger went down the schedule: 11:30 to Potsdam, no. 11:46 to Frankfurt/Oder. No. Or does that stop in Berlin? Yes! At the East Berlin main station at 13:12. That works!

East Berlin main station, what a place he thought. Very historical! It had many different names based on its strategic purpose. First, it was built for the railway connection with Frankfurt/Oder in 1842. It was called the Frankfurter Station. Then, the station got its name from new connections with Silesia that was part of Germany until the end of the Second World War. Then it was simply the East Station and a few other names in between.

Papa's thoughts got him off the real purpose why he was here. Concentrate Ferdi!, he reminded himself. Where is the ticket counter? He stepped aside as two other passengers wanted to have a closer look at the schedule. He searched for the ticket counter and saw it opposite from him ten meters left towards the exit. He walked straight to it and had to wait. Three people were in front of him.

"Did you hear the news?" The second person in front of him, a man with white hair and of some 60 years old with a cane, turned back to the one right in front of Papa.

"They now have stronger security measures on all stations and airports." The other person shrugged his shoulders.

"If they think they have to they must do it."

"Seems too many people do not like the government anymore." He responded with his voice two levels down. Yes, you never know who is standing beside you, Papa thought. Saying this was a big risk already. I could get you arrested now!

Hmm, they increased the security levels. I somehow expected this. No, we expected this, Helga and me. Helga, the children, what are they doing right now? I would love to know! I cannot wait to see them! What a stressful time, what a life changing event. I need to get there, today! Strengthened security levels? Well, it does not matter to me anymore: either I make it or I don't. Wrong, Ferdi! Stay positive! He corrected his thinking and said to himself: "I will make it! I know how to deal with these guys."

He looked around. It was somewhat automatic for him. Always on alert! A bit down one hallway to the right he saw two policemen walking slowly up and down observing the people. Good that they were not near! Surely, they would have taken the white haired man. They had no machine guns, so Papa figured that they were just normal station officers.

It was his turn for the tickets: "Where do you want to go?" the clerk asked him through the round opening in the window. Papa bent down a bit and lowered his voice a bit when he answered:

"Berlin, East Station, return ticket." The clerk took one of the preprinted little three-by-five centimeter brown cards from a box and pushed it into a printer-like device and hit it. He pulled the little card out. Put another one in, changed the wheel on the printer and hit it again.

"Here you are. 5 Deutschmarks 60. The next train is at 11:46, you can make it. Platform Eight. Are you coming back today?"

"Yes!"

"Not sure but there must be trains almost every two hours from Berlin, so you should be okay." Papa put his money into the little turning table underneath the window. The clerk turned it, put in the change and turned it back.

"Have a good trip!"

"Thanks." Papa turned away, put the change in his purse and started to walk to the kiosk. When he reached the counter he realized, "I am so hungry. Some sausages would be good."

Papa always liked sausages. I guess I got this from him. I like them too. I could eat five or six or even more depending on the size. Great with rolls and mustard. The tastiest are the spicy ones with garlic. They are always good for a quick lunch or dinner. Not very healthy on the long run, I have to admit.

Papa reached the kiosk. On a little blackboard it was written: "Thüringer Bratwurst mit Brötchen 1,10 DM". Just what the stomach ordered! Maybe I'll have two! He ordered one and the man with the big white apron put one of the Thuringians into a sliced role and handed it to him. "Anything to drink?"

"You have a small beer?"

"Yes, a Diamant."

"Thanks." Papa never had this beer before; it was a local from the Magdeburg Diamant Brewery. He took the beer and the sausage and took it over to the little stand-up table.

The sausage was great! The beer too, hit the spot. Papa checked his watch: 11:32. Well, still time for another one. He ordered a second sausage and paid for it right away. After another five minutes, he left the stand. Time to go! Now, realizing that he was getting closer to the serious part of his journey, the nervous feeling came back. He was trying to calm himself down. One step at a time. Train first; then we will see in Berlin.

He reached platform eight a minute later. It was 11:41. The train should be here any time.

81.

The Kübel with Reiner Koch and Peter Harder entered the courtyard behind the police building. They jumped out and entered the building. Up the stairs and straight to their office. They knocked and entered after they heard "Come in!"

Their two colleagues were sitting at their desks. One was reading the Saturday newspaper "Das Volk" and the other one read a book. Obviously, they had a quiet afternoon. Nice for them, Peter thought. We should have too but Gebert kept us working!

"Hey, what's new?" asked the guy who read the paper.

"Not too much. We have to write a quick report for Gebert. Did he call yet?"

"No."

"Good. I need my desk for a few minutes." The guy got up and left the office.

"I'll get us some coffee," he said on the way out. "No cake, sorry." He smiled. Peter sat down and Reiner stood right beside him.

"So, what do we tell him? We really do not have any information, do we?" Reiner took a second to search his brain for a good answer: "I think we should tell him exactly what we found out."

"And this would be what?"

"The Hendrichs could not tell us where he is as they were not home!" Peter started typing, click click and cluck cluck.

"And the Bohnes did not know either. They had him over all Saturday and then he went home. He is not home now but they think he will be back this evening as he has to work Tuesday. Something like that."

Every time the typewriter carriage came to the end, it rang a bell. Time to hit the lever and push it over to start a new line. Papa was a fast typer, I watched him many times even though he did not type with all fingers.

After a while, he looked again to Reiner:

"So, I wrote that and also about what the Bohnes said. What else can we tell him? Nothing, right?"

Reiner nodded. Gebert would probably yell at them for such a lousy report. But what could we do? We cannot make something up just to please him. Maybe the new guys have to make the round again this evening.

Peter wrote a few more words and got up:

"Just check and tell me if I have to add something." Reiner sat down and read the report:

"We were at the Hendrich's at 12:15h in Edmund-Koenig-Street 4 where Ferdinand Mann and his family live. We rang the bell twice, nobody answered. We checked through the kitchen window and also walked around the house. We wanted to ask the older couple in the top level of the house, the Hendrichs, but they were not at home either. The same applies for the Pantel family, which we knew already. The Hendrichs could have been in Jecha at their relatives. This would not be unusual. Mr. Mann has to go to work Tuesday morning. The records show this. Therefore we expect him to be home at least by this evening and tomorrow.

We then drove to the Bohne's house to interview them. They were at home at 12:35. We talked to both of them. They told us that Mr. Mann was there yesterday until around 20:00. Then he left for home. They think that he might be at friends. We got the impression that they might know where he is. We indicated that we would come again. We recommend that the policemen on duty should visit both locations this evening to make sure that Mr. Mann is in either one of the locations."

Reiner got up and okayed it. Peter rolled it out of the typewriter, signed it, put the copy on the desk. He took the copy and gave it to the guy reading the book:

"Bring this to Gebert at once. We are still on time as he wants it before 14:00. Or send the driver that's fine."

"We'll send the driver, no problem." The guy put his book down and grabbed the paper, put it in an envelope, addressed it and sealed it and left the office.

Peter and Reiner looked at each other: "Done! Now, let's go home!" They turned to the other guy who had taken his place behind the desk again.

"You guys probably will get the official instruction from Gebert as soon as he sees our report. But I would check on Mann in any case if I were you just to avoid any trouble."

"We'll do it, don't worry. It seems to be important, at least for the Stasi."

Peter and Reiner looked at each other, "Finished, now we go home!" They left the office.

82.

The train rolled slowly but steadily until it came to a halt. Papa helped a young lady with her baby carriage and had to think about Erfurt two days ago. Two days and so much happened already!

He got on the train and looked around for a quiet place. Not too many left, this train was much more crowded. Everybody wants to go to Berlin it seems. It was about 150km away, so time to relax a bit and rest. Papa walked down the aisle between the left and right row of seats. Most were pretty occupied. You could sit with three people on each side facing each other, but this would not be too comfortable. And I do not want to talk to anyone, not now.

The row right against the cabin wall at the end was empty on one side. Space enough for me, Papa thought. Maybe the row was a bit tighter and therefore nobody really liked it. The opposite side was taken by a younger couple. It almost looked like they were on a honeymoon trip or such. They sat very close to each other holding hands.

Papa sat down after putting his satchel in the overhead net. He checked the couple: they were busy with themselves. He looked around and checked every person as best he could. He could not see anything disturbing. He decided to walk the aisle to the rest room in a few minutes just to make sure not to have overlooked anything.

The whistle blew. Here we go he thought. Another hour and a half and he would be in Berlin. The train rolled on after the whistle. Slowly but surely it accelerated; and soon, the world flew by almost like memories of his life. Pictures of Mutti and his children came up in his mind and he again wondered how they were doing.

83.

Mutti was getting real nervous. She checked her watch: 13:28. Ferdi must soon be in Berlin. I wish I knew where he is! Did he make it so far? Or did he have problems? Or is he even already in custody? She shivered. I pray to God, please let him be on his way to us!

She sat in the little front room with Oma and Opa. They were all nervous. Little was spoken as everybody thought about Papa. Too many people in this little apartment, Mutti thought. The situation was already a bit tight: seven people in this little flat. No quiet time for anybody. We were probably too much of a crowd for Oma und Opa after two days – and who knew how long we had to stay. In fact, our travel back home was scheduled for Tuesday of the next week. In other words: eight more days with them in this little space. For Mutti, this was unthinkable and pretty tough. She was not in control and she did not like it. In fact, she never liked not being in control. On the other hand: we were here to visit and have a good time!

Traditionally, there is a coffee and cake time in the afternoon, an old tradition in Europe. Some countries have tea and cookies, other cake and coffee. It's a nice time to sit and talk.

Roland and I were checking out the environment – or should I say cars? We heard Mutti calling us. We ran back from down the street where a few Mercedes limousines were parked. We followed her into the house. Oma had set the table and obviously had baked some cake. She also had whipped cream prepared. I love whipped cream, the more the better. That would make my afternoon! We washed our hands and sat down. The mood around the table was somewhat depressed.

Not too much was said. Oma broke the silence:

"What are we doing tomorrow?" Mutti did not say anything. "Let's go shopping," I said excited. "I would like to see all the toys they have downtown!" Opa smiled.

"That would be nice" Roland answered supportively to my idea.

"I also need some groceries so we have something to eat," Oma agreed.

"We can ride the street train to the Old Market and walk down from there checking out all the shops on Hindenburg Street," Opa continued, "But there is a problem, tomorrow is a holiday. So we have to wait until Tuesday, unless we go just window shopping."

Mutti ate the last bite of her cake and looked up. "Okay, let's do this. How late is it? I wish I knew what Papa is doing right now!"

She got up and went into the kitchen. I guess she had tears in her eyes.

84.

The train was faster than the one from Sangerhausen. It also had more cars. After five minutes, Papa had gone to the restroom as he intended. He needed also to think and concentrate on the next few hours and how he would go forward. In an hour, he would be in East Berlin. What then? Well, not that he did not have a clue. Of course, he and Mutti had talked about it and had some kind of plan. But being so close now to Berlin, it all had to be thought through.

He would arrive at the East Berlin Station. A pretty big station and very probably well observed. Papa was very sure that there would be a lot of Vopos, the policemen. They would be armed with Kalashnikovs, the Russian Army machine gun, named after their famous creator.

Papa would have to avoid them as much as possible; acting normal was sometimes not that easy. You think you act normal or try to and then it does not appear as normal. Well, Papa was trained in such behavior and in all the observation techniques. He knew how to act. Nevertheless, he had to be very, very careful. He did not know at this time how much of the news about his absence at home had spread. The police in Berlin could be informed from the Stasi in Sondershausen; this was the worst case. At best, they did not know anything yet and Papa would have an advantage of about four to five hours before the East Berlin police and/or Stasi started searching for him everywhere: stations, airports, squares, public buildings and public transport. Especially the ones crossing the border to West Berlin.

He sat on the toilet for a few minutes. He was not sure which of the street trains he would use; he did not know the numbers of the different routes they took. But the trains – as in every city – had signs with street names or city areas where they would be going. Next would be finding a good explanation for the border control Volkspolizisten to go over the East-West border, already at the time when he bought a ticket. I have to concentrate on this. On the station would be a plan for the street trains – if I have time to check them out. If not, if I have to leave the station in a hurry, I have to go somewhere and see if I can get some information. Or a taxi driver could tell me. No, not a good idea. I better not talk to anyone. The area in front of the station where the street trains run by should have plans! Let's hope I have an opportunity to check them out.

Papa's thoughts were accelerating: first, I will check out the train schedule now to make sure I know where to jump out. The East Berlin station would be good but I have to have a plan B just in case. "Okay," he told himself, "let's go back to my seat and wait for the arrival."

He left the restroom and stood for a while on the platform between the cars looking at the fast moving countryside: some big fields changing to houses and buildings, plants, a tractor in a field, some cars driving on a small country road and so on. It seemed unreal at the time as if it was just a temporary scene like in a movie. A quick thought on his family: they should be fine, we should be fine!

He turned to the sliding door to enter his car. He slowly approached his bench. The couple was still sitting there the same way: holding hands, leaning on each other. He sat down, smiled briefly at them and looked out the window. His clock showed 12:27. Another 50 minutes or so!

Papa thought to himself, I will get up five minutes before we arrive. It will help me to watch what is happening on the platform on which we arrive. It would be good to know what the situation is: how many policemen are there and if there are any signs of me being looked for. Also, which way is the fastest way out of the station. I need answers!

I could ask the conductor on which platform the train arrives, he should know. He should come to check the tickets anyway. Papa leaned over to look down the aisle. Nobody was coming. He turned back the other way and saw him: he was standing in the aisle in the next car checking tickets left and right. Good. I will ask him. He turned back and looked at the couple. She had rested her head on his shoulders and slept; at least it looked like it. Her friend also had closed his eyes.

A minute later, Papa heard the squeaking door sliding open, the noise from the train got louder for a few seconds until it was shut again. Papa turned around: the conductor. He slowly came closer: row by row he checked the tickets. Papa had taken his out of his pocket and held it in his hands.

"Tickets, please." Papa handed him the ticket. He punched it with his little machine.

"Excuse me, can you tell me which platform we are arriving on at the East Berlin-Station?" Papa looked straight into his brown eyes.

"Good question. Usually, it's number six. But there is so much going on that they change it sometimes."

"Are they working on the tracks?" Papa did not want to ask too directly.

"No, just all these controls they do nowadays." The conductor already stood at the next row.

Controls! Actually not really a surprise but obviously they were on a higher alert. Too many people had left the Republic already. There were rumors over recent weeks that the government had pulled more troops to the borders. It was unacceptable for them that their people would leave their home land. In a few months, it could be that half the people would have left! The country would be dead!

Papa thought about it. The nervousness came back. It was more than being nervous, maybe the feeling had reached the fear level. At least he was forewarned. And forewarned is forearmed they say. He knew that this was very true!

Okay, he told himself. What do I do? Leave the train again before we arrive at the station? Would this make a difference? Probably not. If they observed the stations, the little suburban ones would be too. And being in a crowd of people helps! Berlin was too important and actually most of the people who had fled the Republic already went through Berlin. Was it really easier this way? I wonder.

Of course, being in a big city – and Berlin had probably three million inhabitants – you find cover more easily. And unless they totally closed the borders, all the crossings to West Berlin, there were quite a few possibilities to escape to the West. The thought calmed Papa down a bit. Nevertheless, he had to be on guard. "Watch your environment, not too obvious but thoroughly," he said to himself.

He had decided earlier in the long talks and planning discussions he had with Mutti and Aunt Rosa to take a street train. There were many to take. This decision of which one to choose would be last minute and maybe it would be done in a hurry or on his own gut feeling. When asked why you want to go to West Berlin, a good excuse was always to bring our big friends, the Russians, into the picture. This was always convincing to a certain extent. Not a guarantee but a good start.

His watch said 12:58. Another 20 minutes and the decisive part of my travel will need my full attention. Papa closed his eyes for comfort and tried to rest a few minutes.

He did not plan on resting too long.

85.

The phone rang. One of the 2 policemen took the set:
"Sunday guard, this is constable Schmidt."
"Stasi, Gebert! Anything new on the Mann case?" Schmidt straightened out by the tone and sat upright in his chair.
"No, Genosse Gebert. Nothing yet."
"I need you to go and observe the house before 17:00, understood?"
"Yes, Genosse Gebert. We will do this!"
"And I need a report right after that. And do not forget Bohne!"
"No, we will not, Genosse Gebert!" The phone was hung up.
Schmidt looked at his colleague. "Always this Gebert guy! He can be annoying, don't you think so?" After a few seconds he continued: "We need a car for this!"
"It's only 14:00 hours, come on, we have time enough!"
"But if we do not get a car, we have to walk!"
"We will not, calm down!" But Schmidt was nervous.
"I am going to check if there is a driver and a car at this time. Maybe we can start a bit earlier, around 16:30. What do you think?"
"Okay, but not too early. We can do this in 30 minutes and get him his report around half past five. How does that sound?"
With a silent "yes" on his lips, Schmidt left the office and went down to the court behind the building. When he entered the office, his colleague looked at him with a questioning expression.
"I got it! The driver is gone for now but should be back at around 16:00. I left him a note that he has to drive us for about 30 minutes."
"Good job, my friend!" It seemed that his colleague was not really taking notice – but I guess he wasn't very keen either to walk.
"I'll get us some coffee, okay?"
"Great idea! And some cake with whipped cream!"
Schmidt smiled back: "Did you bring some from home? Hiding it in your desk, hey? I hope so as I will not find a single crumb in the whole building!"
He left the office with their two cups to get coffee.

86.

Papa's head hit the window slightly. He opened his eyes and went pale: we have arrived already. The train had stopped! This is East Berlin! He stared on the platform outside: Many travelers, everywhere – and some green uniforms! The couple opposite stood already in the aisle to walk to the end of the car.

Why did they not wake me up? Papa was a wreck. He could not believe that he had fallen asleep. Aschersleben, again! I am an idiot, how could I do this? He got up, a bit dizzy. He grabbed his satchel and checked himself from the shoes up. All okay, it seems. He brushed his hair back with his right hand. He checked the platform through the window: two policemen were walking up and down and checked the travelers! I have to get out of here with the crowd!

He looked to the front where the doors were. There were still some people standing in line to get off the train. Because of their baggage it went slowly. Thank God, Papa thought. He checked himself again: his satchel in the left, standing in line, he watched the policemen as much as he could. They were walking up and down. If I catch the right moment, they will walk the other way and I will go down the stairs in the opposite direction. Sounds like a plan.

They came back towards the door. It was Papa's turn but he let a couple go in front of him to buy some time. They gladly accepted and Papa even helped them with their bags. The policemen had now passed the door and Papa stepped down the iron stairs. A short look to where the policemen were – and he turned the other way to reach the stairs as quickly as possible. Running was out of the question. Of course, that might have – surely it would have – got their attention. Another 25 meters and he reached the first step. He did a slalom around the slower moving people and reached the floor in 15 seconds.

It was the floor that led left to the exit and on the right to the other platforms. He turned left and tried to hurry but not be too obvious. I have to leave this place he thought. His brain was hammering and his heart was beating faster and faster. Too many green suits here! Probably more up front! Maybe I will take a side exit; but wouldn't they stand and watch there too?

He reached the spacious front hall with all the shops and counters, newspaper stands and kiosks. No time for this now. He looked around and tried to check the hall: "No fast movement, Ferdi!" he told himself. Just find the way out. One of the side exits lead to a street, the other one to a parking area. He could see this through the glass doors. The main front double doors with big glass windows left and right were leading to the area in front of the station; this was where all the taxis were parked and waiting for guests. All the busses stopped there too and the train platforms were located right next to the busses.

'I do not want to take a taxi!'" he ordered himself "Maybe a bus would be okay towards the best route for crossing the border. Or should I take a taxi? Which is safer? I thought about it a hundred times and now I am still not sure! Nuts. A taxi would be faster, no doubt. But they had radio connections. If they were really after me, they would call all of them. What do I do?"

Papa decided to walk further to the side entrance where the parking place was. He stopped and checked his surroundings again. The opposite side door opened just at this second and three other policemen walked in. Well, they were about 100 meters away, so they would not see him right away. Papa decided to leave immediately and opened the door toward the parking lot. He stepped out, walked just away from the door and stood for a few seconds flat to the wall of the station. Not too many people were here, obviously only the ones parking their cars or loading and unloading baggage.

What now? He tried to concentrate. Maybe I am overreacting, maybe they do not know anything – yet. Better be safe than sorry! He walked around the corner of the building so he could see the front of the station. It was a massive open area, pretty busy. He noticed the two police cars being parked right in front of the station. They were allowed to do this. They could do anything they wanted!

Further to the right were the bus station platforms. He saw the posts with the big "H" for "Haltestelle", the German word for bus stop. There were six pedestrian islands where people would wait for the bus to arrive. Each of the six posts had a little frame attached, the schedule for the bus stopping there. Papa was still standing at the corner of the building observing all this when two policemen came out of the station. The ones he saw at the platform where he arrived. He noticed the guns and the one tall guy who wore his hat quite oddly to the side. Papa slipped back around the corner so they would not see him. If it is getting dangerous, I have to walk he thought. Maybe this is a good idea! Follow the bus line and step on the bus at the next stop. It cannot be that far.

He looked again around the building. One of the police cars started and took off. He waited another three minutes. What about a cigarette? No, not now. Papa started walking to the bus stop. He knew from his planning exactly where the station was on the East Berlin map, and the border, at least roughly the part in the center of Berlin. Around the Brandenburg Gate and the few miles left and right of it.

He reached the first post and looked at the schedule: The first bus went the wrong direction, out of town, so to speak. I need to go into the center, Friedrichstrasse. He stepped over to the next platform and checked the schedule there: This bus would go to the next station called Jarnowitz and then to Alexanderplatz but not further to Friedrichstrasse, another station. Friedrichstrasse was maybe 15 minutes from the Brandenburg Gate and not too far away from "Unter den Linden," the street coming straight from the Gate leading into the East Berlin side while the "Strasse des 17. Juni" lead from the Gate straight into West Berlin.

'I need another bus, one which takes me all the way to Friedrichstrasse! He stepped on to the next platform. The schedule was clearly marked "Friedrichstrasse". Great – that's it. From there Papa would take the tram into West Berlin to the first West Berlin station called "Lehrter City Station". I wish I was there already!, he tought to himself.

This was now the right way to go. He looked around: just one person waiting on this island. If he read the schedule correctly the bus should show up in about six minutes. They were pretty frequent in their schedule: every 20 minutes a bus should arrive here. He checked his watch: 13:40. The bus would take probably 20 minutes he guessed. The Friedrichstrasse Station was also pretty big and at least on the Eastern side the closest to the border. Depending on the situation there, he could go and take the S-Bahn in the station and approach the border or wait and check if another station would be a better starting point. He had several chances to approach the border, only one to pass!

Actually the Potsdamer Platz was the biggest inner city traffic square in Europe before the Second World War, 22 streets lead into it from all directions. Now it was pretty much divided into an Eastern and a Western part by the border. But it is south of the Brandenburg Gate and Papa had decided to take the Friedrichstrasse route, which was north of it.

He could still walk a bit; maybe 10 minutes or so to the next station, Jarnowitz, and then hop on the bus. He looked again at the schedule: there was always a little map with just lines and dots where the buses and trams would drive and stop. He had seen that the direction of this bus was okay. It looked like a few kilometers to the center of the city; the bus would need about 20-30 minutes for it, he figured.

"Okay, I'll take the bus," he told himself. Decision made. The good thing about this would be saving time. I can get off any time and walk later if I have to. It was the most direct route to the West sector in his opinion. If anything unexpected happens, I could still leave the bus before I arrive at Friedrichstrasse. Let's do this, he thought. He was not sure about all the stops the bus would make but in the end, it did not matter too much as long as he arrived safely at Friedrichstrasse Station! And if anything happened, he could still change to the subway from Friedrichstrasse towards Potsdamer Platz. It wasn't too far from the Brandenburg Gate and from the center and the Kurfürstendamm, the biggest avenue with the ruin of the bombed Kaiser Friedrich Memorial Church. Of course, those sites were in West Berlin. This plan B would probably make him pass Kochstrasse, also the location with the famous Checkpoint Charlie, the border crossing for the American people.

More people were waiting now beside him. He slowly but thoroughly checked them out. There did not seem to be a problem. He also let his view turn left and right: noone unusual in his sight: younger and older people, men in their Sunday outfit and women dressed up in spring dresses. One almost fell stepping on the platform in her high heels! The wind was blowing a little and every other minute, the sun peaked through the light clouds. There are songs about the Berlin air saying that it has a good smell. Whatever that means!

Another police car arrived in front of the main entrance. Two policemen stepped out and went into the station. They seemed to be in a hurry. Well, I hope they were not at our home yet! Thinking about Sondershausen and the condo, he was wondering if the Stasi would break in the doors this evening if he wasn't home. So far – he guessed – they might have been careful, but not for long. He knew this too well. They somewhat respected the people and their property but not for long. If they "smelled" that there was something going on, they would do whatever it took to prohibit an escape. Papa watched the police car: obviously those two fellows are still in the station.

The bus arrived. It was a single deck bus mostly colored red with two big windows in the front for the driver and the typical row of windows on each side. It must have been quite old. The paint was cracking everywhere and it was noisy, rattling in a way. When it stopped, one door in the front opened. You had to pay the driver. People usually left the bus through the middle door. Papa thought for a second if he should buy the ticket to Friedrichstrasse or just Alexanderplatz, two stations before: take a short break and take the following bus to go the rest of the way. He did not know all the stations and street signs but Alexanderplatz would be an option.

He decided against it. "I have to move forward!" he told himself. He paid the driver and walked the aisle of the bus to the row just behind the middle door as it was roomier. He squeezed himself into the seat. A few more people entered the bus looking for their seat. Nobody sat with Papa.

The bus driver closed the doors and with the typical roar of the motor the bus left the station. Papa's watch showed 13:48.

87.

Our Sunday afternoon was somewhat uneventful. After the coffee and cake, Roland and I left again to explore our environment. So much to see – besides the cars. Just watching the street trains coming and going, stopping opening and closing doors was interesting. The people were also dressed differently from what we knew, a bit more fashionable; at least from my point of view.

We walked up the street for a hundred meters where we saw a sign for an electrical appliances shop. We peeked through the window and saw TVs! They had TVs to sell! Unbelievable. Where we lived, we could not buy them just like this and they were way too expensive. And they showed some portable radios, ones you could carry around and listen to your favorite station.

Very exciting. Maybe someday we could have those too, I thought. There was more: I had never seen an electrical hand mixer to make whipped cream. Mutti always had to beat it in a bowl by hand until it got somewhat stiff. And there was an electric coffee bean grinder! Wow.

We were not supposed to get too far away from Oma's apartment, so we decided to turn around and head back. It was Sunday afternoon and besides the cars and the few shops on the street, there was not much more to see. There will be much more to explore when we go downtown tomorrow – even though the shops would be closed for the holiday!

When we got closer to Oma's apartment, Mutti was already waiting for us in front of the entrance. It seems that she needed a bit of fresh air. The close environment with seven people in a two room apartment was too much for her.

When is Ferdi coming? Is he coming? Did he make it? He must be in Berlin by now. She checked her little wristwatch she had gotten from her parents for Christmas: Almost 14:00. I need him more than ever! If I could just talk to him that would be great!

Her eyes got wet.

88.

The bus stopped for the first time; some people off, some people on. Nothing unusual. No policemen, no strange men, just normal Berlin citizens. It looked that way. But soon, it would be different when he approached the border area between the western and eastern part of the city.

The bus went through the Berlin streets; Sunday afternoon, so it wasn't too hectic. In East Germany, even in East Berlin, few cars were on the streets; it was still a bit of a luxury to have a Trabbi, let alone owning a Wartburg!

West German cars were hardly to be seen. In some of the streets, the remainders of the Second World War were still to be recognized; many of the buildings looked unchanged, not rebuilt and of course, dirty and broken, ruins. Evidence of the bombing that took place towards the end of Second World War. The government had neither the money nor the material to rebuild the town and country. So they left it as it was.

Next stop was somewhere near Alexanderplatz, one of the highlights of East Berlin at the time. A place with such recognition was, of course, kept in better condition. There were too many international visitors to leave it in a run-down shape. They had established quite a cozy atmosphere here with shops and cafes and street restaurants. A few quick looks and the bus had passed the scenery.

Two or three more stations and I am at Friedrichstrasse Station, he thought. I am almost there! It took the bus another eight minutes and the big station appeared around the corner. The driver called it through his loudspeaker and after a few moments, he stopped at one of the platforms in front of the main entrance. Most of the people got off the bus here. This was about a kilometer or so from the border.

Papa stepped out and checked his surroundings, almost like at the other station he thought. Also two police cars in front! They must be in the station, he thought, as he could not see anyone in the cars. It was 14:20. now. I will carefully check where the train to Lehrter Station leaves from. Walking towards the entrance he suddenly noticed that a little police bus arrived from the right, stopped near the entrance, and about five or six policemen jumped out running towards the entrance. Papa stopped walking. What was this? He checked the pedestrians around him. Not that he recognized anything unusual but he tried to make sense of the situation. He also noticed that some people near the entrance had stopped and observed something inside the station. They were after somebody that is for sure! Should he also wait? Maybe. He walked on slowly.

To his right, a middle aged woman was also approaching the station carrying two suitcases. Besides looking pretty, Papa thought that she could help him in this situation. He crossed her way and stopped her:

"Sorry, but that looks awfully heavy for you! May I help you?" She dropped the suitcases to the ground, a bit surprised. Her long blond hair was covering her face and she was totally out of breath.

"Yes, they are heavy and it would be very nice if you would help me at least with one of them."

Papa responded: "No problem, I am happy to help you! Which is the heavier one?"

"The gray one." She looked at Papa and smiled, "Thank you so much, I don't know why I packed so much. I am going on vacation to the Black Sea. Have you been there?"

"No, never, but maybe someday."

Papa lifted the gray suitcase and she took her other one. Together they walked towards the main entrance. There was still something going on in the station; you could not really see anything unless you walked through the doors. Indeed, the suitcase was heavy – but for Papa it was a nice cover. The two must appear like a couple for any other person watching them. A couple going on vacation! Papa was pleased with his sudden idea of helping her.

They entered the station hall. Papa saw the police at once on the left side of the hall. They had two men circled. Not sure what the reason was but it must have been serious. The police had hand-cuffed them both and were interrogating them. At least they are not after me, Papa thought. The lady beside him walked to one of the ticket counters, Papa followed her closely.

"I already have my ticket all the way to Bucharest but have to check with the conductor." She dropped her suitcase and left Papa like he was really her husband.

Women are amazing sometimes. Papa had to smile a little. Oh well, it is good for me; she helps me here. It took five minutes as there were other passengers in line. She came back and said:

"I am all set. What about you? Where are you going?" Papa hesitated. A surprise question. What do I tell her? He decided not to say anything specific. "I am just checking for my trip next week to Erfurt; I need a ticket and information. But that can wait. Which platform do you leave from?"

"It is number four.".

"May I bring you there?"

"That would be very nice of you! I am very thankful." They carried the suitcases and followed the signs toward platform four. The stairs were another challenge they had to master, but they succeeded and ended up at a bench on platform four.

"Thank you so much for your help! I would probably still be in the entrance hall with my suitcases." She smiled again – and before Papa could say anything, she pulled him towards herself and gave him a kiss on his cheek! Papa was a bit stunned, almost blushing. What a nice woman.

"Not a problem! Have a great vacation!" Papa turned around and left. He did not turn back. He suddenly realized that he needed to concentrate on his mission. He went down the hallway to the main entrance hall. I need to figure out the street train that brings me to the West! Ticket, schedule, stations to watch!

On one of the schedules he saw that he indeed could get to the Lehrter Station from here; not a surprise but good to see it confirmed. Always checking his environment: the policemen were gone and so were the two guys they had taken into custody. I wonder what the reason was, Papa thought. Papa went to the nearest window. Two people in front of him, one at the window buying his ticket. They were whispering to each other.

"Did you see them? I overheard the conversation. They were checking them out. Looked like they were trying to go on the train towards the West. Somebody must have told the police."

"I know, they are checking everybody these days. As soon as you buy a ticket."

Papa went numb. Shit! Everybody? Buying a ticket to the West? Actually, I should not be surprised he thought. But they must have reinforced the security! It was his turn.

"Return ticket to Lehrter Station." He tried to sound as normal as possible.

"That's West-Berlin. Are you coming back today?" The ticket agent could have been a trained Stasi officer, who would know! A firm and short "Yes" from Papa and another short thorough look from the agent.

"One eighty." Papa put 2 Deutschmarks on the turntable. Seconds later he took the ticket and the twenty Pfennings out of it and turned away. His heart was pounding. I have the ticket, hopefully I will not use the return portion of it!

He went back to the schedule table. His watch now showed 14:46. The street train left at 15:10 from platform two. I have time, time to concentrate and prepare. The next hurdle, the biggest of all, needs my full attention! I will wait on the platform even though it is not the best coverage. First, a walk to the restrooms and then to the platform.

Sitting on the toilet seat, Papa checked his papers. One thing was certain: everything had to be perfectly set up. The passport, the party book with its bright red cover, the ticket – the speech! What do I say? They will ask me why I am going to the West. What do I respond? This was not the first time he brainstormed about it. He had to make it political, subservient almost to the German Democratic Republic. "I am a true and honest believer in the system. I am a supporter. I am a party member. I am convinced that this Republic of the working people is the ultimate system and best for everybody!" This is how it has to sound. In one word: convincing, doubtless.

"He is not leaving us, this is a good guy." This is what they need to hear in my answer!

15:03. I have to go. He left, washed his hands and went to platform two. The tram arrived a minute later. He boarded it. The tram had two cars.

He sat down in the first one and starred out the window. This is it. The last crusade?! A few other passengers had boarded. Actually, the tram had to stop another time just before the border. Papa did not realize this but the Vopos had to check them. There was no turning back now! Be your best he told himself. You can do this, you learned it: you know how to pretend. All those years with the police!

The street train left Friedrichstrasse Station with the typical rattling of the steel wheels. Every now and then, the wheels were squeaking around the little curves the tram had to take. It passed slowly through some streets; it was noticeable that the streets got more and more empty the further they went. The buildings were not well kept, especially the closer to the border the tram came. More and more looked like the war just had ended. Amazing that they were occupied; you saw curtains and some flowers in the window. Still, you got the feeling of it being a ghost town.

Approaching the border! Papa looked around: it seems that nobody is really taking notice of the surroundings. Some of the few passengers were checking their papers for crossing the border. We must be near. From what Papa remembered, after about two kilometers or so, they should pass the Charitè, the famous hospital where some great doctors worked like Dr. Ferdinand Sauerbruch or Dr. Robert Koch. Right after the Charitè, they would go over the Humboldt harbor bridge that was basically the border. So, the Vopos should board before that.

Papa got nervous, very nervous. His heart started pounding. He tried to calm himself but it was difficult. 15:26 now. He looked around to check out the other passengers again. Some of them showed some nervousness fingering their pockets or papers or simply moving on their seats back and forth. 'You will not do this, Ferdi!'

He noticed a younger guy two seats down from him. It almost looked like that he was on a mission. Papa knew from many investigations how people react under pressure, especially when they had something to hide. This guy did, it looked like. Papa looked out the window; a few more minutes and the border police would enter the tram for the border check. "I will be okay," he told himself, "I will make it."

He checked his watch: 15:31. The papers were prepared: The red party book with the pictures of Lenin, Stalin, Marx and Engels on top; then underneath the passport, then the ticket. Good. What do I say? The sentence was clear in his head. This will work for them; it has to work. Otherwise? Helga! The children!

"Calm down, Ferdi, calm down!" His heart would not stop pounding.

The tram curved around a bigger building and slowed down. Papa saw the Vopos waiting on the platform. They appeared almost like vultures. Ready to take their prey! Green uniforms, boots, guns on their backs and pistols on their belts. Two of them, not really an unfamiliar sight for Papa.

The tram stopped, one woman stepped out. This could be a long stop! The Vopos entered the second car. We won't leave the stop until they have checked everybody thoroughly, Papa knew this too well from other experiences. There were about twenty-five people on board. Papa tried not to stare but did take a little peek to watch them. This would give him the final hints on how it would be best to present himself.

They checked passenger after passenger. Always asking questions and this deep look in the eyes! You should not hesitate with your answer, you should not look away, you should appear as normal as possible. Well, easy to say, Papa thought. It seemed that they let everybody go, nobody was taken off. Anybody would have been handcuffed right away anyway. It took them about 15 minutes.

They looked around again, checking everybody a last time with a serious look. Then they left the first car and came around. Our turn!

The car door was already open. But they did not come in; they waited on the platform talking to each other! One went back to the little station building and disappeared. The other waited on the platform.

Were they called to a phone? Informed about Papa or other possible escapes? This was torture! What if they come back and straight to me? Papa was exhausted. I cannot stand this! Should I leave now? They would certainly find this strange and would go after me. What a dilemma. Another four minutes passed; it was already 15:53. This is taking too long! Another three minutes later the second Vopo came back. They talked again pointing to the tram. Papa froze. Then they walked towards his car.

You heard the heavy steps from the boots when they entered. There was silence. "Grenzkontrolle, Papiere bitte!" The Vopos searched the passengers by looking them straight in the eyes, one after the other. Papa looked at them as there wasn't a problem with their order. After a moment they looked at each other and walked down to start at the other end. They walked by Papa and headed to the last seat. Papa tried to not observe them. But after they had passed him, he took a look.

They must have been in their thirties. Nevertheless, they were trained and dangerous: they knew what to look for. Border policemen had special training for this job. "You are protecting our fatherland against the western capitalist criminals and our republic built by workers and farmers from people who betray us." This is what they were taught. Papa had to learn this too. The woman in the back handed them her papers.

89.

Mutti could not stand it anymore. She walked through the apartment, not knowing if she should sit or stand up or lay down on the couch. I did not recognize it as much as Roland did; he knew about the plan! The situation with Oma and Opa and us five was getting worse. Too many people in one tiny place. No place to hide. It was not really a happy atmosphere, I could tell. I just did not know how serious this whole trip was and the perspective of what could happen. I was simply planning on some toys to take back, looking forward to Monday and the city!

Mutti finally left the apartment. I saw her going down the street. She had taken her light coat. She needed to be alone with her thoughts, thoughts about the future, Papa and the possible consequences of the outcome of this trip. After about 15 minutes – it was getting a little bit dark and some black clouds were rushing in – Opa followed her with a big umbrella. Oma was mumbling something I did not understand. She was obviously not pleased with the whole situation. She tried to be chief in her own apartment but ran into strong opposition in Mutti!

The only thing I remember was that they came back maybe after an hour. Mutti seemed to be a bit calmer and in a better mood – but this might have been just wishful thinking on my side.

This afternoon did not end; it was like the clock stood still. We were all quiet, played with Karin and Brigitte some time. They had some toys. It was always fun to play with the two little sisters! I usually held Brigitte and Roland played with Karin. She could walk. Brigitte still had a hard time. I was hoping that we would have dinner soon. Always hungry!

And still no news from Papa!

90.

It must have been around 15:30. The two policemen had a slow Sunday afternoon, so far. Pretty soon they had to leave to start the investigation on the Mann case. Schmidt and his colleague had read the Sunday paper and exchanged some news, mainly sports. The local soccer team must have lost their Saturday league game against the neighboring town of Bendeleben. Awful.

"I really do not know what this guy is doing. They call him a coach? He does not deserve it! Did you see what his tactic was? Like he will win any game this way! It's a shame for Sondershausen!"

"Well, in one way you are right: they have seen better days and better results. Maybe they should fire him!"

"Exactly what I have been saying for a long time! They should never have hired him in the first place! He should give back his license if they ask me!"

"They will not ask you." Schmidt was moaning something.

His colleague checked the clock on the wall.

"We have to get ready; the earlier the better. Get it over with. Gebert will be delighted if he has his report a bit earlier."

"Okay." Schmidt closed his paper, put it on the desk and got up. He took his pistol from the desk, put it in the holster and took his hat.

"Let's go before another 15 minutes are gone. Hopefully the car has come back!"

Soon after, they left the office to check on the car and the driver. The car wasn't there, neither was the driver. They searched the little office and found the note Schmidt wrote. Obviously, he was not back yet from his trip.

"What should we do? Wait here?" Schmidt's colleague asked him. Schmidt nodded silently. He checked his watch: 15:43. Hopefully he will be on time, he thought. I do not want to be late!

He was about to sit down when he heard the familiar sound of a two-cycle engine. Seconds later, a Kübel came around the building and entered the courtyard. Schmidt walked out of the office and straight to the car followed by his colleague. The driver opened his door and jumped out.

"We can go right away, Genosse."

"Why?" The driver was surprised.

"I have finished my shift, going home for coffee and cake!" He smiled at Schmidt.

"And if you want to go somewhere, you better get gas first!" The grin was pretty big on his face. It was not seldom that they had no gas and could not drive with the car for a day until it was filled up. Supply was sometimes difficult.

"How much gas do you have?" Schmidt wanted to know.

"It is almost empty. Just for a few kilometers, 10 maybe 15 max."

"That's enough. Give me the key, I'll drive!" The driver looked a bit surprised but handed him the key.

"You have to register in the office and write down where you go. Leave the key here on the desk after you come back."

Schmidt just said "okay" and opened the driver's door.

"Come on, we need to go," he shouted to his colleague.

Seconds later, the Kübel left the courtyard and turned left towards Karl-Marx-Allee. They crossed it and went further over Gartenstrasse, turned right and went up the Possenweg to finally turn into Edmund-König-Strasse. The car stopped and Schmidt and his colleague jumped out. The garden gate was half open: somebody must have been here. They took two steps at a time and stopped in the doorway. It was just before 16:00.

"Let's try Mann first and then the Hendrichs, okay?" Schmidt's colleague nodded. Schmidt pushed the button. The bell rang. They waited ten seconds and rang again. No answer. They looked at each other. Schmidt went to the kitchen window and tried to look inside. He turned to his colleague:

"Seems that nobody is home. I'm really starting to wonder." Another ring. They waited.

"Let's try the Hendrichs." They rang their bell, once, twice and a third time. There was a noise – from up above. Schmidt took a few steps backwards to look up over the roof. A roof window opened and somebody yelled:

"Hello, who is it?" Schmidt saw the face of Aunt Rosa peeking out the roof window. When she saw the green uniforms, she almost fainted. They are here, they are really here! What do we do?

"One moment." She went back into the kitchen were Uncle Walter had jumped off the couch.

"They are here, the police! What do we do? We have to talk to them!"

Uncle Walter thought for a second staring at her.

"Yes, we have to talk to them, give them some explanation about Manns, maybe. I don't know!" He turned and sat down. "I can only hope that he made it by now. We cannot control this, we will get in serious trouble ourselves!"

He got up and they both went down the winding stairs. They walked through our hallway and opened the first door. Immediately, the green color was shimmering through the etched glass of the front door. They stopped, looked at each other and Uncle Walter stepped forward and opened the door.

"It's about time!" Schmidt got impatient.

"We have to see the condo of the Manns. Or is anybody home?"

"No, I don't think so." was Aunt Rosa's short answer.

"Do you know where Mr. Mann is?"

"No, we do not know. But he should be back soon."

The two policemen pressed their way through into the hall without a look at Hendrichs.

"Do you have a key to the rooms?"

"Of course not. No." Aunt Rosa tried to act normal but that was not how she sounded.

"We need to open the rooms!" Schmidt was dead serious. He walked to what he thought might be the kitchen and opened the door. It wasn't locked! He walked in and observed it. His colleague went straight to the window and looked outside. Schmidt opened some of the cupboards. There were dishes and in the lower doors also some pots and pans. He walked to the little pantry beside the oven and looked inside. A few jars, some flour and some cherries in glasses. Not too much but nobody had a filled pantry these days!

He closed the door of the pantry and looked at his colleague: "We have to make sure." That was all he said and left the kitchen. The Hendrichs were still standing there in the hallway like statues.

"Is this the front room door? And which one is this?" The Hendrichs were frozen. This was it. They would open the door and see for themselves. It would not take them more than a minute to realize that Manns were on the run.

"I don't know, they are probably..." Schmidt had no time. He had already pushed the handle. The door to our front room opened up! They stormed in and looked around. The furniture was there. Of course, they cannot take that Schmidt tried to think. He opened the sliding door to our bedroom. The kid's beds were there – with covers.

"Check the other room!" His colleague passed Hendrichs and opened the other door to Mutti's and Papa's bedroom.

"Looks okay!" Schmidt came around and entered the bedroom. He went straight to the cupboards and opened them.

"Very interesting!" Mutti had left some cloths, socks and underwear in the cupboards and the drawers; also a jacket from Papa and another coat and two blouses as well as a pair of pants from Papa. But it looked a bit empty. Schmidt stood in front of the open cupboards. He looked at his colleague:

"I think we have some work to do!"

They hurried out of the condo leaving the Hendrichs standing in the dark hall with pale faces. The Kübel roared away down the Possenweg. Schmidt drove back to the office like a maniac. Cutting corners and pushing the pedal he made his colleague aware of what he was thinking:

"We have to call Gebert right away! Forget Bohnes and forget the report. Something is going on here that is for sure."

"Genosse, I do not have to tell you that this is a high alert. Give an immediate notice to all border police, especially in Berlin. Do you understand? This is an order! I'll put a search out at once! We will hunt him down!" was Gebert's response. It was 16:20.

Gebert was furious. They are escaping the Republic and these idiots do not react. He leaned back in his chair and tried to organize his thoughts. "Incredible," he said to himself. This fellow Mann is trying to escape – with the whole family. I always knew that he was not straight; he never was behind our government. I knew it. How could they give his wife the visa? I have to see who signed it!

He picked up a book with phone numbers. There must be someone to call in Berlin. The only way he could make it is by going from East to West in Berlin. All other places he would need to show a visa. Right? Let's see.

Talking to himself he searched the phone book. There, East Berlin Stasi office. Where? Unter den Linden. Must be nice to have an office there! He called. No ringing. These damn phones, they should repair them once! He dialed again. It rang. Crackling and then a "Stasi Berlin, Genossin Tabert". A woman, oh well. Some were really smart and made it all the way up.

"Gebert, Stasi Sondershausen. I need your help!" He told her about his strong suspicion and asked her to give out an immediate order to check for Papa:

"Mr. Mann might be still around East Berlin trying to cross the border. You have to get him!"

"Understood, we'll do our best, Genosse Gebert." The phone clicked. Nothing more I can do now, just hope that they catch him! I have to call Schmidt.

"Genosse Schmidt, I want a full report from you in an hour! That's an order!"

Schmidt sighed, "He still wants this stupid report! I told him everything over the phone, didn't I?" His colleague shrugged his shoulders but refrained from commenting. Schmidt took two sheets of paper and some carbon paper and rolled it into the typewriter.

It was now 16:28.

91.

"Why do you want to go to the West?" The first Vopo looked the younger guy straight in the eyes. The guy could not really cover his nervousness. But being nervous alone would not really trigger them to take him into custody. Everybody was nervous at the border control. But there was a difference. Being nervous as a result of the authorities approaching you or being nervous because you were trying to leave the Republic, intending something illegal. Papa's training at the police academy would help – hopefully!

A second hesitation. "Not good," Papa told himself, "Not good."

"I just wanted to go over and look around a bit and then come back this evening." Not good. This is bad. Papa knew that this was an invitation for them. Not good.

"Please come with us!" One of the Vopos grabbed his arm and pulled him out of his seat. No time for feeling sorry Papa thought. That was not what you should have said, son! Papa tried to stay calm. The second Vopo took the young guy and put handcuffs over his wrists.

My turn. The Vopo took a thorough look at Papa. Papa gave him the little package with the party member book on top. The Vopo recognized it you could tell. While checking it and Papa's passport, he asked the same question:

"Why do you want to go to West Berlin?" The Vopo had again his eyes penetrating Papa's brain.

"I've always wanted to see the Russian Memorial in West Berlin, right behind the Brandenburg Gate."

"I know where it is!" The answer was cold as ice. Papa almost shrugged. The next thing was that the Vopo gave him his package back and turned away. Two more passengers to check.

It was an eternity! Three minutes later, the Vopos left the tram with the young guy. The doors closed and with a jolt the tram started to roll.

A minute later, the street train crossed the Humboldt harbor. The Charitè on the right. Border signs came into view. Signs everywhere. From what are they protecting us?

"You are leaving the German Democratic Republic."

Yes I am! Papa's head fell down to his chest tears running down his cheeks.

92.

Papa's feelings were overwhelming. I made it! I am in West Berlin. I am free! He looked out the window and saw the difference: the buildings looked nicer, painted, advertisements and neon lights, cars, West German ones, not Trabbies! VWs, Mercedes, BMWs. People rushing, dressed nicely. The street pavements were smooth, asphalt, no big holes! He checked his watch: 16:38. Wow, that control took a while. Who cares, I made it! It certainly had not really sunk in yet, it will take probably months if not years to forget the GDR experience. Wrong, I will never forget it, my whole life!, Papa thought to himself.

The first stop was Lehrter Station. I will get off there and see what I can do. I need to go to a police station and tell them who I am! I need a bed tonight and money and something to eat. And I have to call Helga at once! No, I cannot call her, need to send a telegram. She is probably worried sick.

The tram stopped and Papa took the first step into freedom! What a feeling that must have been for him! He jumped down the stairs and stopped: a deep breath of fresh free air! Is it a dream? No, a dream come true!

He checked for the police station. There was a sign on the wall leading to the station office. On the way, he stopped at every shop in the hallway. So much they have to sell! I need some cigarettes first. They have good ones here, he knew. But money, I need West German money! He had heard that there was an exchange rate of probably one to ten. He checked his wallet: around 115 Eastern Deutschmarks. Well, that will not get me very far here.

Nevertheless, he entered the next kiosk and got himself a package of cigarettes; I believe it was Peter Stuyvesant. "The scent of the big wide world" was their slogan. Actually, wasn't he the first mayor of New York? The guy in the kiosk looked at him, "I'll take the money but I have to charge you the 10 times price!" Papa did not care. A Western cigarette would taste wonderful now! Papa gave him the money and got the package. He lit one and enjoyed his new free world. Soon, he would have to tell somebody where he came from and why and the whole story. I have to go to the next police station; they have to help me!

After smoking his cigarette, he looked for the police station. He entered it and went straight to the counter. Behind the counter were two desks opposite each other. One of the policemen sorted some of the papers on his desk. The other one just entered and threw his hat on the desk.

"So, that's done. Just two guys got a bit nasty. Too much beer I guess."

"Okay. Could you please look after that gentleman there?" He was pointing in Papa's direction. The Policeman looked at Papa and walked over to the counter.

"How can I help you?"

"I just escaped." That was pretty dry and straight but how else should I say it? Papa was a bit uncomfortable.

"You escaped? From the GDR?"

"Yes, that is correct."

The other policeman was now getting up and approaching the counter. They both looked at Papa with some questioning expressions in their faces. It was not unusual these days, absolutely not. But still, a guy walking in and just saying "I just escaped?"

"Do you have any papers, passport? Family? Or are you alone?" Well, you can imagine that the conversation was long. It took them almost an hour to get all their questions answered. Papa was of course willing to tell them everything they needed to know. And after all, he could prove basically everything he told them.

"Can you help me to send a telegram? I need to inform my family. My wife needs to know that I made it. She is with the grandparents and the kids as you know."

"No problem. But first you have to sign some papers. Some of them are yours and some are for your registration procedure. This is preliminary. The authorities will do the real ones on Tuesday; tomorrow is a holiday you know, Pfingsten. We also have to get you into Marienfelde Refugee Camp here in Berlin; it was established for all persons coming in from the GDR and others from the East."

Refugees? Is this what we are? Germans entering Germany are refugees? Reality was hitting him. In fact, it showed that there were indeed two German countries with different laws and different cultures and different living conditions. And borders to cross!

Papa signed the papers. The taller one of the policemen handed some of them back to Papa. "I will bring you to Marienfelde. I just have to make sure that they have a bed for you – and something to eat."

"And the telegram!" Papa insisted.

"We'll do that too, let me just call the refugee home."

After a long phone call, the policeman said, "I got you in, Mr. Mann. We have to drive there. Takes about 30 minutes. There is also a tram so we usually do not drive people there. But it is a quiet evening and you do not have enough money. You can stay there for a few days until all the administration is done. When you have your new papers and passports, immigration, registration and so on, you have to fly from here to Frankfurt, and go to the refugee transition camp in Friedland near Giessen. This is where all people are registered, including the ones from Eastern Europe. Then they send you to wherever you want to go or have relatives. Did you know this?"

"No, but I've heard about Friedland. Whatever it takes is fine with me. Who pays for the flight?"

"The government does, no worries. Also, they will give you some money for you and your family. There will be some help. It just takes time, you know." Papa nodded.

"Can we write the telegram, please?" Papa got impatient.

"Okay, let's write it. What do you want to say?"

93.

At Oma and Opa's apartment, it was a quiet evening, but for different reasons. Everyone was with their own thoughts and the best way to not get on to each other nerves was to stay separate – as much as it was possible. Opa listened to the radio; they had no TV. Actually, they did not have a telephone either. I was looking at some newspapers. Roland was reading a book. Our two little ones were sleeping already.

Mutti sat in a chair and looked at some magazines; at least it looked this way. This was Whit Sunday and tomorrow was a holiday. I totally forgot about it. So, no shopping, no toys, not stores, just peeking through windows! Too bad. Well, we have to wait until Tuesday.

The doorbell rang! Opa and Mutti looked at their watches: 19:39. Who could this be? Suddenly, Mutti jumped up. In a quick move, she ran through the little front door. Opa got up too. We were all curious who this could be. Whit and Sunday evening? Mutti opened the door without hesitation. A man stood at the door. Mutti did not know him – but Opa did! He stood behind Mutti and recognized the guy. It was the neighbor!

"Good evening! Excuse me for disturbing your evening but the carriage cannot stay in the entrance way like this." Mutti was stunned. Is that all you are concerned about? She could not believe it. She ran back into the front room, upset and close to tears. Opa managed to move the twin's carriage a bit more out of the way and apologized. It hopefully will not be for long he thought.

"Don't worry about it, Helga. He is always a bit of a complainer. He likes to point out things to the neighbors." Opa sat back into his chair near the radio. The news should be on at eight o'clock. Let's see how the situation is at the borders. They always reported about it these days as so many things happened and so many people escaped or at least tried to.

Mutti picked up her magazine again but was somewhere else. Where is Ferdi now? Did they catch him? Did he make it? She could not go through this for another night. Actually, if something happened to him, we have to pack and go back. It would be unfortunate but I am not leaving him there alone. They will put him into prison, no doubt. A few years behind bars for trying to escape this wonderful Republic! No future for my kids, no future for us. Branded forever and on their black list. Difficulties getting a job, difficulties getting good food, difficulties raising the children and so on. She was close to a nervous breakdown.

It struck eight. The news came on. Everybody had to be quiet. First thing was the situation on the border. It seemed that several thousand people escaped every day! Several thousand, how can this be? How did they manage? Well, there was always the possibility of getting over the border where it wasn't watched thoroughly. Like in forest areas, during the night or actually in Berlin. The way Papa tried to. I was still not aware at this time that we were planning not to go back to Sondershausen.

The doorbell rang again. This time Mutti stayed where she was and Opa went to the front door.

"Could be him again," he just mumbled. The news came on in the radio and Opa would not be pleased to miss part of it. Actually, there was a short conversation at the front door and then Opa came back:

"Helga, it was the mailman. He brought a telegram, I think it is from Ferdi!"

Mutti jumped up, ripped it from his hands and opened it. "I made it!" She started crying and sank into her chair.

It was rather disturbing news for me, I did not understand it!

94.

They drove Papa in the police car through Berlin. It was an early spring evening and many people were walking and window shopping. They passed the Brandenburg Gate, the memorial church right next to the zoo entrance and on to the Kurfürstendamm, the fifth avenue of Berlin.

What a difference Papa thought. Everything seemed to be so much more in order, well kept or at least rebuilt, not as sad and dark as in the GDR. East Berlin was better than cities like Leipzig or Halle. Still, no comparison to this! Then they zigzagged through a few smaller and bigger streets: Charlottenburg, Schöneberg, passing Tempelhof Airport.

Tempelhof, what a historical airport! After the Second World War was over, the Soviets tried to occupy West Berlin and "swallow" it in addition to their East Berlin zone and the middle part of Germany they got when Germany was divided in three parts: the Eastern part went to Poland, the middle part to the Soviets and just the Western part stayed as West Germany. Later, the Soviets cut West Berlin off from any supplies coming from the West, seizing Berlin.

West Berlin was an island and of very important strategic value. The three Allies – France, England and the United States – had only one way to save West Berlin: flying food and medical supplies into Berlin. After almost 12 months, from June 1948 to May 1949, and 200,000 flights later, the Soviets gave up. That's what is known as the "Luftbrücke," or the Berlin Airlift, from then West Germany into Berlin. The Potsdam Agreement about the post-war situation in Germany entitled the allies to fly to West Berlin, but not the West Germans. The inhabitants of West Berlin gave the airplanes a nick name: "Raisin Bombers."

Papa remembered those days. It was really a hard time. Everyone was suffering. Nothing to eat, a cold winter and hardly any paid work. And the winters were severe! He sighed. The fight for a better life seemed to have never really ended – and now we open a new chapter!

The police car finally entered the suburb of Marienfelde. It was a long street, Marienfelder Allee. On the right side, a few larger buildings appeared. They stood in a U-shape. In fact, these were old factory plants rebuilt to give shelter to the thousands of people coming in from the GDR and Eastern Europe daily! In the middle were some wide stony steps leading to the entrance. People were standing around, suitcases everywhere. Whatever those people owned must be in there, Papa thought. Not much of a difference to us. Thanks to Mutti and her plan, a few things were sent in advance so our start into a new life was easier, hopefully.

The police car stopped in front of the stairs. "Here we are, Mr. Mann. I will go with you just to show you were the registration is. I talked to them, they should be expecting you."

"Thank you so much for your help and for sending the telegram!" Papa responded.

"No problem, glad to help!" They stepped out of the Volkswagen Beetle police car and walked together up the stairs. The building was long and obviously had a lot of apartments. Some men and women were standing outside smoking. A few children were kicking a ball. The policeman went in front, opened the door and turned to the left, down a long corridor. He knew the way, obviously. The doors left and right had names and occupation signs.

After knocking on a door with "Administration," someone called,

"Come in." They entered the room and closed the door. Papa was getting nervous; everything from now on was new. What would they say and do? What was the procedure? Would I sleep here or in another place? How do I get something to eat? Where can I wash myself and do they have a bed for me? With others? When can I leave for Friedland?

So many questions unanswered! Papa noticed two officers: a younger woman in her twenties on one side of the big wooden desk and an older man probably around age fifty opposite from her. She looked up when they entered and got up.

"Good evening. Are you the one who called me about an hour ago?" she addressed the policeman while checking Papa with a short glance.

"Yes, I called for this gentleman, Mr. Mann. He escaped using the tram and we registered him at our police office at Lehrter Station."

She nodded. "Family?"

"Yes, but already in Mönchengladbach since Friday, had a visa, luckily. Staying with grandparents. We sent a telegram, they should know by now." He checked his watch.

"Well, maybe soon. We sent it about a good hour ago, so maybe they don't know yet."

She looked at Papa: "Mr. Mann, could I please have the documents, passport and other papers about the family?"

Papa opened his satchel and got everything out. He handed it to her and she started to check them.

"Looks okay so far, officer. If you want, you can go. We will handle the rest here."

"Thanks." Turning to Papa he said: "Well, I wish you and your family all the best for the future." Papa grabbed his hand with both of his and thanked him for everything: the help, the telegram, driving him here and organizing his first steps in the free world. The policeman left and Papa turned to the young lady.

"Do I stay here now? How long until I can go to Friedland?"

"Let's just do the immigration first. Sorry, but we need to do the paperwork first. You will stay here, how long I do not know. Maybe two or three days. We have to organize your trip and need everything signed off by the authorities. Just sit down on the chair beside you and wait. It might take a half an hour. The rest we can do Tuesday. You know tomorrow is a holiday? Don't know if GDR had this too."

"We did." Papa felt sad. Maybe three more days. And then a trip to

Friedland and maybe another three days. It will take a week until I see Helga and the kids!

He sat down on the chair.

The young lady went to her colleague and whispered something. He nodded and she came back to Papa.

"Mr. Mann, you filled in the former employment boxes. You seemed to have worked for the GDR police for quite some time."

"Yes I did. After the war, that was a good chance for me to get a job. Is there a problem?" Papa wasn't sure if he should get nervous. Too many bad experiences with authorities. And now he was depending again on them! But I am in West Germany, why do they almost act like the ones I know so well? This cannot be the case he told himself!

"No problem, Mr. Mann. We are just asked to get all the information straight." Papa did not respond. I hope they do not hold this against me! What are they thinking? That I am a spy?

Papa was exhausted. It finally hit him. What a day! Starting out in Sondershausen, going to Sangerhausen, running in and out of stations, watching the police, then Magdeburg, the train ride to Berlin, almost overslept the station, the Vopos at the border and finally the relief of making it! He realized that he was tired – and hungry too. And a bed would be good!

He heard a voice: "Mr. Mann?" the lady officer stood at the counter. Papa must have been daydreaming.

"Yes?"

"Are you alright?"

"Yes, I am okay." Papa rose from his chair.

"I have everything arranged for you. You will stay here until we do the proper registration. This will definitely take at least until Tuesday, maybe Wednesday. You'll have a bed in a room with another gentleman on the first floor. I will show you later. You will get 50 Deutschmarks from us for your personal spending. In addition, you can have breakfast here and lunch and dinner, if you want."

She looked at Papa just to see if he understood her. There was a little smile on her face. She had friendly blue eyes but nevertheless showed a lot of routine and seriousness in her explanations and her work considering her rather young age. Papa had noticed this at once.

"I should tell you that you have to follow some rules. We want you to be here from 22:00 hours to 6:00 hours in the morning. When you leave, you have to tell us at least when you are planning to come back. Sometimes we have further question or other papers to fill, you know. Or we simply are ready to send you to Friedland. Is this okay with you? Understood?"

Papa responded automatically, "Yes, no problem. One question: Is there a phone I could use? Not today, but maybe tomorrow or Tuesday?"

"There is a public one in the other building, where the canteen is. You will find it. You need a few small coins."

"Thank you."

"Let me show you the room with your bed."

She went back to her desk. Behind her was a big board with lots of keys. She picked one and came around the counter.

"Please follow me." She opened the office door and Papa went right behind her pulling it shut. She went down the hall back to the entrance area. Papa noticed how attractive she was in her blouse and tight skirt. And so did the two younger guys who were just entering the building whistling behind her. She did not take any notice of it, was probably used to it.

"The room is on the second floor, Mr. Mann. Number 208." Papa followed her up the stairs. They entered the hallway to the left. All the doors were numbered ... 204, 206, 208. That's my new home Papa thought. She knocked on the door and waited. No response. She knocked a second time.

"I am coming in!" She opened the door slowly. Nobody in the room; the other fellow was gone.

"Mr. Prock must be gone," she said, "Come in."

The room was some twelve square meters and was of a rectangular shape with white painted walls. In the middle of the front wall was a window with curtains. The room was furnished with two beds, one on the left wall, and one on the right wall. On each side, adjacent to the beds stood a two-door cupboard. There was also a sink beside the door on the right. The floor was simply covered with linoleum. That was it. At least I have a bed and a roof over my head was Papa's first thought. And hopefully this other guy is okay and does not snore all night!

"Mr. Prock, he came yesterday." Papa nodded.

"He is a nice guy." she felt she had to add this. "Towels are in your cupboard. The restrooms are at the end of the hall on every floor; they have two showers each. If you want to wash clothes, there is a washroom on the ground floor. We provide the soap."

Checking her watch she said: "It is now 19:55. Dinner started at 18:30 in the canteen. Dinner is usually cold food with some bread and sausages, maybe a soup."

"Thank you for all your help. I really appreciate it." It was more of a courtesy remark. Papa still had not really mentally arrived.

"You are welcome! If you need anything, we have office hours every day, also tomorrow on the holiday. I will be here all week." She smiled and turned around to leave.

"Thanks again. Excuse me, what is your name?"

"I am Miss Blank. Sorry, I thought I mentioned it." She left and closed the door behind her.

Papa looked around; the right bed was his. Covered with clean bedding, a nice pillow and a blanket rolled up at the end of the bed. He sat down on the bed and bounced to check the hardness. The springs started squeaking a bit. It was one of those metal frame beds with metal springs and a hard thin mattress. Almost like military service, Papa remembered.

He got up and opened both doors of the cupboard; on the left were three shelves, on the right a bar with four hangers. He hung up his jacket and opened his satchel. There was a zipper hardly visible inside. The little pocket inside revealed a shaver, a toothbrush and toothpaste, and a little piece of soap. I have the most important things but I need shaving cream. He put the stuff on one of the shelves and his satchel into the cupboard.

He looked into the mirror above the sink. "You look like hell, but who cares!"

95.

The canteen was in the other building on the right. He found it after asking one of the fellows standing in the hallway. His roommate had not come back yet. Papa was a bit nervous about leaving his belongings in the room but there were only two keys to the room, so if something went missing, it would point to Mr. Prock. Yeah, Prock was his name. Papa wondered what his background was and how he might have managed to escape. Actually, that could be an interesting conversation. Papa took just his passport and money, the little he had remaining. Oh, no they gave me another 50 West German marks. I am rich!

He entered the canteen. Well, nothing unusual here. A rectangular room, probably 40 square meters and a lot of tables placed in a row with chairs and the typical counter where you would get your food after lining up from one side. Gray walls, an old wooden floor and a few windows. No decoration, just a kitchen opening and food schedule in a frame right next to the door. Not very comforting. A few people were sitting on tables eating. Not only Germans, also some Czechoslovakians, Romanians and maybe Yugoslavians, Papa figured. You could not always tell where they came from but then there was the language that gave you a hint.

The line was long, probably some 20 people waiting. Papa checked how the others got their food. Each had a tray with silverware and a napkin and a glass. Obviously, you get also something to drink. Good, I am thirsty!

Papa went to the other end and got his tray and silverware, glass and napkin. People were rather quiet. Just a few little remarks, mainly about the food. Some must have been here for longer! There was also a sign telling you what to expect. Cold meats and bread, butter and cheese. No beer, but water and juice. Papa was now hungry. Anything sounded yummy.

Everyone got a plate full. Papa also noticed the little chocolate on it. He had not had a good piece for weeks. He took his tray and turned around to see where it was convenient to sit down. Or let's say, where he chose to sit down regarding the other people. There was still a free table and he headed for it. He put down the tray and the key and sat down.

Papa leaned back on his chair and thought again of the events of the day. What a day! This morning still in Sondershausen, now in West Berlin. The train rides, the several encounters with police forces, the ride in the private car, East Berlin Station and the last border control. The view of the Vopo he'll probably never forget! I wonder if they came again to the condo and checked on him. Well, there was no question, I am sure they did. Knowing the Stasi, they must have sent the police or maybe even went themselves. But when? I hope that Hendrichs do not have any problems! They have to write us about what happened. The most important thing is that I made it through! I should be happy, shouldn't I? There are still so many things and issues to solve that were basically unknown to him. How would this all work out? It would be nice to talk to Helga! Now would be a good time!

Well, first things first! Let's eat something. His stomach was ready for some good food! While eating he watched the other people. Families, single men, even single women, couples. All caught up in their own destiny: striving for a better life? Probably. "The West" was the magic word. Everything was so much better there, supposedly. But nothing is perfect. There is no perfect place on Earth. I am sure they also have their issues to solve.

Papa was in his own world when somebody shadowed his table. "Is this chair free? Do you mind me sitting with you?" Papa looked up: a tall guy, blond and gray-blue eyes, middle aged, wearing a checkered black and white sweater. Funny, how I always check people out in a second, Papa thought. The police work and training always shows.

"Yes, you may." Papa moved his hand in an inviting gesture. The guy put down his tray and sat down opposite Papa.

"Enjoy your meal!" Papa heard himself saying.

"Thanks. Is it okay?"

"Yes, I was hungry, anything is good, had a long exciting day!"

"I saw the key; guess we have a room together!"

"Are you Mr. Prock?"

"Yes, that's me. How do you know my name?"

"The young lady, Miss Blank from administration, told me when she showed me the room."

"Oh, Miss Blank. Isn't she nice?"

"Yeah, I think so. She was very helpful. By the way, my name is Mann"

Mr. Prock started to put some butter on a slice of bread.

"Did you cross the border today?" Not a real surprising question Papa thought. All these people here were somehow escaping from their countries or at least decided not to stay there for whatever reason. Most of the reasons were based on the political situation at home. And most of the countries in the East could not provide a good living for them as in the West.

"Yes, I did. You too? From where?"

"Erfurt. I left four days ago. Left everything behind. My parents did not want to leave and start all over. But I could not stand it anymore. You know what I mean." He paused and ate. There was sadness in his voice.

"Oh yes, we all know," Papa responded quietly.

"Everything okay with the administration? Your papers?" Papa was curious.

"Yes, but it takes a few days. I have a relative in West Germany, near Wiesbaden. An Uncle. He and his wife made it over right after the war in 1945. I am trying to get them to send me there. I would have a roof over my head for a while until I find work and can afford a place on my own."
Papa thought about what he heard.

"Why does it take so long to fly you out? Your uncle knew that you were coming?"

"Yes he figured it out. I could not send anything as you know, they check all your mail, especially if you have relatives in the West. So, I gave him some indication. The authorities here check all this before they let you go. And then they have a little interview with you."

That last remark got Papa's attention.

"A little interview? What do you mean by this?"

"Well, nothing serious. They just want to know what you did, your occupations and so on. After all, they do not need more spies from the East Block, more than they have already, I understand."

"What kind of questions do they ask?"

"They asked me if I was a Stasi employee or did some work for them. You know. These guys here have sometimes the wrong picture and too little information of what is going on in the GDR. I do not blame them for asking."

While they both finished their dinner, Papa was thinking about the possible interview. I have quite a past with the system: Police, party membership, involvement in political committees and so on. Stasi contacts? Of course. Through the police work, I knew a few of the important officers. They cannot hold this against me!

They got up, had a cigarette together and finally went to their room. It did not take Papa too long to fall asleep despite some worries about the interview coming up.

96.

Whit Monday morning. Except for Mutti, I guess we all had a good night's sleep. Mutti was tossing and turning on the couch and I wasn't too tired. It was an interesting evening for me.

Mutti had finally told me what this trip is all about and that we are not going back.

"We are not going back? But why? I still have my bicycle there and some toys I did not bring!"

"You will understand all these things later. Believe me, it is much better for all of us" Mutti calmed me down. "Someday, you will have new toys and hopefully, we will all have a great future."

That wasn't enough of an explanation for me, my immediate reaction was still marked with disappointment, "And what are we doing now? Where are we living, we have no home? And I have to go to school again!" It was very difficult for me to understand what was going on. In fact, I did not understand it at all. Too complicated for a little boy of the age of close to ten. Roland seemed to be okay with it. Well, he understood it better and he was – at least mentally it seemed – prepared.

I had asked Mutti a few more questions on Sunday evening but it did not help. I do not think that I tried to convince her to go back – why would I. I did not understand a lot of things when it came to politics and the background regarding the differences of the West and the East at this time. Nevertheless, I caught up later and I have realized that this was the best decision my parents ever made!

It was around 9:00 and we all sat at the breakfast table, actually Oma and Opa on the one in the kitchen and we sat in the front room. We had rolls with butter, some marmalade and soft eggs. We like those. They are cooked for about three to four minutes in hot water. The art of making a good soft egg is really to know how long they should cook. Sometimes it is down to 10 seconds! Smaller eggs need less time and of course the bigger ones need a bit more. A good one would still have a bit of a soft yellow middle. You will see this at once when you cut the top off or peel the shell off. We have these little egg holders to put them in, quite common in Europe.

"What are we going to do today?" I needed to know; at least I should benefit from this awkward situation and see some exciting stuff. Shouldn't I? All my toys were gone – and I would need new ones! Opa looked at me, as he did not like talking or conversations when having a meal. You were supposed to be quiet!

I was glad when Oma answered:

"We are going downtown! We will show you guys a lot of new things, some you have never seen before – I think. The shops are closed you know but we can still enjoy the town and maybe have an ice cream." This did not sound too bad, I had to admit.

"When do we leave?"

"Right after lunch." Oma cleared my concern.

I was the first one ready to go! We had to split into two groups: like Friday evening, Mutti would go with Opa to have some help with the twin's carriage and Oma and Roland and me, we would go again with the tram. We would leave a little later so Opa and Mutti would have a bit of a head start. It would take them a good half hour, if not longer to make it to downtown Mönchengladbach, a one and a half mile walk. We planned to meet in front of the main station, where we had arrived Friday evening.

Trams were somewhat inconvenient I thought; you had to go up three steep steps to enter it. It was shaking you left and right when going through curves and back and forth when accelerating or breaking. Well, the trams in the sixties were definitely different from now!

We were waiting at the tram stop right in front of the house. We were told to follow Oma's instructions. You could pay at the driver if necessary. So when the tram arrived and stopped, we entered and Oma paid. He had such a little machine beside his seat loaded with coins in metal tubes and a lockable side pocket attached for bills. The funny thing was that he loaded the machine with the coins he received and pushed buttons to give coins back. Fascinating! I always watched this, never really figured out how he pushed the buttons and always got the right amount of coins out!

The "Strassenbahn" – what we called those trams – started. I almost fell from the jolt and had to hold tight on one of the bars.

"Sit down quickly, boys! I do not want you to get hurt!"

It took us twenty minutes or so to get to the station. About 300 meters from it, we saw Mutti and Opa pushing the carriage together. This was actually hard work. I remember occasions in Sondershausen when we went for walks with Mutti. Roland and I had to help her when there was a little hill or up the Possenweg on the way home from the town.

"You must be very happy that Ferdi made it! We all are!" Opa started a conversation as he noticed that Mutti was absent.

"It would have been terrible if not! Can you imagine what kind of life we would have been facing?" Mutti almost overreacted. Of course, I am happy, of course. This is what we were counting on for ourselves and the children. This was all we were thinking about for almost two years. Being free and being able to do the best for our children. A good education, a nice home, a good job and best of all: no fear. Saying what you think, having the right to do so, reading and hearing what you like. They had heard about our life in GDR, but after all, they have no clue, Mutti thought.

"How do you think that we can get a place to live?" she asked her father. "Any idea?" Opa knew.

"I have talked to Mr. Gillessen in the town registration office. I know him from our club, the one with all the Sudetenland Germans. Remember?"

Mutti answered right away with a short "Yes," hoping that there would be some good news.

"He already made contact with the refugee camp in Friedland, gave them all necessary information and told them that Ferdi should come here to be transferred with you and the children to Wickrath, a little town just 20 kilometers from here. This would be your temporary place until they have found an apartment for all of you."

"That would be great, Daddy! Thanks for all your help!" She grabbed his arm and sighed:

"I hope that we can find work for Papa soon to start our new life!"

When we arrived opposite the station, Oma could not hold us back. A leash would not have restrained us from going five times up and down the escalators leading from the platform to the subway tunnel. When Oma made it into the tunnel, Roland and I were already on the other end experiencing the next escalator leading up to the area in front of the station entrance. We enjoyed this; it was fun. We had never seen them before last Friday evening; so this was our second chance!

I guess I mentioned Roland's and my favorite thing to look at: the cars. All taxis were Mercedes. I heard the name once but did not know how they looked – other than the one we had spotted already on Saturday. They were big cars with four doors. Right next to the station, quite a few were waiting for possible passengers. They were all a yellow-beige color and the taxi sign on the roof.

And then there were the buses: some were dark green and some were the same color as the taxis. The green ones were electric, and had two pantographs on the roof which slid over wires hung between metal masts over the street. Wow. At this time they had those already. I was wondering about this as if the driver would go the wrong way – what would happen? Rip off the wires?

A minute later, Opa and Mutti arrived. We proceeded to the main shopping street, which was called Hindenburgstrasse – named after one of the first chancellors in Germany before the Second World War. When crossing the street, we watched the traffic lights for the pedestrians: A red symbol with a waiting person and a green symbol with a walking person. We saw all the blinking neon lights, one told you to use a detergent in all your washing and showed red, yellow and green colors. And then there was Woolworth's store. Unbelievable what toys they had. It was a pity that it was closed!

The street actually led further, passing clothes stores and department stores, the post office, coffee shops, banks and shoe shops. Well, Mutti checked those out and the nice dresses in one of the boutiques. They had also a little shopping gallery. It seemed to me that you could buy everything in this town. The shops were filled with good products, not as empty as they were in Sondershausen. After all, some benefits I thought!

We finally made it to the ice cream parlor! We sat down, all on one big table. We needed room for the carriage. People were checking it out – and of course the two little girls. Most of the time, Karin and Brigitte were asleep. Mutti always had some warm milk bottles packed in the carriage in case they got hungry.

One thing I remember especially: the ice cream was delicious! We really enjoyed it and it was the first time, in a long time, that I saw a real smile on Mutti's face!

97.

Papa woke up. The light curtains did not block the sunlight very well. He stared at the ceiling. I must have slept pretty well, he thought. He turned and saw that Mr. Prock was still sleeping. How late was it? He checked his watch: 7:48. I guess I slept well! And I needed that!

His brain started working quickly. Yesterday passed in a sequence of pictures and experiences again. One of the most important days of my life, Papa thought. And with the best ending he could wish for: having escaped GDR and to be in West Berlin! There will be a future for us and the children, a better one!

He got up quietly, pulled on his pants and just slipped into his shirt. It was wrinkled but nothing he could do about this now. Papa took a towel from his cupboard and wrapped it around his toothbrush and toothpaste. 'I need to shave later' he thought. Need to get shaving cream and maybe a hairbrush. "Not that there is a lot to brush!" Papa smiled. He had lost a lot of his hair right after the war. Always wearing those tight pilot headsets; that's probably what caused it. By the time he was 26 years of age there wasn't too much left on top.

He opened the room door and closed it quietly. It felt good to be freshened up! I need a second shirt. I cannot wear this another day. There should be a store around here. One thing I have to do tomorrow: shopping for a few personal things. I should have enough money. Have to ask Miss Blank today. He went back to the room and noticed that Mr. Prock was awake.

"Good morning Mr. Prock! Did you sleep well?"

"Good morning, yeah, guess I did. How late is it, Mr. Mann?" He sounded almost concerned.

"Almost 8:30. Time for a good breakfast," Papa responded, noticing that his body needed some food and a strong cup of coffee.

"If you want, I can wait until you are ready and we can go together."

"Okay. It will take me just ten minutes."

Papa looked out the window. The area was an industrial zone with a few factories and companies. Not too much to see other than the big street on which the building stood and a few other apartment buildings down the road. There was quite a lot of traffic for a holiday on this early morning. People were walking, all dressed up for the holiday. Papa sat down on his bed waiting for him to come back. He was hoping that this day would pass quickly so he could fly out. I should send a letter to Helga or at least a card from Berlin!

98.

Tuesday morning. Finally! Let's get going and move forward. Papa was nervous. I need to go, get the whole family announced in Friedland and go to Mönchengladbach. He could not wait. Maybe I will go to the office and ask Miss Blank right after breakfast about the next steps and a place to shop for my stuff.

Today, Papa hurried with his breakfast. His brain was going through his plan for the day: first Miss Blank, then shopping, then finalizing the papers and maybe tomorrow leaving for Friedland. It was just after 9:00 when he knocked on the door of the administration office.

"Come in!" He opened the door and entered. Besides Miss Blank, the other officer was sitting behind his desk; the same one that was there on Sunday evening.

"Good morning, Miss Blank!"

"Good morning Mr. Mann! What can I do for you?"

"First of all, I need to know where to buy a few personal things and a new shirt. Then I would like to ask about finishing my registration and getting to Friedland."

"Okay. There are several shops just down the road on the left side, about 500 meters from here. Drugstore, a little clothing shop and a grocery shop. I guess this is what you want?"

"Yes. Thanks. That will be fine. And what about my papers and the flight to Frankfurt and going to Friedland?"

"This will take probably 3 or 4 more days, I am not sure Mr. Mann. We have to schedule a few meetings first with the authorities."

Papa was surprised and got impatient:" 3 to 4 days? For what? I thought I gave you all the information and that everything is okay?"

"There is nothing wrong, Mr. Mann. Just some formalities we have to follow. Sorry."

The other officer got up and walked to the counter.

"Miss Blank, I will take it from here." She turned and went back to her desk. Papa was now afraid of what was coming next.

"Mr. Mann, I am Mr. Koch. I am the responsible officer here. There is really nothing wrong with your information, your papers and so on. But with persons coming from the GDR as well as for people coming from other countries we have a certain procedure."

Countries? Papa thought that Westerners always thought of one Germany and not two German countries! Mr. Koch continued, "You were in high political positions; you were a party member, police work for many years. Our authorities would like to talk to you about these occupations, your experiences and activities."

Papa could not believe this! He felt like he was back in the GDR. Hearings with authorities? Cross examinations? That was common where I came from, but here? Am I in the West or not?

Mr. Koch saw Papa's face and read his mind:

"There is nothing to worry about, Mr. Mann. As Miss Blank said: just formalities. As soon as we have this done, you are free to fly out and go to your family." Papa still did not understand. After a few seconds, he came up with a clear question:

"When will this happen? I want to leave here as soon as possible! Can you tell me when we will have the hearings?"

"Not yet, but we should know by noon. Maybe you could stick around so we can reach you after lunch. Or come when you have finished lunch."

"I will be here!" Papa did not say anything else but left the office. It was like a setback for him. They do not trust me!?

He went down the street shopping but his mind was on the upcoming hearings. "They will not send me back just because I worked for the police! And everybody had to be in the party, if they wanted it or not. At least it was mandatory for people like me being a police officer." Papa said to himself. "I cannot wait until this is over!" He was trying to look forward to his flight to Frankfurt.

The shops carried exactly what he was looking for; shaving cream – he looked almost like a criminal after 2 days – some deodorant, little scissors, a new toothbrush and a hairbrush. He also needed a post office; a card from Berlin to Helga and the kids would be great. Telling them what was going on here and when I could be in Mönchengladbach. He asked the lady in the shop. In fact, the post office was another 100 meters down the road on the other side of the street. He got a postcard and wrote on it inside the post office, got a stamp and sent it. This really felt good! At least, they would know by tomorrow or latest on Thursday what the situation was.

Next was a shirt and some socks. Papa wasn't really a big shopper. Mutti did everything for him – always. So, the first light blue shirt with long sleeves is mine, he thought walking into the shop. The problem was that they had several! What should I buy? Or better: which one would Helga buy for me? He made a good guess and bought one with some fine red stripes. The socks will be easier, just black and done with it, he thought. The shop also carried different black ones! He grabbed the first, paid for the shirt and socks and left.

It could actually have been a wonderful day if there wasn't this interview. "I am not a criminal! They will not send me back, I am sure. All I did was follow rules. I did not kill anybody or do anything which could concern them." Papa tried to ease his mind. Still, there was a little nervous feeling around all this. Was there anything that concerned them?

He saw a little coffee shop and decided to sit down for coffee and a cigarette. It was just before 11 and he had still some time before lunch at 12. A cute waitress came and he ordered his coffee.

While smoking and drinking coffee, he realized that all of this would come to a good end. "It has to!" Just sitting here and watching his new environment was a good change! The pedestrians were dressed in better quality clothes, the cars were much better – and so was the air. The pollution from the two-cycle engines was horrible in the GDR. You coughed all the time and it smelled oily. Here, they are all four-cycle engines, they do not produce the same kind of pollution; maybe something else but at least it did not make you cough! Also, he noticed that the factory plants and chimneys were not puffing out dark yellow or black fumes that made the air hard to breathe. People seemed to be in a better mood, too. Did they have less to worry about? Maybe.

Papa really enjoyed this break! For the first time he had some time to sit down and really enjoy a cigarette. The waitress came and he paid for the coffee. It was now 11:35. He went back to the building and went to his room. Mr. Prock wasn't there. Good timing! He shaved, freshened up, put on his new shirt and put the other stuff in the cupboard. "I might wash the other shirt and my old socks. Who knows when I'll have time and a place to do this." He went to the ground floor to check out the washing room. An older woman was washing her clothes. She was right in the middle of loading it. Good thing, Papa thought. She knows how to operate these machines.

"Excuse me, can you tell me how to get the other machine going? I am not that familiar with washing machines!" The understatement of the year! He would not even find the button to switch it on. "I do not know anything about this." And never in his later lifetime would he have known how to operate a washing machine! That was women's field of expertise.

"What do you want to be washed? Just the shirt and the socks?"
"Yes, that's all I have for now."
"Give it to me, I'll put it in with mine."
Papa had no time to react, she grabbed Papa's little bundle and threw it into the machine.
"And how do I get it back?" It sounded more like a protest than a concern.

"It'll take an hour. You can come here and I will give them to you." There was a "Thank you" coming from Papa's lips. Oh well, nothing I can do now. Hopefully, I will get my stuff back.

"And do you know where I can hang my shirt up for drying?" "There is a clothes line in the other room. You can hang it up with clothes-pins or take one of your hangers from the closet."

"Thanks again, I will be here after lunch." That was actually a good idea, hanging the shirt from a hanger. "I would never have thought of that." Women seem to have some kind of a practical sense!

Papa had a quick lunch. He wanted to be ready for whatever was coming up with this interview. And before that he had to get his shirt and socks back!

They had schnitzel today with potatoes and some beans. He did not see Mr. Prock in the canteen. Prock mentioned that he might leave today or tomorrow. Is he gone already? I have to ask in the office. Miss Blank would tell me.

It was a good schnitzel! Some good food they had here. Also, the desert was good: peaches.

Mr. Prock walked in and waved at Papa. He got his tray and meal and sat down with Papa.

"Everything okay? How is it going for you?" While he was starting with his meal, Papa told him about his little shopping tour in the morning and the upcoming interview or whatever it was supposed to be.

"That's okay. Unless you have something to hide you will be fine. Every bit of information helps them to understand what is going on in the GDR. You have to understand their position. They cannot ask for better informants then we are." In a way, he is right, Papa thought to himself. And it is free of charge! Still, I will feel better when it is behind me. He finished his desert.

"Do you know when you get out of here?" Papa asked.

"Oh yeah, I will leave later this afternoon. It is about time! They will fly me out in the evening and my uncle will pick me up from the airport. It is not too far to Wiesbaden and he has a little beetle Volkswagen. I am happy."

"This is great, I am glad for you. Maybe we should exchange addresses and keep in contact? I am not sure where I'll end up but it should be somewhere in Mönchengladbach I guess. My wife's parents live there."

"Sorry, where is that?"

"Not too far from Köln and Düsseldorf."

"Let's do this!" Prock responded.

"I will leave a note in the room with my uncle's address. For a while, I should be reachable there."

"I certainly wish you all the best for your new life, Mr. Prock! I hope I can start it soon myself!"

"You will! Time is on your side. Soon you will take the plane to Frankfurt. All the best to you too and I hope I hear from you, Mr. Mann!"

They stood up, shook hands. A short wave goodbye at the door and Papa took a turn to go up to the room while Prock proceeded to the office. Papa took a hanger from his cupboard and went down the steps to the washing room to take care of his laundry.

Again, Papa could not stop this nervous feeling coming up again. He checked his watch: almost 13:00. Good timing. Hopefully he will know what the next steps are in a few minutes.

Papa knocked on the door and entered the office. Miss Blank was not there. Maybe she was on her lunch break. The officer sat up behind his desk when Papa entered. He saw Papa and got up.

"Mr. Mann, good day! How are you?" He tried to be friendly. Why is he so friendly? He is hiding something, right? Papa knew the psychology too well when it came to situations like this. They are trying to calm you down – because they have something to hide!

"I am okay. Is there anything new about the interview? When is it scheduled?" Papa went straight to business. No time to waste. Get it over with!

"Well, we got a call from the BND. They would like to talk to you. Again, nothing to worry about, just a few questions."

Papa was stunned, the BND? He knew the abbreviation: Bundes-Nachrichten-Dienst, equivalent to the American CIA. Prock hadn't mentioned this!

"The BND? What do they want from me? I have done nothing which should concern them!" The officer looked at Papa and just repeated what he told him:

"Just routine, Mr. Mann. I cannot say more."

"When?" Papa was short now; it bothered him. The BND wants to talk to me. What is this all about?

"This afternoon. They will come and pick you up at 14:30." They'll pick me up! Like I am going to prison or in custody, Papa thought.

"I will wait in the entrance way at 14:30" Papa responded, turned around and left the office. His head was spinning. The BND. Why don't they send the FBI or the CIA or MI5!? He knew all these organizations by their abbreviations from certain schooling with the police. Not too much information they would give you but enough to understand how those guys operate and what their intentions are. And the Soviet equivalent was the KGB, a similar organization.

Papa went up to his room. Prock wasn't there. Maybe he had left already. Yes he had; there was a little note on his bed with the address. "I wish I could fly out today!" Papa sighed. He lay down on his bed staring at the ceiling. This might be an interesting afternoon!

99.

Someone knocked on the door! Papa must have fallen asleep, or at least done some daydreaming. He checked his watch: 14:28. They knocked again and a voice called, "Mr. Mann, are you there?" Papa jumped out of bed and checked himself briefly in the mirror.

"Yes, just a moment." Seconds later, he opened the door. It was Miss Blank. "Sorry, Mr. Mann, but they are waiting for you in the hall downstairs. I'll tell them that you need another minute, okay?" Papa nodded. She left and Papa checked himself again in the mirror. Where is the hairbrush? Not that it will help too much but at least I should look halfway decent for them. He quickly brushed his teeth and got his jacket. Now he noticed that the new shirt did not go with the jacket – I should leave the shopping up to Helga!

He closed the room, locked it and went downstairs. There they were: two men, dressed in black pants and jackets with shirts and ties. Just like in the movies. One was a bit taller than him, the other just Papa's height. They were about Papa's age. Not looking too friendly. They probably felt important, maybe they were.

"Mr. Mann?"

"Yes."

"We are supposed to pick you up. I am Mr. Grode and this is my colleague, Mr. Praus. We have a car waiting outside. Please follow us."

Papa did not say anything; this was really a bit too much, wasn't it? He felt like a criminal. But nothing I can do about it now.

He followed the guys to the car. An Opel limousine. Papa jumped in the back with Grode; Praus sat in front with the driver. They left towards town.

If nothing else, at least Papa saw more of Berlin. Nice city! Monuments and big buildings, wide streets and shops. The smaller streets all had condos and apartment buildings. Trees were blooming! Well, it was spring after all.

The car went down one of the long avenues and turned into a side street. The building was noticeable because of its big iron gate and fence around it. The gate swung open but a barrier prohibited anyone from entering the courtyard. There was a guard in a little house beside the gate. When he saw the car he opened the barrier. He must know all the license plates by heart Papa thought. The Opel stopped in front of the entrance.

"Just follow us, please, Mr. Mann." Praus and Grode led the way through the door. It was a two wing wooden door with windows and iron gates covering them. A few steps up and a long corridor to the left. Praus opened one of the doors on the left and entered.

"Please wait here, Mr. Mann." They left.

Papa stood in a small room with a table and three chairs. The window had bars in front and it gave him the feeling of being imprisoned. He was a bit afraid of what was coming.

"Maybe I am really overreacting? What could they possibly want from me?" Papa did not sit down but walked up and down the room.

It must have been an eternity until the door opened.

"Mr. Mann? Would you please follow me?" It was Praus. Papa followed him to another door. Praus opened it and entered a bigger office room. It had two windows and some curtains, no flowers. It was furnished with a big desk, two high-boards attached to the wall beside the door with a lot of files. A single chair was standing in front of the large desk. Two officers dressed in suits and ties were sitting behind the desk. One had some files opened in front of him, the other one a pad of paper.

When Papa entered they rose and said, "Please take a seat, Mr. Mann."

The whole setting really did not make Papa comfortable. It had the similar feeling of his police days when he was interrogating prisoners or criminals or political suspects.

"Am I a suspect of some kind? Does this all make sense? What did I do wrong?"

Praus had not left the room; just Mr. Grode was gone. Praus leaned against the wall between the two windows with his arms crossed over his chest waiting for the officers to start.

"Mr. Mann, thank you for coming. You know Mr. Praus already; I am Mr. Kunze and beside me, this is Mr. Hausmann. We know that this must be an uncomfortable situation for you but there is nothing to worry about from your side! We know that you just escaped and we know about your family and your intention to stay in West Germany. We also know about your police position in Sondershausen and your other engagement with the GDR authorities, especially the Stasi. If you do not mind, we would like to ask you a few questions about that time." He paused looking at Papa. He did not answer. This was too serious for him. He felt like they put a rope around his neck. Involvement in Stasi actions? I know a few people but I wasn't one of their agents!

"Let's just check your personal data quickly just to make sure that everything is correct." The one with the open file started to ask Papa names and birthdates, addresses, occupations, other family data. He then wanted to know about Mutti and the children and the visa and how they made it over to the grandparents.

That was easy. Papa told them everything and how he made it over on Sunday. Actually, talking about it calmed him down a bit. He got used to the chemistry in the room. He figured also that this was the easy part of the investigation.

"Thank you for the details, Mr. Mann, , we appreciate it." While Papa was talking, the second officer wrote down notes. All three were listening but never interrupted Papa.

"We need to talk with you now about your police work and Stasi contacts. Let's just start with the police. Please tell us exactly what your occupation was, title, your tasks. We would like to know also names of colleagues or superiors." Papa tried to start with the easy part, his employment, dates, his progress, trainings and promotions within the police department. A little bit about his daily work. He also told them that he hated the system, the politics and the living conditions in the GDR.

"For me and my family, it was just no longer acceptable. We were worrying about the future and we especially wanted to provide a better education and better future for our children. You must understand this, don't you?" Papa said it a bit like an accusation telling them that this whole meeting was not reasonable from his point of view. The reaction was immediate.

"We can imagine how you feel, Mr. Mann. But we also have to take care of our system here and we want to know who we let into our country." There was a serious undertone.

"We can only ask you for your cooperation here."

Papa went quiet. The two officers exchanged a short look while Hausmann pointed to something on his pad. Kunze nodded. He turned to Papa.

"During your time in the police, you had contacts with the Stasi. Why did you work with them? And did you at any time work for them as an undercover agent?" Papa swallowed. Here we go. Now they are getting serious. But I have nothing to hide! I was against the system, I did not support them other than doing my routine police work. Sometimes I had to sit in when they interrogated political suspects, too. But this wasn't my choice. I was always on the side of people having their own opinions.

"First of all, I was not a Stasi agent. I never worked as an undercover agent for them. On the contrary, I had to be very, very careful not to reveal my true opinion about the whole system. My family and I had to always be very careful in what we were saying. Even with relatives or friends, we seldom talked politics. It was simply too dangerous. They might not intend it but could easily say something negative while being investigated." Papa stopped here. He wanted to give his statement a certain importance. They should know that I did not cooperate.

"When you worked with the Stasi, you say that it was forced on you or that in the course of your tasks it was a necessary obligation?" They wanted to know were Papa stood.

"As I said," Papa continued, "I had to deal with them. For example, they asked the police to investigate certain people and wanted reports on them. So, we had to do this even though we hated it. It could have been a neighbor or a friend. Imagine! At least I hated it. It was the interaction between Stasi and police that brought me into contact with them, not that I wanted to. One of the reasons why I quit my police job was how the police treated me after my mishap during the training in Aschersleben. The other major reason was that I could not cope with a situation anymore that was opposite to my personal view of things and my passion for having my own opinion. Do you understand this? That is the reality over there!" Papa's statement was emotional now. All he left behind came back into his mind. All the years of being pressed into a suit which did not fit him, so to speak.

"What happened in Ascherleben?" Kunze asked. Papa told them the story and how the police tried to undermine his position and how they treated him and basically left him no choice other than to quit. The officers listened carefully.

"I can imagine that this was a difficult decision for you. No job and a family of six."

What do you think!? You have no idea! Papa had to hold himself back speaking out loud. You people have no clue!

"Yes it was! My wife was very supportive and through friends, I found the new job. From then on, our decision was clear and transferred into a plan for escape. That my wife got the visa for herself and all four children is still a mystery to me."

The guys looked at him. Papa thought about the discussions he had with Mutti during many evenings. The decision they made. The plan and procedure of sending packages with important personal items to relatives and friends. The fear of being discovered accompanied with all of this. The farewell in Erfurt not knowing under what circumstances we would be together again. These officers somehow felt what we went through – probably. But you can not understand if you haven't gone through something like that yourself!

"In which political events were you involved and to what degree?" Kunze asked. Of course, this was a logical question. Western Germany was very cautious at this time to not invite any subversive forces. Not that there was a real danger to the West German government but better to be safe than sorry was the motto.

Papa started with June 17, 1953. The small revolution in East Germany. The whole environment such as living and working conditions were so bad that the workers and farmers as well as other groups of people went into the street demonstrating against the government. It was very critical for the government so they involved the Red Army with tanks to put the revolution down, like they did later in 1956 in Hungary. "I was called to enforce the security that day. The entire police force was needed. The main activities were in the big cities like Berlin and Leipzig and Halle, not so much in Sondershausen. So, my involvement was more passive."

"You are a party member of the SED, right?"

"Yes, as a police officer I had to be a member." I knew they would ask this. Papa was not surprised.

"And it was not that you were convinced about their philosophies or their doctrine?"

"Of course not!" How often do I have to tell them that I was against the Communist and Socialist system the way it was run in the GDR?

"As for your contacts with the Stasi: Could you give us some names of Stasi officers you worked with?" A simple question but a difficult answer. Papa did not want to wipe out his honest cooperation here by saying that he would rather not mention names. On the other side, would they ever hold it against him?

"What consequences will this hearing have on me and my family, Mr. Kunze?" Papa thought it is time to ask questions himself before giving them any more help. If they are open as they seem to be, they will answer my questions straight without any excuses or "ifs" and "whens".

"We don't think that there will be any, Mr. Mann." was the response.

"Yes or no?" Papa needed a clear response to make sure.

"No. There is nothing to be afraid of, Mr. Mann. This is for our books and files." Maybe it was hard for them to admit that they did not know enough about the GDR and the system over there.

Can I trust them? I have a few names and if I give them the names, will they let me go now? Being suspicious was a natural reaction coming from an environment where you always had to be on guard. On the other hand, the Stasi had probably no way of pursuing me in West Germany anyway – I hope.

Papa gave them a few names of officers in the local Stasi he worked with starting with Gebert. They wrote the names down. Papa did not feel good about the whole hearing but he had no choice but to cooperate with them. After all, he wanted to put it behind him and go to Helga and the kids – as soon as possible!

Hausmann and Kunze exchanged a look and a silent nod. "Okay Mr. Mann. Thank you for your statements and remarks and your cooperation! We appreciate it. If you do not have any other question for us, Mr. Praus will bring you back to your quarters."

"Yes, I have another question for you." Papa responded. The officers sat down again.

"And what is your question, Mr. Mann?"

"Will this be the one and only interview?" Kunze hesitated a bit but said:

"As far as we are concerned, yes." That left a possibility for more interviews Papa thought.

"Who else would need to talk to me?"

"We are not sure at this time, Mr. Mann. We are an island here in West Berlin, secured by the allies France, USA and Great Britain. Sometimes, they are also interested in talking with former officers of the East German system."

"When will I know if there is another interview?"

"As far as I know you will be informed shortly." Hausmann and Kunze got up again.

"Thank you again, Mr. Mann. All the best for you and your family!"

There was no sense in asking more questions Papa thought. They will not tell me everything they know anyway. Papa was just glad that it was over. He turned around to the door and left the room followed by Praus. They went silently side by side through the long corridor. Papa felt empty and stressed out. Obviously, the West Germans had their system too with secret services and Stasi-like institutions. The difference was that you could say almost everything what you wanted to and their constitution stood for a free society.

The car was waiting outside to bring Papa back. Praus did not go with him and said goodbye. The driver brought him back to the refugee barracks while Papa was reviewing the whole interview. In one way, it was over and Papa felt good about it. It really did not seem that the interview would harm him or his family in any way. And there was really no intention to send him back. He never really thought so but it was good to have it confirmed.

On the other hand, the remark by Kunze about the allies left a bit of an uncomfortable feeling with him. Would they really want to interview him too? Same questions or maybe more details of certain events? I was never involved with any international matters. I hope they proceed quickly now so I can fly out. 'I will ask the officer in the administration office first thing tomorrow morning!'

After dinner, Papa went to bed right away. His last thought before falling asleep this evening was Helga and us children. Maybe 3 or 4 more days until I see them!

100.

Opa and Mutti left early on Tuesday. "We have to go to the town registration office and see that we can get registered here in town."

"Can I go with you?" My mind was on the shops and the toys I might miss seeing today not going downtown. The shops were open today, great. But staying home with Oma would not be as much pleasure as shopping.

"No, you have to stay with Roland and Oma until we get back. This is important for us. I have to go with Opa. Play with Karin and Brigitte for a while." I have to admit: that was always fun for us brothers. But the toys and shops were new!

Mutti and Opa left and took the tram downtown. They went to the main station and crossed over the bus stations to "Westland House." That was the building's name. It was partly the mayor's office but also hosted a lot of the city's administration such as public services, registration office, office for the public regulations, passports and so on. They went in and Opa went straight to the elevator. He knew where Mr. Gillessen's office was. He had visited him before to ask him to help us.

The elevator was small but better than walking up the stairs to the 4th floor! Opa checked quickly and said, "It must be on the right side, the second or third door as far as I remember, Helga." They searched and found it. Third door, Mr. Gillessen, Einwohnermeldeamt. The German word for the registration office of town habitants. If you are going to stay in the town and live there, you have to register within three months. That's still the rule today. It would also be the place to have documents signed and passports or ID cards initiated. Good rule! There were unregistered persons not to speak of illegal people. But it was public knowledge where a person lives or lived before.

Opa knocked on the door. A loud "Come in" came from inside. Opa opened the door and let Mutti in and followed her closing the door behind them.

"Guten Morgen, Franz!"

"Same to you, Emilian!" They shook hands.

"This is my daughter Helga Mann, Franz." Mutti also shook hands with him.

"Sit down here, please. Just a moment, I'll get another chair." He grabbed a second chair and placed it beside the other one in front of his desk.

"I am glad to see you here, Mrs. Mann! I heard about your trip and the possible escape of the whole family. Where is your husband now?"

"He made it to West Berlin Sunday evening. I am so very glad!"

"That is great, I am very happy for you all!"

Opa added, "He will be in Friedland in about two or three days we think and as we talked about earlier, we have to see that they get a place, maybe in Wickrath. Did you organize anything yet as you intended last time we spoke?"

"No worries, Emilian! I have made contact with Wickrath, the temporary homes for refugees from the GDR. It was not easy but I got a room for the family!" Mutti was relieved and thanked him right away.

"Thank you, Franz! When could we transfer them to Wickrath?"

"I still need the final confirmation from the managers there but I should have it by tomorrow. When do you think he will be here?"

"Two to three days to Friedland and then maybe another two days from there. So, probably by the end of this week?" You could see in his face that Mr. Gillessen was thinking.

"It might take longer than this. Up to ten days from now. That would be the middle or end of next week. I will see what I can do. Maybe you could call me Thursday. I should know by then."

Mutti thought about the stressful and overcrowded environment they all experienced at the moment. Six people in a little apartment, seven when Papa arrived! Plus the babies! Her parents were very helpful but in reality, they probably wanted their life and space back as soon as possible. You would never hear any complaint from Opa; he was very content in almost any situation. But Mutti and Oma could easily step on each other's toes. There was more than one occasion in the past when it sparked between them.

Mutti was also curious about any other material or financial support we would get for our starting a new life. Before she could ask, Mr. Gillessen must have read her mind and answered her question.

"Mrs. Mann, you probably know that we will provide you also with money and will help you to find a place to live after the temporary home in Wickrath. There might be also some furniture or beds or other household goods we can provide to help you get started. But this is not so important right now. May I ask you if your husband has any idea where to find work? What is his profession?"

Mutti told him briefly about the relationship between the company in Göllingen where Papa worked until the escape and the company in the neighbor town of Rheydt. There was a business and commercial relationship between the two companies and Papa wanted to see if this could help to get employment there. At least, it was planned that he would apply for a job there first.

"That is very good!" Mr. Gillessen responded. "The earlier, the better. There is enough work out there but of course it should also suit your husband and his experience."

He looked first at Opa and then at Mutti with a questioning expression: "Any other questions?"

"No, the rest we can discuss later." Opa responded on their behalf. Mutti nodded, she was happy that things were moving forward.

Opa and Mutti got up, thanked him for his personal support and left the office. "Everything will work out, Helga, I told you!"

I think that everybody was happy to hear that we would leave the apartment soon. A few more days, not easy but doable, Mutti thought to herself. Hopefully Ferdi is okay and will arrive soon!

101.

Wednesday morning. Papa woke up. He looked at the other bed and it was empty. Of course, Prock is gone he reminded himself. So I have the room all for myself. It was around 8:00. Thirty minutes later, he went to the canteen to have breakfast. "This is my third day, I hope that there won't be many more here!" He always ate the same thing: rolls, marmalade – Papa liked marmalade, always – a soft egg and some good coffee! It was now a routine.

Again, he thought about the hearing yesterday with the BND. Maybe I should ask the guy again in the registration office if he has heard anything new. Or Miss Blank. Someone should know. He decided to go after breakfast and ask. He looked around and saw some new people. More and more were coming from GDR. All escaping, just with a few things in a suitcase or a bag full of personal belongings; everything else was left behind. Freedom was more important!

Papa finished breakfast and went straight to the administration office. He knocked and entered, not waiting for a response. As usual the officer sat behind his desk moving papers around and Miss Blank was on the phone. Papa said good morning and waited until she put down the phone.

They both responded nodding. Miss Blank got up after her call was finished and went to the counter to see what Papa had on his mind.

"What can I do for you, Mr. Mann? Did you go to the interview already?"

"Yes, I did yesterday. I was wondering if you heard anything about another one scheduled for me?" He ended his sentence on a question mark. She said:

"No. But let me ask my colleague." She went over to him and whispered something Papa could not understand. She came back with a stunning surprise.

"Yes, Mr. Mann. There will be another interview tomorrow. With the Americans. So, it is better that you be here tomorrow all day. It might be in the morning."

Papa went pale. The Americans? That would be the CIA! What in this world do I have to do with them? Yes, they are one of the allies Kunze talked about. But the CIA?

"Everything okay, Mr. Mann?" Miss Blank asked Papa, obviously noticing that he was beyond surprise. Papa needed a second.

"I am okay, thanks Ms. Blank. When would this be?"

"As I mentioned already, probably in the morning."

Papa took a deep breath and finally said: "I will check with you in the morning tomorrow."

He left the office and went straight to his room. He lay on his bed wondering why the Americans would be interested in his story. What did I do that is of interest to them? They have their spies everywhere; they are probably very well informed. But as Kunze indicated there might be certain things they would like to ask me about. But what do they want to know is the question!

Papa spent the rest of the day wondering about the answer to it. Even the nice afternoon walk, the coffee in the shop down the road while smoking two cigarettes, the smiling waitress, nothing could really destroy the uneasy feeling.

He finally fell asleep over it. But he had some wild dreams!

102.

There was loud talking. People in the hall were discussing something. It woke Papa up. His watch showed 7:35. He rubbed his eyes and his first thought was: "CIA interview!" He remembered all the brainstorming he did yesterday evening with no hint after all – other than the obvious and the things the BND was interested in earlier.

Papa got up and went to the door. For a while, he listened to the conversation. After he felt that it wasn't of importance to him, he got ready for the day. What a day this will be! I have to be prepared. He decided to go to breakfast and go over his time with the police: from the very beginning in 1947 to his forced departure. Maybe I can think of something.

Breakfast was good and rich. He made sure that he had enough to go through lunchtime in case the CIA will pick him up around 11 or 12 o'clock. He sat in a corner of the cafeteria to be alone and not disturbed while brainstorming.

Yesterday evening, he could not really remember anything that might be of interest to them. But with the West Germans the situation was the same: they had nothing really specific – other than his police time and his Stasi contacts. The damned Stasi. Always the cause of problems! If you were one of them or not, if you were a normal citizen or an official or an officer, no matter where you stood in East German society: the Stasi was always like the sword of Damocles swinging over you.

He got up and went to his room, brushed his teeth and checked his outfit. He packed all his papers and laid them on his bed.

"What about a cigarette, Ferdi?" he said to himself. He left his room and went down, leaving the building through the front door. It was a nice day again with some clouds, not too warm. Some of the other refugees had the same idea: they stood around smoking. These cigarettes were really good. Taste and tobacco and even the paper it was rolled in.

Papa watched the street; the CIA probably came in a black American limousine. One of these heavy six meters long vehicles. I don't know. I have never seen them in the GDR. Just during some of the trainings, our guys mentioned them and how to spot them. Today is Thursday, he thought considering his departure from Berlin. "If I get through this today and there are no more interviews, then I could fly out tomorrow or at least Saturday

Helga! She would be so happy to see me – and me too to see her and the kids!" He finished his cigarette and went back to his room. I can only wait!

He lay on his bed staring at the ceiling. So many things happened during the last six days: Helga left, the talks with the Bohnes, the hiding, the police chasing me, the telegram, the trip to Berlin, the trip into the West with the check at the border and now here. What else will happen? How does our future look?

He was snoozing when somebody knocked at the door.

"Mr. Mann?" It was Miss Blank. Papa was a bit dizzy and got up. A short look in the mirror and he opened the door.

"The Americans are waiting for you in the hall downstairs. Are you okay?" She looked at him with a pitiful look.

"Yes, I am, thanks. Just dozed off a bit."

"Are you coming? They do not like to wait as you can imagine."

"Two seconds, I'll take my jacket and the papers and money." Papa grabbed everything and followed her down the stairs.

It has never been difficult to spot these agents. At least Papa did not have a problem identifying such characters; even though they were dressed like normal people. These agents always had a special behavior and look. The two men – one leaning on the wall – were no different. Dark slacks and black polished shoes, white shirts and jackets with two slits in the back, American style jackets. And thin ties around their necks. When Papa came down following Miss Blank they turned their heads.

It seemed that Miss Blank was more of interest to them than Papa! Miss Blank looked very attractive today with her pink blouse and short skirt and heeled shoes. The two men were all over her with their eyes.

"Sergeants, this is Mr. Mann. If I can be of any further help, let me know." She turned and went down the hall to her office while at least four eyes were following her every step.

"Mr. Mann, I am Sergeant Hunt and this is Sergeant Long. Pleased to meet you. We are going to our office. The meeting is scheduled for 13:00 o'clock. Did you have lunch or do you want to grab a bite to eat?"

Papa shook his head, "No, thanks, I had a good breakfast."

"Okay, let's go then!"

Hunt had this thick American accent when he spoke German. His German was not too bad but his grammar was ugly. Well, it would be nice to speak English as well as he speaks German, Papa thought.

Long had not said a word yet. Hunt turned on his heels to walk to the car waiting fifty meters down on the other side of the road. It was black and it was long! A driver was leaning against the door smoking. When he saw us coming, he flipped the cigarette on the street and stepped on it. He jumped behind the wheel and started the engine.

Not sure but maybe a Chevrolet, Papa thought. Hunt jumped in front on the passenger seat and Papa and Long went in the back. It was roomy, enough room to stretch your legs. Not like our Kübels, Papa thought.

The car went down some roads probably towards the center of town. Papa wasn't sure if they would tell him?
"Where are we going?" Papa wanted to know.
"Our office is more in the center of Berlin. Actually, do you know where Checkpoint Charlie is?" Hunt asked him.
"No, not exactly." Papa had heard about the border control point and knew that this was the famous one for all American citizens if they had the desire or duty to go to East Berlin or the GDR.
"It is close to there on Kochstrasse." Long had not said a word since they met but answered the question. His German was bad, more like adding some words together rather than building a sentence. His accent was different from Hunt's but Papa had no idea what accent he spoke.
Papa had to pinch himself: I am driving in a car with the CIA in West Berlin, almost like a VIP. I am free – hopefully – and we will start a new life when this is over! The only question still remaining was: what do they want from me!?
It took them about 30 minutes to get to Kochstrasse. A villa type building with a little front yard, it almost looked like an embassy. To a certain extent, Papa enjoyed the ride. He looked at all the many new things and impressions. What a city Berlin was! Buzzing and energetic!
They jumped out of the car and Hunt lead the way through the front gate up a few steps towards the massive wooden front door. He opened it and Papa and Long followed him into a bigger entrance hall with old marble floors and a big stairway in the middle that lead to the first floor. On the left was a reception desk. A secretary sat behind it. Her appearance was like the ones in the American movie Papa had seen once. The police had a few films for training purposes. She was blond and well proportioned with hair down to her shoulders, tight blouse, skirt and makeup. Right; that is what they called the colors women put on their face Papa remembered! If Helga would ever wear makeup?

Hunt spoke English with her; Papa could only identify the words 'yes' and 'no'. That did not help. She picked up the phone and dialed a number.

"Yes, okay, first floor, 218."

"Sergeant Hunt, first floor you heard it, they need another ten minutes or so but you can go up now and wait." All three went up the stairs, made a right turn and went down a short hall. In front of the room with the number '218', they stopped.

"Just a few minutes, Mr. Mann." Papa nodded. That's it, he thought. The nervousness was back. There was one name on the door and a title: Lieutenant Marvey. A level up, I guess.

"May I smoke here?" he asked.

"No problem, Mr. Mann. But when we enter, please stop. There is an ashtray on the window sill there, see it?" He pointed to the next window. Papa lit his cigarette and took a deep drag. He looked out the window and saw the silhouette of the Reichstag, the old German parliament building. And beside it, just a bit hidden by the trees, there was the Brandenburg Gate with the Quadriga on top. This is the four horse Roman chariot.

"All we ever wanted is to be free, say what we want and do what we want, learn what we need and progress the way we can for a better life." It looks like we can start now!

"Mr. Mann? Sorry, we've been called in." Papa was in his own new world for a moment. He did not hear the call from behind the door. They entered. It was a big office, a nice one. A large desk with a lamp, a sideboard and a cupboard. Pictures, one of John F. Kennedy, their president. Papa recognized him from newspaper photos. Beside the picture, the American flag: stars and stripes they called it. In the front of the desk were two chairs side by side. The windows were open and a light breeze let the curtains tangle. The guy behind the desk was older than his sergeants, maybe fifty-five. He was in a brown suit. He was a bit over-weight and his face was puffy. Nevertheless, his eyes were open and alert. He seemed to anticipate an interesting conversation.

He lifted briefly from his chair and greeted Papa:

"Mr. Mann, please take a seat." He paused until Papa sat down. The two agents were leaning against the windowsill. Funny how similar this whole scenario is, Papa thought. There is not much of a difference between a hearing with the BND or the CIA!

"My name is Lieutenant Marvey. My two agents Hunt and Long you know already. We are from the CIA, I guess you've heard about our organization." He paused. His accent was again different from the other two but at least a bit clearer. Also his grammar and comprehension of the German language seemed to be better. Maybe they trained the upper level better.

There was certainly some importance in his statement and he wanted to make it clear that this is serious. Papa understood quietly. He was often enough in those interviews or interrogations. Of course, now it was all about him and his family's future.

"May I offer you a coffee, Mr. Mann? I would appreciate if you do not smoke. Thanks."

"A coffee would be nice, with cream if possible."

Marvey checked with Hunt and Long; they nodded. Marvey picked up the phone and ordered four coffees. After he put the phone back he started the conversation.

"We can skip the basics; as you can assume, we have checked all your identity and those of your family, relatives and so on. The BND gave us the information. We would like to get straight to the things we are interested in and want to ask you a few questions about your time in the GDR. We realize that you just escaped from there last Sunday. Please tell us a bit about how you managed it and how your family made it over to the West."

Okay, same question, same long story. Papa started but was interrupted when the "Marilyn Monroe" from the reception desk downstairs opened the door and brought in the coffees. The coffee was hot and the agents could not refrain from staring at all the other hot parts. She left with a wild swing and closed the door knowing that she made an impression. Papa put the cream in his coffee, stirred it and took a sip. Not bad. Then he continued and told them how the escape was planned and executed, about the visa and his own escape. He also mentioned something about the background with the police and the decision that was basically forced on them as a family by the circumstances. They listened and did not interrupt. Papa ended his statement with a sigh:

"I am very glad that we made it!"

"Very well. We appreciate your information." Marvey was up for more.

"We know that during your time with the police department, you were also dealing with the Stasi, right?"

"Yes." Papa left it there, let's see where they are heading.

"You were in contact with them as what? An informant or intelligence?" That is a bit aggressive and maybe unfair Papa thought.

"No, neither. I just had to deal with them when it came to certain felonies or criminal acts."

"Why would the Stasi get involved in the normal daily activities of the police? Isn't that unusual?"

"They were not always involved; only when felonies were suspected to be politically motivated." That was a difficult answer as it would indicate that Papa would have worked eventually with the Stasi to support them pursuing and prosecuting political criminals. In fact, he was a political criminal himself now but fortunately outside their influence.

Marvey wanted to know it exactly. "Mr. Mann, when there were criminals based on GDR law and it turned out that all they did was only a political failure in the sense of the GDR's laws, did you work with the Stasi during the prosecution and the trial? Or support their findings with interrogations?"

Papa had to think about it for a moment. Actually, yes – but no. He remembered cases where he brought a guy into custody because he broke into a shop and further along in the investigation, the guy made accusations against the state and the government and protested against the poor supply of groceries or something. Those reports were also seen at the Stasi office; everything related to political matters was forwarded. So, what could you do?

"Did you understand my question?" Marvey got a bit impatient.

"Yes I did, Mr. Marvey." Papa paused.

"No, I would not be involved if it was just a political case. I see that you want to find out if I was really cooperating with the Stasi or if I was an informant." Papa looked him straight in the eyes with confidence just to give his statement a bit more emphasis. Marvey showed no reaction, no hint of what was in his head.

"Let me repeat: I was not a Stasi informant or if you want a co-worker! In my position as a senior police officer, I got involved in many cases of felony or other criminal acts. I could never choose beforehand if I wanted to be involved or not. Therefore, sometimes, I was drawn into cases where there was a political background to the act of the particular person. But as soon as this was clear, we forwarded the case to the Stasi as the political aspect was of higher importance to them than the criminal one."

Marvey looked at Hunt and Long; it was a look something like, "we've heard this before." There was some doubt in their view. It was hard for them to understand how a state like the GDR operated. It was more like a dictatorship and the authorities mirrored this in their actions and in the way they operated. It was that easy.

"As a senior officer," Marvey continued, trying to get his information in a different way, "Who were your contacts local, regional or countrywide? We would like to know how the Stasi was structured and to what extent you could be ordered to support them as a police officer."

Papa thought about this question for a while as he did not want to give them more ideas that he had been involved with the Stasi. He was only involved with the local organizations in Sondershausen or seldom with the one in Erfurt. That was no lie! And at the end of the day: who had escaped here? Me! Isn't that proof enough that I did not want to support the GDR and authorities like the Stasi?

Papa explained as much as he knew about the Stasi organization and made it clear that he did not get involved in their activities. Papa had to deal with them. I remember how we were trained as children to be careful and walk quietly when passing the Stasi office. It was located in the street where the villa was in which the chess games took place. We had to pass it coming straight up from town. We did not even turn our heads to look at its office windows! Papa hated the GDR politics and their authorities and the negative influences on his and his family's lives. This is why he was here in the West, finally!

Marvey, Hunt and Long listened to Papa's remarks. They must have heard similar statements before. There were certainly other officers who escaped and the BND and the CIA were of course interested in interrogations and the information they could gain from it. The difficult part was maybe to find out who was really a supporter and came to the West as a possible spy. Marvey took a little break. He concentrated on the papers he had on his desk. Obviously and not surprisingly, a few notes were written down beforehand. He needed time to rethink.

"Sergeants, any questions?" He looked at them for help. They looked at each other and said something in English. Marvey overheard it and nodded.

"Mr. Mann, we have another question. It is about your SED party membership. Is it correct that you joined the SED right after you arrived in Sondershausen. Why did you do this? We understand that there was no pressure to do so."

"At the point of my subscription for the SED membership, there was no immediate request to do so, especially as I actually had no intention to be a member. This is true. But what you do not know is that I was about to make an application for the police service and it was clear that it would be easier to get a job with an SED membership. It is that easy, I had to do it. After all, the police job was essential for me to be able to start my family."

"Why did you not escape right away as it would have been easier at this time, wouldn't it?"

"Maybe a bit easier. As you probably know, Mr. Marvey, most of our relatives escaped at this time. Not without danger and by night! But we had the chance to start our family life in Sondershausen with this good job with the police. So, we finally decided not to go. And of course, who could have known at that time how GDR would develop?"

That was a good question! Who could have known? West Germany was not in such great condition at that time after the war either!

Papa took another sip of his coffee; it was now almost cold. It was symbolic in a way as the heat of the meeting was gone. The lieutenant seemed to be satisfied with what he had heard even though secret service agents never made the impression of trusting the answers totally. Papa knew this from being an investigator himself often enough.

"When do you fly out to Frankfurt, Mr. Mann?"

"I hope tomorrow. Why do you ask?" Now Papa had rising doubts that the meeting was over. What else can I tell them?

"We have a few specific issues, but they are related to the central organization of the Stasi. I guess you would not be able to answer those."

Was this a trick? I told them that I do not know anybody outside the local organization.

"I can only repeat that I do not know people outside the local Stasi. I would not be of any help to you."

Marvey nodded like "I hear you but I do not really believe you." He looked again at his agents and waved his hand, "I think you can bring Mr. Mann back. Unless you can think of anything else to ask?" Marvey was finished. They declined in English. Marvey got up; he seemed to be a bit disappointed. "Maybe the information I gave him was not good enough, maybe he expected more. Sorry, Mr. Marvey that is all I know."

Papa got up too and said goodbye to Marvey. The two agents mumbled something in English. Papa did not care. He was glad that it was over. Finally, I can fly out. Maybe tomorrow. Two more days, maybe and I will see Helga and the kids!

They drove him back. It was 14:40. It was not that long of a meeting but it was somewhat exhausting. I need another coffee and then I will go to Miss Blank and ask her what the next steps are. She will still be in the office then.

The sun was still out when he had dinner. It was an early dinner. The food wasn't great but Papa had developed a good appetite that day. Miss Blank would work on his flight tomorrow! She had promised him that she would arrange it that afternoon, probably for Friday.

I will write Helga another postcard!

103.

Thursday. Mail came always at around 9:30. Mailmen are on time! And it was exciting mail. Opa had the card in his hands when he walked into the kitchen. Oma and Mutti were doing dishes.

"Ferdi wrote a card!" Mutti almost dropped the plate she was drying. She practically ripped the card out of Opa's hands. We overheard this and went to the kitchen door right away. Mutti read the card out loud:

"Dear Helga, as you know by now, I made it through! I am now in the refugee camp and trying to get a flight to Frankfurt. Hopefully this will be soon. Love you and greetings to all!"

Mutti started crying. Opa took her in his arms. Mutti was so happy!

"When is Papa coming?" I needed to know.

"Well, maybe in three or four days, he did not say. He probably did not know yet," Mutti sobbed. She looked at the card again and read it again. A few more days, hopefully soon, she thought to herself. "Papa has to go to Frankfurt first and then to Friedland for our registration, address and to get a room in Wickrath." She paused, "Opa, do we have to go to Mr. Gillessen again or is everything arranged?"

"I'm not sure; maybe we should go to him again tomorrow now that we roughly know when Ferdi is coming." Mutti nodded:

"Let's go tomorrow morning and ask him. We need this room there until we are transferred to a proper condo or apartment."

They went Friday morning and made sure that we would be transferred during the next week as soon as Papa arrived. "It will be such a relief!" Mutti told herself. She was ready to drop.

The only thing she did not like was that Oma's brother came with his wife from a town called Jülich, about 40 kilometers away from Mönchengladbach. Uncle Walter had a little plant doing recycling work for fabrics and wool. It was an hour away and they wanted to pick up Roland for a few days so the condo was less crowded. They would bring him back to Wickrath once we have moved there. Mutti did not like the idea as she needed Roland to help her. He was thirteen and Mutti relied on him when it came to watching me or the babies or simply for carrying heavy stuff.

Well, Opa and Oma had decided this, and she had to agree. Soon, Mutti would be her own chief again; she could not wait for that moment to arrive!

104.

Papa was first in the office that Friday morning. Miss Blank told him that he had to wait another day; it was just that the logistics had not worked out. He would fly to Frankfurt on Saturday and go from there by train to Giessen, the town near the general refugee camp for all people coming to West Germany.

Friedland was a famous location. Everybody knew about it and saw the pictures in the newspapers or on TV of the thousands and thousands of people coming, mostly from the GDR, but also from Eastern Europe. This was the place where everyone got their final registration papers and were sent to towns and cities where either relatives lived or where they wanted to go. Sometimes, opportunities were given for special professional circumstances, and people were asked to go to certain locations where there was work for them. Finding work was not a big problem; after all, West Germany was in its booming years that they called the "Wirtschaftswunder." Growth of the economy was a given and besides the East Germans, many other nationalities were coming into the country as "Gastarbeiter," a workforce that was considered guests for a while helping Germany with its reconstruction after the loss of the Second World War. Well, many of these "guest-workers" stayed for a long time or forever.

At least, Papa now knew that this would be his last day here in Berlin, and he would be able to go to his family! No more hearings, no more worries about the authorities, no more question marks about when he could leave. This was encouraging!

Saturday morning at 10:38, the Air France flight took off from Tempelhof airport towards Frankfurt am Main. Papa had to convince the older lady beside him that flying on a plane is really not such a bad thing after all – especially when you fly to a free country! It was her first time on a plane and she was scared.

105.

Friedland turned out to be a shorter stopover for Papa than he had expected. Two nights in a camp with many thousands of people looking for a free and better future for themselves. Most of them just had fled the GDR, others came from Eastern Europe and felt that Germany was after all their "land of the free." There were days when over 12 thousand left the GDR: during the night over the unobserved portions of the border, via neighboring Eastern block countries, from East to West Berlin, with daily visas to never go back, leaving everything they had behind them.

The authorities already had the information that Papa – and his family – wanted to stay in Mönchengladbach, close to Mutti's parents. Wickrath, the little suburb not too far away from Mönchengladbach would be our home for about six to eight weeks. Opa had arranged this with his friend, the officer he had visited twice with Mutti. And it all worked out!

Papa received the registration forms and it seemed that everything was organized for him and us. He would soon be with us. After spending Saturday and Sunday there, Papa left on Monday morning by train.

At the time, Friedland was a very crowded place and would stay like this until several years later. Today it is a memorial.

106.

It was June 2nd. After we had our Papa back, we left Oma's and Opa's apartment with the little we had to move to the camp in Wickrath where they gave us a room with four bunk beds like in the military, a table and four chairs. Adjacent was a tiny little porch that could function as additional storage or even as a refrigerator during cool nights. It was not that warm these days. Nevertheless, we were happy. We could leave Oma and Opa's tiny apartment. Don't get me wrong: we were very grateful for the help that Oma and Opa gave us – and would give us in the future – but it was an unbearable situation with eight people in a two room flat. I guess that everyone was relieved when we left Mönchengladbach to move into our temporary home in Wickrath!

We had to share the bath and the restrooms with about 20 other people as well as the kitchen. Washing clothes was also a shared event. Mutti was and still is a master of improvising. In a day's time, she had made it a "home" for us with some pillows, a few nice blankets, some pictures and a tablecloth. We had gotten some money from the town and could buy groceries and other necessary household items. This is where I celebrated my 10th birthday. In West Germany June 17 was a holiday, they called it the "Day of the German Unity," in memory the revolution in 1953. For many years, my birthday was always a holiday.

Papa was busy looking for work while we were put in the local school. What a difference! The kids were so not like the ones in GDR. Maybe in some ways they were more mature, but in another way they were way behind in their educational level. Roland and I knew more than the other kids our age. We would be able to skip at least a grade! But they had nice toys and watches and better clothes. We looked poor in our hand-me-downs!

Life was like it was on hold. Many things were temporary; we knew this. This was definitely not our last stop. We wanted to get our own apartment, wherever it would be. But first things first. Papa needed work and an income to support us.

There was an opportunity! His connection from the company in Göllingen where he last worked last with the company in Rheydt helped him more than he would have expected. He went there and introduced himself and left them his application. A few days later, he had an interview! We were very nervous about the outcome. It really would have helped us tremendously. Several days later the mailman brought Papa a letter of acceptance; he got a job in the material planning department! This was something to celebrate – if we could. But life has its own twists and turns and sometimes your destiny hits you so hard that you think you will not survive it.

Brigitte got sick! Mutti was a registered Baby nurse and tried to figure out what was wrong with her. Brigitte had stomach pain and did not eat. Her belly got quite big and she was crying almost constantly. Mutti and Papa went to the doctor with her and Mutti pointed out to him that it could be an inflammation of the appendix.

"I don't think so Mr. and Mrs. Mann, I think it will go away. We will give her some medicine for her tummy and she will be fine." Mutti was not satisfied.

"But what if it is an infection of the appendix? What if it bursts? You know that could be her death!" Mutti was loud – but wasn't heard. Nothing against doctors, I think they do a great job – most of the time. But they also make mistakes!

I do not want to go into further details here, it makes me sad to think about my little sister who could not say anything or Mutti who could not get through with her opinion. I do not think that it would happen today with all the modern technology and diagnostic methods, hopefully! It was the most devastating day when they could not save her after the appendix broke and Brigitte died. I cannot tell you how absolutely horrible that was for us – probably it would have been for anybody.

But in our situation! The start of our new life was taking a big toll. It took all our strength and courage to overcome this. I will always remember when we stood at the grave during the funeral and this little tiny white baby coffin was laid down into the ground. We still think that the doctor is to blame as he hesitated too long. But it will not bring Brigitte back. As hard as it was, we had to get through this and look forward to our future.

When we lived in Mönchengladbach, we always went to her grave in Wickrath. We did not have a car for several years and public transport took two and a half hours each way. It did not matter; we always went to see her!

107.

It was August 13. A wonderful Sunday morning with blue sky and sunshine: a day to rest. Even today, Sundays in Germany are quiet as almost all shops are closed, and people rest up from their work. I like this: no hassle, no running around shopping, driving here and there – and getting stressed out even on your day off!

We had moved to a new apartment the authorities arranged for us. It was located about two kilometers from downtown in a housing block with two entrances; each led to six apartments. But it was lived in by two families at a time! All these thousands of people needed homes and West Germany was still in rebuilding the infrastructure for millions of people after the war. So we had to live in two rooms in a 78 square meters rented apartment while the other two rooms were occupied by another family. The problem was that they were not refugees, and they were not very keen on sharing "their" condo with us. There was no real bathroom as each family needed a kitchen. So the actual bathroom was remodeled and we had a common toilet. Not much of a difference from our camp in Wickrath. Still a step forward, believe it or not. And we knew that the authorities were trying hard to get the families moved into their own apartments as soon as possible. There was light at the end of the tunnel!

We had lived there for almost a week when I came back from my little cure. I had been sent from Wickrath to a three-week cure with other kids as I was often sick, and Papa and Mutti thought that this would help me to get stronger. Well, I did not like it. One reason was that it felt like a prison and we were watched all day and the nurses told us every move to make. A tight schedule with times for breakfast and lunch and dinner and time to go to bed and sleep! Was I happy when I could leave and go back to my family? Yes, very much so! Very happy! So I missed the move from Wickrath to Mönchengladbach on August 8th.

Papa had not started work yet and we had a few days to get settled. The front room was also my parent's bedroom, and the other room was our bedroom. The little kitchen was barely furnished and we had to get some used furniture. The beds were all like in Wickrath: bunk beds. With a little help from Oma and Opa, we got the most important things we needed for our new daily life. Brigitte was just four weeks gone and the sorrow was hanging like a black cloud over us. We got our news from an old tube radio and the daily newspaper.

On Sundays, Papa always wanted a newspaper and some cigarettes. He still smoked. Western tobaccos tasted so much better! Maybe it was just the paper the tobacco was rolled in. There was a Sunday paper called "Bild am Sonntag." It is still published today. Maybe not the most intelligent comments and articles, but it was a popular newspaper. Big pictures, big headlines, a sports section, provocative in some ways.

There was this tiny kiosk at the tram station not far from us. You had to go down the street, then down a pedestrian tunnel under a railway track and then to the right to the station. Many of these tram stations had little shops or kiosks for cigarettes and cigars, newspapers and magazines and some sweets. This one opened on Sundays for two hours! Papa gave me two Deutschmarks. Wow! At that time, this was enough to buy a pack of cigarettes and a newspaper – and you got money back!

I had my new pants on and a white shirt. I will never forget that day! I went to the kiosk. The guy was around mid-fifties; perspective changes when you get older, he might have been younger than I am now. He knew me by then and gave me a friendly greeting.

"Good morning, one Peter Stuyvesant and a Bild am Sonntag, please," I said to him. He smiled at me, turned around, took the cigarettes from a shelf and the top newspaper from the stack on the counter.

"Here you go, young man," he replied, handing me the paper and the pack of cigarettes.

I gave him the money and he gave me the change. I wished him a nice Sunday and left.

I was ten years old, and going back home I started at once to read the newspaper. There was a big headline: "Tanks in Berlin." I looked at the picture and realized that what it showed was two Russian tanks that I knew from seeing them in real life and soldiers, German soldiers. The picture gave the impression that it was taken at a construction site; they were building something! I read further, stopped walking and finished reading the article. It explained why it looked like a construction site; they had started to build a wall! Brick by brick with layers of barbed wire in front of it – all controlled by Vopos! Not that I understood right away the full impact of it, but it certainly looked scary.

It was the day when they started building the Berlin Wall!

When I came home, the first comment I heard from Mutti and Papa was: "We knew that something was going on. It was about time for us to leave!" Mutti and Papa hugged each other and Mutti shed some tears.

Just why did we have to pay the high price of losing Brigitte? It could have been so perfect for us here in West Germany!

Epilogue

After 14 months, the other family left and we had the whole apartment to ourselves; now with a real remodeled bathroom, front room, bedroom for the parents, two little rooms for us three children, and a little kitchen. Oh, and a balcony. As long as Karin was small, she slept with Papa and Mutti in their bedroom and us boys had the two little 11 square meter rooms. I lived in that room until I finished college!

Those 14 months were hard, and not without fights and harsh words with our "neighbors." Neighbors? Just imagine you walk into an apartment with a six meter hallway and the three rooms right after the door left and right are yours but the "neighbors" always walk through your hemisphere to reach the three rooms further down the hallway? And you hear everything and you see them, you have to be quiet, you always feel watched – and you have to pass them when you go to the bathroom! 78 square meters is not a lot of room for eight people; they were three and we were five. And we thought the situation with Oma and Opa was tight. Think twice.

Remember the twin carriage we moved all the way to West Germany with the two little babies? Mutti was worried about it when we were checked at the border and during the whole trip. There was a reason for it!

Well, on some of these busy long evenings in Sondershausen, Mutti and Papa had opened the carriage's sidewalls! They were made from a cheap carton: two cartons parallel in a sandwich-style leaving a gap of two centimeters with the top clipped together with a cheap plastic material. Mutti and Papa had opened these walls carefully from the top and had put all of Papa's stamps into the gap, bedded in cotton. They had taken them all out of the albums and fed them into this two centimeter space, piece by piece! Then they covered it up again with the plastic seal.

When we were in Mönchengladbach, there were weeks of busy evenings and weekends to get them out carefully, clean them and sort them again. It was hard for Papa, but we had to sell them finally! We got a lot of money for the collection, worth about a two-months salary at this time.

We got more and more settled. This applied to us children with school and kids and the different life style of West Germany and also for Mutti and Papa. My parents always wanted us to study hard and get a good education, something Papa was lacking due to his early draft during the Second World War. He would have loved to be an engineer!

Roland and I made it through gymnasium and apprenticeships; further education in colleges and finally became engineers. Karin learned a more creative profession: she is a master florist. Roland's particular interest was always vehicles and engines, sports cars to be exact: he even built himself a Chevy Cobra later in his life. I was not that into to cars, even though I repaired my first cars from bottom to top myself, same as he did. Also, my old first Diesel Mercedes always needed TLC but served me well during my time as a student earning my engineering degree. I love limousines! And I love driving!

My interests were a bit different from Roland's. I liked to play chess with Papa for hours – while Roland welded his first go-kart together with a motorbike engine. I have to admit, it was fun driving it! I remember when we drove on our street at some 60 kilometers an hour! You could not do that today, too many cars, too much traffic – and a big ticket from the police!

I also found my special interest in soccer; Papa was a fan since Sondershausen, and we went to almost every game of our local team, especially when they made it finally into the Bundesliga and even played some great international teams. I have very fond memories of these events and special times I spent with Papa. The team is still my favorite!

Mutti never changed – and will never change! She is the most loving and caring mother I know, other people think so too! She sacrificed a lot in her life – and so did Papa – to keep our family together and make us a real home! There is nothing she would not do for her family! All the girlfriends Roland and I brought home were always welcomed, and Mutti even had the tendency to treat them like "she" could be the one for our entire life. Same with Karin: her boyfriends were treated nicely and everybody felt immediately like part of our family. Mutti earned some money on the side and spent it – on the family, not on herself!

Sometimes, we sat together and asked ourselves: What if? What if Papa and Mutti had not had the courage and preparation to escape? Had not the will to provide for a better life for our family? The barricades were high and sometimes seemed insurmountable. The final fall of the Berlin Wall in 1989 and the reunification would have come too late for us; well, maybe not too late but we would not have reached the same comfort level in our lives, we would not have achieved owning houses and properties or achieved our professional levels – providing certainly for a better than average living standard.

The escape was the turning point in our lives.

We all got married, Karin, Roland and myself. It took me two attempts to find somebody very special. Maybe because I was travelling a lot in my early career days, and because I was always looking for an improvement in my life, my first marriage did not work out. My international career in sales took me to many foreign countries, and an unbelievable destiny also helped me to find my precious wife, the love of my life – on the other side of the world, in America.

But that is another exciting story.